HIGH PRAISE FOR
PERRI O'SHAUGHNESSY'S BESTSELLING
LEGAL THRILLER

MOTION TO SUPPRESS

"WITTY, COMPELLING AND DOWN-TO-EARTH
. . . a tasty legal thriller that leaves you hoping there will be
more to savor in the future."
—*The Orlando Sentinel*

"*MOTION TO SUPPRESS* DELIVERS! Suspense, plot
twists, and legal thrills make this a real page-turner."
—Darian North, author of *Criminal Seduction*

"This courtroom drama maintains a swift pace. . . .
Keen detective work, smoldering romance and ongoing
consciousness-raising . . . create a Roman candle of a
novel that just may rocket O'Shaughnessy to pop-lit fame."
—*Publishers Weekly*

"*MOTION TO SUPPRESS* IS NONSTOP EXCITE-
MENT! O'Shaughnessy combines the mystery of a masterful
whodunit with edge-of-the-seat courtroom drama, and
mixes in plenty of riveting psychological intrigue. The por-
trayal of the glitz and the underbelly of the casino world is
top-notch and the characters are finely drawn."
—Jeffery Deaver, author of *Praying for Sleep*

Please turn the page for more extraordinary acclaim. . . .

BY PERRI O'SHAUGHNESSY

MOTION
TO
SUPPRESS

PERRI O'SHAUGHNESSY

Dell

Published by
Bantam Dell
a division of
Random House, Inc.

NOT FADE AWAY. Words and music by Charles Hardin and Norman Petty. © 1957 MPL COMMUNICATIONS, INC., and WREN MUSIC CO. © Renewed 1985 MPL COMMUNICATIONS, INC., and WREN MUSIC CO. International Copyright Secured. All Rights Reserved.

THE ARCHER METHOD OF WINNING AT 21. © 1973 by John Archer. Published by Wilshire Book Company. All Right Reserved.

YOU BRING OUT THE BEAST IN ME. Words and Music by B. C. Cole. International Copyright Secured. All Rights Reserved.

ISBN 0-440-24317-3

Reprinted by arrangement with Delacorte Press
Printed in the United States of America
Published simultaneously in Canada

Dell paperback edition published in August 1996
Dell paperback reissue published in June 2001

1
OPM

To Helen June O'Shaughnessy
In memory of Roger Charles O'Shaughnessy

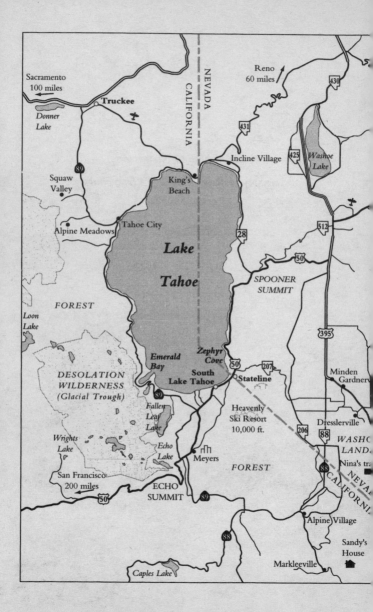

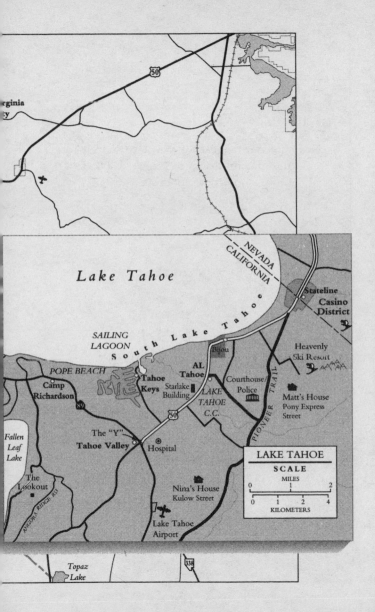

Thanks to our families for their love and support. And grateful thanks to Nancy Yost and Marjorie Braman.

My love is bigger than a Cadillac
I try to show it and you drive me back
Your love for me got to be real
For you to know just how I feel
A love for real'll not fade away
A love for real'll not fade away

April 26, Midnight

LET ME TELL you the way I remember it.

I worked the four-to-twelve shift at Prize's Thursday night, April 26.

One thing I learned my first year at the casino, a lot of gamblers hate snow in April, and they don't come up the hill. Maybe they've already stowed their parkas in mothballs, or it's 1040 time and they're hurting. Maybe so many drought years in a row in California made them forget how to deal with snow, so they hit Vegas instead of Tahoe. Maybe they're all tired out from skiing in their shorts.

But Tahoe casinos stay open night and day, no matter how slow it gets, just in case some big loser might show up in the dead of night. I was glad to be working even if it meant looking busy when there was not much to be done.

No high rollers showed up that night to gamble away the money that, if they had any sense, they had already kissed good-bye, so most of the staff was pretty low-energy, including me. A few local guys slumped at their stools, flipping over cards at the twenty-one tables, sweating into their hiking boots, waving cigarettes and sucking in the smell of saloon mixed with cleaning fluid. Along with the junketers who come up once a month from Sacramento and San Jose, and the floaters—guys who stay for a night or two on their way somewhere else—they play lousy and tip worse.

The dealers silently handed out cards at the ten or twelve

tables that had any players. They don't let us wear watches, but we all knew what time it was exactly, and exactly when the next shift would take over our stations so we could return home to our loving spouses.

I was feeling a wicked twinge in the ball of my right foot every time I walked. They make you wear these killer spiked heels, black patent, like something out of an S/M movie, supposed to keep everybody awake, I guess, players included. Even though I had been taking it easy whenever the shift supervisor wasn't watching, it was late and I was really tired.

By the Tonga Bar, a man with shiny brown boots and a cowboy string tie was watching me. He had caught me by the quarter slots earlier, but I'd seen something I needed to do across the room. This time, he moved in fast. My back was against the wall and these thin, hard lips started whispering about his room upstairs. I pushed him off me, spilling his house bourbon, and Security came to the rescue.

I remember thinking it was a good thing it wasn't Anthony behind the mirrors, watching. He blames me when I get cornered.

That night I was working swing, which I usually like. Swing shift I get home about one in the morning, so I have afternoons to do the shopping and errands around town, but that night I felt bad, and it showed. I decided to shine a bunch of smiles around in my last ten minutes to make up for the rest of the night, maybe up the tips a little, even though underneath I felt like hell, because no matter what happens with me and Dr. Greenspan and Anthony, I need that job.

I had seen Dr. Greenspan just before I went to work that night to tell him Anthony wanted me to quit treatment. I did some crying in the parking lot afterward. See, when I started my therapy, I told Anthony I thought it would help our marriage, which was a lie. I guess he finally figured that out. He told me the day before that Daddy, meaning Dr. Greenspan, was not going to get me out of this one. He was sick of me exposing our private life to a stranger and I was going to shape up and act like a wife. He'd told me he was done paying for crapola that made him look bad.

Dr. Greenspan told me I could make payments each month and cut back the hypnosis sessions to twice a month. He warned me that we were at a crucial point in the therapy, where things I had buried were just coming up. The sessions were starting to get painful. He told me that was a good sign. But Anthony was saying no more.

All that evening—passing the rows of slot machines, giving free liquor to players at the blackjack tables, saying, "Cocktails?" in my nicest voice, letting the guys look down the front of the skimpy outfit I had to wear—I had been trying to think of a way to continue my treatments. I knew my parents wouldn't help; they're Christian Scientists who would make me go to a Church healer.

The thought of asking Tom for help crept into my mind just as I leaned over to pick up my first big tip from the guy losing on third base at Table Four. He was an amateur who had spent the evening pouring free drinks down his throat, and now, practically horizontal, flashed his money and tried to stuff a bill down my front, but I saw it coming. I straightened up fast and he ended up handing it to me before he fell off his stool. Two other people at the table laughed.

I hated to ask Tom to loan me money. Supporting a wife and three children on a school principal's salary, he was stretched. It wasn't like he owed me anything.

Plus, Anthony was going to find out about Tom if I kept going to the doctor. He's an ex-cop and a suspicious type. Bad for Tom. Very bad for me.

The last few minutes of my shift that night took forever. When Brenda showed up about ten after twelve, a few minutes late the way she always is, I ran into the employee lounge. Off with the black satin Playboy-bunny knockoff, which I folded and put into my cubby, off with the mesh stockings and heels, which I stuffed into a canvas bag. I washed some of the junk off my face, and got into warm leggings and my down coat. The parking lot at Prize's is just down from the mountains at Heavenly. You can't imagine the wind and cold some nights.

A couple of inches of new snow covered the ground by the time I got to our house. It's in the Tahoe Keys and we have a piece of the lake with a little dock in the backyard. No boat, though. We can always use Rick's. Anthony doesn't like owning anything he can borrow. I could see into the picture window through the heavy flakes. Anthony wasn't lying on the blue couch, but the fire was bright.

"I wanna love you night and day/ You know my love'll not fade away." The CD player boomed out ancient Rolling Stones, and when I heard it, I almost drove away. That music meant he was awake, drunk, and waiting for me. I sat watching the dashboard ice over long enough to hear him start his favorite song up again.

I got out. I locked the car, because Anthony always checks. Then I saw some boot tracks leading off toward the side of the house, recent, because the snow was fresh. I couldn't figure out what he would have come outside for, but I called anyway and got no answer.

Anthony had left the door unlocked, so I sneaked in quietly. When I got inside, I could only see firelight, a few candles burning, orange flickers on the wall and a lot of shadows. I didn't see him and that was a relief. I took off my parka and sat down on the couch to take my boots off. I pulled too hard, and knocked a plate and fork onto the floor. The bedroom door opened.

"You're late, Misty," Anthony said. His feet made the

parquet tiles crackle when he walked. He pulled the tie belt into a knot on the maroon silk robe from China he had filched from somewhere and dug around in the pocket. His hand came out with a crumpled cigarette pack that he stuffed back inside. His hair stuck out, and his eyes were puffy and red-rimmed. He walked over to turn off the music.

"I thought you were out there in the snow," I said, waving at the window. Anthony grunted, sat down in front of me on the coffee table, and picked up my foot to take the boot off.

"I can do that myself," I said, pulling my foot back.

"Okay, I'll get you a drink."

"No, thanks."

"Take it." He jammed a stiff Yukon Jack into my hand and I knocked it down fast, saying to myself oh, what the hell, holding the glass out for another, feeling my face heat up. It takes two to make me brave.

"Anthony, I've got to tell you something."

He took hold of my chin and yanked my head up so I had to look at him. "Hurry up, now. I got work for you in bed," he said, like he hadn't heard me. "Did you bring your work shoes home, pretty girl?" His mouth turned down. He felt sorry for himself about something. It was a mood I hated.

"I'm not sleepy yet." My voice sounded like it sounds at work, calm no matter what. I was hearing a rap song over and over that some fake had bleated all night from the lounge beside the gambling room. Inside my head the sound was louder than his talking, "Uh-oh, no, no, uh-oh," making me want to throw my boots through the plate-glass window. I drank down the second drink and pulled off my sock.

"I guess you didn't hear me, huh?" He spread his hands, palms open. The robe split open onto dark hair and shapes. I tried to look away.

"You go on," I said.

"I figured something out," Anthony said. He slid his hands down my neck, over my breasts, then grabbed my shoulders with thick, security guard's hands. "You don't care, do you, Misty? You just don't care. You'll never love me how I love you. You're givin' it away, and I don't even get to take your boots off."

"You're drunk," I said.

"Tell me you love me, then. Dance with me."

I couldn't help it. I know I flinched when he touched me. "I want out." That's all I said. He knew what I meant.

"You bitch!" He was trying to get me to stand up. I just went limp.

When he spoke again, he was real quiet. "All day long I waited for you, thinking about how to make you love me." The way he was holding me I knew I would be black-and-blue in the morning. "You want it over with me, maybe. But I'm not through with you. I'll never be through with you."

And then he started the ritual, our good night scene, this part just like we had done it a million times before. "Bedtime," he said. He lifted me up, holding my arms down. I smelled whiskey on his breath and was scraped by stubble on his jaw when he pressed me against him.

"Let me down, Anthony, please." But he held on. I could beg, but he would still carry me to bed. I tried to picture the next morning. With any luck he'd be cheerful, handing out money and orders to buy myself a present.

"Shut up."

I let myself drift off into the dream where I was someplace else, where it didn't matter what he did to my body. This time it didn't work. I felt pain from his hard fingers. I smelled his unwashed skin. I knew better but I couldn't stop myself; I struggled to get free. It wasn't part of the ritual.

He set me down and, still gripping me with his left hand, he gave me a hard knock in the head. When I opened my eyes again, I could see him looking down at me, breathing hard.

He was smiling, enjoying it. Like always.

Without thinking I reached behind him. My right hand connected with a crude carving of a polar bear, made out of gray rock, very heavy. I hit him in the back of the skull just right, with a nice, loose wrist, as if I had trained for this moment, solid as when you bowl, hitting the pins just off dead center for the strike.

His eyes closed and he fell forward. Then I saw the blood coming down onto his neck. I tried to catch him going down, but I dropped the statue on the table. Glass shattered and I swear the sound of it tore something apart in my brain. I managed to get him onto the couch, scared shitless, in a bad movie, knowing things had changed forever, already thinking about what he would do to me for this. He was moaning. I was too.

I left him on the couch while I ran for the cordless phone. It wasn't in the kitchen where it should be. I heard a thud, as though he had slipped down to the floor.

And then, what? I was so tired that night, tired and scared of him and sick of my life. I remember heading back toward the living room, but I guess I found my way to the bedroom instead. I don't even remember my head touching the pillow.

The clock radio said seven-thirty. My head was killing me and I was still dressed under the covers. Anthony had gotten up before me, which surprised me; I thought that meant he was on day shift. The floor felt ice-cold because the fire had gone out in the night and we're always too broke or too cheap to keep the heat going, so I pulled on a pair of grubby

socks I found under the bed and went into the kitchen, kind
of woozy, to get a cup of hot coffee from the automatic
coffeemaker that Anthony always set up after dinner.

Then I saw the cordless phone on the floor by the stove. I
remembered hitting him. I ran into the living room, burning
myself when the coffee went flying. He wasn't on the couch.
I was thinking, is this some new sick game of his? Is he
hiding in the hall, or behind a door, ready to pay me back
for the night before? I was careful as I checked around. Not a
sound.

Outside, blinding April sun on fresh snow, Lake Tahoe
out back just blazing blue against the sky, but no sign of
Anthony. The footprints from last night were buried in the
snow.

Back in the house, glass on the rug from the coffee table.
Blood on the couch pillows. No polar bear statue.

No Anthony.

1

NINA REILLY CALLED her son from a pay phone on the street outside San Francisco's First District Court of Appeals, barely able to hear his voice above the traffic when he answered, but reassured by his cheery hello. "I'm going to stop in at the office, honey. Can you stick something in the microwave?" He would eat something cold instead, she knew. Bobby had picked up on her husband Jack's reluctance to do domestic duty around the place. Changing into comfortable shoes she kept in her briefcase, she trotted back toward Montgomery Street, outdistancing the winos on Market, reverting to heels when she hit the lobby.

One of the elevators wasn't working, so she waited a long while, watched the crowd take their time unloading when the car eventually arrived, and jumped in, taking a hit from the impatient doors. On the thirty-fourth floor nobody was at the reception desk as she passed by to pick up her messages.

Early evening fog flowed into the high canyons of the Financial District outside her office window. Across the street, also thirty-four floors up, she could see fellow office workers hanging on the phone, rushing around with papers in their hands, holding meetings in their conference room, which looked a lot like her firm's conference room. Watching her competitors across the chasm, she was reminded of Bobby's hamster, Cheeky, circling in her wheel through the monotonous night.

Before she could pick up the phone, Mel Akers, one of the senior partners, came in.

"Heard you were back, Nina. How'd it go today?"

"Get ready, Mel. I'm ninety-nine percent sure I won."

"Oh. Good job, Nina."

"Maybe one last chance for this appellant to get out and straighten up. Let's hope there's no fourth strike. I never thought he deserved life in prison for what he did, Mel. He's not a bad guy, just a loser."

"Not today though, huh, Nina? You deserve a pat on the back."

She smiled at the thought, at his unusually unenthusiastic reaction. She had more to say, but he clearly didn't want to hear details. A win in the Appeals Court counted for more points than most wins. She had expected Mel to invite her out for a celebratory drink, at the least.

"Can I sit down, Nina?"

"Sure, Mel," she replied, instantly sensitive to this departure from routine. Mel usually had a quick joke for her, and then flashed off down the hall to spread it before she could. Instead he tapped his well-manicured fingers on her desk like he did just before a big court appearance.

"I have some tough news, Nina. You know how mid-size firms are having to specialize to keep up with all the new laws that get passed each year? And the recession is killing our clients. Hardly anybody pays anymore. They just sue us if they lose. We should have gone to medical school. Then people wouldn't hate us so much."

"Maybe so."

"Malpractice insurance eats up half our profits."

"Yep."

"And the State Bar, they've got this new industry, inventing new ethics rules and sending their stone-faced inquisitors around to haunt honest practitioners. . . ."

"So . . . what's your point, Mel?" Nina said.

"Well, you know, at the partners' meeting last week we decided we had been a bit hasty opening up a couple of departments. With the economy like it is we have to consolidate our resources. The days of the general-practice firm are numbered."

Mel's watery eyes behind their specs looked slightly past her, out the window, as though she were becoming as insubstantial as the fog outside.

"Unfortunately, we don't feel we should try to keep our appellate and family law departments going anymore. That's you and Francine Chu. We just don't have the depth."

"Huh."

"It's nothing personal. You've done a great job."

"So where are you putting me?" The firm had other departments—corporations, taxation, securities, insurance defense—where the money was, and the turgid paperwork that drove lawyers mad.

"Well, we might be able to fit you into our construction litigation department. Ralph Teeter is looking for someone. I don't know if you have the interest." Now his eyes located her. Would she stay or would she go?

"What else do you have?"

"Nothing, unfortunately. Francine has decided to join her uncle in private practice in Marin County."

So Francie was leaving, her best friend at the firm. That hurt.

Soul-sucking work, construction litigation. Her professional life would consist of endless depositions of soil-subsidence experts and aerated-concrete engineers. She would become an expert on dirt, roofing materials, cracked and shifting foundations. It was big business in California. The quickie subdivisions of the eighties had led to the latent-defect litigation of the nineties. The lawyers took their tithe whether the construction was good or bad.

"Ralph Teeter's getting on to seventy now, isn't he?" He needed a strong, healthy, workaholic flunky. He would never retire. He lived with his ninety-two-year-old mother and he was well-known for arriving at the office every day at six-thirty A.M. "I'm not sure Ralph and I would be a good mix," Nina said.

"Well. Think about it. I'm authorized to offer you a three-month severance package should you decide to . . . uh, seek new opportunities. Of course, we'd be sorry to see you leave. Obviously, you've done good work for us, Nina."

"A generous offer," Nina said. Mel relaxed visibly. He must be thinking Nina was not going to get hardnosed on him. She would bow out gracefully, not sue for wrongful termination. "Six months' severance would be even more generous," she continued.

"I don't know if the partners would go for it."

"Six months, and medical insurance for the rest of the year."

"I suppose I could propose it, but I—"

"Think about it," Nina said. Within an hour Mel called back and agreed.

She left at six, early for her, fighting the traffic back to Bernal Heights, taking forty-five minutes to drive what she could have walked in twenty. Her son grabbed her and absorbed her attention from the minute she walked in until, homework done and bath completed, he got tucked into bed. She pulled out a bottle of Clos du Bois blanc and made good progress on it for the rest of the evening, waiting for her husband. When Jack came home, looking tired and tense, she was lying on the couch in the dark living room, the glimmering city lights her only illumination. He gave her a distracted kiss and disappeared into the kitchen.

When she finally got to the bedroom a few hours later, he was snoring. She poked him. He lurched over to his quiet side, still buried in his dream. Too tired and dispirited to wake him, she composed a new day in her mind, saying witty, powerful things to Mel, coming off even better than she had. She didn't get to sleep until late. When the alarm rang at six-thirty, Jack was already gone.

The next day, in jeans, mustering the bravado she usually saved for the courtroom, she went back to Montgomery Street to clean out her desk and arrange for her cases to be transferred. People she had joked around with for five years wore solemn expressions. Her farewell luncheon felt like a wake. Jack didn't get back to the condo until almost ten, and went immediately to bed.

In the morning, he joined her at the table on the deck that sat on piers overhanging a cliff. The city towers, rectangled, pyramidal, and mirrored, bathed in their usual silvery morning light, looked exotic as ancient castles and as remote from her.

"Cold out here," he said.

"Yes, it is." Nina set her orange juice glass solidly in the middle of the railing, respectful of the distance between it and the ground.

He picked up the newspaper, apparently contented with this repartee, and began to read.

"Jack, I've got to talk to you."

The way he slapped the paper down told her he would rather not have a conversation. "Okay." He folded the paper and refilled his coffee cup. "What about?"

"They let me go." The shock on his face made telling him almost worth the wait. "Mel gave me the bad news the day before yesterday."

"Jesus, Nina. Jesus. This is terrible."

Instead of feeling gratified by his response, she found herself vaguely disquieted.

"I squeezed six months' severance out of them," she went on, but Jack was still shaking his head in disbelief.

"You didn't do a damned thing to deserve this, Nina."

"I'm almost sure I won the appeal too. Judge Ritty asked a question about their citations that gave a pretty clear indication of the Court's direction on the judgment."

He said nothing, just pulled on his mustache.

"What would they have done if I had lost it? You have to wonder." Her lightness didn't help. He pulled her hand across the table, squeezing too hard, shifting into a mood that had recently become familiar, which she realized suddenly she did not like, a mood that was intended to comfort her and instead felt awkward, as though they were strangers.

"Bastards," he said, his voice crisp and workmanlike. "Listen. I'll call Drew. He knows a shark who'll bloody them for you."

"I'm not going to sue."

"You can't let them get away with this."

"I'm ready to go, Jack. I need a change. I thought it might be good for us. . . ."

"You *need* a job."

"We can make it for a few months without if we have to. What are you so afraid of? That I won't be able to get another job?"

"Of course. Of course I'm afraid you won't be able to get another goddamn job." He got up. Throwing his napkin onto the table, he jostled her glass with his elbow. It went over, falling in a long, quiet moment during which they looked at each other in mutual dismay. The sound of glass shattering, when it came, seemed distant and anticlimactic.

★　★　★

The violence of Jack's reaction lingered with Nina all day. He was out of the house the next morning, dropping Bobby off at school by the time she woke up. That night and the next, he came home after one in the morning. When she stayed up very late the second night and tried to talk to him in bed, he yelled that he needed his rest, he had court in the morning, and turned over to sleep.

Which possibly explained why, on Nina's third full day at home for the first time in five years, she was feeling lonely down to the soles of her feet. She had nowhere to go and nothing to do except laundry. The frustration and despair that had smoldered for days made her by turns restless and apathetic. Home free. She ought to start looking for a job. Instead she got a load of clothes going. She took a long shower, returning to find sudsy water undulating across the kitchen floor. Calling the condo plumbing service, she parked herself on the couch with the newspaper to keep her company.

Within an hour there was a knock on the door. She got up and opened it. The condo's plumber came in smiling, and looked her up and down. Making a gesture of vanity suitable to his youth, he reached up to his hair, next to the golden-brown eyes and big nose, setting a small silver cross in his ear swinging. She directed him to the mess and went back to curl up on the couch. When he was finished in the kitchen, he came in. He stood beside her, eyes on her shirt, on the place where her bra ought to be.

"What a shame, having to bill such a pretty lady," he said. The curtains were closed. The machine noise cut out abruptly, its stillness inspiring a shared recognition that nobody else was home.

"You listen to the ads, you'd think those old washers would go on forever," he said. "I put in a new hose, but you better start looking for a new machine." He showed her the cost of the hose on the bill, leaning his head in close to hers while his finger traced over each item. He smelled like detergent, fresh and fragrant from his labors.

Nina raised herself as gracefully as she could out of the plump cushions. She walked over to the table for her purse, aware of his eyes on her bare legs, aware of his body and the tight jeans over his rear end.

Turning, she found him close behind her, his long lashes narrowing around tiger eyes, the swinging earring hypnotizing. She had trouble getting her checkbook out. "Not feeling well today?" he said.

"Why do you ask?" she said.

"Last time I was here, you had to take off work to let me in. I remember." She scrounged through her bag as she recalled the occasion and the conversation they had had. He had lived in Bernal Heights all his life. He loved the City. He worked for his father, over on Valencia. He wanted to take over the business. He wanted to learn to be a pilot. He went hang gliding at Fort Funston every chance he got, finding a fling off a cliff about the most invigorating thing he could imagine. She knew so much about him. Why couldn't she remember his name? While she considered, he edged in until the hairs on their arms touched.

His body so close to hers seemed larger, surrounding her with an aura of wild threat and protection she found herself unable to categorize or resist. Caught in the dangerous spell, she didn't do the proper thing. She didn't move away. "You have beautiful hair," he said, his hand reaching out to stroke it. "Brown like milk chocolate. Silky."

His hand slid under her head, lifting it, and then suddenly, he kissed her, wrapping his arms around her in a hug as warm as bear fur. His fingers touched her hair so softly, she felt soothed and thrilled at the same time. She found herself touching his earring with the tip of her finger, discarding the cool knowledge that she should not be doing this, tracing the curve of his ear instead. Somehow he had kicked off his shoes and he was on the couch with her, murmuring how nice she was, how beautiful, how smooth her skin felt. He moved around her with an easy familiarity, as though he had known her forever.

Dizzy with her own desire, she moved her hands down his back and heard him sigh. Then he stopped, moving only to turn his head to one side, then froze. Above the roaring in her blood she heard somebody saying, loudly, coldly, precisely, "So this is how it is. This is how it is." The boy jumped up and she tried to sit up, looking at her husband. For a long instant Jack stared at them with a look on his face she did not recognize. Then he turned away. The front door slammed.

"Sorry," the boy said. "This really sucks. Your old man?"

Nina had no reply.

He tied his high-tops and came over, rubbing her head lightly. "You going to be all right?"

"I'll be all right."

"Your husband looked pretty pissed off. There's no chance he'd . . . hit you or something?"

"He's a lawyer." Now, didn't that say it all?

"Uh-oh. Worse." He started for the door and then turned back toward her, clearly reluctant, his face a question mark.

"Oh," said Nina. "I'll leave the check under the mat, okay? You can pick it up later."

"Great," he said, ducking out of there. "And thank you for calling Jiffy Plumb."

Not funny. But she appreciated the gesture. She really did.

Ms. Cherry, a brisk-sounding woman who identified herself as Jack's attorney, called her at home the next day.

"No, he'd prefer you don't try to contact him at the hotel," she said.

"He has to talk to me sometime. He can't just call it quits after five years without talking to me." Nina tried to sound businesslike and failed. "Jack loves to talk. . . . We can work this out, if he'll just call me." She couldn't believe she was pleading, groveling to this stranger. So that was how her divorce clients' spouses felt when she called to notify them the locks were being changed and they'd be getting some papers.

"I'm afraid his decision is final," said Ms. Cherry, her tone neutral. "He has instructed me to file the petition for dissolution as soon as possible. I will be sending you a marital settlement agreement for your review. We'll need to sell the condo."

The words impaled her. Just like that, she was going to lose her husband and her home. Correction. Not just her. Bobby. "I understand that Mr. McIntyre is not the boy's biological father, and never formally adopted your son," the lawyer went on, reading her mind. "He wishes to maintain contact with him, and we would like to work out informal visitation."

"Well, you tell Mr. McIntyre that he can kiss my ass," Nina said.

"I'm sorry you feel that way," Ms. Cherry said. Nina used that line, too, when people had tantrums over the phone at work.

"He has to talk to me," Nina said. She hung up the phone and stood for a long time, her hand on it as though to pick it up again. She couldn't think of anyone to call except Jack. Since she couldn't do that, she wanted to run away to work, using it like exercise to relax her, but that option no longer existed. She walked out on the balcony. Pine needles from a tall tree on the hill behind their house twisted through the mist to speckle Jack's blue canvas chair. An ambulance led by two police cars screamed along the street, bearing its unfortunate cargo to the hospital up the hill.

The week before, she had been a married, respectable San Francisco attorney with a well-settled future. Now all she had was Bobby and her law degree.

If only she had agreed to work with Ralph Teeter. If only Jack hadn't come home early.

If only she had done the grocery shopping instead of the laundry.

Strange days, indeed.

2

WHEN BAD THINGS happen, people often leave town. Also, they turn to their families. Nina's brother, Matt, lived at Lake Tahoe, and he had a spare room. They drove there the next day.

She was pretending, for Bobby's sake, that she was her usual self.

They ate lunch just north of Sacramento, at a big barn called Schulz's, one of those self-consciously old-fashioned stores where you could buy candy straight from bins filled with licorice, saltwater taffy, and caramel corn. They ordered huge hamburgers. Bobby left most of his, cadged a pocketful of change, and dove into the noisy adjacent room with its kiddie rides and video games.

Nina sat at a nearby table, reading the news while she ate french fries. The governor wanted to cut welfare again and siphon off still more money earmarked for public schools— not bad enough for California to be next to last in spending on schools out of the fifty states. The deficit was worse than the legislative analysts had ever dreamed, at least before the election. Car-jackings were up; Apple Computer stock was way down. Still reeling from a series of earthquakes, fires, and coastal mudslides, California wasn't recovering from the recession.

The second section told the horror stories, the ones about stalkers and molesters and new carcinogens found in the diet.

Money and the environment and the pervasive aura of violence. Same old shit, Jack would say. You couldn't take these things personally; they occurred on too vast a scale. Was the Golden State named for the Gold Rush or its dry, golden hillsides, she thought, zipping to the comic section, purposely redirecting her thoughts.

Her eyes fell upon Madame Zelda with her crystal ball, sitting in a dusty trance in her glass cabinet a few feet away. She got up and dropped in a quarter. Zelda's face lit up under the ragged scarf. The machine hiccuped and a yellowed card dropped into the slot.

> Love's little dove has flown away, leaving you filled with
> sad dismay.
> Fear not! Great happiness lies ahead.
> You have a tendency to be obstinate.

Obstinate: grim, logical, and conscientious. The brain of a cyborg, the heart of the Grinch. In short, a standard member of the legal profession. She thought again of the alacrity with which she had succumbed to her friendly plumber. Obviously, something else was inside her, too, something suppressed and raring to receive some attention.

By three o'clock they had driven another seventy miles and seven thousand feet up to Echo Summit. This high up it was still winter, and the road wound between dirty walls of snow. Just past the ski lifts at the top they followed the last sharp curve into the immense Tahoe basin.

From their vantage a thousand feet above the Tahoe valley, the whole oval of the lake, seventy-two miles around, twenty-six miles across, more than sixteen hundred feet deep, radiated intense turquoise into a baby-blue sky. The lake was already more than a mile high, but the snowy mountains that ringed it passed the two-mile mark. Between the mountains and the lake, the landmarks were close enough or tall enough to materialize like mirages above the dense forests: on the south shore, the tiny town of Meyers and nearby the landing strips of the Tahoe airport, then the high-rise casinos glamorizing the lakeside town of South Lake Tahoe. On the north shore the small towns of Incline and King's Beach disappeared in the distance; but Tahoe's highest mountain, Mount Rose, pointed the way to Reno.

The Bronco wound down from the granite summit into the town. The temperature had dropped thirty degrees from Sacramento, but Matt Reilly, Nina's younger brother, was chopping wood in the front yard in his Giants baseball cap and an old T-shirt. He gave Bobby a hug and said, "Troy and Brianna are out back," then put an arm around Nina. "I thought you'd be all bandaged up, on crutches maybe, like a Crusader fresh from the wars," he said.

Matt had moved to Tahoe five years before, when their mother died, and married Andrea later the same year. They had two children, Troy, Andrea's eight-year-old son from a previous marriage, and Brianna, who was four. In winter Matt drove a tow truck and in summer he ran a parasailing business at the foot of Ski Run Boulevard. He looked slim and sunburned. Nina had always tried to protect him when they were children. This time she needed his support. "I hope you'll stick around," he said. He helped her unload her suitcases to the spare bedroom, and let her try her hand splitting kindling when she asked for something to do.

Andrea came home from her Sunday shift at the Women's Shelter at five, a tart redhead with the fast moves of a working mother, handed Nina a bag of groceries, and took charge of the household. She looked pleased to see her sister-in-law; her work in the field of domestic violence had involved her in several legal hassles, and she would now have her own in-house counsel for a while.

By nine the three kids were asleep and Matt had washed

the dishes. The adults collapsed by the fire, talking about the day, the chores, the fresh prespring air. Nina told them her story, giving them credit for not laughing when she came to the part about the plumber. Especially Matt.

"Do you want to keep trying with Jack?" Andrea said. She lay entwined with Matt on the couch, while Nina adjusted herself on the floor by the fire, settling for an oversize pillow.

"When we got married, he still loved someone else," Nina said. "I needed him so much then, I shotgunned him to the preacher. All he wanted then was to handle a few cases and the rest of the time lay low in his cabin at Big Sur and listen to music and read poetry out loud. So naturally I got my first big job in the brightest lights I could find and moved us out of Carmel to San Francisco. Bobby went to day care and our home life consisted of *hi*'s and *good-bye*'s and Sunday afternoons. Now Jack's caught me squeezing another man's butt. So mortifying. So banal. *I* wouldn't want me back."

"Well, screw him then," Matt said. "He cheats at Monopoly, anyway."

"Oh, yeah, I want to get hostile and trash him, Matt. That's how my divorce clients get through their first few months. The former love-of-her-life turns into a monster. But I can't do that. I'm the one who turned into Mr. Hyde and precipitated this whole thing." Yes, that was it, a low and shambling fragment of id had been cavorting around in her mind, making trouble.

Andrea said, "Now you mention it, you could use a haircut and a shave." Nina threw Matt's slipper at her. Andrea went on, "Can't you always find another job in the City?"

A vision of Ms. Cherry's life rose unbidden in Nina's mind. She didn't know Jack's Ms. Cherry, but she knew the Ms. Cherrys of San Francisco: the empty home life; the long hours; the demanding partners; the continual rushing

around; the relentless, grinding pressures of their caseloads.
. . . She ought to know. It was her own recent existence
she was describing to herself. There had to be another way
to practice law.

"I'd rather be staked to a sandhill and eaten by fire ants,"
she heard herself say. Matt and Andrea laughed. "But for
Bobby's sake, I better decide something soon. He's going to
miss Jack. Jack's the only father he's ever known. And the
condo where he's lived all this time . . . it'll be sold."

"Stay here and think things over as long as you want,"
Andrea said. "And try not to worry. Bobby's adaptable.
He'll survive this."

"And Tahoe's excellent in the spring. It's fab and gear and
all those other pimply hyperboles." Matt failed to hide a
huge yawn. "Age is a terrible thing. As soon as I hit thirty I
couldn't stay up past eleven anymore."

Andrea got up too.

"Think I'll stare into the fire for a few minutes," Nina
said. She didn't want to go to bed and sleep alone. She fell
asleep there, woke up at two, found the fire down to embers,
and finally climbed under the yellow covers. She dreamed
she was back in high school, on the first day, and she'd
forgotten her locker combination, and her books were in
there. She was late. The bell was ringing. She had blown
high school, and she couldn't think of a thing she could do
about it.

On Wednesday, while out shopping for chocolate Easter
eggs, Nina passed a small office building. A cardboard For
Rent sign on a post, dangling crookedly from one nail,
caught her eye. The building fronted on Highway 50, the
main drag in town. There was plenty of parking in back. She
returned the same way, and this time she turned into the lot
and entered through the double doors on the side. Inside,

she walked along a carpeted hall with ten office suites, five on each side.

The property manager, evidently glad to see her, showed her a small corner suite with a reception area where a secretary and a couple of client chairs might fit. There were two inner doors, one of which led to a long room that would make a nice combined law library and conference room. A big closet with several electric sockets could stow a fax, copy machine, and supplies, even a small refrigerator.

When she raised the blinds on the side wall in the main office, she could hardly believe her eyes. Lake Tahoe, tufted with whitecaps in the wind, less than a mile away, dominated an unobstructed view of marsh and trees. Other than a dirt road, there was no evidence of human activity in that direction.

The manager followed her eyes. "Great view of Tallac," he said, pointing to a jagged peak across the southern portion of the lake. "I climbed it last summer. It's a long day, but worth it." In his sixties, skinny in his beat-up jeans, he wore what Nina had already come to recognize as Tahoe's trademark, a plaid wool shirt. He pulled the other set of blinds on the wall next to the highway to show the busy street, sidewalk, traffic lights, gas station on the corner across the street, and Mexican restaurant on the other side. "Parallel universes," he said. "You choose when you pull the blinds."

"How much?" she said.

"Seven-fifty a month."

Insanely cheap by City standards. She made an instant decision, took out her checkbook and wrote him a deposit. He told her he'd get a sign made. By the time the installer hung the sign three days later, she had bought two desks, a long table, lamps, office supplies, and several chairs at the local office supply store. They were delivered the same day, set on an old Oriental rug Andrea loaned her that she'd owned since college. She hung the two Ansel Adams prints she found in boxes of papers from her San Francisco office, and considered them with satisfaction, stark and elegant on her new reception area wall.

NINA F. REILLY, ATTORNEY-AT-LAW the sign on the building read in large, raised block letters. She called Andrea and Matt and they opened up a bottle of champagne while the man outside struggled to attach the sign to the stucco. Several of her new office neighbors came out, an elderly accountant named Frank and two ladies from the real estate brokerage at the other end of the hall, happy to break up the day and drink Korbel out of a paper cup.

On Sunday and Monday of the three-day Easter weekend, leaving Bobby and a huge Easter basket with Andrea, Nina drove hastily back to Bernal Heights and packed up the place. She also left recordings on the respective answering devices of Ms. Cherry, Bobby's school, Francine Chu, and Mel Akers. By Monday at midnight she was back in Tahoe, dead beat, packing a lunch for Bobby. She would enroll him at the John Muir Elementary School, where Troy attended school and Brianna had preschool, the next day. On Tuesday afternoon Matt helped her unload the small trailer with its computer and printer and boxes of books and toys into the garage.

April sixteenth.

Fourteen days since she lost her job: ten days since Jiffy Plumb sent its representative over to wreak havoc.

"Historical change," she said to Matt as they puffed their way into the garage with her box of pots and pans.

"Historical? Or hysterical?" Matt said. "Really, you move ahead like a tidal wave over all obstacles. I'm in awe."

"It's all very logical, everything I'm doing," Nina said.

"Sure, Nina! Like moving to Tahoe. Very logical!"

"What do you mean by that? Here, set it on top of the TV."

They set the box down and straightened up. "In case you haven't noticed," Matt said, taking off his cap and wiping his brow and exhibiting a prime case of hat hair in the process, "there are ways besides using logic to make decisions."

"Like what?"

"Like using experience and intuition."

"I guess. So what do you think, Matt? Is life a tragedy or a comedy?"

Matt placed his cap carefully on his head. "You've asked the right person that question. And my answer is, let's go inside and put our feet up and have ourselves a beer."

3

Her announcement had come out in the paper the day before, along with her ad for an experienced legal secretary, but the phones sat unused and the silence bothered Nina more than she'd expected. She thumbed through the *Attorneys* section of the yellow pages, marveling at the half-page ads. At least twenty lawyers practiced right here in town, for twenty thousand people. Either the people of Lake Tahoe had an unusual number of legal problems, or lawyers loved living here enough to eke out a precarious existence.

No clients, said the neat magazines in the reception room, and no prospects. Andrea said she would steer clients her way, but there was no predicting when that might be.

She should get up and go find the local Rotary. They let women in now, reluctantly. She started a list. Join the Lake Tahoe Chamber of Commerce. Call the Municipal Court and see if she could line up some misdemeanor appointments. Play racquetball. Make herself conspicuous.

She was hanging her purse on her shoulder, about to go over to the courthouse and introduce herself to the clerks, when the outside door opened. Through her open office door Nina watched a short, very wide older woman in a brown raincoat step in. She sat down, out of view, in one of the client chairs.

Nina pushed her chair back in a loud squawk.

"Hello," she said, walking into the reception area, her

hand extended. The woman looked at it, then gave her own. Her grip was firm, warm.

"I came right over," she said. "I'm Sandy Whitefeather."

Nina escorted her into the office and pulled out a Client Interview Sheet. "Can I get you a cup of coffee?" she said.

"Sounds good." Sandy Whitefeather looked around the office with interest while Nina brought them both coffee.

"Well. How can I help you today?"

"You can hire me, Mrs. Reilly. I'd like to be your secretary." She drank some coffee, comfortable, looking straight at her.

"Oh! I see! I thought . . ."

"You thought, 'A client.' Looks like you could use some." Nina put away her form. "I assume you have a résumé?"

"I didn't have time to put one together. I figured you were in a hurry."

"Right. So, Ms. Whitefeather—"

"Sandy."

"Tell me about yourself."

"I'm a Washoe."

"I'm sorry? What's a . . . ?"

"Native American. Local tribe."

"How interesting. But—"

"You want to know why I would be a good secretary. I'm taking secretarial courses at the community college. I know every kind of word processing program, Windows, whatever. I've lived here all my life, and I know the town."

She was still wearing the raincoat and it wasn't raining. Nina had an idea of the secretary she wanted in the back of her mind, and Sandy Whitefeather wasn't it. Her idea was of a sharp girl, fast, somebody the clients would like to chat with when they were waiting.

"I've been working for the big firm, Caplan, Stamp, Powell, and Riesner, over by the Grand Auto down the road.

File clerk. They're never going to make me a legal secretary, so I'm applying to be your secretary."

"Why won't they promote you?"

"I won't bring the coffee. I'm not cute. I wear clothes I like." She opened the raincoat. She was wearing a full blue skirt and a tan blouse, with tennis shoes. "They hired me for affirmative action," she said, and smiled. "So I'm taking my own affirmative action. What do you pay?"

"Seven dollars an hour," Nina said.

"It's not much."

"It's what I pay."

"Well, I guess I could live with it. Assuming prospects for a raise when you get going."

"I'm not offering you the job yet," Nina said.

"I'm not taking it yet," Sandy Whitefeather said. "Are you going to do some pro bono work? Or are you gonna be like the rest of 'em, only take the paying cases?"

Who was being interviewed here, anyway? "Yes, I'm going to be working with Andrea Reilly at the Tahoe Women's Shelter. Some pro bono. Some sliding scale."

"Andrea? Good."

"She's my sister-in-law."

"She does good work. What kind of cases do you want to take?"

"I do mostly criminal law, civil litigation, family law. . . ."

"And whatever comes through the door, like the rest of 'em, for a while." She sipped her coffee. "I've got some people who need a lawyer."

Was this woman intentionally insolent, or was she just one of those people who skipped the usual mental edit before opening her mouth? Nina couldn't tell. Not a follower, this one. Not the assistant type.

"Give me the name of your supervisor."

"Jeff Riesner," Sandy Whitefeather said. "What a prick."

"I'll let you know, Ms. Whitefeather."

"Sandy. Don't get me wrong, Mrs. Reilly. I'm glad you're in town. We need a hotshot woman lawyer. That's what you are, right?" She was definitely kidding.

"Two out of three ain't bad, Sandy," said Nina.

The woman's face did not move, but deep within her eyes Nina saw sly intelligence appreciating the joke. "Word of advice, Mrs. Reilly."

"Nina. Or Ms. Reilly."

"The lawyers in this town are dog-eat-dog. Don't expect much. I know 'em all."

"What do you think about the judge? Judge Milne?" Nina asked, off the track, but too curious to miss an opportunity to hear something useful.

"Doesn't matter what I think," she said. "He's the Big Chief. Do what he says and you'll be okay."

"Well, thanks."

"We'll do fine," Sandy Whitefeather said. She gave Nina a wink and walked out.

During the rest of the week two more women came in to apply for the position. One couldn't spell, and the other couldn't use the computer software. Nina put their résumés in an empty drawer.

On Thursday her first clients came in, a divorce and a fender bender. Each offered a $250 retainer, which she took. Each had been referred by Sandy Whitefeather.

That night, while Matt was out back with two of the kids looking through his telescope at the Great Nebula in Orion, Nina asked Andrea if she knew Sandy Whitefeather. Andrea, who had assigned Troy the dinner dishes, hovered nervously around the sink, trying not to notice as the plates flew from his hands into the drainer. "Yeah, everybody knows Sandy," she said.

"She applied for the secretary job."

Andrea looked surprised. "Is that what she does for a living? She's active politically. She raises money for the Shelter, I don't know how. She's a leader in the Native American community here."

"A flaming liberal. Just what I need to attract the older, white business types who have the money to hire me. And she has an attitude. Referred to her current employer as a prick," Nina said.

"Why doesn't that surprise me?"

"I'd be nuts to hire her."

Andrea caught a dish hurtling toward her and toweled it till it sparkled. "You disappoint me, Nina. For a lawyer, you're hardly standard issue. And Tahoe has plenty of potential clients with money who appreciate a little nonconformity. There are the showgirls, the roadworkers, the ski instructors, the gamblers, the dopers, the battered wives . . . lots of legal work if you broaden your thinking a little. And I can tell you Sandy has my deepest respect. Have you talked to her boss yet?"

"No, but I guess I might give him a call."

She called Jeffrey Riesner the next day. The secretary said he was in court and would be back about four, then put Nina on hold twice to field other calls before she took the message. Riesner's office was obviously very busy. Nina got to work on her divorce case.

Just before five the phone rang. "Jeffrey Riesner, returning your call."

"Thanks for calling back."

"Sure. Welcome to the Tahoe legal community. Let's do lunch sometime." The voice was commanding, wary, and brusque.

"That would be fine," Nina said. "I'm calling about one of your employees, Sandy Whitefeather."

"What's she done now?"

"Nothing. I mean, she's applied for a legal secretary position with me. She says she's a file clerk and you are her supervisor. I wondered if you could give me some idea about her qualifications for the job."

"She told me she was looking around. I can't imagine where she got the idea she could do legal secretary work. She just alphabetizes papers and sticks them in the files."

"She says she's used Windows."

"I wouldn't know. She doesn't use computers in our office." He waited for the next question.

"How would you rate her as an employee generally?"

"Can you keep this confidential, Ms. Reilly?" Riesner said. When she said yes, he went on, "She's a troublemaker, but we get points for having her around."

"Troublemaker?"

"She doesn't know her place."

"Which is?"

"Keep her mouth shut and do what she's told. I can't recommend her, to be honest with you."

"Well, I appreciate the information."

"Anytime. So what brings you to Tahoe?"

This seemed too hard to try to explain, so Nina said she had always loved the area.

"Practicing law up here is hard. But hey, there'll be some gals who need divorces who would prefer a woman. You'll be all right, if you keep your expectations down. Criminal law is my thing. I do the big felonies up here."

"I do criminal work too," Nina said. "Thanks again. And now, if you'll excuse me, I have a call on another line." She hung up, thought a minute, and then called Riesner's office again, asking for Sandy Whitefeather.

"Great," Sandy said, when she offered her the job. "I'll be there Monday morning."

"Shouldn't you give notice?"

"Leave that to me. See you Monday. By the way, I lined up some people coming to see you at ten on Monday. You said you wanted some divorce work, right?"

"Yes. Thanks," Nina said.

"You're welcome," Sandy said. "Her name's Michelle Patterson. Everybody calls her Misty. She'll haul Tom Clarke along, I bet," she added before hanging up. Like everyone knew him already. Well, Nina guessed by Monday she'd know him too.

4

THE SUN SHONE on a light layer of new snow on the mountains above town on Monday morning. Nina erased her lonesome weekend from her mind and eased into her work. At the door to the office, decked in the same clothes she had worn to her interview, Sandy waited, arms folded. "Nine o'clock," she greeted Nina, her expression a lecture on early birds and worms. Nina led the way in and showed her the marital dissolution papers she had drafted.

"Just fill in the originals like I did the copies, then bring them in and I'll look at them. Have you ever seen these forms? Judicial Council Forms? When we're finished, we file them at the courthouse."

"Mm-hmm," Sandy said. Nina went into her office. A few minutes later Sandy came in with hot coffee.

"I thought you don't do that."

"I don't do it as part of my work. I do it because it's a good thing to do," Sandy said. "I take care of you. I take care of your clients. Both of them."

As Sandy turned away, they heard a knock on the outer door. "Once they come through that door, they're ours," she said, and went out, pulling the office door halfway shut.

Outside Nina's town-side window, the cars slogged through the slush on Highway 50 on their way to Heavenly Valley, full of people on vacation from reality in Sacramento or San Francisco, from jobs for which they sat in traffic jams half the day, in which they slaved away fifty weeks a year. Up here in Tahoe, they could forget the mortgage and the taxes, adopting the current uniform of the rich and carefree: neon spandex. No money? No problem—fake it with credit, enjoy the clean, forgiving air and the fun of heading for the slopes at—she looked at her watch—nine-fifteen on a Monday morning. Nina heard some chatting, something about Sandy's kids.

Michelle Patterson came in first. Young, early twenties. A real Barbie doll, the original, politically incorrect Barbie with long, pale hair and impossible boobs, a ridiculously tiny waist and an invisible tummy. Nina's first reaction was disbelief. Looking more closely, she saw the face was not Barbie's, not by a long shot. Straight, dark brows and a stony expression hardened the heart-shaped face, and a long cigarette hung out of the luscious little mouth. Tom Clarke, Nina assumed, followed, wearing the first suit and tie she had seen at Tahoe.

"Please sit down. Can we get you some coffee?" she said. They said sure, frowning. They had cast a swift glance at the office and settled down into their chairs. The girl's hand reached out and found Tom Clarke's hand. He pulled it away with a slight movement.

Sandy brought in the mugs, taking her time with the setup.

"Got an ashtray?" Michelle Patterson said. Her voice was high and girlish, with an edge.

"Sorry, but smoking gives me cancer," Nina said. "Mind putting it out in the outer office?" The girl's eyes narrowed, but she got up and went back out the door. When she returned, she stretched out her long legs and sprawled in her chair.

Something about her didn't quite jibe. She wore no makeup. Her white T-shirt was rumpled and frayed at the

neck and that long, Scandinavian hair needed washing. She
was braless and cold enough so it showed. Dark circles shadowed her eyes. It didn't matter. There was too much grade-
A basic equipment there for the bad maintenance to detract
much.

"I'm freezing," she said. "Tom, give me your coat.
C'mon." Clarke took off his suit jacket and hung it around
her shoulders. His own shoulders were massive, leading
down a barrel chest to a tight stomach and a nicely filled pair
of gray flannel slacks. Aviator glasses and a well-trimmed
beard framed a red face, sensual and fleshy. He smelled like
cherry pipe tobacco. She'd have to do something about the
ventilation system, Nina noted, wondering if they could
smell the chocolate Easter egg she'd had for breakfast.

According to the intake sheet, Michelle Tengstedt Patterson, who called herself Misty, had come for a consultation
about a divorce from her husband, Anthony Patterson.

"Thanks for fitting us in," Clarke said. "Sandy told us you
were booked weeks in advance."

"No problem."

"Sandy said you are a top-notch family law attorney.
We're lucky to have you here in town."

"I'm pleased to be here."

"I'm the principal at Pineacres Elementary. Misty is a barmaid at Prize's. The casino. She needs some advice."

"The initial half-hour consultation is free." The local attorneys' ads said so, and Nina could do no less.

"The Tahoe attorneys are all good old boys. I want Misty
to retain somebody who will try to understand her situation.
She's in real trouble."

"Tell me why you aren't looking for a good old boy,"
Nina said to Clarke. "What can I do to help you?" She sat
back in her high-backed chair and waited.

"Well, I know most of the other lawyers, and I can't afford

to have my name bandied about. Misty wanted to talk to a woman family lawyer, and you seem to be it. I should mention right away, since we made the appointment to see you last week there's been a new complication."

He hesitated. Misty Patterson's face was turned toward him, her hair swinging down to obscure any expression.

"Misty's husband is missing as of Friday." His left hand rose to caress the beard, then moved as if it couldn't help itself to the girl's shoulder.

When he stopped there, Nina said, "Can you tell me what happened, Mrs. Patterson?" And then, when the girl remained silent, "Is Tom here with you as a family friend?" She looked directly at the young woman.

"No," Tom Clarke answered.

Nina ignored him. "Tell me about it," she repeated.

The girl sat up straighter. "Okay," she said. "First of all, call me Misty. Second, I'll try to explain about my husband. His name is Anthony. He and I . . . we had a fight Thursday night. It never went this way before. I hit him. He . . . I guess he left home during the night. I was very scared, so I slept in a down bag in my car the past three nights, hiding from him. I called in sick at work. I couldn't let him find me." Her head tilted toward the floor, and her hair made it hard to see her face.

"How did you hit him?" Nina asked.

"Good and hard. Just one time. Bad enough so he bled a little, but his eyes were open after. I didn't think I hurt him all that much." She added something under her breath that Nina couldn't hear.

"What?"

The girl twisted in her chair, looked at Clarke, then turned back to Nina. "He was hurting me with his hands, trying to . . . you know . . . force me. . . ." Tom Clarke puffed up and looked explosive.

"You fight often?"

"He pushes me around, that's all I mean. He doesn't beat me or anything. I get him mad sometimes. And it all depends on how high he gets on the drink-o-meter."

"I've seen bruises," Clarke said.

"Why would he just take off like that?" Nina asked, flicking on her desk recorder.

"I don't know," Misty Patterson said. "It's not like he's gonna let me off the hook for whacking him. My guess is he's got something special planned for me. He's not a guy that forgives or forgets."

"Tell me exactly what happened the night he disappeared," Nina said, and she started to fill up her tape with the story of the fight the Pattersons had on Thursday night. Her new client's voice was emotionless as she talked, but her face set itself in the lineaments of fear.

Tom Clarke sat back, no longer interrupting and not touching her either.

"Okay, Misty. First of all, why didn't you call a doctor? You said you were going into the kitchen to call a doctor."

"I woke up in my bed. I don't remember after the kitchen."

"Have I got this right? You have a furious battle with your husband. You tell him you want to leave him. He attacks you. You hit him so hard that he bleeds and falls to the floor. You're terrified that he'll retaliate, so you head straight for the bedroom and fall asleep?"

The girl shook her head. "I have trouble remembering things sometimes. I block things out. I've been seeing a therapist. It's weird, I agree."

It wouldn't do for an answer, but she seemed to have nothing further to offer on the point. "Have you checked at Boulder Hospital?" asked Nina.

Misty nodded. "I called his doctor. He said he hasn't seen

Anthony in the last couple of days. He's not in the hospital. As far as I know, he hasn't filed any charges against me, not that that surprises me. He always says the law's not for players. It's for wimps who can't take care of themselves. Guess that's one reason he made a crummy cop."

She lifted a long leg and slid it over another, seemingly oblivious to Clarke's flushed stare. "His parents are dead. I called the only guy I know Anthony hangs out with, Peter La Russa? He's a pit boss at Prize's. He wouldn't even talk to me. I couldn't tell if he'd talked to Anthony or not. Oh, and I called his ex-wife, Sharon Otis, in Sparks. She told me to go to hell. Not the first time." She rubbed her nose.

"Okay, let's look at other possibilities. Where else could he be?" Nina said, struck anew by the girl's physical impact, the long, slim fingers waving gracefully in the air, the curve of cheek, the blush of blood pulsing under her skin. Too much woman. Nina felt like a dried flower arrangement.

Tom Clarke said, "Dead. Misty hit him, and he crawled off someplace." He sounded pleased. "He deserved it. The son of a—"

"Dead," Nina repeated. "That's an extreme prospect. You've checked all around the property?"

"The yard's mostly scrub, not like an acre of trees," Misty said. "The house fronts on one of those canals leading out onto the lake."

"What about Prize's? You say he works there too?"

"He's missed the whole weekend. They told me when I called in sick, so I told them he hurt his back," Misty said.

"It's uncommon, but occasionally people get amnesia from blows on the head," Nina said.

"Or maybe she hit him just right and he's a goner," Clarke said.

Nina turned to him, her brown eyes staring into his.

"He abuses her," he said.

"I have to go get a cigarette," Misty said. She left. Nina listened for the hall door to close.

Clarke jumped up and started pacing around the office. Nina was reminded of the jungle cats alone in small cages at the zoo in San Francisco, tense, captive, and impotent. She stopped her thoughts and waited for him. "We have been seeing each other," he said.

"You're married."

"Very. Happily, I thought. And I have three kids. But when I met Misty, I was knocked out." He walked back to the desk and leaned over Nina. Now the tobacco smell mingled with English Leather. An aftershave wearer. Maybe his wife bought it for him. "I never intended for anything to happen. But Misty wanted me and she let me know it. . . ."

He stopped at the picture window, glowering out at traffic moving slowly through a green light. Nina took the moment to examine him, wondering how he stayed so fit, what he did with those hands, why he was endangering his career and marriage with an affair. "I hate this," he said.

"You must be worried her husband will find out."

He turned back and she saw fear and anger in his face. "Not only is he the violent type, he's the devious type. He could ruin my career, my whole life. Easily. Meanwhile, where is he? I'm hoping this ends with him dead."

"Before you hope that, you'd better hope it won't end with Misty in jail," Nina said. Misty opened the office door and slid into her seat. "What do you think the chances are your husband knows about the two of you? I mean, my assistant knew."

"Sandy only knew because I told her when I said I wanted to see you. I know her from one of her kids who works at Prize's. She'd never blab about it," the girl said. "I'm very careful." Clarke said nothing. He was busy contemplating Nina's file cabinet. She wondered what he wasn't telling her.

"Do you want to stay married to Anthony?"

"No."

"That makes it easy. We can get a divorce proceeding started," Nina said. "Give me authority to apply for some standard restraining orders for you, to keep Anthony away from you and the house. Report him missing."

"Problem is, how do I make it, up here? Cocktail waitresses make six bucks an hour and tips, and it's off-season. The checking account is in his name. He handled everything. And I can't go back home."

"Half the property and money is yours. I can help you with that. How long have you been married?"

"Three and a half years," Misty said.

"I gotta go," Tom Clarke said. "I have to work this week even if the kids are on Easter vacation."

"Sure, Tom, you go ahead," Misty said. She stood up and handed him his coat.

He pushed his chair back. "Glad to have you on board, Miss Reilly. This conversation, our visit, is entirely confidential, of course?"

"Of course. There's a back door that will take you directly out to the parking lot."

"Misty, I'll call at lunch. Don't worry, now. You're in good hands." As he moved to leave, he cast Nina a look that Misty could not see, a look that said, "She's all yours."

"Bye, Tommy," Misty said, waggling her fingers like one of his schoolgirls.

As soon as Clarke left, Misty Patterson straightened up and pushed her hair out of her eyes. Nina told her she would need a thousand dollars for a retainer for the divorce, less than half what she would have requested in San Francisco. Misty said her parents in Fresno would pay for it. They talked about moving her into a motel for a few days. Sandy must have been listening, because she buzzed Nina. She said she knew a safe place and called Art Wong, the manager at the Lucky Chip Motel right at the Stateline—Lake Tahoe border. He said he could put Misty in a single for twenty-five a night, under any name she liked.

Sandy brought in the petition and the application for the restraining orders.

"Okay, let's get your date of marriage."

"Three years last September twentieth."

"Children?"

"God, no." She paused. "Anthony's not the daddy type. He wants all my attention."

"Do you have friends, relatives around here?"

"I talk to some of the girls at work. Other than that, just old boyfriends. I've been waitressing a year and a half. I wanted to work, and Anthony wanted to keep an eye on me."

"For good reason?" Nina said gently.

She shrugged.

"Where are your parents?"

"Fresno. We moved there from the Subic Navy Base in the Philippines, where we lived until I was ten. No brothers, no sisters, just me."

"Do you see them much?"

"Anthony and my father argue so much . . . and then my mom gets all upset and goes to her room. Sometimes my dad comes up and rents a boat and he and I go fishing. We get along better now that we don't live together. I didn't like my dad as a teenager. He really overinflated when I started getting interested in boys." She gave Nina a little smile: defiant, shamefaced, and secretive.

"Earlier, you said you didn't think Anthony knew about your . . . friends," Nina said.

"I told you, I'm careful. And I try to do whatever he wants, otherwise. That protects me. At least, it did till last week." She closed her eyes, then opened them and smoothed her forehead with bare fingers. Noticing Nina's eyes, she said, "Tips are better if you skip the wedding band. We all do it."

"Let's get a quick listing of your assets and debts for the petition," Nina said. They spent ten minutes listing the maxed-out credit cards, the cars, the VCR and the stereo, the jewelry and the ski equipment. No IRA's, no Keogh Plan, no stocks, no retirement. Anthony Patterson was the sole signator on the checking account statement Misty had brought. It showed a balance of over forty thousand dollars, an amount that Misty couldn't explain. Nina made a note to ask for a court order accessing the account. She explained that the judge required specific facts to support the request for restraining orders, and asked if Anthony hit her frequently.

Misty said, "Like I said, he pushed me around. Usually he won't leave a mark. But Thursday he was so pissed off, I'm still bruised up. Look for yourself." She pulled the T-shirt casually above white shoulders mottled with splotches like purple finger painting. An ugly multicolored bruise defiled her right breast. "Feel my scalp," she demanded. Nina probed under the hair. "Ow!"

"I need pictures of those bruises," Nina said, thinking, that'll make some judge's day.

"I'll get Tom to do it."

"Does he abuse you in other ways?"

"He squeezes and twists my arms. He takes me to bed whether I want to or not. He holds back on money when he's unhappy: gas money, money for lunches. By December last year, I was drinking a pint of Yukon Jack every night and smoking dope every day before I went to work. I had no friends, you know? Just guys I picked up and got rid of after a few sessions."

"Is that what made you see a therapist?"

"No. Just partly. I had this other major problem. See, I can't remember much of anything about my childhood. We lived in the Philippines until I was ten, but all I remember are small details—you know, warm air, palm trees, rainbows, flowers, and bugs. What I can't remember is me there. Okay, so who remembers that much about being a kid? But I started having these nightmares. God, they scare the life out of me." She shivered. She swallowed some coffee, and when Nina said nothing, she continued slowly. "In them, my father is a kind of . . . monster from the dead."

She was way off the matter at hand, but Nina was interested.

"Did you ask your parents about all this?"

She shook her head. "I tried, but my dad told me not to be ridiculous, my childhood was fine. He refused to say any more about it. They never talk about Subic."

"Why'd they leave the Philippines?"

"Mom and Dad had some kind of run-in with the Church there. I don't know the details. They're less involved now, but seem much happier in Fresno.

"Anyway, I was scared to sleep and got so I couldn't get out of bed in the morning. Anthony, big help, told me I was full of shit, pretty much. Told me I looked better smiling.

"He always has something going at work, some deal that is going to make us rich, or somebody who's done something that bugged him, who he has to pay back, you know? My troubles bore him or make him mad. Sometimes he closes the curtains and lies down in the bed with me on our days off. He gets out the booze and he . . . uses me. I lie there thinking about the next time I can see Tom, or thinking, if I die now, who cares? A dumb animal, like a dog, chained to that bed and that man and just worth nothing."

"Why do you stay?"

"Seems so easy to someone like you, doesn't it?" Misty asked unexpectedly. "I bet you never lost control of a situation in your life. Ever had somebody tell you they'd much rather see you dead than lose you? How about that somebody used to be a cop and knows how to use guns? A guy who cries over sappy songs, a guy who tells me he loves me thousands of times. A guy that watches me every second, who complains when I wear certain clothes, not because he wants me pretty for other people, but because he thinks I should always think about how to please him. A guy I cheat on and don't love anymore . . . but he is not going to let go. Never! So Thursday . . ." She paused.

"That night . . ." Nina prompted.

"I knew I wanted to go. I didn't know how to leave him. I didn't know what to say. And when I got there, the mood was evil. Ax-sharp, ready to chop. Before I even said anything." She looked thoughtful for a moment, then sighed. "Do you think he read my mind? Dr. Greenspan says we have a lot of ways of communicating our intentions. But it seemed like maybe he had worked through something, or decided something. . . ." Neither of them spoke for a minute. "Angels passing," Misty said softly, pointing toward the ceiling.

Then she put her elbows on the desk, cupping her face in her hands. "One night a few months ago I went into the kitchen and looked at the oven, thinking, how do you do this? Because I'm not very mechanically inclined. I mean, how do you get the gas to come out without heating it up so you bake to death? How do you stuff yourself in so you won't fall out?"

She sounded bad, lost, incredibly sad. The only thing Nina could think of to say was, "You didn't do it."

"That's when I first went to see Dr. Greenspan, over near the hospital. I asked him to give me some pills, something to cheer me up, but he wouldn't. He won't just hand out pills; he tries other things. He gave me some good ideas about eating better, not that I always do, but at least now I think about it. And I've been doing hypnotherapy with him, 'cause I feel like if I could just figure out this dream, everything would be fine." She let out a little laugh. "Sure. Even he says that's not bloody likely."

"And Anthony? What does he think about the therapy?" Nina asked.

There it was, that hard look again. "He didn't know what kind of a doctor Greenspan was at first. Now he says I have to stop. When he ran off last week I called Dr. Greenspan for a short emergency session this weekend, to help me through all this."

"All right, Misty," Nina said. "I have enough to draft up the paperwork and get you started. Go straight to the police department on Al Tahoe Boulevard and tell them you have a missing persons report. Tell them you and Anthony had a disagreement, without getting into details. Say you've been hiding from him and you're afraid. Tell them I'm getting restraining orders for you. Then check into the Lucky Chip Motel. Come back tomorrow morning and you can read and sign off on the paperwork and sign the retainer agreement."

She nodded. "Okay."

"One more thing. What did you do about the mess from Thursday night? The coffee table that broke and the statue?"

"The statue was gone when I woke up. I guess Anthony took it somewhere. Everything else I cleaned up the next morning, before I left. That stuff went out with the trash."

"Why?"

"I was just about to leave and I thought, Anthony'll come back and he'll get reminded. Well, not if I can help it. I even scrubbed off the blood on the couch pillow."

Sandy walked her out and Nina went down the hall to brush her hair and get a drink of water. When she got back, Sandy said, "Mrs. Patterson said she forgot to tell you the police were over at her next-door neighbor's. Something about his boat."

"Make a note and stick it in the file," Nina said.

"Come in, Mr. Sandoval." Another new client, thanks to Sandy. My, she was a busy lady. "Sorry to keep you waiting."

Something in the interview needed revisiting. She had it for a moment, then lost it. Something the girl had said suggested . . . what? She thought hard, closed her eyes to the sight of an unhappy man turned brutal thug, attacking his wife in a scene that happened all over every night, but nothing else came. Opening her eyes, she glimpsed Misty standing on the corner outside her window, waiting for the light to change, tall, pale, young, and lovely, hugging herself against the breeze. Old Mr. Sandoval struggled over to the window, leaning on his cane, and watched her move across the street.

"Ah," he said.

5

NINA BROUGHT MISTY'S paperwork down to the court just before five on Monday, but the hearing examiner who handled temporary restraining orders had already gone home, and Judge Milne had left at three.

"Call in the morning and I'll let you know if you got your signatures," said the clerk who had been left in charge.

"After looking at our declaration, don't you think we have an emergency here?" Nina said. "The husband may find her tonight." The petition for restraining orders was always accompanied by a statement of facts by the petitioner, showing why the petition should be granted. Most states used affidavits; California used a special form called a declaration.

"He hasn't found her in three days. He couldn't be looking very hard," the clerk said. She was a small, unruffled black lady who had seen it all. There were other people in line behind her, scared-looking young women with kids and a couple of rumpled men who must be lawyers. "That's the best I can do," she said.

On Tuesday, when Sandy called the court, she was told that an additional declaration would have to be filed showing why the respondent hadn't been given advance notice that orders were being sought against him. "Why didn't you tell me this yesterday?" Nina said, getting on the phone line.

"Thought you knew what you were doing, so I didn't

check through the papers as carefully as I would for a *pro se* petitioner," the clerk said. "If you want, you can come down and fill out a form in handwriting and sign off like the wives do."

"I'll do that." She went straight down to the courthouse, filled out the form, and said pleasantly that she would wait for the orders, hiding her annoyance. Every county had its own peculiar procedures, and sometimes you didn't find out about them in advance. The orders came back in twenty minutes. She took them over to the sheriff's office. As long as the papers were on file with the sheriff, the sheriff could make an immediate arrest if Anthony came after Misty.

One problem remained about enforcing the restraining orders. By law, Anthony Patterson had to get notice of the orders before he could be held responsible for violating them. Most of the time a friend of the wife's could go to the husband's workplace or the local bar and serve him. Here, unless she mounted her own search, that could not be done. Misty could carry around a spare set. If Anthony showed up, she could serve him, though the law said a party to the action wasn't supposed to do so. Nina went hunting for Misty at the Lucky Chip.

Between the Stateline casinos and the Lakeside Park Beach, on the California side, a warren of anonymous motels had sprung up to accommodate vacationers in various states of financial disarray. The Lucky Chip, with its small, empty pool and small, empty parking lot, had absolutely nothing to recommend it except its nightly rate. Nina wondered why Sandy had chosen this particular one. A young woman in sweats, talking to a baby in an infant seat on the counter, looked up as she came in, and Nina had her answer. Sandy's young clone. "I'm looking for Art Wong," Nina said.

"He's the owner. He's not around. Can I help you?" The

baby flung things on the floor in a kind of disgusted commentary as they talked.

"I need to leave some very important papers for one of the people staying here. Michelle Patterson."

"Sure. I can see her room from here. I'll catch her when she comes in."

"Don't forget."

"Sandy would call up a devil if I did," the girl said.

"Any idea where Mrs. Patterson might be?"

"Nope. She did say she goes to work at four, so she'll probably be back before then."

Where was Misty? Should she try to reach her through Tom Clarke? Not a good idea. Misty was a secret in his life and Nina would hate to be the one to drop the gossip bombshell. Anyway, she had a feeling that now that the going had gotten tough, Tom Clarke would be going. That would be tough for Misty. She was used to depending on men, Nina imagined.

Misty arrived at the motel at a little after three o'clock, a bottle tucked under her arm. She waved toward the office, dropped her keys, picked them up and dropped them again. Fitting the key into the lock took some time.

She changed into her skimpy tuxedo, threw a long sweatshirt over it, and headed out the door wearing run-down shoes, a bag with her heels swinging by her side. As she walked to the casino, letting the wind give her a nudge now and then, she sang to herself. "I'm gonna tell you how it's going to be. You're gonna give your love to me. My love for you has got to be real. I want you to know just how I feel." She crossed at a busy corner and resumed her song. "My love is real, not fade away." She walked for a few minutes before she stopped dead in her tracks. The booze wore off too damn quickly these days. That was his song and she was trying hard to forget.

She hurried to her job, resolutely silent, and worked the entire shift with an ache that began in her head and cruised throughout her body in the course of the evening.

At midnight, in the locker room, history repeated itself, as it had every night since she'd last seen her husband. She changed the clothes and wiped off the makeup, horribly conscious of her habits and the fact that tonight she would not be going to the house at the Keys, but to the Lucky Chip. Not even Tom would be there to keep her warm. He was avoiding her. Two police officers from South Lake Tahoe met her in the Lucky Chip parking lot. "Mrs. Patterson?" one said.

"That's me," she said. "What can I do for you?" She used the polite words she used at the casino every night with certain types of men to subdue her reaction to seeing them, which was fear.

"We need to talk with you."

"What about?"

"Your husband."

"What about him? Do you know where he is?"

The cop cleared his throat. "When did you last see your husband?" he said.

"Thursday night. We had a bad fight."

"You haven't seen him since?"

"No. I didn't want to see him again. Are you going to tell me what this is all about?"

"I'm sorry. I have to give you some bad news. He's dead, Mrs. Patterson."

"Oh, no!" Misty wailed. "Where did you find him?"

"At the bottom of the lake."

And then Misty did something that surprised everyone. She took off at a fast trot across the parking lot.

"Mrs. Patterson, wait. Come back here!" The two cops took off after her, one talking into a black box, the other running like a man who knew how to run fast.

She got through the lot to a side street, and started up the hill toward Heavenly's looming ski trails. Amazed at her own strength, she quickly outpaced her pursuers. She veered off onto Pioneer Trail, losing herself in a path she remembered.

Hearing but not listening to sirens, she found the flat granite rock she and Anthony had picnicked upon when they first came to Tahoe. She stopped, panting, and wiped her wet face. On a blue-and-white cloth decorated with roosters, she had laid out the meal. They drank wine from the bottle and settled in to snuggle on the ground, leaning against the rock. Everything had been so perfect that day, hadn't it? He must have told her he loved her a hundred times. Strange how, thinking back, the words had been so hard for her even then, the glare of his feelings eclipsing her own pale light.

A long time later, they found her there. "I didn't mean to kill him," she said. "I didn't think I hit him that hard. I can't believe he's dead." They looked at each other. The tall one nodded.

"You have the right to remain silent," said the small one, the one with the stiff hair, Sgt. Higuera. He talked on.

The other one stood her up and put her hands behind her back. He clicked handcuffs neatly into place.

They led her toward a police car with an open back door. She called up every technique she ever had for controlling herself, imagining herself elsewhere, imagining herself dreaming, imagining herself dead.

She heard herself screaming, but couldn't stop.

The man in the front seat, the one scribbling into a notebook, looked back at her. "We'll be there in just a couple of minutes. Settle down. Try to enjoy the ride."

"It was just another fight like a million other fights!" But it wasn't, she knew it wasn't. She had hit him and now he was dead. "Guilty as sin," she murmured. That's what her mother always said, and the words seemed right. She knew she should shut up but she couldn't. She said a few more things, then she rested her head back against the dirty vinyl and let herself cry.

6

THE PHONE CALL came after midnight on Tuesday. Nina had been lying between cold sheets, thinking that if she jumped up to get another blanket, her cold feet would freeze solid. The moment she heard the ring, she knew who it would be. She knocked her water glass over when she reached through the dark, shattering it on the floor.

"Ms. Reilly? It's me, Misty Patterson. Anthony is dead. My husband."

"I'm listening," Nina said. "If I interrupt you, stop talking right away."

"First off, I'm in jail. They say I killed him!" This the girl followed with an incoherent curse.

"Stop right there. Have you been booked? What's the charge?"

"Murder."

"What have they told you about your husband?"

"All I know is they found him in Lake Tahoe. You're my lawyer. You have to get me out of here right away before I start screaming again, please. Whatever it takes. I have to get out. . . ."

Nina knew an emergency when she heard one. This girl was having trouble holding it together. She made her voice as level as she could. "Keep your head. You have to tell me what you know about Anthony."

"Get me out of here!"

"I'll talk to the officer on duty right after we talk, but from what you've said nothing can happen until tomorrow. Mrs. Patterson, Misty, listen—"

Sobbing on the other end of the line.

"You're going to get through this. This may not be as bad as you think."

"I'm dying in here!"

"You're not a kid," said Nina softly. "And I'm not your mother. They're only going to give us five minutes. Understand?"

After a long pause, a shaky voice replied, "I understand."

"I'll be down there in the morning. I'll call your parents then, if you haven't had a chance to. Two things. First, think of all the people you know who've spent the night in the hoosegow."

"I don't feel safe in here," she said, in a sullen tone that told Nina she had calmed down.

"I'll be looking out for you there, I promise. Second, if anyone wants to talk to you or ask any questions, tell them you are exercising your right to remain silent and refer them to me. Say that back to me."

"I'm exercising my right . . ."

"To remain silent."

"You are my lawyer and they should talk to you."

"I'm depending on you to do that. Can you do that, Misty?"

"Sure," Misty Patterson said, crying again. "Whatever."

Turning on the bedstand light, Nina sat up on the side of the bed, pulling the covers around her. The icy night air crept into cracks around her body, and she could just hear Bobby's light snore from the kids' room.

Picking up the phone again, she located the officer on duty. Misty Patterson had been booked for the unlawful killing of Anthony Patterson. If Nina wanted to appear at the arraignment, she would need to talk to Collier Hallowell, the deputy district attorney who had signed off on the arrest warrant. Misty would have her own cell, because it was a Tuesday night, not too much action. That was all he knew. Nina lay back on the bed, her mind working busily.

She left the shards of glass for morning and finally sank back into her own troubled dream, in which Tom Clarke, looking disappointed, spanked her, then pulled her pants off and screwed her. She woke up feeling angry and cut her foot getting out of bed.

Off Al Tahoe Boulevard in a grove of pines, the county jail took up almost one floor of the low redwood building that also held the Municipal Court of the Lake Tahoe District, County of El Dorado. Nina spotted the crowded ski runs at Heavenly Valley through the trees as she approached. Spring wind whirled eddies between the parked cars. Soft green grass poked up through the last of the snow. Nina wrapped her coat around her and walked from the parking lot past a dry fountain, ringing a bell on the wall. A voice in a metal grate crackled, "Who is it?"

"Nina Reilly. I'm Michelle Patterson's attorney. She was brought in last night." The door buzzed and she grabbed the handle.

Partway down the hallway a fresh-faced guard with slick hair and a spiffy clean uniform checked her California State Bar card from his glass kiosk, scrutinizing her with the alert curiosity required in his line of work. "Hi," Nina said, extending her hand. He shook it. "I need to see my client."

"You're her lawyer?"

"Yes."

"This is a criminal case. Don't you mostly do family law?"

He laughed at her expression. "It's a small town here. We hear rumors. Everybody talks."

"I am . . . was representing her in her divorce."

"Oh. So she'll be looking for a good criminal lawyer. You know, Jeff Riesner's the local expert."

Lucky Jeff, to have the police chasing their own sirens on his behalf. "I've heard."

"Hey, Gordy," he said. "Get Patterson. Her lawyer's here." While they waited for Gordy to return with Misty, he flipped through papers.

"He's got the town locked up pretty tight, does he?"

"I'm not dumb enough to say a word against the man," he said. "You here to shake things up?"

Sensible Nina said no. Perverse Nina said, "You never know."

She walked past the kiosk and was buzzed into one of the visiting cubicles. She sat down. Misty Patterson came in and sat down in a chair on the other side of the glass partition, her hair pulled away from her face this time in a ponytail. Her eyes hid inside deep sockets. She looked about sixteen. Nina picked up her telephone, but Misty didn't budge, wooden as the furniture. Nina pointed to the receiver. "Pick it up," she mouthed.

"Good morning, Ms. Reilly." Misty said formally into the receiver. "Don't ask how I slept."

"How are you feeling?"

"Are you going to get me out now?"

"It doesn't work like that. You're charged with a serious crime, but there will be a bail hearing tomorrow."

"My dad'll bail me out. He'll be royally pissed off, but he'll stand by me."

"There's a problem. It's hard to get bail on a charge like this. The DA's office thinks you're a flight risk. Remember how you ran when they came to arrest you? They're going to ask to keep you here pending trial."

"Oh, no! No!"

"I'm sorry," Nina said. "I need to find out more about what's going on, then I'll see what I can do for you. So, help me out here."

"The South Lake Tahoe Police picked me up just after my shift was over at Prize's. Probably nobody even knows where I am." Nina thought they would probably know this morning, when the *Tahoe Mirror* came out. "I got to call my parents this morning. They're coming up. I gave them your name."

"Tell me what you can about your husband, Anthony. And what you said to the officers."

"They read me my rights. I'm not sure what-all I said at first." She sounded a little evasive. "Then they tried to get me to say I knew Anthony was dead all along. They said they knew we were having problems. They wanted to know why I didn't report him missing."

"What? I thought you were going to go straight to the police station when you left my office."

"I wanted to make sure I didn't miss Tom's call, then I was going to go. Remember? You wanted pictures and he was supposed to call me. But he didn't call." Her voice wavered from high to low. "My neighbor, Rick? He's a real decent guy. He always let us borrow his boat. Anyway, he reported it stolen when he got back Sunday night. So somebody spotted it, not so far off the Keys yesterday sometime. That's what they told me. When they went to get it they found Anthony. In the lake, the boat floating above him . . ." Her voice faded. " 'Terrific visibility in Lake Tahoe that night,' one guy said. 'Like the old days.' "

"Are you okay, Misty?"

"I wish I could see him." She locked eyes with Nina through the glass. "I don't believe he's dead."

"You need a lawyer right away to represent you on this charge."

"You're my lawyer."

"Not on this charge. You consulted me about a divorce. You and your parents need to talk about who to retain as your counsel. I know you'll want the best representation you can get."

"Forget that. I want you as my lawyer. Sandy said you're famous in San Francisco, and not just for family law. For criminal defense."

"Sandy exaggerated," Nina said, thinking she'd have to put a muzzle on that woman. "My experience is limited. I handled criminal appeals. I've never defended a client against a charge of murder in a trial. I'm not confident I could represent you competently."

"I have to unload something, Nina, even if it gets me into trouble. When the police came? I panicked and it wasn't because they arrested me. I panicked because I figured I did kill him."

"Misty, wait—"

"I want you to hear this. If I killed him when I hit him, how did he end up in the lake? I'd never take Rick's boat out by myself to dump him. I'd call Tom or somebody to help me. I just don't remember what the hell happened that night after I hit him. I'm thinking maybe it's like this stuff with my past, another thing I'm blocking out, something traumatic."

Murder certainly qualified as traumatic. Didn't Misty realize that her loss of memory about the events that night, if real, pointed as surely to her guilt?

"I never intended to kill Anthony. I wasn't mad like that. I just wanted it to be over with him."

"Were you afraid for your life? Can you at least remember that?" Nina couldn't keep the skepticism out of her voice.

"He never hurt me like he wanted to kill me. Mixed in with all the love talk, I know he hated me sometimes. I think he wanted to make my life a living hell. But I never once thought he wanted me dead."

"Of course, you did strike out to defend yourself. Maybe you hit too hard. That's hardly premeditated murder."

"Aren't you listening? I just don't think I hit him that hard. Believe me, I've seen a couple of bar fights. You can whack a guy pretty good without killing him. I didn't kill him. You have to believe me."

"I believe you're being as honest with me as you can." That was Nina's standard line to a client who was probably lying. But sitting there, looking through the glass at the girl, having talked to her three times now and listened to the blunt and ingenuous revelations, she couldn't imagine Misty had invented the whole ball, loose and tangled with strings dangling in all directions. Why not make up a tighter story? Even Misty must see that the actions she described were not logical.

"You think any other lawyer can defend me? I don't even know what I did. And one look and they're going to be like, 'Ditz. Airhead. Don't go betting your allowance on that tootsie roll.' Most of the time I don't care what they think, but if your lawyer thinks you're a piece of shit, that matters."

"Oh, Misty." She didn't have any idea what she was asking Nina to do.

"I need you on my side."

"You need a good lawyer."

"You."

Nina felt herself wavering. "I can't promise anything now, but I'll let you know by tomorrow."

"Talk to my parents. I'll give you the number. Tell them what you need for money."

Nina said, "Listen, a couple of things for now: Stay calm and keep your mouth shut. If anybody bothers you, call me. I'm leaving some money at the desk for you. Remember, don't talk about your case. Don't talk about your dead husband."

"My dead husband." Misty closed her eyes, her chest heaving. Terrified, exhausted, she sat drooped in her chair, one hand clasped to her breast, tendrils of soft hair escaping from the rubber band. She looked tragic and melodramatically beautiful, a belle demoiselle weeping in a dungeon.

On her way out to the car, stepping over the mud puddles in the asphalt, Nina walked with her head down, thinking about Misty. Andrea said that most wives of battering husbands lived in fear. They generally tried to keep the batterer calm by behaving as close to perfectly as possible. This young woman did not seem to fit that mold.

Why had she married Anthony Patterson? Did Misty even know the real answer? He must have had something, Nina finally decided, to sweet-talk her into marriage, because whether she knew it or not, Misty could have her pick of the males of the world.

Nina shouldn't take the case, not because she couldn't handle it, she told herself, but because she should start small here, build a reputation block by block. She should avoid splashy cases with muddy circumstances. She should build a life. Jack would say . . . Oh, the hell with what Jack would say. But Matt would be horrified. The community at large would not welcome her.

Yes, there was a sensible way to approach things, and she prided herself on her good sense and rationality at the same time she was feeding the cyborg ice cream. She wanted to take this case.

She would sleep on it. In the morning, she would know what to do.

Mulling, she reversed direction, walking back toward the building, this time turning into the offices of the El Dorado County District Attorney.

"Mr. Hallowell is in court in Placerville this morning," a clerk guarding the window reported. A square-faced Asian-American sailed out of an inner office, his arms full of files. The clerk called out, "Mr. Lam?" As he passed her desk, she tucked an envelope on the top of the pile.

"Mr. Lam? The new deputy DA, right?" Nina asked, falling into step beside him as he pushed through the double doors into the courtyard. She introduced herself. "I've been asked to represent Michelle Patterson. Do me a favor and tell me what you can about the charge."

"Really? Hmmm. That's going to startle a few people," he said, slowing down to study her. "You're new here, also, I understand."

Nina nodded.

"Well, I heard she is one good-looking . . . defendant," Lam said. His broad face under the heavy glasses spread into a big smile. "Really, you should wait and talk to Collier."

"I'm good about favors," she said. Whatever it was he thought she meant, it worked. His eyes were calculating.

"You can call me Burton, and I hope you will," he said. "On one condition. You didn't hear this from our office."

"Duly sworn. Just tell me what you know about the body, Burton."

"Ah, yes, the corpus submarinus . . . Well, I heard the Coast Guard found a stolen boat floating empty out on Lake Tahoe, about a half mile out from the Keys. They found traces of blood in the boat. Maybe somebody had sloshed lake water around in the galley or maybe the storm last weekend got it, because it was semiwashed, but the blood wasn't totally gone. Because of the blood, a diver was sent down to have a look around. Bad luck for the defendant." Lam shifted his files. "I have to be in court two minutes ago."

"So tell me fast," Nina said.

"You know all the stories about Lake Tahoe being so deep and cold, people who drown never get seen again? It's normally a couple hundred feet deep there, and murky from the boat traffic. The lake was much shallower than usual a long way out and was unusually clear yesterday, like in the old days. They picked him off clean sand thirty-five feet down. You know why bodies don't float on Lake Tahoe? Because it's melted snow. And corpses sinking into melted snow don't decompose like they would in warmer water. They don't form gases and puff up.

"Probably a bunch of dead things hanging around on the bottom from way back," he added thoughtfully. "Like in a dinosaur tar pit. Bodies just waiting to be discovered. The diver said Patterson wasn't lying there. He was sitting, leaning over a little, head up and bobbing. And his eyes and mouth were open. Looked like he was just about to say something. Not a nibble on him. Perfectly preserved, like a woolly mammoth. Or good ol' *T. rex.*"

7

NINA MARCHED BY the jail for the second time just as an older couple stopped in consternation at the locked door. "Push the buzzer," Nina advised, passing them on her way to the county clerk's office. First-timers. It was not what most people expected when they went to visit a jail. She walked on, hearing behind her some argument over the intercom.

"Tengstedt," the man at the door said, and began to spell the name.

"No visitors until five o'clock, sir."

"But my daughter—"

"The hours are posted on the door," said the voice on the intercom firmly. The man stared fixedly at the grille, as if considering ways to damage the speaker. His wife took his arm, leading him to a concrete bench in the shadows.

Nina walked back and introduced herself. "You must be Misty Patterson's parents." Nina held out her hand and Misty's father, after an initial hesitation, clasped it in a crushing handshake. Nina had forgotten to squeeze hard and was sure she had lost a few points already in the appraisal that was being made.

"We can't see Michelle until five," Carl Tengstedt said.

"They have visiting hours only twice a week," Nina said. "Since you drove all the way from Fresno, it's fortunate you picked one of the two days. At least you'll get a chance to see her today."

"Our daughter is in jail," Tengstedt said. "Of course we got here as soon as we could."

A short man, uncomfortable in a pin-striped suit, he looked as though he missed his uniform. "You say you are her attorney?"

"I do represent Misty, in another legal matter. I just learned about her arrest, and I talked to her a few minutes ago. She asked me then to represent her in the criminal proceeding," Nina said. She suggested they reconvene in her office. They walked out to the cars in strained silence.

"Misty. I guess Anthony Patterson gave Michelle that nickname. Young lady," Carl Tengstedt said a half hour later from the tapestry chair facing Nina's desk, "just what kind of law do you practice?" He looked at the certificates on the wall, showing she had graduated from the Monterey School of Law five years before, showing she had been admitted to the California Supreme Court the next year, and the Ninth Circuit Court of Appeals about then. Suddenly the prized certificates seemed a little skimpy.

Tengstedt continued looking around the room, his unfriendly gaze lighting upon the stacks of paperwork on the floor she kept meaning to pick up, photos pinned up and not yet framed, the rug that needed vacuuming because people had tracked in mud from the parking lot. He was about sixty, but his hair was still reddish, what you could still see of it. His left hand, on her desk, made a fist as though he still had some use in mind for it.

"I didn't say I have agreed to represent your daughter on the charge against her," Nina said. "Up here, like most of the attorneys, I practice whatever law is required by the client. Everything but tax and workers' compensation."

"You handle divorces," Tengstedt said.

"Those too."

Tengstedt leaned forward, while his wife sat still beside him, her shoulders curved in toward her body. Nina had a sense of déjà vu. Misty had sat just like that before Nina had stopped listening to Tom Clarke and forced her to tell her story. Barbara Tengstedt wore her blond hair in a smooth chin-length pageboy. She wore a beige wool skirt and sweater. She had Misty's pale skin and slimness, but hollow eyes and thin lips aged her.

"What I'm trying to figure out is why you think you can take this case," Tengstedt said. "No offense."

"None taken. I understand you want your daughter to be well represented. There are several other attorneys in town she could retain. The most experienced one is Jeffrey Riesner at Caplan, Stamp, Powell, and Riesner, and I'll have Sandy give you his phone number so you can talk to him. I don't know him personally, because I am new here, but if Misty wishes, I can refer you to San Francisco counsel." She heard a sniff from the outer office, and got up to shut the office door firmly.

"As it happens, I do have some experience in this area. For the past four years, at Rothman, Akers, and Teeter in San Francisco, my practice has emphasized criminal law as well as family law. Although my criminal trial work hasn't specifically included a homicide to this point, I have handled appeals of people convicted of homicide. I argued the appeals in the First District Court of Appeals and in the California Supreme Court. I'm current on the law."

Tengstedt did not seem impressed. "You defended people convicted of murder?" he asked finally, his voice thin. She could see it in his eyes, hear it in his voice. Her office was too small. Her secretary looked like a refugee from the homeless mission. Looking at herself through his eyes, she saw a young woman with brown hair that was too long and a skirt that was too short. No gold jewelry, no Mont Blanc pen, no Chanel suit, none of the trappings of a rich and successful businesswoman. Even his coffee mug advertised the local Thrifty. He wanted bigness, a deep voice, an impression of physical power. For him, the physical and mental power showed up together. Nina blamed Raymond Burr.

"Well, I would like to get some references."

"Sure," Nina said.

"And I'd like to know how much you would charge."

"Twenty-five thousand dollars as an initial retainer, billed against my usual hourly rate of two hundred dollars per hour. Plus expenses," Nina said. "Including the investigator's time."

"I'm sure you can understand we need to talk to Michelle about this," Tengstedt said.

"You know, she can also request a public defender. You aren't obligated to pay for her attorney," Nina said. "And it appears she may have some funds of her own." If she could get into Anthony's bank account.

"No, no, we can help her. We just . . . need to know where she stands. You say she has already asked you to represent her. Do you think that's a good idea?"

"I don't have the same amount of felony trial experience as, for example, Mr. Riesner. But other factors in a particular case may balance that out. For one thing, your daughter has expressed confidence in me, and—"

"She hasn't got a clue about people," Carl Tengstedt said. "Look who she married."

"Let me finish," Nina said. "I believe that she has told me the truth, at least as she understands it, about the events surrounding Mr. Patterson's death."

"So?"

"Some of the things she has told me are, frankly, hard to believe. And another lawyer, who does not believe her, might be inclined to handle the case in a very different way than I would."

"So?"

"I think it is important to her case that her ideas and feelings not be disregarded. We have established rapport—that could mean the difference between success and failure in a situation like this one, where there's a lot of confusion to clear up."

Tengstedt's frown had been deepening as she spoke. "Sorry," Tengstedt said. "You've lost me. We'll talk to her and get back to you."

"Please keep in mind that I have not agreed to represent her yet. I told her I will let her know tomorrow. There is a bail hearing coming up and I would suggest that I at least cover that for her, since I'm familiar with what's going on."

"That would be helpful," Tengstedt said, seeming to soften slightly. They talked about the no-bail recommendation for several minutes.

"Fresno is three hours' drive from here," Nina said then. "If I do represent your daughter, I'll need to ask you to come up again very soon to meet with me."

"I run an auto dealership specializing in four-wheel-drive vehicles. I'm my own boss. I can come up anytime," Carl Tengstedt said with some pride. He seemed to be weighing something in his mind.

"Me too," Misty's mother said. She looked down at her hands. "I have arthritis, and I don't drive anymore myself."

"My mother had an arthritic condition too." Nina said. "Thank God for aspirin."

A deep silence greeted this pronouncement. Nina remembered, too late, that the Tengstedts were Christian Scientists who usually did not take medications. "I understand Michelle lived in the Philippines until she was ten," Nina said hastily.

More silence.

"She spent her adolescence in Fresno?" Nina had the feeling each question she asked offended them in some way.

"She used to be a pretty good student when she was little," Mrs. Tengstedt said, kneading her hands. "It certainly is cold in here."

"She got into some trouble with boys," Tengstedt said suddenly. "We told her, we tried to protect her, but by the time she was sixteen she was sneaking out her bedroom window. Up till then she had been such a good child."

"What caused that change in her personality? Do you think it was just adolescence?" Nina asked. Carl Tengstedt shot his wife a warning glance. What had she said that was so threatening? Nina could understand why Misty could not just ask her parents about the past.

"Hard to say," Tengstedt said. "Now we got to go find a place to stay tonight before we go back to see Michelle."

"You know, you haven't asked me anything about Anthony's death," Nina said.

Again, the hard military man and his wife sat rooted in their chairs. They were holding themselves together with great effort, Nina realized. Her questions, which seemed so innocuous, were adding to their pain. At length Mrs. Tengstedt said, "Whatever Michelle did—was involved in—we are going to stand behind her."

Nina thought about her words for a moment. "Mrs. Tengstedt, Misty told me two hours ago that she is innocent of this crime. You seem to have some doubts. Can you tell me why?"

"This is our daughter's life, Miss Reilly," Carl Tengstedt said. "Not some movie with a surprise ending. Michelle had her reasons, that we do not doubt. I'm not going to disown her. Maybe we protected her too much, drove her too much the other way. She ran off with the first animal to break open the gate. And in the end he got what he richly deserved."

"Don't be so quick to assume your daughter killed her husband, Mr. Tengstedt," Nina said. "I don't make that assumption."

"She's vulnerable," Tengstedt said as if he hadn't heard her, "to so many influences." He wound his thick watchband around his wrist. "We forgive whatever she has done and we believe Almighty God has forgiven her too. She'll take her punishment, but we'll make sure it is tempered with mercy. Did she tell you we had Anthony checked out before she married him? He was with the Fresno Police Department. They fired him after two years because he was crooked. The worst kind, one of those creatures that strongarms small business owners in return for 'protection.' Punished the ones that couldn't pay him off with broken arms."

"She didn't tell me that, no. This is very helpful," Nina murmured when he stopped.

"When we told Michelle everything we found out," he went on, his face betraying great emotion, "she took off. We never expected that. God knows what's been going on here."

"Carl knows about stress," Mrs. Tengstedt said. "He was a prisoner of war in Korea, shot down in his plane in the South China Sea. And he held on to his navigator in seas ten feet high until they picked him up. He's a war hero." She spoke as if she had memorized the lines. "Then he was caught by the North Koreans, and they—"

"Please, Barbara, enough," Carl Tengstedt said.

"But you were a hero!" she said, and now her voice beseeched him. What was she begging him to say?

"Let's go now, Barbara," he said, not looking anymore at Nina, looking inward at some private pain she could not begin to comprehend. His wife rose obediently. Carl Tengstedt offered his hand this time, and Nina remembered to prepare for the grip.

She walked with them to the front and asked Sandy to help them with a motel a grade above the Lucky Chip and to give them Mel Akers's phone number in case they decided to call for a reference. She also provided Jack's phone number at work. Maybe they'd have better luck reaching him. She knew he would say he had a high regard for her professional capabilities, if nothing else.

Her stomach was cramping with hunger. She ate a tuna sub and stopped by the Baths, a casino across the highway from Prize's. She passed into the timeless red-carpeted smoke, changed a twenty into quarters, and played the quarter slots. The cocktail waitresses here wore tiny white Roman togas that, as always, emphasized their secondary physical characteristics. They managed to look bored and anxious at the same time.

At two-thirty she was at the courthouse on another case she had just taken, entering late in the game for a small businessman who had been representing himself. The settlement conference went on all afternoon, because there were a half dozen Sacramento insurance company lawyers wrangling over who should have to pay for the damage in the warehouse fire that had destroyed her client's business. The client had told her to settle it and had given his parameters. By some miracle, and the heavy hand of the visiting Alpine County judge, a ferocious ranch owner named Amagosian, the case was settled.

Her client had been waiting outside. When she told him it was all over, at a figure he had said would be acceptable, he nonetheless expressed doubt about the settlement. He knew it was just; he knew he had let the main policy lapse a few days before the fire; he knew he was lucky to recover anything from his insurance broker; but he still hated taking a loss. "It's a good settlement if everybody comes out mad," Nina told him. She knew after he calmed down he would be relieved to still be solvent, and sure enough at six o'clock he stopped by with a bottle of Dom Pérignon. He popped the cork and Nina and Sandy helped him celebrate his deliverance from the legal system.

Before leaving, Nina drafted another letter of apology to Jack, which she added to the other yellow sheets in the wastebasket. She drove by the lake heading back to Matt's, admiring the starry night in spite of memories it inspired, which she moved fast to quash.

At home at last, she hugged Bobby before changing into jeans. The living room, warm and redolent of garlic, olive oil, and wood smoke, enfolded the family in its atmosphere, muting the children's voices, and the song of their mother, who made up words to an old tune, with the children's names featured prominently. Matt greeted her, then went outside for wood, saying this would be their last fire of the season. "Summer's coming," he announced. "Green sky at sunset."

"Is that really real, Uncle Matt?" asked Bobby, who was working on a page of multiplication problems on the floor.

"Good question, Bobby." Matt stroked his chin. "Brings up the issue of real reality versus virtual reality. Save that one for your mom at bedtime."

Nina's plan had been to say nothing. Instead, she unloaded a censored account of her day on Andrea, who stirred hot noodles, strained them, and snapped fresh green beans in between sips of hot apple cider.

"Here you go again, Nina."

"I wish everyone would quit saying that. Bobby is starting to patronize me too. He's started saying, 'Figures,' when I ask him to do anything, like brush his teeth. I don't think

I'm so predictable. I surprise myself more than I care to admit."

Andrea smiled and passed her a noodle. "Too soft, huh? But the kids like them this way." She dug around in her cupboard for a can of tomatoes. "I have to make one batch for them, without any visible ingredients, your basic white noodles and smooth red sauce, and one for us, the lumpy, clean-out-your nose, spiced-up version." She pulled some sausage out of the refrigerator and chopped it. "You said you were going to work four days a week, start slow, leave lots of time for a rich and fulfilling personal life."

"I did say that, but not as eloquently."

Andrea poured oregano, chopped onion and garlic, pepper and salt into the pan where the sausage hissed and spit.

"This case will receive some attention, establish my practice. The money will set me up for a while."

"You could go at that more gradually," Andrea said.

Nina chewed on a breadstick. "I'm not the gradual type. Besides, I'm already in it. She wants me, whether her parents do or not. I hear Riesner's competent, but this girl has a special problem."

Andrea handed her a pile of mismatched knives and forks and motioned her toward the dining room. "Which is?"

"She's too fucking beautiful, if you'll excuse the expression. She's existing in sex-object limbo, with only male relationships. She would do better with a woman lawyer who could see past her body."

Andrea called from the kitchen, "What I would have given for such a problem in my salad days. But don't you try to avoid tangling psyches with a client? I mean, you can't fix everything. All you have to do is the legal part, right?"

"You know from the Tahoe Women's Shelter how that works, Andrea. Poverty, divorce, support, mental illness, physical disability, employment problems, truant kids, aged grandmothers, bounced checks, alcohol, self-hatred—you name it, the social problems women have are always intertwined with their legal problems."

"But it's too overwhelming to take all that on. Each of us professional helpers steps in to fix one little part of it, so we don't end up all together in the psycho ward."

Nina sat down at the table, remembering a custody hearing a few years before. Just before the case was called, she had been arguing vehemently with the opposing counsel that her client, the mother, should have physical custody. After a couple of minutes the lawyer, an imposing, elderly man, had stepped back from her and said in an accusatory tone, "Why, you've become completely personally involved!" So what? Her client was about to lose her kids! But back then, all she had felt was shame, the shame of acting like a human being when she was supposed to be acting like a lawyer.

"I care enough about her to want to fight a legal battle for her. She's got her own rounds to go, starting with her father."

After the spaghetti was wiped off the three smaller faces and Popsicles were inserted in their mouths, Matt pushed himself back from the big plank table he had built for his family. "Ever notice—"

"Don't say it, Matt."

"How murder fascinates you?" he finished. In the silence that followed, Nina could feel her heart beating, fast.

"I hate it when you get so dramatic, Matt," Nina said to her brother.

"Murder fascinates you," he repeated. "The appeals you did in murder cases got you involved but kept you at a nice, safe, intellectual distance, but this is different. You'll be dealing with the people and the raw emotion."

"I'm a big girl," Nina said.

"Wouldn't it be wiser to take the conservative path here?"

"I expected it, but I'm still surprised at you, Matt." Nina reached to push the curtain back on the window and sighed.

"Oh, just being brotherly. Talk to Jack yet?" Matt asked. "Not that it's any of my business, but on the one hand you say you want to work things out with him, and on the other hand you move to Tahoe and leap into what looks to be a long, heavy case." Andrea gave him a look that silenced him.

"No, I haven't. You'll be the first to know."

"What the hell," he said. "I never did a safe thing in my life." He tugged his wife's hair and smiled. Raising his voice so that the children could hear, he cried, "I'm going outside to look for the moons of Jupiter. Moons of green cheese with goats to eat it." Children ran for coats and gloves while Andrea shook her head.

"Nobody's ever going to believe you if you keep that up," she told him while he maneuvered the telescope toward the French doors leading to the patio.

He stopped on the way out to rub tomato sauce from a finger onto her cheek and then kiss it. "What's life without little mysteries?" he said.

Nina took some plates into the kitchen, stacking them too high and holding them too tightly. Matt and Andrea were afraid for her and it was catching. She didn't want protection, she wanted support.

Standing there at the sink, yawning while she waited for the hot water, she realized one reason why she wanted the case. Misty trusted her. This time, she wouldn't betray that trust.

8

Nina awoke Thursday morning to rain drumming on the metal roof. Carl Tengstedt called during breakfast. In a formal tone, he asked her to represent Misty. Just as formally, she agreed.

Misty had won. Now it began.

She drove Bobby and his cousins to school and arrived at the courthouse early. Misty's bail hearing and arraignment had been scheduled together for 9:00 A.M. With twenty minutes to burn, she climbed the stairs to the second floor.

Nina peeked through the glass in the door of the main Superior Court courtroom and saw that court was in recess before entering. Collier Hallowell was joking with another man in a suit, his back to the door.

"Sorry to interrupt," she said. "I just wanted to introduce myself. I'm Nina Reilly. I have the Patterson case."

Collier Hallowell turned, and she had an impression of kind eyes in a tired face. "Hi, Nina," Hallowell said. "Good to meet you. Do you know Jeff Riesner?" She shook hands with both men in turn, while Riesner's eyes moved as furiously as an electric screwdriver through her. She wished she were wearing toweringly high heels. Their bodies, between her and the light, shadowed her. Both men had dressed their part. Hallowell wore an inconspicuous gray suit that looked like it had come off the rack of the Men's Wearhouse, downplaying the terrible power of the State. Riesner was resplendent in tailored blue pinstripes and an Armani tie, to show judges and juries that the defendant had persuaded a man of substance to accept his story.

"Ah, the famous criminal lawyer from San Francisco," Riesner said. "Gracing us with your presence. I've certainly enjoyed hearing the phony stories you're putting out to try to rope in some business. You're quite a little self-aggrandizer."

"Shucks. I guess that means you don't want to do lunch after all," Nina said.

"Don't mind Jeff," Hallowell said. "He's our resident dickhead."

"I wonder if I could have a minute of your time, Collier," Nina said.

"I guess I'll be running along downstairs," Riesner said. "Oh, one last thing, since I have your attention: Stolen any new clients from me recently?"

This time Hallowell did not come to her rescue. "They've all been over," Nina said, "but I have my standards."

Riesner smiled a smile so hollow it sucked up the air. "You're in way over your head on the Patterson case, deeper than the dead guy. Maybe your client will get that in time."

"Good-bye, Mr. Riesner."

"See you around," Riesner said. "You betcha."

After Riesner left, Hallowell sat down on the counsel table and folded his arms. "You look at home," Nina said.

"With what the county pays me, it's about all I can afford." She saw now that the tired eyes were friendly gray ones with an engaging smile for follow-up. Women jurors would like his style. "It's true, I spend my days here."

"How many deputies are there here at the Lake?"

"Four, soon to be down to three in the next round of budget cuts. One for Child Support, one for Muni Court, one for Superior Court, Judge Milne's bailiwick. That's me.

If we need to we can borrow from Placerville. Where are you from, Nina?"

"San Francisco for a few years, and before that, Monterey."

"You like pretty places."

"Yes, I do. How about you?"

"Born and raised in Tahoe, except for law school at Boalt. It's a good town, if you can stick it out the first year or two. Quite a few lawyers come up the Hill for a season and decide to move on."

"I'm staying," Nina said.

"Glad to hear it. So we'll be working together. I have to tell you, the reports have been slow to get to my desk. I don't have anything to offer in the way of a plea bargain at this point."

"I didn't come for that. I'd like to be sure I get all the reports you have as they come in."

"Sure. Judge Milne has a standing discovery disclosure order. You don't even have to ask, we have to give you everything. You can pick up what we have tomorrow morning. You married?"

Should she zing him for that one? "Yes and no," she said. "Why do you ask?"

"Know your enemy." He flashed a winning smile, then checked his watch. "We'd better get downstairs. Judge Flaherty awaits."

"You're going to do the Muni Court work this morning?"

"Just the Patterson case. I like to work the murder cases from the start." Hallowell walked downstairs with her.

Defendants and their families filled the Municipal Courtroom aisles and seats. The defendants who had not made bail or who were here for bail hearings had already been led in in their orange jumpsuits, sitting together in their own set of pews up front like a bad boys' church choir. Misty was there, in the back row, an attractive nuisance, her teased hair a flag for the bulls. It was hard to take her seriously. She looked like a babe in a heavy-metal video. Nina gave her an encouraging smile.

The attorneys lounged up front, too, in their own special row of seats near the action. Riesner sat on one end, deep in conversation with an older man who laughed in a low voice as she came up and sat down at the other end. Collier stepped up to the counsel table on the right and started pulling out files. The public defender, a mournful-looking young man with the expression of one who has endured much, had already set up his stacks on the other table.

"Remain seated," said the bailiff. A regal rustling preceded Judge Flaherty to the bench. He popped out of some hidden place, a white-haired, rotund man with a ruddy face.

"Mr. Hallowell?" he said immediately. "You have something down here this morning?"

Collier said, "Just one case, your Honor. Patterson. Bail and arraignment."

The judge riffled through his files and said, "Okay, People v. Patterson. Bring the defendant up. Is she represented by counsel?" Nina already stood at the counsel table, and a deputy walked Misty over to stand by her.

"Yes, Your Honor. Nina Reilly, representing the defendant."

"We'll do the bail hearing first. Mr. Hallowell?"

"As the Court can see from the paperwork, it's our position that no bail be granted at this time," Collier said. He spoke softly, drawing attention to every word. "Ms. Patterson has no family here and no other real ties. She rents her home and has lived in the area only three years. The charge is as serious as it gets. She is a flight risk."

"Mrs. Reilly?"

Mrs. Reilly would do, though there had never been a Mr. Reilly, except Dad. "There are no statements or actions to show this defendant would flee the jurisdiction, Your Honor. This lady has a full-time job locally, which she has held for eighteen months. The charges against her will certainly be reduced if not dismissed at the preliminary hearing. She has never been charged with any other offense, much less convicted of one. There is no indication that releasing her would cause any danger to others. Request bail be set in the amount of fifty thousand dollars."

The judge raised his eyebrows. "Mr. Hallowell, fifty thousand dollars is ridiculously low for the charge, but three years is almost an old-timer up here. And this young lady has no priors. There are allegations of a struggle just prior to the incident. Is it likely that the Murder One charge will be reduced?"

"It's too early to say, Your Honor. But she took off when the police tried to question her, Your Honor. If the Court is inclined to grant bail, we would request it be set in the amount of two hundred and fifty thousand."

"Too much," the judge said. He stared at Misty for a moment, then said, "Split the difference. Does one hundred and seventy-five thousand sound reasonable, Mrs. Reilly?"

"I think the defendant's parents could make one hundred thousand dollars bail, Your Honor. Her father owns a small car dealership in Fresno. The defendant has no assets at the moment, as we have not been able to access a separate bank account of her husband's yet."

"Mr. Hallowell?"

"Way too low, Your Honor."

"Bail's set at one hundred and seventy-five thousand dollars," the judge said. "Let's arraign her."

Nina accepted a copy of the charges and waived a reading. "How do you plead?"

Misty looked at Nina, who nodded. "Not guilty," she said.

"Want to set a date for the prelim?" Judge Flaherty asked Hallowell, who already thumbed through his appointment book.

"Three weeks from today, if the defendant is willing to waive time," he said.

"Contingent on my receiving the police reports by to-morrow, we'll waive time," Nina said. She had no need to consult an appointment book yet. "May twenty-fourth is fine."

"Ten o'clock," the clerk said.

It was over. "I'll be over to talk to you in a minute," Nina whispered to Misty as she was led away.

Collier Hallowell headed for the hall, with a cluster of people around him. He waved as she turned toward the outer doors.

Nina had checked him out. He had won a statewide repu-tation for ten years of successful prosecuting. He'd had many offers to move up to the big cities, but he refused to leave Tahoe. He would be running for district attorney next year.

Collier Hallowell, not Jeff Riesner, worried her, with his good looks, mild manner, and that sweet self-deprecation. He was the good old boy to beat.

Misty Patterson looked glad to see her back at the jail. "My dad said he left a check for you at your office in the slot last night, Nina. Did you get it?"

"Haven't been by there yet, but he called this morning to tell me."

"He's not exactly . . . but I'm glad you're going to be my attorney. I felt safe standing next to you today."

Nina shook off the superstitious shiver inspired by this

vote of confidence from a girl who did not seem to have the good judgment of a fly. "I'll do everything I can."

"I believe that." Misty looked slightly more relaxed today. Her eyes showed signs of life.

"How are you?"

"Better. I met somebody I can talk to in here, Delores. That helps. The food is terrible. That makes me want to throw up."

"Don't trust anybody," Nina said.

The girl rubbed her hands together. "Yeah, I got you. You told me not to talk about my case. I don't."

"Good. I talked to your parents a few minutes ago, Misty. They are going to have to get a loan on their house. Unfortunately, that means we can't get you out of here immediately."

"Oh, no."

"We'll get you out as soon as possible. I promise. I'm going to need some time to investigate the facts. I won't even have the lab reports and police reports until tomorrow."

"I keep going over and over it in my mind," Misty said. "I hit him, but I swear he was conscious when I went into the kitchen. I told him I was calling the doctor and he nodded his head. Want to hear something totally odd?"

"What?"

"I miss him. Inside, all the old feelings are still there, comfortable, like his old shirts I used to wear, only there's no place to hang them."

"Some of those feelings can't have been good ones," said Nina.

The girl shook her head and chewed a piece of hair. "I used to feel lousy about going home in case he was in a bad mood, but I was kind of used to that. Now I'm pretty much tripping all the time. I don't have a clue about what to do, and Anthony is still harassing me. He's still deciding what I wear and get to eat, where I sleep. Like he's not really gone, he just figured out a way to squeeze me tighter. It will never be over now, I've got my own private ghost."

"It doesn't have to be that way. . . ."

"If I killed him, I wish I'd done it better. I should have hid him out deeper. If nobody found him, I wouldn't be in jail, would I?"

"Let's talk about something else. Who were Anthony's friends, business associates? Can you give me a list?"

"All I know is his ex-wife, Sharon Otis, the one I told you about already. He still did some business with her, I don't know what. And Peter La Russa at Prize's. He and Anthony used to go out drinking together. Then there's Rick Eich, our neighbor, who used to sit out on the deck with him in the summer. Anthony never talked about his Fresno days. Before that, I know he grew up in Philadelphia and his mom supported him and his sister. He was smart but he couldn't afford college."

"Where's his family?"

"His sister is somewhere, but they don't get along. She's got some problem. She's disabled or something. He started working when he was fourteen, he told me once. I think he lived with an aunt for a while."

"Did he stay in touch with his sister or his aunt?"

"I don't think so."

"Had anyone threatened him? Who were his enemies?"

"Anybody who crossed him. Nobody specific I know of right now. He always had some kind of deal going. He did make enemies."

"Tom Clarke was angry at the way Anthony treated you. He wanted you to leave him. How serious are you two?"

"He hasn't tried to call me once since we came to see

you. I think he's all done with me. I was just a diversion for him. He was just interested in the sex."

"I don't get this," Nina said. "Misty, tell me something. Since you started going through adolescence and all that, how many . . . relationships have you had?"

"With different guys?"

"Different men. Things you never thought would last."

She was quiet for a minute. Then she looked into Nina's eyes. "Twenty-five or thirty guys," she said. "Maybe more."

"No herpes, no hassles, no pregnancies, no AIDS?" Nina said in wonder. "You're telling me Anthony never found out?"

"Luck of the Vikings," Misty said. "I'm careful. For a long time I don't think it even crossed Anthony's mind that I would dare sleep around on him. At first he liked it when men looked at me, especially before we got married."

"Why so many men?"

"Oh, I don't know," Misty said. She looked embarrassed.

"You like sex?"

Her face changed. "I'm good at it. I'm sick of talking about this, Nina. Somebody asks me, I come through. Think about it the way my husband thought about it. I'm a dumb, ugly slut."

"No, Misty," Nina said. "You're so wrong."

"I belong here," Misty said. Then came tears, and Nina waited until she finished.

"Misty, dumb sluts don't have the sense to hire me. And you must know you are a very beautiful woman. You must see how people react to you."

Misty looked hard at Nina. "That's the first time a woman ever said such a thing to me. My mother always says looks don't count and don't last. Men . . . well, sure, they tell me I'm gorgeous, but men lie."

"Can't you see it? When you look in the mirror?"

"See what?" Misty said, frantically combing her fingers through her hair. "What are you talking about?"

Nina had nothing to say. Her pen stayed poised above the pad. She collected herself, and said, "Okay, let's move on. Tom says you were seeing somebody else within the last few weeks."

"One time I was really drunk," Misty said. "I mentioned to Tom that I went up to Steve Rossmoor's suite one night a few weeks ago. He's the general manager at Prize's. Just the one time. Well, twice. I made a big mistake mentioning it. Maybe that's why Tom dumped me."

"Anybody else?"

"Maybe there was someone," Misty whispered. "But I don't know who. . . . I mean, there used to be someone in my dreams . . . who really loved me . . . always there. . . . Sometimes when I was with Tom I pretended I was with him."

"Was he a real person?" Nina said gently. "Or only a dream?"

The girl frowned. "Well, just a dream. I told Dr. Greenspan about him. He says that was an ideal that I . . . put in the place of a flesh-and-blood man. He says I needed a . . . fantasy."

Nina couldn't imagine why, given such an active real life. "Any other flesh-and-blood men?"

"Umm, three guys last year, before I met Tom. One was a painter, but he gave that up and got a job in computers in L.A. Then there was Jammer. He was a clerk at the convenience store by my house. I saw him for a month or two. When I stopped for milk and bread." The corners of her mouth turned up.

"Where is Jammer now?"

"I don't know," Misty said. "He got married."

"And the third man?"

"Davey," she said, and now her face was downcast. "He was skiing the Siberia run at Squaw last December and a lady from Marin County came flying out of the woods and knocked him down. I went to see him at his apartment the next day and he seemed all right, just sore. And then he was getting up from the bed and he had this awful pain in his back and down his legs. His mom had to take him back to Sacramento to take care of him."

"Did you have any continuing contact with any of these men? Did any of them call you or try to get together with you again?"

"No," Misty said. "Except I sent Davey a get-well card." She looked over her shoulder. "It's lunchtime soon; I'll have to go or I'll miss it."

"Sure. Is there anything you need?"

"A quart of booze. Couple cartons of Winstons. A few doobies. Ha-ha. Another toothbrush. Mine disappeared. A hairbrush, if they'll let me have one. Some magazines or even romances to read."

Nina wrote it down.

"Tell my mom. She knows what I like and it'll keep her busy. Don't mention the doobies though, even as a joke. You don't want to walk in front of her when she's on the way to church."

Nina picked up a burger and some milk at the drive-up window at McDonald's and drove her car to Pope Beach. The rain had let up; above the white crags a powerful wind blew the clouds back down to the Nevada desert. She just sat there in her car, leaning her head back and relaxing her neck muscles, letting nature put on a show for her. After a while, slowly, she drove back to the office.

The check from the Tengstedts decorated the middle of her desk, a twenty-five thousand dollar retainer plus an advance against costs, and a signed retainer agreement. Nina closed the door and sat down in her office chair, feeling the paper in her fingers.

Money. She had been getting along financially on her savings but this meant so much more: She was really in business, not just fooling around until Jack decided to forgive her; she was committed to the case, whatever it took; she might be trying a homicide in a few months. She hadn't felt so simultaneously brazen and terrified since Bobby was born. Pulling out a legal pad, she started her list, buzzing for Sandy at the same time.

Sandy entered, leading with the appointment book. Today she wore cowboy boots, a flowered, full skirt that billowed in her wake, and a purple blouse. Her usual calm and skeptical expression controlled from the top.

"Okay. Here's what we have for the next week. The Sandoval personal injury. Have Mr. Sandoval sign an authorization. Send it to the hospital with a letter asking for complete records and billings. Review the file for any other damages, like wage loss. Draft a claim letter to the insurance company and ask for five times the amount of his specials. Use the letter I just sent out on Pal, our other PI case, as a model. Give it to me to look at when you're finished."

Sandy wrote, head bent. She had smooth, plump hands with silver rings. Her notes looked unreadable. Nina hoped it was a private shorthand.

"The ski accident case, Hopkins. Call the client and ask him to bring over his copy of the accident report. On Mrs. Washington, we have a hearing for temporary support on Monday. Calendar the day before to make sure we have the proof of service on file." Nina went down her case list, which was short. Mrs. Washington had been referred by Sandy. Mr. Hopkins had formerly retained Jeffrey Riesner.

Remembering Mr. Hopkins's comments about his former attorney, Nina smiled.

"Turning to Patterson, write a letter of representation to the DA's office and sign for me. I'll open up a separate trust account with the cost check and put the retainer in the regular trust account. Do what you need to do to obtain the police reports and lab reports as soon as you can. Set up a file." She paused to shuffle papers. "Write a letter for my signature to the Tengstedts acknowledging the check. Send an authorization to Misty's doctor, what's his name, Frederick Greenspan, and set up a meeting with him for me. You'd better start a Rolodex for yourself. Here's the number for Bruno Cervenka at UCSF. Call his office and set up a telephone conference with him for four o'clock today if you can. Sandy, I know I'm loading a lot on you. If there's something you can't do or don't understand, ask me."

"Don't worry," Sandy said. "Piece of cake."

"That's it for now." But Sandy remained sitting.

"Yes?"

"You need a better rug in the outer office. A big plant," Sandy said. "I can get a good rug for you."

"Where?"

"The Washoe Center over by Gardnerville sells rugs."

"Right."

"And a radio," Sandy said.

"Okay. And Sandy? Thanks for all the business you've sent my way. But remember—"

"I heard you the first time," her secretary said, and went out, firmly closing the door behind her.

Nina was already picking up the phone and punching the 1 for long distance.

"Paul, it's me, Nina Reilly."

"Nina! How are you? I got your card. What are you doing practicing law at Tahoe?" She could hear the baseball game get suddenly muted. Did he work at home? She pictured Paul van Wagoner, long legs draped over the arm of a soft chair, files open on his lap, watching the Oakland A's get trounced.

"That's a complicated tale, Paul. Listen, I have a business question for you. You went private, right? Know of anybody up here that's in your line? Somebody good? It's a murder case."

"I know just the guy. Sharp. Experienced. Reasonable. Humble. Snappy dresser. Warm without being cloying."

"Wait a minute."

"Adventurous but steady."

"You?"

"Good going, Watson."

"But you're in Carmel."

"I can come up there for a while, give you a few days now and more time as you need it. Say the word."

It had never occurred to her that Paul would want to come up himself. One of Jack's oldest friends, they hadn't seen much of him since they moved to San Francisco. Now the thought of him and their shared past felt cozy as an old sweater, a feeling that begged to be scrutinized.

"Well, shoot, Paul. I'd love to hire you." Damn the torpedoes.

"I can drive up day after tomorrow. It's about four hours—"

"Driving a Concorde?"

"Ah, Nina. It's such a delight to hear your voice," he said. "Now tell me how I find you."

Nina couldn't get through to Bruno Cervenka at the UC Medical Center in San Francisco until four-thirty. He was teaching a seminar in something called depth psychology.

Bruno was old, ancient. The school had been trying to get

him to retire for years, but he refused, forcing a compromise. He continued to teach a couple of graduate courses and consulted on legal cases; the school still carried him as a full professor. There wasn't anything else they could do. Bruno had many friends, and an unalterable conviction that if he ever retired, he would die instantly. "Like old Sarah Winchester, who had carpenters building onto her house until the day she died, convinced that if they stopped, she would die. Work is life," he had told Nina once. He had testified in many capital cases, always on behalf of the defendant. Nina's firm in San Francisco had used him as a consultant on several appeals.

His age and his orientation toward the defense weakened his credibility as an expert witness at trial. On the other hand, as Nina had learned working with him on the appeals, he was a brilliant clinician. He understood people. He had no preconceptions. This made him much more useful than a sharp-edged Stanford Ph.D. who mainly manipulated computers and lab rats.

"I have a case for you, Professor," Nina said. "A young woman who has total amnesia about her childhood to about age ten. She's beautiful, unfaithful, and struck her husband on the head with a statue a week ago. She says she went to bed and fell asleep while he lay bleeding, and still breathing, on their couch. Her story's so outrageous I'm wondering if she simply doesn't remember what happened. Her husband was found in Lake Tahoe, apparently pushed off a boat. She says she knows nothing about it. She's been charged with murder."

"Has she ever received psychiatric treatment?" Cervenka asked, sounding frail and far away. Nina wondered if he could make the trip over these mountains or if the elevation change might kill him.

"A few months ago she began having emotional problems.

It sounds like she was suffering from some form of depression. She went to an M.D. who does hypnotherapy. From what she says, she was feeling better, but the therapy still hadn't resulted in recovery of her childhood memories."

"Are her parents still alive?"

"Yes, and she has asked them about it. They say she had an ordinary childhood. She has no brothers and sisters. I don't know if it's part of their religion or what—they're Christian Scientists—but they don't have any old photo albums around to jog her memory."

"Does she have other episodes like this, in which she has lost important memories?"

"Just her entire childhood and the episode with her husband."

"Traumatic amnesia, with denial and repression mechanisms. Epilepsy. Fugue. Multiple personalities. Prevarication. It could be anything, based on what you tell me," Cervenka said. "There are probably two separate sets of precipitating events to account for each of the amnesias."

"Prevarication . . . you're suggesting she's a liar, Professor?"

"Naturally. There is a rather serious charge against her. If she does not like what she remembers, perhaps she is simply not telling."

"She could hardly make it worse for herself. If she did watch him die, then took the body out and dumped it, we still have a case for self-defense. He was assaulting her at that time and previously. What I can't deal with is not knowing what happened."

Cervenka said, "I would have to know much, much more to help. I could talk with the young lady, perhaps hypnotize her myself. We can start with her physician's treatment records. Who knows? Maybe the physician was negligent.

The hypnotism could be adding to her amnesia trouble instead of helping."

"Can you come to the mountains, Professor?" Nina asked, a little tentatively.

"Whenever possible, the mountains must come to Mohammed, my dear," he said, sounding almost jolly. "I am currently using a wheelchair until my new hip cooperates better. So send me her records, and then we will make arrangements."

"Within a week, Professor. Thanks for being willing to look into this."

"You may not need me at all," Cervenka said. "Many traumatic amnesia cases clear up on their own. What does her physician say?"

"I'm meeting with him next week, to pick up her records and find out what he knows," Nina said. "But I want you on the case, Bruno. Her doctor is a treating physician. His thoughts and records are going to be freely available to the DA. I need your help as a consultant."

"My pleasure," the old man said courteously on the other end of the line. Nina hung up, ignoring the unpleasant feeling that Bruno had given her. He made it seem too complicated. Misty blocked unpleasant things out, that was all. Amnesia controlled her, not lies. Okay, give credence for a moment to the concept that Misty was lying. That still made the charge manslaughter at worst. . . . With Nina's smarts, a top investigator, and a great shrink, what could Riesner offer that was better?

9

NINA PAID HER two bucks and took her ticket. Andrea waited for her inside the old Elks' Club building. She could feel the backbeat vibrating through her spine without being able to identify a recognizable tune. The crowd rushed forward and carried her in.

"Good excuse to celebrate," Andrea had said earlier, when Nina told her about the Tengstedt check. "Let's go to the Firemen's Ball."

Nina had been sitting on the couch, the manila envelope from Ms. Cherry's office she had just opened in her lap. In it she found the marital settlement agreement; twenty pages precisely dividing up assets and debts, outlining the procedure for selling the condo, providing for attorney's fees to the prevailing party in the event of a breach of the provisions. Jack's large, familiar signature was sprawled across the bottom of the last page, just above Ms. Cherry's.

"The Firemen's Ball is the highlight of the spring social season," Andrea went on, pseudo-Boston. "You get your Crab Feed in two months, and then the big Pancake Breakfast in August. But this is where you get your dancing."

"Hmmm."

"To the Movers, the wildest electric guitar playin', bass-thumpin', screamin', poundin' rock 'n' roll band this side of East Sacramento."

Nina had sat there, the papers loosely clasped in her

hands. Seeing the envelope at the post office, she had known right away what it was. A wet pain slipped roughly around inside her chest like a bloody scalpel.

Friday night tonight, and she felt allowed. She would close and lock her bedroom door, removing the leather shoes, the stockings, the suit skirt and jacket, and finally the underwear. Over her head she would throw the long green silk nightgown. Then she would lift the yellow spread from her soft mattress, curl up and disappear.

She would apply something she had learned in the past: You could adjust to anything after the first twenty-four hours. If you could get to sleep, the time went that much faster. The ego erected a membrane of rationalizations and defenses around the pain, fragile but efficient as the bubble of a blister. By tomorrow, she could bear it. "No, Andrea. I'm more dead than alive. It's been a long week. I need a long, hot bath and bed. . . ."

"A long week? I've been slopping around in freezing muck for five months. I'm sick and tired of being buried by snow and too cold to count on my fingers. Let's go someplace warm." Andrea had tilted her head, surveying her. "Sleep is not what you need. You're always so damn fierce and serious. Why don't you ease up for tonight? Tonight's an old Tahoe tribal tradition to celebrate the end of the cold season. Everybody comes to dance, except kids and their baby-sitters and your brother, who hates crowds even more than you. This thing's our opera, ballet, and off-Broadway." She took her sister-in-law by the sleeve and tugged. "I don't want to go alone, so you're coming."

Nina shook her head. "Don't push me. I'm not budging."

Andrea plucked the envelope from the couch and hit Nina on the head with it. "Admit that you won't be able to sleep."

Andrea kept after her until Nina washed her hair, let it

dry, ran a spiky brush through it, put on a red sweater she thought might distract from the winter pallor of her skin, and went with her.

She drove Nina to a barn outside town, lit up in the middle of a field. The moon had not come up, but the stars clustered so brightly in the sky that the grass in the meadows shone white. Four-wheel-drive vehicles in all shapes and sizes pressed up against the brush alongside the road anywhere the trees had been cleared, for what seemed like miles.

Inside, the town whirled. Behind the long bar in back, dozens of white-shirted amateur bartenders passed out paper cups of beer and wine. Peering through the darkness, Nina could see a few long tables lined up with benches, mostly empty, surrounding the dance floor.

"Good love . . ." The band played old rock 'n' roll songs off somewhere in the gloom. Andrea passed her some red wine. Everyone else was singing and moving, sloshing beer from the cups they clutched. She drank the cup and went for a refill. Warmed by the wine and moiling bodies, and overloaded on all sensory fronts, Nina soon found herself part of a blurry group of friends. "Lay-la," they all sang. They danced together, alone, in groups, bumping everybody else, beer flying in a constant thin spray, laughing and yelling.

Hundreds of pounding hearts, thumping and mindless, carried Nina along as the band launched into a fast-forward version of "Brown Sugar." A few minutes later, on her way to search for a sip of water, she took time to unstick the damp sweater from her body.

Leaning against the bar, trying to attract the bartender, she felt a hand clasp her waist. A firm arm steered her from the corner to a stool. "Excuse me, ma'am, but I'm moving through, here," said the man, disappearing into the crowd. The touch, like a flash of electric light, woke her up. She saw the men, the bodies under the clothes, and they looked good to her, very good. Not San Francisco jogging types, these guys had weight and muscle. Maybe it was all that wood chopping they did. And she'd never gotten over a predilection for beards.

For five years she hadn't gone out without Jack. They'd critiqued all the known Japanese restaurants in the City; watched, then postmortemed, the Kurosawa flicks at the Castro Theater, and caught up with music when they could. They'd read *The New York Times* all day on Sunday. They had gone through her mother's death together, talked law together, filed their tax return together. But mostly they had worked, six or even seven days a week. Where was her son in all this? And where was the rest of Nina, the dancing part?

She drank water, then some more wine. Downing the dregs of her cup, she set it on the counter and jumped back into the crowd. She shouted and the people nearby smiled at her. She stamped her feet and the wooden floor bounced.

She danced until she saw Paul van Wagoner pushing his way over to her. Disconcerted, she looked around for Andrea, but Andrea had melted into the color wheel. Then Paul was in front of her, and he was . . . dancing, his limbs loose but awkward. He reached out, grabbed at her with a brusque confidence, and began pulling her toward him, twirling her, catching her, keeping the beat, while her surprised body remembered the old moves. His hair was plastered to his head and his blue denim shirt and jeans looked lived-in. He had been there awhile. He didn't try to speak, and neither did Nina.

The band relaxed into a slow tune. He pressed himself tightly against her, closing his eyes. Swaying slowly, they relaxed into each other, into an easy, familiar-feeling rhythm: his hip slides, her hip slides, their hips slide together. After a few songs they edged toward the door a step at a time. When Nina could feel the evening's cool on her hot cheeks, he took her hand and maneuvered her gracefully through the jovial phalanx that blocked the door.

Outside, couples leaned against the wall or sat in cars with the doors open. Two kids on skateboards raced through the parking lot. Nina could suddenly hear her fast breath mixed with a ringing in her ears. Sweat dried cold on her forehead: A cup of red wine appeared to have fallen onto her white pants. She released Paul's hand and stood at a slight distance. "You got here fast. How'd you find us?" she asked. "Oh, you went to the house and Matt told you."

"He sent me here," Paul said, looking up at the night sky. "More stars here than in Monterey. That's why I rushed." He'd had a beer or four, Nina realized suddenly, and he hadn't shaved, and he'd popped a button on his shirt, exposing some soft blond chest hair. At her glance, he also looked down at his shirt, shrugging and grinning at the same time.

"See you tomorrow," he said, still smiling, and disappeared into the darkness.

"Nina." Andrea came up. She, too, showed the effects of the dance—shirttail out, face shiny, and a slight limp. "We've got to go before I cripple myself."

They started for the car. "You don't waste a minute, do you?" said Andrea, watching the departing back.

"Give me five minutes to get divorced, Andrea. Paul's an old friend. He's doing some work for me."

"You like him, though." They walked in silence until Andrea said, "He's an old friend of Jack's, isn't he? I think Matt told me something about him. You dated him, right? Rough stuff, right?"

"Matt ought to mind his own business."

Nina crawled under the comforter, her body still humming with music. Tossing, punching up her pillow, checking the clock, adjusting the sheets, she could not find a comfortable place. Finally she took the second pillow and lifted her leg over it as a man substitute. It was right then that she discovered the iron band constricting her solar plexus, encircling her so tightly she could hardly breathe. Breathing shallowly, she tried to suck air into her belly, wondering how she could have been walking around like this, without even noticing. She couldn't breathe, much less sleep. How long had she been in this condition? Why, she was barely alive.

She hoped nobody could hear her, because there was nothing she could do to stop what presently became a pitiful display. Stuffing her face into her pillow, she soaked it with tears and snot until she had to get up and blow her nose: her face in the bathroom mirror—now, that was something to cry about.

Bobby woke up about six and came into her room softly, climbing in beside her. She put her arm around his warmth and they both fell back to sleep, awakened finally by the pounding of cousins on the door about nine.

Saturday. Washing her face with cold water, she marveled at her swollen eyelids.

"What happened to you?" Matt asked, when she walked into the living room.

"Fun, fun, fun," Nina croaked.

Matt let out a chuckle. "The Firemen's Ball has a way of wringing the blood right out of you. Let's go for a hike up the hill behind the house. I'm taking the kids."

"I have to go to the office. The reports on the Patterson case ought to be in the mail today. The guy you sent to the Ball last night? Paul van Wagoner? He's a private investigator now and I'm hiring him to do some work."

"That explains why he came sniffing around in the dead of the night. He's a pro." He said it without being mean. "I remember him from Monterey."

"That seems like a long time ago. Sometimes I miss Monterey."

"This is a good place to settle, Nina," he went on. "Know why I love Tahoe? The trees. Millions more trees than people. Towns of trees, nations of trees, hermit trees, incense cedars, sugar pines, lodgepoles, ponderosas, white fir with snow so heavy on it the branches bend into curves . . . so many people hardly notice what's all around them. The mountains are too high. The lake is too big and deep. The trees soften all that scary grandeur."

It was a long speech for Matt. But taking her coffee to the porch, watching sunlight drift through the morning woodstove haze, she understood what he was trying to say. A hundred feet above the ground, the trees had turned together toward the sun, and the tips of their branches wore a new, brighter green. They lived and grew in a slower time frame, serene, ignoring the human hullabaloo beneath their canopy of light and shade.

She wanted to stay and she knew Bobby would be happy here, but she wasn't ready to consider happiness for herself just yet. She buried the marital settlement agreement under her bed before she left.

Paul came through the office door about two o'clock while Nina was copying the Patterson reports on her newly leased machine. She turned around and saw him more clearly than the night before, daylight revealing a few deeper creases in his face and dark blond hair longer than in his police days. He waited, measuring her degree of warmth, and she was obscurely embarrassed by the night before, so she said, "Paul!" and held out her hand, trying to look cool and professional.

Jack and Paul had gone to Harvard as undergraduates. Jack had gone on to law school, but Paul moved into criminology. She had met Paul through Jack five years before, when they all lived in the Monterey area. In fact, she had gone out one interesting evening with Jack and Paul and another woman, and she couldn't remember now who had been dating whom. In Monterey she had known Paul as a hard cop, very physical, with a cynical, rather patronizing attitude toward women and a quick, dangerous temper.

Nina had heard stories from Jack about Paul's insubordinate attitude for years. It was a testament to his abilities that he had been promoted to homicide detective. She had been attracted to Paul, but she had chosen Jack. Since then they had seen Paul occasionally on his infrequent visits to San Francisco, Paul always escorting a new woman. Nina remembered suspecting once that he brought the women by for Jack's stamp of approval. Who knew about these male friendships?

Last night at the Elks' Club, dancing with him, she had thought, he hasn't changed. He's too uncivilized. He thinks he's God's gift to women. He likes to throw his weight around. But then she had thought, he hasn't lost the old charm, or that nice broad set of shoulders.

So now he would be her investigator. She would keep a professional distance between them. Paul could be . . . *predatory*, that was the word, and right now she felt too exposed.

He, too, was measuring her, though his face expressed nothing but a mild friendliness.

Nina wiggled her bare feet into a pair of soft shoes beneath her desk.

"I spent the whole week cooped up. Let's go down the trail to the lake."

In the front office, Sandy had also just arrived and was tossing an embroidered bag on her desk.

"Sandy, this is Paul van Wagoner. He's an investigator, a former police officer, up from Monterey. He'll be working on the Patterson case with us. What are you doing here today? It's Saturday."

Sandy opened her eyes as wide as an owl's. "Guess what? I had work to do." Paul and Nina headed out the door, Nina shaking her head.

"I admire your choice of help," Paul commented after they had turned south, taking the trail that led toward the lake.

"You or her?" Nina smiled. "Oh, sometimes she's just a royal pain, but I need her and she knows it. She's bringing in most of my business at the moment. I hired her for all the wrong reasons and she's made herself indispensable on every front. She's so sure of herself."

"So are you, Nina. You're handling this breakup with Jack with a lot of courage."

"Does it look like that to you? I feel like I'm scrambling uphill, just feeling for a toehold in gravel."

"What's happened with you and Jack? I haven't talked to him lately."

She wondered if it was true. "He served me with divorce papers."

"I'm sorry to hear that. As you know, I've been there."

"Doesn't surprise you?"

Paul thought before speaking. "At first, when I heard you two had gotten together, I thought you had a lot in common. I like Jack and you're a good woman."

"Thanks."

"You're both lawyers who seemed, at least back then, not to want to take a fast track. You've got that 'save the world, spare the innocent' type thing in common. Also Jack wanted a family so much, and you and Bobby made an instant one."

"Instant family, that's a good one. He got more than he bargained for."

"More than he deserved. He inspired the break?"

She hesitated. "No. It was me."

"That surprises me. Jack is bad at the long haul. Steady jobs. Long mountain-climbing trips. Whatever. When it comes to figuring out where do we put all this sewage we've generated, he's gone. For him, it's got to be fun, new, or challenging. Otherwise, he fades out. He gets bored." He noted her face. "No offense, Nina, I don't mean with you. With Jack, who would always rather be in Fiji."

Her hackles were up. She recognized it, but couldn't do a thing to quell the anger she felt at his words. "I imagine Jack will tell you all about it, if he hasn't already. The truth is, I cheated on him and he found out."

"Oh, it's all your fault, huh? That simple?"

"Yep. It is."

"Okay. But why did you, Nina? And why did he give up?"

"That I don't know, Paul," she said. She cupped her hands behind her head, then lowered her arms again, taking note of the way he looked at her, and thinking suddenly of Misty, how not knowing what happened was the hardest part. "Maybe I don't get to know. And now it's your turn."

"Not much to add to what I said already. I never much fitted the cop mold, had a number of problems in the department. Maybe Jack regaled you with a few over dinner," Paul said. "Things that didn't seem humorous at the time have acquired that beloved patina of age. Sometimes I miss the people. Mostly I don't. I've got a small office going. I'm a corporation. I have a secretary and a license and a Rolodex."

"You didn't get married again, Paul?"

"Now, why mention that? You know someone who's looking?"

The trail meandered over a footbridge across the upper Truckee River, which cascaded down to the lake a mile away. Vivid new green showed on the tips of the spruce trees. Purple lupine and blue columbine poked from the pine cones and pine needles carpeting the floor of the forest.

"What a place. Disneyland without the traffic," Paul said.

"I could hardly believe it when you agreed to come. I hope I can afford you." She meant that in every way. Now that he was here, this loose tie to her old life, she felt the complication of him. They strolled out of the forest into the soft, waving grass of the Truckee Meadow proper. At last, through the berry bushes along the shore, Lake Tahoe gleamed under a cloudless sky. Paul climbed a smooth granite rock and gave Nina a hand up.

"Tell me about your case, Nina."

She told him Misty's story, all of it, and he listened without interrupting, creasing his brow when she talked about Anthony Patterson sitting at the bottom of the lake. They looked across it toward the north shore. A warm breeze played with her hair, and she realized spring had finally arrived. "What's your take?" she said.

"There's a question mark at the heart of it. She says she hit him with something that could have killed him. She says he was coming around and she went into the kitchen to call a doctor. After that, she says she went to bed. Nobody is going to swallow this story. How does the prosecution make this whole thing work?"

"I imagine they're thinking she lured him out to the boat after the first blow and then hit him again, which would explain how she got him out there without having to carry him, or else she hit him both times out there. As for swimming back, you know they'll play up the adrenaline rush stuff. Superhuman feat, et cetera."

Nina continued, twisting needles off of a pine branch. "From my point of view, either she killed him on the second blow, and dumped him somehow, and is repressing it or lying about it, or she really did go to bed as some sort of shock reaction, and some third party took him out, hit him again, and dumped him."

"Who?"

"How about her dad, just for the sake of argument? Now, here's a guy who is a terrific swimmer, from what I hear. And he'd want the body not to be found, thinking that way Misty would be protected both from her husband and the law. Say he took the boat out to hide the body, ran out of gas, and jumped ship, hoping it would disappear quietly?"

They explored that theory, but without knowing more than she did about Misty and Carl Tengstedt, Nina couldn't believe it. "After all, by then she'd been married for years, and she wanted her parents to butt out. They seemed to accept her choice, even if they didn't like Anthony Patterson."

"How about this? You say she saw some footsteps in the snow when she got home. Say someone was already in the house, one of Misty's lovers, or an angry former pal had climbed through a window. When Misty hit her husband and then conveniently ran off to bed, whoever it was took the opportunity to kill him. Someone who didn't realize the water was so shallow where he was dumped in the dark, who thought the wind would blow the boat so far away there would be no way to link it with the body. Then Patterson wouldn't be found at all."

"That raises interesting questions. Why not bring the boat back to the dock? Why not worry about not being able to get out all the bloodstains? Why swim back in that frigid water? Next, who was this person really trying to protect by hiding the body in the lake? Misty? Or someone else?"

"Maybe he came after her again, only this time she realized he was so violent he might kill her, so she connected again. Maybe that's what she's blocking out. A much more

traumatic interaction. Let's go back and look at the reports,"
Paul said. "Just because it looks like a turkey and smells like a
turkey . . ."

On Monday, April 30, the Tahoe City police department
was contacted by Rich Eich, a homeowner in the Tahoe
Keys who claimed his twenty-two-foot Catalina sailboat had
been stolen. An Officer Tomlinson, who spelled like a third
grader, had been dispatched and prepared the report. Eich
had been on vacation in Hawaii and noticed the boat missing
from the mooring off his dock on his return Sunday evening,
April 29.

Late Monday, the Coast Guard reported seizure of a boat
found drifting about half a mile out from the Keys. An
onboard thermometer recorded a water temperature of
forty-eight degrees close to the surface of the lake. The gas
tank was empty, which might explain in part why the boat
was left to drift. And sailboats needed wind if their backup
motor gas tanks were empty.

In the small cabin traces of what appeared to be dried
blood were discovered on the flooring, and subsequent investigation showed apparent blood traces on the deck. Further conversation with Mr. Eich revealed that neighbors
sometimes borrowed the boat. He was worried about the
blood and the possibility of an accident. Consequently, the
Coast Guard searched the area and sighted, through clear
waters, a shadow on sand approximately thirty-five feet
down. A scuba diver found the body of Anthony Patterson.

Like all gossip, deputy district attorney Burton Lam's held
a grain of truth. Patterson appeared to be sitting—in fact his
body was loosely arranged, feet on the ground, and head
seeming to pull the body up into a sitting position. Underwater photographs, taken with a flash, showed his face, the
eyes probing another world. His bathrobe, now untied,

floated around him like a shroud. With some difficulty, he had been hauled up in a fisherman's net. Preliminary examination showed a concavity to the skull, which might be either accidental or intentional. Anthony Patterson was identified by fingerprints on file for two previous Fresno arrests. His file showed his current residence address: 226 Tahoe Vista Lane.

The second report, typed by Lt. Julian Oskel, South Lake Tahoe City Police Department, described a visit to the Patterson house. On Monday, April 30, at 2200 hours, Oskel, along with Sgt. Juan Higuera, arrived at the residence in the Keys with a search warrant. Finding no one at home, they went through the house, finding no particular signs of violence. They discovered a small plastic Ziploc bag full of cocaine in a sock drawer in the master bedroom. From pay stubs located in the den they determined that the subject and his wife worked at Prize's Casino. In the trash can they located a fresh garbage bag that held large amounts of broken glass, along with wads of stained sponges and cleaning utensils.

The Douglas County, Nevada, sheriff's department was called in, but was unable to interview subject's wife as she had just completed her shift and couldn't be found. Brenda Angelis, a co-worker, was interviewed and stated subject's wife, Misty (Michelle) Patterson, had told her that evening that she had been fighting with subject. "He didn't want to pay for her therapy anymore. That pissed her off," the report quoted, and continued in damning detail.

Nina groaned. "She does talk," she said.

"An argument for either innocence or stupidity," Paul said.

Misty Patterson was arrested at the Lucky Chip Motel on the California side of the state border late Monday night. Branding Misty Patterson as "hysterical" upon arrest, it reported verbatim every word the officers heard from the time she was Mirandized. There were many.

"Oh, Misty, Misty," said Nina, reading the words with sick dismay. "I thought *I* had a big mouth."

The suspect was taken into custody and booked at the South Lake Tahoe jail facility. After refusing to make any further statements, she made one phone call.

A third report was prepared by the U.S. Coast Guard diver. "Interstate waterway," Nina explained to Paul. "Comes under federal jurisdiction."

"I knew that." The diver remarked on the extremely good visibility in the lake due to the lateness of the season. He requested and received permission to search underwater in the area where Anthony Patterson's body was found. About two hundred feet closer to the Keys shoreline, the diver discovered an Eskimo soapstone carving, Aleut or Inuit, approximately ten inches tall. The polar bear, duly marked, went to the South Lake Tahoe police. A subsequent underwater search of the same area the following day resulted in no new findings.

Nina was up and pacing. "We need the autopsy report."

Paul left the room for a minute. "The technicians in Placerville are backed up. It's done. You just can't have it until next week."

"I'll call her doctor today. He's going to have to give me something," said Nina.

"You have somebody lined up to look at the physical evidence? The statue, the trash? The body?"

"You're lined up. You think it's necessary to see the body?"

"Sometimes the forensic guys interpret what they see based on what they want to see. There are judgment calls to make. Patterson will still be at the morgue in Placerville. I should go see the body," Paul said.

"Yes. We should do that first thing Monday morning."

"You don't trust me to look over a dead body, Boss?"

"I want to see him, Paul."

"We could go tomorrow," he said finally. "Speed things up."

Nina thought. "Could we take some kids along? They could play at the park by the town offices. I feel like I never see Bobby."

He paused before his reply. "I guess."

That's right, she thought. He had told her once he never wanted children.

"What else needs doing?"

"I'd like you to talk to the parents, the Tengstedts. Maybe her father will feel more comfortable with you. These people are keeping too many secrets. Then visit the casino."

"The Peter La Russa character. Guy who was a pit boss could have gotten mixed up in all sorts of things."

"So we meet Anthony tomorrow, the one person who knows exactly what happened that night."

"And he's in no mood to talk either."

"Too bad."

Paul said, "Don't expect tomorrow to be fun, Nina," and left her without the option of a last word.

10

PAUL HAD DONE what had to be done to arrange for them to visit the county morgue in Placerville on Sunday. What that entailed, Nina didn't know or care. He had even offered the use of his precious van, a sleek new red Dodge Ram customized with water and electricity hookups and a pop-top. Bobby and his cousins, despite seat belts, bounced up and down while Paul gripped the wheel and held his mouth shut so tightly his lips turned white.

Almost at Placerville, at a place called Apple Hill, Nina asked him to pull off the highway to where the small farmers on the hill sold seasonal fruit, vegetables, and baked goods.

"Think they might have apple pandowdy?" she said. "I always wanted to know what that is."

"Wrong season for apples," Paul replied, diverted for a moment out of his mood.

"You're right; I should know that."

He stopped the van at a roadside stand and bought a sack of nectarines. The proprietor stared when Nina asked about apple pandowdy.

"I'm from Mexico," he said. "We don't have this dowdy."

"You realize your credibility is shot?" Paul said as they loaded the kids in back. "Remind me to go somewhere else for local lore."

"Never mind. I'll show you seedy underpinnings while

you're up here. We'll start at Harvey's with the White Ghost slots, which give you a second chance to line up three bars. The Krazy Klown—you can triple your money. The Megamachines, hooked into slot machines all over the world, in Russia, Tanzania, the Galápagos . . . and the blackjack machines, the ones that let you double your bet and play again right up to 999 quarters . . . the poker machines, with kings that wink and jacks that smile . . ."

"Smart locals don't play slots," Paul said. "They play the only games you can win at, blackjack and maybe craps."

"What do you know? You're just a *turista*."

"I know more than you think," Paul said. "And you think you know more than you do." Before she could react to this provocation, he went on, maneuvering nonchalantly around a hairpin curve with just his left hand, "You have to learn blackjack. It's an essential survival skill living at Tahoe, like knowing how to make snowshoes from rabbit tendons if you're caught in a snowstorm."

"So teach it to me. Not the rabbit tendon stuff, the black-jack. I like to win."

"Sometime soon we'll sit down with a fresh deck of cards. Right now, let's find out what you know. For example, have you learned to beware of gambler's ruin?"

"Gambler's ruin," Nina said meditatively. "What's that? Getting sloshed on free drinks?"

"No, no, although that is a well-known pitfall. Gambler's ruin is a mathematical term for what happens when you don't start out with enough of a stake."

"So how much of a stake do I need?"

"Assuming you practice my system, about two hundred times your minimum bet. Which in your case is the minimum house bet for blackjack, or three bucks," Paul said.

"I'm supposed to sit down for a little friendly card playing with six hundred bucks? I usually go down there with a twenty," Nina said.

"You and the other marks. Okay, I'm the dealer, showing a six. It's a fresh deck; you're holding a pair of sixes."

"Stand," Nina said.

"Nope, you split pairs of twos, threes, sixes, and sevens against the dealer's two through six. With a fresh deck, always assume the dealer's going to have a ten as a hole card. When he turns that over, he's going to have to hit the hand again, and chances are he's going to bust. You both have terrible hands, but odds are you'll win both hands, because the dealer hits first. Also, you can hit each six and maybe come up with something better than a twelve on one or both."

"Or the dealer will pull a five to add to his sixteen. And I'll lose twice as much," Nina said.

"Blackjack is no game for cowards. It takes faith, discipline, and an iron stomach," Paul told her. His stomach had a bodybuilder's flatness under the khaki polo shirt, she couldn't help noticing. "Something like what you'll need today, viewing the remains. Actually, you will have a two percent edge over the house just knowing basic strategy."

"And just how much will I be making per hour, practicing your system with a six-hundred-dollar stake?"

"About ten bucks an hour," Paul said, "but you're your own boss."

"Well, how will I do if I just keep on with my friendly slots?"

"The house edge is over ten percent. Stay home, eat popcorn, rent a video before you do that. I guarantee that way you'll come out ahead."

They pulled off Highway 50. They had entered the foothills between the Sierra and the Sacramento Valley. On the left, the road turned into the main street of Placerville, population 6,500, formerly known as Hangtown. On the right, the road wound along the American River a few miles north to Coloma, where the ill-fated James Marshall discovered gold at Sutter's Mill in 1848. Spring runoffs had brought out the weekend prospectors in their campers, causing a traffic jam at the light. The price of gold had made even a few flakes a real find.

They found the morgue, in the basement of the stone courthouse on Main Street, next door to a lush green park with advanced play equipment. "Back shortly," Nina called as the two boys ran toward a tall contraption made of net and old tires, little Brianna following after in her sparkly new shoes.

"Aren't you afraid to leave them alone?" Paul said, following them with his eyes. "Ever the ex-cop. Scares me."

"We're right next door. And Bobby and I stay in touch. He keeps his in his fanny pack," Nina said, holding out a small black object for inspection.

"Well," he said. "A folding cellular phone. Pocket-size. Top of the line. Welcome to techno world, a place where people can have the illusion of safety. I don't like it."

The implicit criticism angered her. Danger all around, kidnapping, yes, but these kids deserved a life outside prison, didn't they? And so she had made a conscious decision to give her son as much freedom as she could without being eaten up by fear. Nina eyed a bearded old fellow steering his shopping cart toward the park. Still, there were three children, and Bobby had fast feet. She was nervous, but she would let them play.

"Welcome to parenthood in the nineties," she said. "Do you still feel sure you don't want children?"

"It's not that I hate kids. It's just too nerve-wracking. A kid might keel over, fall down the stairs, disappear, drink poison, grow up to be an addict, marry someone I hate, crash my van . . . too hard for me. And I would be linked to a particular woman forever, whether I wanted to be or not." He gave her a sidelong glance. "You asked. Give me a nice, peaceful homicide." Paul began the descent to the basement, and quickly left her behind, his footsteps echoing along the dank passageway. "Ready to visit the under-world?" he called, then fell silent. Nina, behind, tried and failed to forget what was ahead. By the time she arrived at the black-lettered door, Paul was knocking. Observing her face in a pool of sickly yellow light, he asked in a Cockney accent, "Wot 'ud become of the undertakers without it . . . ?"

"Let's get this over with," she said.

A white-coated man wearing a tag that said DR. CLAUSON showed them in, wiping frameless glasses as he marched them down yet another corridor. Behind the door marked FORENSICS he showed them a sheet-covered body laid out on the table. Up to this point he had spoken not a word.

It was Paul's show. He did not look at the body, but asked, "Were you the examining physician?"

"I'm the medical examiner," Dr. Clauson said. "There's only me."

Nina took out her notepad, which the doctor did not seem to notice. He sat down on a chair and shook a cigarette out of a pack of Camels, ignoring the NO SMOKING sign posted prominently on the wall. Taking a long drag, he said, "So what do you want to know?"

"When was the autopsy conducted?"

"Tuesday, May first, five-thirty P.M. White male, six feet even, dark brown hair and brown eyes, brought in by the South Lake Tahoe Police Department."

"As you know, Ms. Reilly here represents the defendant, the dead man's wife. We'd like to know when we can expect to get a copy of the autopsy report."

"You don't have it yet, eh? It's the budget cutbacks. There's only one secretary for the whole County Health Department. You'll get it in another week or two. What does she want to do with the body?" he said suddenly, turning to Nina.

"Who?"

"The widder," he said. It took a moment to register that he meant Misty.

"I have no idea," Nina said. "I'll talk to her."

"Got to get him out of here in the next couple of days. We're too small to store bodies for long. Two more came in last night. Drunk driver took the turns too fast at Strawberry."

"Do you have your examination notes?" Paul asked.

"Nope. I put it on tape as I go, then hand it over for typing. I remember the general stuff, but if I'm wrong on something you can't hold me to it."

"Fair enough," Paul said. "Okay, let's take a look at him." The doctor shrugged and pulled off the cloth.

The photographs in police evidence had been too crude for Nina to form a real impression of the man. She had been expecting her own image of an Anthony: short and stocky, neckless, big-bellied and extremely hairy except on top. This Anthony, except for the extreme bluish pallor, the bloating, and the concave portion of his head, had been a young man with a big, strong body and a wonderful face—a real man's face, with a clean Roman jaw, prominent cheekbones, a full, firm mouth, long eyelashes, and heavy brows under a high forehead. Broad, square shoulders tapered down to a lean waist over long, well-muscled legs.

Nina stood there, wishing she could see his eyes. Where was the monster from that night Misty had described? She looked again at the face, uncreased with the anger and bitterness that must have marked it in life. "A few cc's of water in his lungs," the medical examiner said. "First thing I checked. He wasn't dead when he hit the water. But he was unconscious, judging from the relatively small amount of water I found."

On Patterson's index finger shone a ruby ring set in gold. It was all he was wearing. Well-hung, Nina thought. It was amazing how large and important his genitals looked on his body, like a whole separate animal with its own desires had lived at his center. His head had fallen to the side, his mouth a little open. All his meanness had leaked away with his life.

"Why don't you just summarize the major findings," Paul said.

"Sure. Fingernail scratches, here and here," said the medical examiner, pointing to Anthony's chest. "Couple old scars, one from a bullet, here and here." Nina looked more closely and could see where Anthony had been cut open.

"Inside, everything looked normal but the lungs. Looked like a carcinoma in situ was developing in the right lobe. And the water, of course."

"He had lung cancer?" Nina said.

"The beginnings of it. Looked highly malignant. I saved it to ship down to the research center at UC. Want to see it?"

"No! No. Would he have had any symptoms?"

"Not necessarily. Sometimes just a slight cough. Would have taken a chest X ray for him to know he had a problem." Dr. Clauson shrugged again. "Oh, and he was drunk. Have to wait for the lab reports to get his B.A. level, but you could still smell the alcohol when I opened him up."

Maybe Paul should have come alone.

"Two blows to the head, blunt instrument, an hour or so apart in time. The second blow was the serious one, gave him a shallow skull fracture."

Dr. Clauson held Patterson's head in his hands, and he was twisting it to the side. "See? The temple is a bad place for a fracture, usually causes immediate severe subdural bleeding like it did here. Doesn't take much pressure on impact to cause unconsciousness. This other one in back must have hurt, but there was no fracture. The bash in the back of the head might have knocked him out for a while, long enough for her to get him out on the water."

Nina started to speak and thought better of it.

"Tell me again, Dr. Clauson," Paul said. "Which blow did he take first?"

"The little one in back," the doctor said, laying Patterson's head down none too gently on the gurney.

"Any idea what the blunt object was?"

"Oh, yeah, the police brought it in with the body to see if it matched up with the wounds. I think it's up in Tahoe in the evidence locker now. It's a polar bear statue, about eight pounds. She grabbed it by the head and struck him with the base. You could fit the right corner of the base into the cerebrum wound. The smaller wound in back fits along the edge of the base. Diameter of the edge fits the wound. I understand they pulled it out of the water not far from where the body was found. Anything else?"

"Cause of death," Nina said. "Did he drown?"

"I'd say so. I'd say he never noticed hitting the water, though. The second blow, ma'am. The second blow knocked him in the water, and the lake did the rest in a couple minutes. The second blow alone might not have killed him, even with the bleeding."

"How do you know the second blow caused him to fall in the water?" Paul said.

"Only way it makes sense to me," Clauson said. "I'm not on the witness stand. I'm just telling you what I think, right now and without the lab reports. She hit him in the back of the head. She dragged him out to the boat. Then out on the lake she put him on the railing and bopped him one more time to keep him from swimming around and raising a ruckus after she pushed him over. The railing on those boats is only about eighteen inches high. At least they found him. Lot of missing persons reported in this area. I figure they're down there. Every year they find one or two, dredging the Keys channel."

He was lighting up again. The cigarette smoke plus the disinfectant smell drifted across the body. Nina breathed it in.

"Thanks," she mumbled, and ran for the door. She felt better at the park, gathering up the happy kids, but the curving road after Apple Hill was too much. She got carsick and they had to stop by the side of the road at the Audrain turnout.

Paul drove over Carson Pass on Monday morning just about dawn, stopping when he got hungry. Here, wagon trains from the staging point at St. Joseph, Missouri, had rolled across Nevada to settle California. Struggling up almost nine thousand feet of steeply inclined massif, the pioneers came at last to the same place he was standing, looking west out over the pass, past the peaks of the western Sierra to the fertile, golden-green valleys of California.

Turning from the view and pulling up his collar against a brisk breeze, he entered a one-horse casino and ate a platter of bacon and eggs.

He had an appointment with the Tengstedts in Fresno and a pocketful of questions Nina wanted answered.

"Talk to the father, Paul," she had said that morning. "Find out more about her childhood memory loss. Bruno thinks she may have had a similar memory loss on April twenty-sixth. Bringing back one memory may bring back the other. Try to get more on Misty's relationship with Anthony. Give me your impressions of the parents. Oh, one other thing. Find out what Carl Tengstedt was doing on the night of the twenty-sixth."

"You think he might have visited the Lake?" Paul said.

"He and Misty used to go fishing now and then. You do that in the early hours, right? Maybe he got the urge, came up late the night before without calling her. Or maybe Misty called him and he drove up. It's only three hours. Maybe he just disposed of the body for her."

"With all the other males around your client, why are you looking so hard at the old man?"

"Just a feeling about the parents. They do have some kind of secret, and they're very frightened about whatever it is. And one other thing."

"What?"

"Remember, I mentioned he was a swimmer? Tengstedt's wife said that he was shot down in Korea in stormy seas and managed to hold on to another man for hours before he was rescued."

"So?"

Nina had said, "The boat was drifting out there, out of gas. Whoever took Anthony out on the lake had to swim half a mile back in frigid water. It took a hero to do that and survive. I don't think I could do it, and I'm a pretty good swimmer."

Now Paul pushed his notes aside and leaned back on the vinyl back of his booth, observing his bleary-eyed fellow customers. Just outside the open door of the coffee shop, he could hear a pleasant ringing and the jingling of coins falling into a slot. Some lucky bastard had actually won something in a slot machine.

He loved his job. He was making a lot more money than he could have dreamed of as a cop, and he got to roam over the countryside in search of the facts, answerable only to the IRS.

Just before leaving, he had called his secretary and playmate, waking her from a sound sleep in the water bed in her cottage in Carmel. Marilyn told him to come back with a big check. Since leaving the police force, besides the independence of having his own investigative business, he was enjoying his first financial success. Certain large corporate clients, most of whom he farmed out to reliable subcontractors, footed the daily bills. He missed being on the force, but he was not stupid enough to go back when he wasn't welcome. There was a certain type there, and he wasn't it.

In addition to an increased financial payback, he was now able to pick off the plums, like this job, and indulge a well-honed interest in people. He had always been very self-contained, but as his work threw him into situations that demanded it, he discovered the fine pleasures of instant intimacy. People in trouble were vulnerable. Interviews were so much more gratifying when you could ignore police procedure. He had a talent for getting people to tell him what he wanted to know, and he was no longer averse at all to sharing select pieces of himself, particularly when he knew he would never see the person again. In return he got friendship, advice, and an instant relationship. It was remarkably like a one-night stand, only nobody expected a callback.

Nina had changed over the five years with Jack. She still liked to joke around, and she had the same voluptuous figure he remembered from their first meeting, but five years of lawyering had sharpened her. With her brown bangs, intent brown eyes, head thrust forward and shoulders squared, she now looked more like a little hawk. The tentative girl in law school, the unsure one, had seemed softer, needier, more approachable. It was just too bad. He would protect her now as well as he could, but she didn't belong where she was in the first place. He didn't like having as his boss a woman on the loose, the sole support of a child, running her own business. He was sick and tired of these pushy broads trying to take over. They were all stressed out and divorced, just like she would soon be.

How exasperating it was that precisely this kind of woman always attracted him. He couldn't resist their convolutions and moodiness, their direct speech, their self-doubts, their strength in the head and their weakness in the heart.

She needed him, even more than she knew.

He got back in his van. Behind the wheel once again, he flipped on the news. A San Francisco station two hundred miles away tried to create some radio excitement out of gridlock on the Bay Bridge. Out the window a line of snow-covered peaks receded into the sharp, bright air. Highway 395—someone should write a song about it, because it had to be one of the most beautiful roads in the world. An hour to Mammoth Lake, around Yosemite, cutting across the top of Sequoia National Park . . . he turned off the news and searched for a jazz station.

If he thought of Fresno at all, he thought of a hot, dry, dull agricultural town. Today, however, deeply into spring, the whole San Joaquin valley lay strewn with yellow mustard flowers. Fruit trees dripped with blooms in pink and white. It was the pioneer's dream. The town boiled with the scents of flowers and fertilizer.

Tengstedt had agreed to meet him at home, before going to work at the auto dealership. The house was in the old part of town, a mock Southern plantation house from the thirties, painted white, its lawn disciplined into a military buzz cut. The Tengstedts must be doing well.

He walked under an arch into the green front yard. Carl Tengstedt was there, waiting for him. "Beautiful day," he said.

Paul agreed and they went inside. Mrs. Tengstedt, a worn-out-looking blonde, was sitting at the kitchen table. They sat down and had some coffee, talked about the case and got used to each other for about twenty minutes.

Then Mrs. Tengstedt got up and said she had things to do and invited Paul to dinner. Paul said thanks, but he was on a tight schedule and was driving back to Tahoe tonight to get on with the investigation. She kissed her husband on the top of the head and went out the door.

"Okay, then," Carl Tengstedt said, settling himself on the striped couch in his living room. "You said you wanted to know more about Michelle's background. Well, you're looking at it. This is her home. She's a good daughter and we love her."

It was so quiet, Paul could hear the tick-tock of the pendulum clock on the mantel. He looked around him. A doily adorned the top of the entertainment center; a Winslow Homer print decorated the other wall. A neat pile of Fresno newspapers sat in an ornate brass container. Mr. Tengstedt had his recliner, Mrs. Tengstedt her rocking chair and cushion, and even a sewing basket on the rug next to it. A big Bible rested on a mahogany stand in the corner. The all-American living room, Penney's catalog, circa 1960, and in this home Father clearly knew best.

Tengstedt was nervous. Paul could see it in the hands folded tightly, the stern expression on his face, but he had the stolidity of a burgermeister too. He looked honest. The good-citizen type. Very effective with a jury, likely to be believed. He said, "We're putting a lot of faith in Ms. Reilly, Mr. van Wagoner. I wish I could believe it's well placed."

"Nina Reilly is an excellent attorney," Paul said, hoping it was true. "I've known her for years."

"Then she can settle this quickly. Is it possible Michelle could be sentenced only to probation? After all, this is her first offense, and that man was violent. He was arrested before."

"Michelle doesn't believe she killed Anthony," Paul said. "There may be a trial."

"That would be very foolish, from what you have told me about the evidence and my daughter's statements. Michelle has always had difficulty accepting the consequences of her actions."

"You seem so sure, Mr. Tengstedt, that your daughter's a murderer," Paul said. "I hope you'll allow Michelle's attorney to handle this as she sees fit."

"We don't have any choice, do we? Michelle has made that clear. Tell Ms. Reilly the loan on the house is coming through next week, and we'll post Michelle's bail. But we want Michelle home with us."

"I'll pass that along," promised Paul. Some of it, he would.

Tengstedt changed the subject abruptly. "You know, we would have got her back somehow after she ran off to Tahoe, except for one thing."

"What's that?"

"I strongly disapproved of her marriage to Anthony Patterson. I felt it would be disastrous for Michelle to link her life to his. But I have to say this one thing about Patterson: He really loved Michelle. I could see it when they were together. I never dreamed he would strike her, harm her. He seemed to idolize her. We prayed for her happiness."

"Of course," Paul said. "I understand that you are Christian Scientists."

"Science of Mind, yes. My wife and I both were practitioners, you know, spiritual healers. No longer."

"You left the Church?"

"No. We left that particular congregation when we came back to the States from the Philippines in 1982, of course. But we are still followers."

"Why did you leave?"

There was a pause. "We had some irreconcilable religious conflicts," he said finally. "And we found ourselves at odds with our neighbors. It seemed better to leave."

"Mmm-hmmm," Paul said.

"I joined the Science of Mind Church at a very young age. My grandparents had been members of the Boston congregation, the Mother Church, for years, and they were close to Mrs. Eddy. Mary Baker Eddy, the founder of the Church. Barbara joined the Church when we married."

"Tell me a little about the Church," Paul said.

"There are thousands of congregations all over the world. I'll give you the book, *Science of Mind,* if you'd like. Basically we're Protestants, one of the few Protestant churches that was born in America. We believe the crucifixion and resurrection of Jesus Christ was the central event in history, and we believe that heaven is located right here on earth, if we can develop the attitude of the Christ mind."

"Heaven right here on earth . . ."

"You see, the material world is nothing but a hypnotic construct. Belief in a world of matter is what causes sin and suffering. So we believe that disease is merely a delusion of the material world, and that prayer and understanding through Bible study can rectify any problem."

Tengstedt said this as though he had said it many times before, with complete conviction. Paul listened hard for the point of this earnest religious statement.

"So I was a practitioner, healer. A doctor of the spirit, you might say. I ministered to the nationals as well as to people on base in need of help."

"Tell me about Michelle's life in the Philippines," Paul said.

"I don't know why you're so interested."

"For us to understand Michelle, we need a few details about her life growing up," Paul said.

Mrs. Tengstedt appeared in the doorway, a ghost in a white apron. She carried a tray toward them and set it on a table nearby. "Please help yourselves to some refreshment. You've had a long drive," she said to Paul. As she stood up, she looked directly at her husband. "Michelle has been our greatest blessing, also our greatest heartache," she said, moving toward the kitchen.

"Will Michelle be told about the things we discuss today?" Tengstedt said.

"It depends. I believe you know Michelle cannot remember the first ten years of her life. She has forgotten some events of the night of April twenty-sixth as well. Nina feels that if she were helped to remember her early childhood it might help her remember the more recent events."

"She's on the wrong track. She's not going to take her to some quack psychiatrist, is she?"

"I don't know if Nina plans on bringing in a doctor." Tengstedt had jumped up from his recliner as if he had been bitten by a Filipino snake. "Take it easy, Mr. Tengstedt. Ms. Reilly would never do anything that would hurt your daughter."

"You tell that lawyer for me that Michelle's first ten years are not something we're prepared to discuss at this time. Events from long ago could not possibly influence the legal problems she has."

"I hope you'll reconsider your decision, Mr. Tengstedt. We think it might have some relevance."

Tengstedt said nothing.

"Do you mind talking about Michelle's life in Fresno?" asked Paul, moving on to what he hoped would be less explosive territory.

"I put in my time and I retired. My family was here in Fresno, so we moved back," Tengstedt said shortly.

"Go on," Paul said.

"After we moved here, things steadily went downhill for her. She got wild, got secretive, did poorly in school, though she tested out as very bright," he said, a sad note of pride in his voice. "And then she ran off with this backstreet thug, Patterson. Who's been killed." He fingered a picture on the mantelpiece of a young woman in a yellow dress and hat, haloed with golden hair, a flat Easter backdrop behind her. "It broke my wife's heart to see her throwing herself away like that."

"I was so afraid that something like this might happen someday." Barbara Tengstedt was standing in the entryway between the kitchen and living room, smoothing her hands over her apron. Her husband walked over to her, put his arm around her shoulder. They were about the same height. The effect was almost comically bland, Mr. and Mrs. America in their living room, but it was a tableau, with a frozen, waiting quality. It seemed to Paul as though, by touching her, Carl Tengstedt had silenced his wife.

"Not knowing is causing her pain right now," Paul said. "Look, whatever it is, we can deal with it together. Why not just blurt it out?"

"You don't know how to take *no* for an answer, do you, Mr. van Wagoner? But you will have to accept my judgment on this."

"Okay, let's talk about April twenty-sixth. A Thursday night. Just for completeness' sake, I need to know where you and your wife were," Paul said.

Tengstedt clapped his hand to his forehead. "Now he's accusing me of murdering that slime!" he cried disbelievingly. "Mr. van Wagoner, perhaps you ought to leave our house."

Paul was about out of patience himself. "Did you or your wife go to Tahoe on April twenty-sixth, Mr. Tengstedt?"

"No! How dare you!"

"Where were you?"

"Right here in this house all evening. Barbara!" He commanded her, squeezing her shoulder. "Tell Mr. van Wagoner here that we were in the house all that night. He's accusing me of something!"

"Keep your shirt on, Mr. Tengstedt," Paul said.

"We were right here," Barbara Tengstedt said in a tremulous voice. She twisted away from her husband and sank into her chair.

"Sure you didn't go for a swim in the lake that night? From what I hear, you like swimming."

"Out! Out!" Carl Tengstedt roared.

11

❧

NINA DROPPED THE kids at school on the way to work that same Monday morning. Troy and Bobby played out their boyish identity struggles together in the backseat, arguing over who kicked a soccer ball farther; who ran faster; who multiplied quicker; who bullied meaner; and Brianna, in the front seat, took advantage of her final bit of privacy to squeeze in a little thumb sucking. Before Bobby left the car, he offered up his cheek for a kiss. "I like it here, Mom. But I'm getting kind of tired of living at Uncle Matt's. When are we going to have our own place?"

Good question, Nina thought, but she had no answer. Not yet.

By nine o'clock, Nina stared through a purple haze out her office picture window at Mt. Tallac, raising her pencil to a sheet of paper with nine dots in three rows.

She began running it around the dots. Matt had said you could touch the pencil to paper once and make four straight connected lines join all the dots. Bobby had solved the puzzle immediately, but Nina couldn't, and it bothered her. Her pencil scraped satisfyingly as she moved it around. It looked so simple!

She knew two ways to approach any puzzle. You could be methodical and linear, eliminating false leads one by one until only the solution remained. The police investigated this

way, and Paul would investigate this way based on his training.

Start at the beginning, logically. She put the dot puzzle
aside and made a list for Paul to work on. Check on the
photos of Misty's bruises that she had promised to provide.
Talk to Rich Eich and look the boat over. Interview Tom
Clarke. Interview Stephen Rossmoor, the manager at Prize's
with whom Misty had had a fling. Look at the physical
evidence listed in the police reports. Talk to the ex-wife,
Sharon Otis, and Peter La Russa, Anthony's friend.

And then there were those footprints in the snow, heading
toward the back of her house, that Misty had noticed and
assumed were Anthony's. Sic Paul on that.

She set Paul's list down, and started making her own. Take
care of the legal questions. Research search- and arrest-war-
rant law, and make sure the police had made no mistakes on
the night Misty was arrested. Find every hole in the police,
autopsy, and lab reports, and every conflicting inference.
Research the crimes of murder and manslaughter, looking
for ways to reduce the charge.

So much for the logical method. The second method was
her own little secret. She turned the lists over and picked up
the piece of paper with those infernal dots again. She
stopped analyzing and stared at the piece of paper for a long
time. She almost had it. . . .

Now, quickly, still staring at the dots, she turned her
mind to the case, coming up on it sideways, like a crab.
There it was, blurry and huge, the center, the question that
burned, flamed, demanded to be answered, made every
other question inconsequential: What had happened after
Misty left her husband and went into the kitchen? Nina
drew a quick sketch of the living room, the door to the
kitchen, the man lying on the couch, the glass from the
broken table, as Misty had described these things. A bright

fire in the fireplace. A maroon robe. Two glasses, and a bottle of Yukon Jack. Dirty dishes. Footsteps in the snow outside, and a polar bear statue.

Misty could not remember. Why? *Theory One:* Misty remembered, and she was lying. *Theory Two:* Misty had been tired and gone to sleep, as she said. *Theory Three:* Misty was repressing the memory. *Theory Four?* Nina couldn't think of anything else.

Theory One: In spite of her own conviction that her client spoke the truth, to be thorough Nina had hammered at Misty a few times. Her story remained the same; not one detail changed. *Theory Two:* Misty was completely immune to normal human feeling and had indeed fallen asleep in the heat of one of the most violent scenes in her marriage. *Theory Three.* Nina drew a circle around it and the thought came to her again, as it had visited her persistently all through the weekend: Misty suppressed memories.

She would do the legal work later. Today was Theory Three day. She would talk to Dr. Greenspan. Later she would call Bruno again.

Drawing the nine dots again, she failed with her pencil one last time, then set the puzzle aside on her desk, hung her heavy briefcase off her shoulder, and left the office.

Dr. Frederick Greenspan's office was a rustic but well-kept bungalow a block from Boulder Hospital, off Winnemucca. In a quaint reception room furnished with lace curtains and a Baldwin piano, several older people lounged on chairs. Others could be seen through the interior door, lying on narrow cots with tubes snaking out of their arms. The receptionist, unusually tall for a woman and incongruously elegant in yellow and black, offered Nina a cup of herbal tea and said the doctor would be right with her.

The people waiting did not seem impatient. Talking and

whispering, reading and shifting in their chairs, they seemed at home, friendly with each other. Nina, who hated waiting, picked up the holistic healing brochures from the spindly table beside her. The first, a short four-color extravaganza on hypnotherapy, promised that clients could regain lost memories, heal emotional problems by learning to relax, end addictive behaviors, and intensify the therapeutic relationship through this miraculous "new" treatment.

The second pamphlet covered chelation therapy. The article, written with a folksy touch by a satisfied patient, extolled its virtues. The writer had suffered a heart attack and after chelation therapy was "now regularly cleansed of free radicals and will not need the surgeon's knife in the future." Chemicals suffused into the bloodstream at a steady rate for a few hours each week vacuumed up free radicals and unsafe ions, the implication being that aging could be slowed. That explained those people with tubes. But what about those chemicals? And what about the good ions? How did they avoid the vacuum? No details here, even in the fine print at the bottom of the last page.

The doctor came out within five minutes and shook Nina's outstretched hand, then showed her to his office. In his fifties, tall, gaunt, and angular, with a heavy brow, sunken eyes, jutting cheekbones and prominent ears, he carried himself with the mien of Moses about to hoist his staff and command the Red Sea. "I'm sorry to keep you waiting," he said, sitting down at his desk and taking off thick glasses, while Nina revised her impression. The voice still spoke with a Brooklyn accent, and the brown polyester slacks with patterned anklets reduced him to unmiraculous. The office was too warm; a thin sheen of sweat blanketed his forehead.

Nina sank into a deep-blue easy chair, the only other chair in the office. Obviously clients sat here, eyes directed toward certificates displayed on the opposite wall. She read in a moment that Dr. Greenspan had completed a course in hypnosis at J.F.K. University and a course in Zen practice at Shasta Monastery. He had earned his M.D. at Temple University in New York twenty-five years before.

Misty's file sat on the desk. "Thank you for seeing me today. I'm hoping you'll give me total access to my client's file."

"You haven't really told me what this is all about," Dr. Greenspan said, spreading his hand on the file. "But I have my patient's authorization to give you a copy of her file and discuss whatever you wish." Up close, he smelled like soap. His cheeks had been scraped clean in what must be a painful daily process.

"The file is a start. I am sending it to another doctor at UC in the city who may serve as a consulting psychiatrist in this case."

"Does he intend to try hypnosis?"

"Yes. Don't worry, Bruno's very good."

"I hope he will be very careful."

"He has written extensively in the field. An expert, you could say."

The receptionist came in without knocking. "Frederick, I'm leaving now. Now, remember, your file clerk says she'll cover the desk for the rest of the afternoon. Keep an eye on her." Turning toward Nina, she smiled. "She's new, and needs extra help. Our nurse, Rhea, is going to be busy with patients." Nina had seen the file clerk in the front office, a plain, soft-spoken girl with gray teeth, who looked remarkably similar to the nurse, except for the nurse's bifocals. Walking around Dr. Greenspan's desk, the woman planted a kiss on his forehead, then curled her lips into a grin, saying, "Don't worry. We're married."

"Oh, good," responded Nina, trying not to look at her watch.

"Good-bye, Ericka. I won't be late." Dr. Greenspan led his wife to the door. "I won't be a minute," he said, closing his office door behind him. Through the wood, Nina heard murmuring that went on for several minutes. "Instructions for the nurse and so forth," he muttered when he came back. "Now, where were we?" He looked pleased to see the file still on his desk, apparently untouched. "Misty Patterson. How is she?"

"Her arrest came as a terrible shock to her. I'm not sure they knew whether to take her to jail or a mental hospital. She's worked hard to pull herself together and is trying to adjust."

"It's disturbing to hear this. To my knowledge, she's not violent or insane," the doctor said. "She shouldn't be locked up."

"We hope to have her out soon."

"I haven't seen her since right after her husband disappeared, in a brief emergency session. She did call me this Friday, explaining that she could use some help and asked if she could see me. I told her I'd talk to you today about it."

"You mean, you'd continue to treat her?" Nina paused and thought. "Well, first of all, Doctor, Misty's medical records and your testimony are probably relevant to a number of issues in this case. If there is a trial, as you're still her treating physician, I expect you'll be called as a witness to discuss her state of mind. Anything Misty said at this point might be discoverable. It's too risky."

"That may be so, looking at the situation purely from a legal point of view, Ms. Reilly, but I am concerned about Misty's health. To suddenly terminate the treatment she is receiving would be damaging. She needs therapy, you know. With due care we could maintain the progress we have already made, and keep her stress at a manageable level. I believe we could keep away from any discussion of the events leading up to this charge."

"Maybe," Nina said. "But I have to call this one. I think we have to put her treatment on hold."

The doctor shrugged, a little angrily. "I suppose I'll have to defer to your judgment, then."

"Tell me about your work with her."

He picked up the file and began flipping. "She started coming in right before Christmas. Here's her paperwork." Nina read rapidly through the form. Misty's handwriting was round and large. She dotted her *i*'s with circles.

Under *"Why did you come today?"* she had written, "I am so sad." The statement stood out in stark contrast to the girlish handwriting.

"We had only ten hypnosis sessions. It sounds like many, I know, but she had a long way to go. I believe she initially consulted me because she wanted to know why she felt compelled to be unfaithful to her husband. Later she indicated some interest in her forgotten childhood, which she had come to realize played a role in the person she had become. It took three sessions for us to understand that the two problems are connected."

"You mean, some kind of shock in her childhood caused her to suppress those memories and led her to the reaction-formation of sleeping around?" Nina said. The words felt mealy in her mouth.

They must have sounded thick to him too. He frowned. "I suppose you could put it that way."

"What was this childhood trauma?"

"We hadn't gotten to that point."

Deeply disappointed, Nina forged on. "You have no ideas? After all this work with her?"

Dr. Greenspan didn't seem to be listening. He gazed out

his own window, which framed the soothing sight of a dark blue-green spruce forest.

"Dr. Greenspan?"

"Frankly, I would be very skeptical about anything her father tells you about her childhood."

There was a word hanging out there, a word Nina hated and didn't want to hear. She swallowed and said, "You suspect her father of . . . abuse, is that it?"

"She has no specific recollection," Greenspan said. "Nevertheless, her behavior is classic, the compulsive quality of her sexual life, the alcohol abuse, the depression, the abusive marriage, the low self-esteem, the amnesia itself. This is a very troubled young lady, and her trouble appears to stem from her childhood. I suppose some other trauma could be involved. Let's just say it's a possibility."

"How would hypnosis help her?"

"Well, accessing suppressed memories is one of the most well-known benefits of this type of therapy. You can't deal with an emotional problem as long as it's unconscious. Hypnosis brings it up, with the appropriate emotional reactions, and living through the experience again may cure the compulsive activities.

"If the old memory is not brought up, it manifests in other ways in adult life, in generalized emotional pain, perhaps in a drinking problem, perhaps in an unconscious repetition of the childhood psychodrama. I believe Misty was acting something out in her adult life that stemmed from her childhood."

"And you say you were making progress?"

"Misty is an excellent subject. She is able to achieve a deep, deep trance state. This has taken some time to develop. In the last sessions we were beginning the age-regression. She had to work her way through some strong emotions."

"What type of feelings did she express toward her husband?"

Dr. Greenspan said, "That's difficult to explain. I would say . . . in the beginning she loved him in a rather immature way, but once they were married she found it necessary to . . . wreck the marriage. She was repeatedly unfaithful, you see, and her husband reacted predictably with jealousy. She denied to herself that he suspected something and didn't link his treatment of her with her own actions."

"Oh, I love this, Dr. Greenspan. You're saying she asked for it, right?"

"I believe I'm trying to say a great deal more than that. I hope you will not let your feminist sympathies blind you to the truth about your client," Greenspan said calmly.

Nina felt manipulated, as if her own work were being subtly trivialized. In the same way, the doctor was trivializing Anthony's physical and emotional abuse of Misty. He was grating on her, sitting there with his knobby hands folded together, talking such a good line, a line that would remove all lingering jury sympathy for Misty.

"You seem to have made a rather harsh assessment of your patient," she said. "I'm trying to understand. Are you defending the way her husband treated her?"

"In a way. Marriage is a primal drama. The partners receive something valuable, which they need, or they part quickly."

"And Misty needed . . ."

"To be punished—and to punish."

An awful glow to these pronouncements, like atomic bombs going off one by one, blew Misty Patterson sky-high. Greenspan's interpretation had an evil simplicity. In those six words he would tell a jury that, driven by her unconscious, she had engineered Anthony's harsh treatment of her and eventually found a reason to kill him, all to get back at dear old Dad.

Another enemy had stepped out from behind a tree, shaking a weapon in her face. Why he would assume such an aggressive stance in this preliminary interview seemed clear: For some reason he did not want to be involved or to testify. He wanted the case settled without a trial.

"He had told her to terminate her therapy with you," Nina said.

"Yes, we talked about that. Although she seemed all right at the time, it doesn't surprise me that she was quite angry. She had come to depend on our therapy. She would feel cut adrift, ending our professional relationship so abruptly, without conclusion."

"Did she threaten Anthony, then or at any other time?"

"No, but—"

"She didn't tell you anything on the phone from jail, did she?" Nina asked.

"No, no. I know better than to elicit that type of information," he said. "Tell me, is it true that Misty says she cannot remember the events just after striking her husband, as it says in the paper?"

"What would that tell you, Dr. Greenspan?"

"Such amnesia would indicate a strong connection to the unconscious motivations we discussed."

"You're saying, the amnesia proves she was carrying out her unconscious agenda of killing her husband."

Dr. Greenspan steepled his fingers, looking regretful. "I'm afraid so."

"Do you know something, Doctor?"

"Yes, Ms. Reilly?"

"I think you are full of shit, and if you go into court spouting this pseudopsychological crap, I'm going to fix it so you leave crying for your mommy."

"Ms. Reilly," he said, standing up, smiling. "Should you ever consider help for yourself, I can recommend a good therapist."

On her way out Nina stopped at the front desk for a résumé of Dr. Greenspan's experience. A different receptionist handed it over without comment, and returned to her computer monitor. Nina went down the walkway, reading it over before inserting it into Misty's file. According to the résumé, which recapped the certificates on his wall, Dr. Greenspan was a family-practice physician interested in holistic health. There was no mention of a specialized psychiatric background or training.

She could fire effective mortar at his background on the witness stand.

But what if he was right?

Turning the key in the lock of her car, she had the sensation of being watched. A moment later, Dr. Greenspan's wife appeared by her door.

Mrs. Greenspan had perfect hair, upswept, curved into a French twist, not a hair fluttering loose. Up close, she looked somewhat older, about fifty. Her makeup foundation, slightly darker than her skin, ended at her neck, and the corners of her dark-lipsticked mouth were beginning to pull down in what the plastic surgeons call marionette lines. Still, in her yellow dress with the black belt she made a handsome, if somewhat overdramatic, appearance. She stopped a couple of feet away and said, "I wonder if I could speak with you for a minute."

"What about?" Nina asked.

"Oh, nothing much. I heard you in there, with my husband. You were quite rude at the end." She sounded a lot like Nina's Aunt Helen, who talked with the same disappointment when trying to teach Nina to play the piano.

"I thought it was a private conversation." Nina imagined Mrs. Greenspan's shell-like ear compressed painfully against the doctor's solidly paneled door.

The older woman brushed the reproof aside. "You misjudge my husband, Mrs. Reilly. He has helped so many people, so many troubled people like Mrs. Patterson. If you had only given him a chance to explain—"

"Does your husband know you're out here, talking to me?"

"Now you want to cross-examine me. How interesting it must be to be an attorney! Of course, in my day girls still found their fulfillment in marriage. I actually met Frederick in college, and believe it or not I had planned to go to medical school. But I was lucky to find a wonderful—really wonderful—husband. Someone I could help. I have spent many years helping Frederick build up his practice."

"Would you mind telling me what this is all about? Because I have five people waiting for a good excuse to lose their tempers with me back at my office."

"A little patience goes a long way, don't you agree, Mrs. Reilly? Or is it Miss?"

"Ms.," Nina said.

"Aren't you the liberated woman! Such a silly thing to call yourself, though, isn't it? I thought that went out of style quickly, like the Susan B. Anthony dollar." She favored Nina with a severe smile. As she spoke, she moved closer and closer to Nina. Despite herself, Nina took a step back. "You're married?"

"Yes."

"Your poor husband! Oh, now it's me being rude! It's just that I can see your important career keeps you from home so much." Nina was now feeling strangely guilty. She put her luckless marriage firmly out of her mind.

"I'm sorry, Mrs. Greenspan. I have to go now."

"Yes, your clients are waiting, I understand. And I hope you understand that I am very proud of my husband and I wouldn't want—"

Nina was jingling her keys, and this interruption seemed to upset Mrs. Greenspan.

"Some female shyster with a sicko client to try to—"

Key in lock. Open door, with the words ringing in her ears. Get in, turn key in ignition.

"Smear him. So you watch out, you little—" Mrs. Greenspan's well-bred voice expressed mild perturbation, but her words had begun to flow like a stream of toxic waste.

"Hold that thought," Nina said, slamming the door, and hightailing it out of there.

That night at eleven-thirty, Nina called San Francisco from the quiet of her bed. "Sorry to call you so late, Professor," Nina said, "but I'd like to make an appointment for Misty and me to come and see you as soon as possible. I'll fax the file from Dr. Greenspan."

"I'm too old to sleep," griped Bruno, sounding not at all displeased to hear from her. "What is your impression of this hypnotherapist?" he asked. Nina could hear Jay Leno reducing the day's events to audience laughter in the background.

She summarized her conversation with Dr. Greenspan and the stranger one with his wife. "I think Dr. Greenspan is a dangerous phony. And his wife seems like a certifiable wacko in the grip of a mid-life crisis. But you know me. I don't trust anyone, especially a man with certificates in frames that cost more than his college education."

"Check his credentials," Bruno said. "Anybody can get a hypnotherapy certificate with a few hours of coursework and practice. Lets the M.D.'s slide in the back door of the psychiatric profession. Then they start thinking they're Freud, though they don't know a goddamned thing about psychiatry."

"That's what I like about you, Bruno, your devotion to maintaining the highest professional standards," Nina said.

Bruno let out what sounded like a bark. "This is serious, Nina. Remember Pope's warning about a little learning? 'Shallow draughts intoxicate the brain.' That's hideously true when it comes to psychotherapy. The dangers? Beware the unanalyzed analyst. He can project onto the patient. He can interpret the patient's dreams in terms of his own psychic troubles. He can misdiagnose a patient and send him out in worse shape than before. He can countertransfer, creating an unhealthy emotional fixation or relationship with the patient instead of encouraging a healthy transference."

"I get you." She scribbled on a yellow pad. "Any other thoughts?"

"Well," said the old man, "this Dr. Greenspan has to worry about malpractice. He's been hypnotizing a girl for how long, three months? Now, presumably, she's killed her husband. Certainly he must worry at some point that his professional acumen will be attacked. Or he's afraid you'll sue."

"Funny you should say that. His wife accused me of trying to find a way to involve him in what happened. He didn't seem to be thinking along those lines. I think he just wants to stay out of a messy case."

"He just hides his thoughts better," Bruno said.

"Now we're psychoanalyzing him."

"Yes. Isn't this fun—" said Bruno drily, "playing around in people's psyches. That has its own dangers. I recall my constant advice, to take it slowly and carefully. . . ."

"I don't have much time," Nina said. "When can we come to your office? I want you to see her."

"Any day between three and six. Those are my office

hours and I can be flexible. We talked earlier about hypnosis. Shall we try?"

"It's risky. If she says something I don't want to hear, we couldn't use you as an expert to testify at trial, but that's okay. Your name would never have to be brought up. As long as I don't name you as an expert witness and you stay a nontreating consultant, the prosecution can't question you. It would be attorney work-product and privileged."

"I see. You're thinking she may confess to me, and the physician is afraid I'll have instant success with his balky patient. My concern is different."

"And that is?"

"Well, if she is a borderline personality, I want to be very careful not to press her too hard and possibly bring on a full-fledged psychosis."

"Unlike the doctor, I'm not much worried about you dealing with his patient. I trust you. And if we can keep this session entirely private, and you thereafter do not work with me or act any further as my expert, I don't have to give your name out, and the consultation can remain forever private."

"Fine," Bruno said. "So my job is to remove the memory your client is repressing in the hope that she will remember this hypothetical person who struck the fatal blow."

"Or establish beyond doubt that my client struck the second blow, which, I admit, is much more likely. At least I can work out a defense strategy at that point."

"You realize that the first and second episodes are linked. She has clearly locked her past up tight. If we cannot see into her childhood, we may fail."

"You can do it."

"All this, in one session?"

"But, Bruno, you're a genius."

"Depends on what test you're using, my dear. And this

one may be written by the devil in hell insofar as your client is concerned."

"We're gambling here."

"You find it exciting to take risks."

"Do I give that impression? Because I really only enjoy gambling when I win. God, we have to be careful."

12

⚜

THE NEXT DAY, back at Tahoe, Paul ate breakfast at the Heidi's on Highway 50 where it ran along the foot of Ski Run Boulevard. Outside, wind rustled through the pine boughs. A flock of gulls careened out of the south, flying back to nest on the beaches. Granite crags, distantly visible out the window, defended the lake, brilliant white snow still showing high up on green and speckled gray. . . . He would take a few days, do some free-climbing on the granite this summer.

"More coffee?" A waitress paused in her flitting. She looked fresh out of junior high school. How mortifying that she should be sexually mature but twenty-five years younger than he was. She poured him a third cup, which he drank while he examined a geographical map and guidebook to the lake. He liked to be oriented, and maps were another way to have information at his command. His attention was drawn first to a name, Desolation Wilderness, then to the vast area extending behind Emerald Bay on the California side. Here was a great glacial valley headed by a roche moutonnée, a huge steep-faced wall of granite rounded in back. He took a red fine-point pen and circled the area on the map. July would be a good month.

Meantime, better get on with today. He reread Nina's list. Time's a-runnin' out, boy, he said to himself, and rose, glimpsing himself in a glass door, a big man, rugged—he liked to think—outfitted for anything in a windbreaker and running shoes.

The El Dorado County sheriff's office covered the east end of a long building that had at its western end the windowless jail where Misty Patterson was incarcerated. In the middle were the courtrooms, mediators between law and disorder. A deputy took him right through the security door and in back to the evidence locker.

"You got it made, working up here. I worked San Francisco and then the sheriff's department in Monterey. Great guys, don't get me wrong."

"Not as much action here as the City," the deputy said. "But we get our share."

"How many homicides do you get a year?"

"A few, mostly drug-related. We run a tight ship. The tourists appreciate it."

"I can see that," Paul said. "Is this all that was taken as physical evidence?"

The deputy nodded, looking over Paul's shoulder at the four Ziploc bags now spread out on a metal table.

The first bag held the contents of Misty Patterson's purse and other personal articles, a few credit cards, Mervyn's, the Emporium, a Visa card, and about ten dollars. A small cardboard box held old papers, souvenirs of Misty's. He unscrewed the lid of a small silver flask and sniffed, wrinkling his nose. He put the bag away. "Can she get this bag back if she fills out the form?"

"If Hallowell calls the jail. Set it up with him."

The second small bag contained the Eskimo statue. Paul reached in for the statue but was stopped by the deputy, whose badge read BELTINE.

"The cold water wiped the fingerprints," noted Paul. "At least that's what the police report said. I need to take a closer look."

"Use my handkerchief. And if you drop it I'll be looking for a job," Beltine said. Paul nodded and took out the heavy statue.

A ten-inch polar bear, gray and massive, stood erect on its hind legs. The style, detailed and impressionistic at the same time, was Inuit, Paul thought. He recognized soapstone, looking remarkably like granite but softer, on a heavy base. Searching for bloodstains, not finding any, he hefted the statue. The head fit easily into his hand, anchored by the bear's ears. He swung it experimentally, imagining the *thunk* as the base connected with Patterson's skull.

Inside the third bag he found some badly decomposed cigarette butts, a rusty pair of pliers, and paper trash. "From around the outside of the house," Beltine said. In his urge to move on, Paul almost missed a small piece of metal in the bag. He pulled it out of the paper and held it near the light. "What's this?" he said.

"Let's see," the deputy said. "Harley wings. Looks like real silver. Pretty nice work."

"It's barely tarnished. Where was this found?"

Beltine looked over the inventory. "Small silver pin, found in the back of the house, under the window into the bedroom."

"Does anybody know anything about this pin? Whether it belonged to the guy's wife, or . . ."

"Nobody's checked this stuff out since it was brought in. You're the first."

"Now the last bag." Upholstery from the living room couch, neatly labeled, bore marks of what looked like bleached bloodstains. Samples of cloth from Rick Eich's boat galley carried darker brown stains. A small plastic bag, neatly taped, held a few grains of white powder. A small inner bag held belongings found on the bedside table, keys, a leather wallet with a photo of a girl in it that had to be Patterson's wife.

He stopped to study the picture. In a silky, skin-colored bikini, the girl was lying on a gleam of white sand in front of Lake Tahoe near Emerald Bay somewhere, with the reddened sky turning dark. Her body, a soft swoop of shoulder, breast, and belly, looked challenging, poised and ready to leave this spot soon. Long, curvy legs stretched out, crossing slightly at the knee. A haze of gold over the sand must have been roused by the same wind that tangled her hair into snakes around her head. She looked straight at, and somehow beyond, the photographer, her eyes staring inside rather than out. An arch expression, and full lips with a hint of smile capped the stunning beauty that had so beguiled Anthony Patterson.

So here was the famous Misty, the Misty who probably killed her husband, in spite of what her lawyer wanted to think. The ex-cop in Paul knew that an arrest meant they usually had the guilty party. That picture of her reminded him of something. Something about the attitude, the kind of daring, hussy pose was familiar, but he couldn't think what it was.

He turned his attention to a hundred-dollar Prize's chip; credit and I.D. cards, driver's license, and receipts. Anthony was four years older than he had told his wife. "Six twenties were still in the wallet," Beltine said. "We got that in the money locker."

Paul held up an even smaller plastic bag, containing a still-damp comb, a Chap Stick, and an empty cigarette package showing some water damage.

"All still in the pocket of the guy's robe."

"Man, life is cold," Paul said.

"It does have that poignant quality," Beltine said.

* * *

Paul drove around town for a half hour, timing his walk into Tom Clarke's office at the elementary school on Bijou Street for five minutes to twelve, and he caught Clarke walking out the main door, surrounded by children. He fell into step beside him, offering his card. "Excuse me, kids," Clarke said. They dropped behind. Clarke said, "I don't need this."

"You have to talk to me," Paul said. "So let's go have lunch somewhere."

The Pineacres Elementary School principal looked around and waved to some parents. He pointed east. "Around on the Nevada side. Okay? Let's go to the Thirsty Duck at Round Hill."

"How about we make it the Chart House on Kingsbury? Farther away. Better food. And I'll buy," Paul said.

"I'll meet you there," Clarke said.

"This way, you're anonymous," said Paul, opening the door to his van. Clarke, casting a final furtive glance toward the school, climbed inside. They rode along the highway around the lake into Nevada while Clarke, a classic bad passenger, issued orders and directions Paul didn't appear to hear.

They each ordered a pint of Anchor Steam and salmon steak for lunch. From their raised table the two men could see across the lake to the west shore, toward Mt. Tallac and Emerald Bay. They were paying for the view, and Paul couldn't take his eyes off it, but Clarke ignored it, looking around as though expecting the jig to be up any second.

"What do you want from me?" he said. "I have a wife and kids. If the *Mirror* gives out my name, the district won't renew my contract and my wife will leave me. I got Misty a lawyer and that's all I can do."

"April 26th. Thursday night."

"Home with my wife."

"That's it, then. Home with the wife. Anything you want me to tell your girlfriend?"

"Have you met her yet? Misty?" Clarke said.

"She's still in jail." Paul pictured the photograph and this time recognized the image instantly. Misty Patterson was not, by a long shot, the romantic Botticelli Nina described. This woman had too much animal for that rarified company. No, at least in that picture she was a blond ringer for Manet's "Olympia" model, the shady lady that shook the world.

"Don't go getting all self-righteous with me until you've seen her. I met her one night at Prize's. She suggested we get together in the parking lot after her shift. It was December, snowing, nobody out there but the snowplows. She gave it to me in the backseat of her car under a sleeping bag, the windshield frosted over. It was like being eighteen again." Clarke sat back, his hands holding the edge of the table. "She wanted to meet again and she set it up. We went on from there."

"How many times?" Paul asked.

"Quite a few. Hey, I didn't count. I wish, honest to God—I wish it could have gone on forever. I liked her, loved her in a way, and it wasn't just the sex. Her husband treated her like a hound dog to kick around, and she needed my affection. I'm only human. You have to see her."

"So she talked about him with you." The waiter set down a steaming plate in front of Paul. The smell of garlic and lemon was too much for him. His mouth full of fish, he went on, "Did she talk about killing him?"

"No! She was afraid of him. I had a hard time convincing her . . ."

"To leave him?"

"If she had, this wouldn't have happened," Clarke said. "She almost made it. I had her talked into the appointment to start the divorce, but he went after her once too often, and this time she fought back."

"And then she dragged him next door, bleeding, and loaded him in her neighbor's boat, and went out on the lake in the middle of the night in a snow flurry with the bear statue and threw him overboard, and swam a long way to shore in freezing water, and she was all tired out so she hit the hay and had forgotten all about it by the next morning."

"It does sound bizarre," Clarke said. "You ever read about the incredible feats of strength people perform in desperate circumstances? That's the way I see it."

"How about the forgetting part?"

Clarke put his fork down and leaned over. His lips were red and wet under the beard. Paul recoiled a little. "She's telling the truth about that. She called me the next morning and she was very scared about Patterson being gone. She couldn't fake that. How she could forget all the rest of it, I don't know. It was shock or something. She wasn't thinking straight. She should have called the police the minute she hit him, and showed them her bruises. She never should have tried to cover it up."

"You saw bruises?"

"No. Nothing I could testify to."

"Sure you did. You were going to take some pictures of the bruises for Nina Reilly."

"Never did. I decided I'd done what I could, like I said."

"She says she didn't hit him a second time." The salmon was gone. Paul ordered a slice of Mississippi mud pie and coffee.

"What? The papers said he got hit twice. So she did. She's forgotten the boat, and she's forgotten that too."

"You've got it all worked out, don't you, Mr. Clarke."

"Right."

"And the interesting thing is, the way you worked it out, you don't have to come into the story at all," Paul said.

"Right," Clarke said again. "I had no involvement." He looked at his watch. "I have a Curriculum Committee meeting at two. We're reviewing a new social science textbook. You know, lots of pictures of minorities and the handicapped, girls fixing cars and boys cooking dinner. Nobody's going to have a problem with this baby. But I have to be there."

"I heard your wife and kids moved out the same night Patterson died," Paul said. The school secretary had been indiscreet in a phone call the day before, but Clarke would never know it.

"You heard about that," Clarke said. He stood up.

"So I'm curious about this happy evening at home with your wife you were telling me about." Paul signed the American Express slip, scratching his head as he figured out the tip.

"Janine found out, I don't know how. I admitted it. She was loading the kids in the station wagon, and I was trying to talk her out of it. She left anyway."

"I can imagine how you must have felt that night."

"You can't imagine."

"Maybe you went by Misty's house later that Thursday night for a shoulder to cry on. It was late enough for her to be off her shift, and they have those sliding glass doors in back that open out onto the yard and the Keys. Easy to see if she was alone, right? You could just peek in and see if the coast was clear. What did you see? Did you see him come after her? And her hitting him with that statue?"

"I spent that evening with my wife trying to patch things up," Clarke said dully, and then more vigorously, "I wish I had been there to finish that bastard off. Oh, hell, what's the point? Look, I told you, I have to go. It took awhile before

Janine moved in again. It's been rough. Things are better. Not fixed. Can we go now?"

"Do you own a bike? You know, a motorcycle?"

"I knew I should have brought my own car. Yeah. I have an old Honda 400cc. A Hawk. So what?"

"Just wondering." It was hard to imagine Clarke wearing Harley wings on any article of clothing. He would be too worried about the school board.

"You ask me one more question, Mr. van Wagoner, I'm going to call a cab," Clarke said.

Paul looked surprised. "All you had to do was ask," he said mildly, pulling out the van keys.

Misty lay on her bunk wishing she could sleep. The guard had just finished the afternoon cell check, and the wing remained relatively quiet, though so stifling that she imagined she could see wavery heat lines. "There probably hasn't been any fresh air in here since the place was built," she said to her cellmate.

"Could be worse," Delores said. She stood in front of the six-inch metal mirror above the sink, trying to comb her thick black hair into French braids that would fold back into her scalp. "Come here and help me with this." Misty climbed off her bunk. "You move slow, like a big girl," Delores said.

"This place is making me sick. I hate the food. I want to sleep but I can't get enough," Misty said.

She held Delores's hair in place and stuck in a plastic comb.

"I just need to get out of here," Misty said. "Three more days, my lawyer says."

Delores said, "How do I look?" She turned in a full circle. Delores was fifty-three years old, but, as she kept telling

Misty, that helped her on her shoplifting excursions. The clerks at K mart paid more attention to the young girls.

"Even without makeup, you look great," Misty said. "It's your smile."

"It's my joy de vivre," Delores said, but she cut her laugh short as she watched Misty fall on the bunk again and close her eyes. "Babe, you are in a tough situation. Why don't you get up and fight?"

"What if I did it?" Misty said from the bunk, her eyes still closed.

"Hush, now. The walls have ears."

"I've been thinking, Del. I'm the one who ran around on him. I'm the one who made him crazy. He wasn't like that in Fresno. If he knew what I was doing, it would explain a lot."

"He could have left you instead of hitting you," Del said.

"He still loved me. I guess I hurt him a lot."

"He stayed home and took it."

"Maybe I'm not worth saving," Misty said.

"You're bad, just plain low-down bad."

"Yeah."

"You'll never be happy."

"Mmm-hmmm."

"Now look at me. I am a beautiful, very damn smart, and hard-lovin' African-American woman, in jail right now, yeah, but going to rise above it. You can call me every bad name in the book, but it won't stick because I know who I am. I decide who I am, and I figure out how to make myself happy." Del sat down with an emphatic thump on the bunk next to Misty. "Do the same. You're a big girl now."

"Who I am is just plain bad."

Del rolled her eyes up. "No. No. Listen to me. I'm going to tell you this one more time. Doesn't matter who they say you are! Only thing that matters is who you decide you are!"

"I'm a nobody. My work is to say 'Drinks? Drinks?' and mosey around with my butt hanging out. And where I'm heading is worse."

Del laughed. "You thought it was hangin' out before . . . Guard! Guard! Get me out of this cell with this no-account woman! You make me want to take you by the shoulders and shake your head clear. You have a new situation now. You don't have a husband, and you probably don't have a job either. Today is today and you have to fight!"

"I'm afraid," Misty said. Del got up, shaking her head.

Late that night, when it had cooled down a little, Misty had a nightmare.

She dreamed she was living in an old town, a jumble of brightly colored houses and swaying trees like they had back in the Philippines, with her small daughter. Her father, a famous and kindly doctor, had died a while back. Then one day her beautiful mother took ill and was about to die. An operation could save her, but only her father could perform it.

Misty mixed up a potion so he could arise late in the night in a house across town where her mother lay. He would walk across the floor to her mother's curtained bed, fix her, and then he would rest in peace. He loved Misty's mother so much, he would come back from the dead.

Night came, and Misty and her daughter walked through the dark streets and pools of yellow lamplight with the potion.

As they approached the house, Misty became afraid. She knew what she was doing was unnatural, but she had to save her mother. They went up the stairs. Her daughter clutched the brown bag lunch that she was proud to have made herself. In the room, her father's coffin lay in a murky corner.

Her mother, still as death on the bed, lay with her hands folded across her breast, lace falling from her sleeves.

Misty set the potion down on the floor, took her daughter's hand, and ran out the door. She had done her duty, and now she ran from an awful fear.

I forgot my lunch in there! her daughter said, her white face turned up toward her mother.

Misty said, no, you can't go back, but her daughter pleaded, saying, oh, please, I'll run fast. Misty thought of her father, the good, kind man. Okay, hurry!

Her daughter rushed back up the stairs. Misty waited, reeling with dread for her father, her mother, her child, herself. She heard her daughter shrieking, and she wanted to run away, but she ran up the stairs and threw open the door. And there he was—a radiant white skeleton, dressed in his black hat and carrying his doctor's bag, advancing toward her, closer, his arms outstretched, looking stricken and suffering and murderous, and there was her daughter tossed like a bloody doll in the corner, and she knew he would have to kill her, not out of malice but because he had degenerated into something inhuman now, and she stood there terrified, paralyzed, holding her mother's car key pointed at him like a talisman while he reached out for her . . .

She woke up, shuddering in anguish and fright, and Del was holding her, saying, "Hush, now. Hush, now."

13

Five-thirty. Nina's stockinged feet, propped on her paper-strewn desk, were the first things Paul saw as he came in. Behind him, Sandy was saying, "Knock!" in a disgruntled voice.

"Six toes," Paul said. "I suspected you were hiding something."

"Just tired feet, Paul."

"How's the legal research going?"

"Not good. The search and arrest warrants are probably valid. I mean, Rich Eich had reported his boat stolen, so they sure had a right to board. Then they saw blood. The diver found a body with obvious wounds. A co-worker of the wife's told them about Misty's fight with her husband. Misty gave them lots of ammo before and after they read her her Miranda rights. They obtained a warrant before searching her house. They had plenty of probable cause. I have to file some motions to cover all the bases, but the motions won't go anywhere. That's the bad news."

Paul lifted an eyebrow. "The good news?"

"Matt is revving up the barbeque for the first time tonight. Want to come over? You can tell me all about Fresno and your look at the evidence locker."

"Sure. You'll be interested to know that your client's father threw me out. In case he calls to fire you."

Nina had bent down to put her shoes on. She straightened up quickly. "How come?"

"I asked him for an alibi, but I doubt that was the real reason. I pulled too hard on his chain, pestering him about Misty's childhood in the Philippines when they lived at the naval air base at Subic."

"Did you learn anything?"

"Not a damn thing. He told me to lay off questions about Misty's past."

"We can't let this fall by the wayside, Paul. We have to take it further."

"How far do you want to go?" the detective asked. "We don't know that the moldy family laundry has anything at all to do with this case. Are you trying to be your client's lawyer, or her psychiatrist?"

Nina said thoughtfully. "Maybe we should send you to the Philippines."

"Who's going to pay for it? Tengstedt? Travel thousands of miles to a military base to ask questions about a child who lived there thirteen years ago? Come on, Nina, we've played enough with this idea. Let's start thinking about how somebody else could have killed Patterson."

She sighed and pulled on the other shoe. "I just have this feeling. Maybe it's the cases I've been reading. Did you ever hear of a legal concept called the fruit of the poisonous tree?"

"Seems like I have. Defense lawyers talk about it in hearings to suppress evidence."

"Exactly. It's used in a motion to suppress. The idea is that if a judge decides a search warrant is invalid, the judge may also, under certain circumstances, suppress the evidence obtained from the use of the warrant. Remember the bloody glove found on O. J. Simpson's property before the police got a warrant? The judge could have ruled that any testimony about the existence of the glove was inadmissible, which would have maimed the prosecution's case. The idea is, if the tree, which in this case is the warrant, is poisoned, then the fruits of the tree, that is, the evidence obtained from use of the warrant, is also poisoned."

"Tainted evidence gets suppressed. Everybody pretends it doesn't exist. Fine. What has that got to do with Subic?" Paul asked.

Nina swiftly sketched a tree on her legal pad. On the trunk, she marked *Subic*. She drew a big apple on a branch and labeled it.

"Anthony dies," Paul read aloud.

"The fruit of the poisonous tree," Nina said. "Misty had suppressed the tree and the fruit, just like a judge might." She looked at the drawing.

Sandy had come in and was also peering down.

"I believe that Subic started the chain of events that led to Anthony's death," said Nina.

"Well, that tainted old tree's too far away to visit," Paul said.

"Auntie Alice!" Sandy announced suddenly, loudly.

Paul looked at Nina significantly and tapped his temple with his forefinger. "No, Sandy, Auntie Alice is still in Kansas with Auntie Em."

"Maybe yours is," Sandy retorted. "My Auntie Alice is a payroll clerk at Subic."

Daylight saving time had finally arrived. Only the first week in May, but not until eight did a few shreds of magenta and orange chase each other across the sky.

Paul knew he had eaten too much grilled steak and baked potato, but it had been worth it. He was in the living room with Matt, lying down on the couch and watching the Giants beat the Dodgers. The women were off putting the kids to bed. Matt had built a big fire, and there was another can of Coors on the burl-wood coffee table. For a brief moment Paul wondered if he shouldn't settle down with Marilyn, buy a place by the beach, give in to a couple of kids who would kiss him on the cheek at night and call him Daddy, like Matt's kids did.

Nah.

He got up and put on his windbreaker. It would be a relief to get back to fact-gathering, away from the intuitions Nina passed off as reason. Fact: Anthony Patterson had been chief of security at Prize's. Fact: Peter La Russa was a pit boss at Prize's, a friend of Anthony's. Fact: The client had a reputation with men.

As far as he was concerned, the yellow brick road led straight to Prize's.

Life in the nineties had lost its glamour, Paul thought as he walked down the gift-shop aisles toward the playing area of Prize's. Glitter, diamonds, tuxes, limos, flashy shows, liquor, parties, late nights, gambling, even recreational sex had been put away as frivolous and unhealthy in this dour decade.

But glamour lived on in the pleasure domes of Tahoe, if you squinted and suspended your disbelief a little. As he crossed into the huge gaming room, past the shouts from the craps tables, past the croupier stacking chips at a packed roulette table, past the shiny red BMW rotating seductively in front of the Megamachine slots, past the Tonga Bar with its thatched roof and bubbling aquariums, past the long line for the nine o'clock show, Paul felt ready for some action.

Near him one of the dealers, a woman about forty, stood with her arms folded, a single deck displayed on the green baize cloth waiting for customers. "Peter La Russa on shift?" he asked her.

"Right over there," she said, pointing out the pit boss.

Her table was in La Russa's group. On impulse he pulled out a chair, sat down, and handed her a hundred-dollar bill.

"All nickels," he said. She pushed over a stack of green chips, scooped up her deck, and started shuffling. Paul set two of his five-dollar chips on the table. Very fast, her pretty hands twinkling with rings, she dealt him his hole card and turned over a ten for herself, then dealt him a three. He looked at his hole card. Damn, a ten. He tapped the table lightly with his cards, and almost before he was finished tapping received a jack. Bust. He turned his cards over and she showed her last card, another ten, before she took his money.

Next hand, she dealt herself nineteen and he lost with a queen and a seven. For the next ten minutes he played with all his concentration, following the basic strategy, but his stack shrank relentlessly. It seemed like he had hardly sat down when she said, "Bet?" and he saw he'd lost it all. He decided not to drag out his wallet again right then.

"Cocktails?" a voice said as he was rising. He looked down at a nice-looking girl, about thirty-five, her little breasts served up in the black satin like dinner rolls in a fancy napkin, her face inert with boredom. He pictured Misty in that outfit, that night in April. Was her smile as cold? "No, thanks," he said. "Could I talk to you for a minute?"

Her smile dropped back into a thin line. "About Anthony and Misty Patterson," Paul said, but he already knew it was hopeless, she was looking around for help. La Russa came over as though she had called him. The cocktail waitress slipped away.

"Mr. La Russa?" Paul said. "I need to talk to you about Anthony Patterson."

La Russa slicked back greasy gray hair, which matched his shiny gray suit. Soft, beautifully manicured hands laden with heavy gold rings gestured to the wings. "Come on over here," he said. He led the way over to an empty bank of tables and they sat down at one of them.

"Know Anthony Patterson?"

"Yeah. Why do you ask?"

"Know he's dead?"

"I heard. So tell me again why I should talk to you."

"I'm an investigator for the attorney who represents Misty Patterson," Paul answered, passing over his card.

La Russa jumped up so quickly, he knocked over his club soda. "Shit," he said. "You looked like a cop. I don't have to talk to you."

"No, but it will look strange if you don't," Paul said.

La Russa said, "Anthony was a friend of mine. He never should have married Misty, 'cause she made him goddamned unhappy, but I'll say this, then you can get the hell out: Patterson had a lot going for him, and it's a fucking shame." He walked rapidly back toward his station inside the next bank of tables. Paul followed. "What were you and Patterson into, Peter?" he said loudly.

"Get Security over here," La Russa told his assistant, who picked up a phone and punched a number. All the dealers were watching, surprised to see a civilian enter the pit area, some of them smoothly dealing out cards at the same time.

A massive shadow stepped forward. Obviously, security was good at Prize's. "Problem?" he said.

"I have an appointment with Mr. Rossmoor," Paul said. "Could you direct me?"

Stephen Rossmoor waited at the door of the penthouse suite.

"Sorry about your luck tonight," he said, waving Paul to a plush couch under a large, bright painting. "Call me Steve." His grip had just the right pressure, and he was smooth, but he looked young for the job, in his early thirties.

"You I.D.'d me fast," Paul said, looking around him. The penthouse living room was as large as his house back in Monterey. One wall was window, looking down over the sparkling lights of the gaming district. Through the inner door he could see a desk and conference table. The whole place seemed to be carpeted in pale gray fur and furnished with antiques older than California. "You live here?"

"My home is in Zephyr Cove, but I spend the night here now and then. Drink?"

"Whatever you have," Paul said. It was Chivas, straight up. Rossmoor sat down at the other end of the couch. He wasn't drinking.

Paul had done some background checking on Rossmoor. Yale '82, Princeton for his master's, a miserly Connecticut grandpa who had left him a bundle. Paul knew and despised Ivy League, the buttons on the Oxford shirt collar, the hair a little mussed but short enough, the class ring, the scuffed but expensive loafers, M.B.A.'s sliding easily into the jobs of men who had worked their way up. Rossmoor fit the stereotype, except he had the fresh-air browning of a tennis player or swimmer, a big difference between him and the pasty faces Paul remembered from the East.

Inherited money always bugged Paul. It might not buy happiness, but it bought the deep-seated security and ease that Stephen Rossmoor possessed. Paul had been a scholarship-and-loans boy. He resented the rich kids.

"Mr. La Russa didn't want to talk to me," Paul said.

"I told him not to," Rossmoor said.

"What kind of liability is the club worried about?"

"Just the usual risk management, Paul. How is Misty? Is she having trouble putting up the bail?"

"She'll probably be out tomorrow."

"Great. And her parents are helping her with the legal fees?"

"Why do you ask?"

"I want to help. I'd like to see that she gets off as lightly as possible. My attorney says she might be offered a plea bargain for probation if you push the self-defense angle."

He sounded sincere. Paul said, "Nina Reilly should talk to you directly."

"I'll talk to her."

"I need to ask you a few questions about the Pattersons."

"Be my guest."

"Fine," Paul said. "Let's start with your relationship with Michelle Patterson. Misty."

"She's an employee, has been for over a year." Rossmoor scratched his head. "I admit to a personal interest in Misty. It would be hard to find a male employee who didn't have one, actually."

"You're close?"

"No, I wouldn't say that. I wanted a relationship, but she didn't."

"Tell me about it."

"She came up with me for a drink before work just a few times. We talked, got to know each other a little bit. The truth is, I found myself rather suddenly getting serious about her. She didn't seem to want that."

"When was this?"

"The early part of March. She was working till midnight, and Patterson worked midnight to eight A.M., graveyard. I never deluded myself that I was the only one she was seeing," Rossmoor went on. "But I didn't want to know."

"Patterson might have had a nasty reaction if he found out," Paul said.

"He never found out, I don't think. And from my point of view, she was another man's wife but she was unhappy and trying to get up the strength to divorce him. I'm single. My intentions were . . . honorable."

"She stopped seeing you?"

"She dropped me, to be honest. I don't know why. I wanted . . . a lot more. Actually, I still do."

"Does she still have a job here?"

"Sure, if she wants it. Sure."

"I don't know, I'm just asking," Paul said. "I mean, she's supposed to have killed another employee here. You'd think his friends would be unhappy to see her again."

"Maybe Peter La Russa. I don't know that Anthony Patterson had any other friends," Rossmoor said. He seemed more relaxed talking about Patterson. Paul pressed on.

"So what was it they were doing? You know, what kind of scam were they running?"

"You know, Paul, talking about that sort of thing might cause trouble for the club."

"I know. I'm not simpleminded," Paul said.

"Let me guess," Rossmoor said. "Let's see, community college in California, army or marines, maybe finished up at UC. Career as a cop, left because you couldn't get promoted. How did I do?"

"Born and raised in California. Harvard undergrad. Northeastern for my M.S. and then the Peace Corps. The cop part is right."

"College in Boston but a California boy. I knew some West Coast fellows at school. They didn't much like Yale. They thought we were all snobs, but California snobbery is the worst. I should have known by the way you looked down your nose at the antiques," Rossmoor said. He was smiling, inviting Paul to join in. It was hard not to like him.

"Look," Paul said. "You tell me you have a thing for Misty, you want to help her. You're privy to some information that might help her, about Patterson and Peter La Russa. Are you going to give it to me or not?"

Rossmoor got up and moved to the window, hands behind his back.

"Suppose the information might lead to the arrest of someone else and free her?" Paul said. "Which wins out, the corporate or the personal interest?"

"My turn," Rossmoor said. "I want to know if you can prove somebody else struck the second blow, the one that was fatal."

"Where'd you hear about that, Mr. Rossmoor?"

"Steve. Of course we obtained the police reports."

"Help me out here, Steve."

Rossmoor fell silent. He finally said, "It doesn't seem relevant, but I'm willing to give you the general outlines of a problem the club had with Anthony Patterson, on condition you don't talk to the press, look into it quietly, and keep it all confidential unless something important to your client does turn up."

"Fair enough."

"Patterson knew his job, I'll say that. For the first year or so he did really well. Knew how to peg the bad guys, knew where to lay the blame and how hard to come down to keep the peace."

"Would you describe him as violent?"

"You're an ex-cop; so was he. Would you describe yourself as violent? He manipulated violence like an expert, the same way he could use any other kind of weapon. If he blew, it was a calculated blow."

"What changed after a year?"

"Purely speculating, his marriage started to sour. After that, aside from his hobby of controlling his wife, he devoted most of his attention to pursuing easy money. He could be quite persuasive and attractive when he wanted to be. I admit he had me fooled at first. Anyway, he and La Russa brought in a card counter, a really brilliant blackjack player who's on the Gaming Association's blacklist."

"Hey, I didn't last thirty seconds out there before you knew me."

"They put him in a wig and glasses and he played only at a table La Russa supervised. He played big money. That set off the alarm bells, but Patterson shut them off. The counter won about twenty thousand, as near as we can tell, before I got into it and watched Anthony protecting La Russa, who was protecting the counter."

"I got the internal report at the beginning of April. Patterson was due to be fired, but Misty called him in sick on the twenty-seventh and twenty-eighth, Friday and Saturday. He was off Sunday. Then he was found on Monday. La Russa we weren't sure about until this week. The final word on him is coming in tomorrow. He's already retained an attorney from Carson City. Considering everything, we'll probably just let him go quietly."

"What happens to the counter?"

"If we see him again, we run him out. It's a gray area legally, so we probably wouldn't try to prosecute."

"Do you report this kind of information to the Nevada Gaming Commission?"

"Not if we can keep the lid on it," Rossmoor said. "And I've been instructed to do that."

"You're taking a risk."

"I'm not as conservative as I look."

"I don't suppose you stopped by to check in with Misty or Anthony on Anthony's last night."

"No. I wasn't there. Ask Misty."

"Where were you?"

"In bed, here at Prize's that night. We're working on some new security for the parking lot and I got hung up.

We've been having some problems with cars being vandalized. And we prefer happy customers."

"Alone?"

"Yes, alone."

"Any witnesses at all who can place you here?" Paul persisted.

"Security," Rossmoor said. "They videotape the hallway outside the penthouse."

"You *must* be in love," Paul said.

"What do you mean?"

"They videotape the hallway. . . ." Paul repeated.

"What are you getting at?"

"I assume they don't just videotape the hallway, but they watch the tapes later?"

"It's something I'm so accustomed to, I don't think about it."

"He knew about you and his wife," Paul said.

Rossmoor was a professional. He smiled and blew it off. "That's not . . . that wasn't Patterson's area. Chances are another guard would see those tapes and wouldn't think a thing about them. Meanwhile, hate to say it, Paul, but I have another appointment."

"Sure," Paul said. "Just a couple more questions. Do you drive a motorcycle?" He didn't expect a positive answer. A Bentley, yes.

"I've got a nice Harley, but I haven't been out on it since last summer," Rossmoor said. "It's about time to grease it up, now that the ice is gone, not that I get your drift here."

"Idle curiosity." Paul rose. "Any chance I could have a look at your internal reports about Anthony?" he said.

"It would be difficult. I'll think about it. Are you in town long?"

"If I'm not around," Paul said, "you can always talk to Nina."

"I didn't mean that. Play tennis, Paul? I'm always looking for a good game."

"I was thinking you were probably a swimmer," Paul said.

"Always on duty, I see. I swim, but I don't swim on Thursday nights. Nice to meet you, Paul."

Paul walked past him. "Just one last thing," he said. "Got the name of the counter?"

"Al Otis. He lives in a trailer park in Sparks, we understand. His wife is Sharon Otis, once Patterson."

"What do you mean?" Paul said.

"Anthony Patterson's ex-wife," Rossmoor said. "For what it's worth." As the door closed, Paul watched Steve Rossmoor head for the bar and pour himself a very stiff one.

Back at Caesar's, where he was staying, Paul went down to the club and worked out on the Nautilus equipment, then swam laps. The recreation area was almost deserted. They must be losing money, he thought, between the off-season and the recession. He rode up the tower elevator to the seventh floor, where his room was, and got into the hot tub with his phone.

This time Nina answered on the third ring.

Paul told her most of what he had.

"You've been busy," she said when he was finished.

"It's always like that when you start looking into people's lives," Paul said. "We're much more complicated than we think."

"So in early March Misty was seeing Tom Clarke and Stephen Rossmoor at the same time. Carrying on two affairs after marrying a jealous husband."

"I don't know how heavy she was with Rossmoor, but there's definitely something there. As for her husband, she was blind if she didn't think he was keeping a very close eye on her behavior. Rossmoor's an idiot too. In one breath he tells me about the security cameras on his door, and in the next he tells me he doesn't think Anthony knew about him and Misty."

"Does she really believe he never knew or does she just want to believe it? My biggest problem with this client has to be understanding her. Do you think she was looking for punishment?"

"Who knows why women sleep around?" Paul said. "All I know is, it hardly ever seems to be out of simple lust."

"Let me assure you, it happens. Anyway, if he did know, you've got to assume he would be upset."

"Not the type to forget, by all reports."

"By the way, she had him buried by a funeral parlor in Placerville today. A few people from Prize's came. A relative in Philadelphia sent a wreath. He died before he got his revenge on his fickle wife."

"I thought I'd go to Sparks tomorrow, talk to the Otises," Paul said.

"Okay, you do that."

"Want to come along?"

A pause, then Nina said, "Okay. Misty's parents are definitely posting the bond for her. She gets out tomorrow. She says she needs to spend a day or two by herself at the Lucky Chip before I take her to see Bruno."

"Makes sense. See you tomorrow morning, then."

"Yeah. Al and Sharon Otis. This couple I *have* to meet," Nina said.

14

WHEN PAUL CAME down the next morning he found a message from Nina saying she would be a few minutes late, and a sealed envelope at the reception desk. Rossmoor had sent the internal report on Patterson to him by messenger. Apparently even his temporary digs at Caesar's had been noted.

In the casino coffee shop, nicked cup in hand, he scanned its pages. He found it refreshingly grammatical.

Anthony Patterson, as chief of Security at Prize's, had responsibility for spotting professional "casers," the blackjack card counters. The Reno and Tahoe clubs traded their information in monthly memos, complete with photos of the card counters taken from the glass ceiling while they played.

The casinos did nothing to stop the occasional weekend big winner, who they realized had useful publicity value, but vigorously fought the real pros that tried to confuse their spotters with camouflage. Besides changing clothing and facial hair, professionals called upon innocent-looking accomplices and played each club for only a short period of time, jumping from table to table with the shuffle. The best card counters jumped from Vegas to the Bahamas to Atlantic City, and stayed away from northern Nevada, where the rules on doubling and surrender hurt the player's odds.

Semipros tended to be locals who showed up at the same clubs over and over until convinced by repeatedly being eighty-sixed out the door that the time had come to move on or retire. Although it was not strictly illegal anywhere, very few people had the combination of big stakes, chutzpah, and concentration to make much money counting cards. All the clubs took precautions.

The report listed Albert B. Otis as a pro. According to the report, he was balding, but sometimes wore a toupee; about five six, but sometimes wore lifts, and had gray hair, but sometimes dyed it black or brown. Sometimes he wore glasses.

But there was one thing he always wore, a gold ring with a diamond-shaped onyx, and he twisted it while he waited for the cards to turn up. This mannerism had been discussed at a recent northern Nevada club managers' meeting, where the decision was made that it wasn't a cue for anyone else or a method of counting, just a useful affectation. One flash of that ring, and Al had been escorted out of the MGM Grand and the Luxor in Las Vegas and Harvey's at Lake Tahoe.

For about a month before Anthony Patterson died, Al had been gambling at Prize's without the pinky ring, undetected. The thick new reddish mustache and beat-up 49ers football jacket helped for a while, but eventually a dealer on the graveyard shift remembered Otis's Southern accent and told the pit boss, Peter La Russa, who was supposed to tell Patterson in Security.

The same dealer noticed Otis an hour later, playing a twenty-five-dollar minimum at La Russa's tables, black chips worth at least $2500 stacked in front of him. Patterson, on shift then, had to have seen him, so the dealer reported the incident directly to Stephen Rossmoor's assistant.

The assistant didn't touch Al, since what she really wanted to know was why Patterson was letting the man play. During one of his off-shifts she viewed the security videos for preceding days, which showed a ringless Al, in various hair colors and getups, winning thousands. He always left when Patterson's shift was over.

So it was that on April 24, the watchers in the ceilings had turned their cameras on Anthony Patterson. The next night, the night before Patterson disappeared, Otis returned to play a table at Pit Four, one of Peter La Russa's tables with fifty-dollar minimums. In three hours he was up $4750, a substantial but not too conspicuous profit.

Afterward, Al and Anthony Patterson met outside the front door to the club. They were followed to the parking lot, but the watcher was unable to overhear their conversation.

The report recommended that Patterson be terminated when he reported for his shift the next night, and that updated descriptions of both men be circulated among the clubs. La Russa was to be called in for questioning. For reasons not given, no report to the Nevada Gaming Commission was recommended.

Patterson failed to appear for his shift on Friday night. His wife called him in sick. Patterson's wife also called the next night, Saturday, and reported Patterson would be out with back problems. Sunday night Patterson was off duty. The following day his body was discovered.

Once over Spooner Pass, Paul slowed down to negotiate the hairpin turns so that Nina could relax and marvel at the view of the high desert plateau to which they were descending. The road led through Nevada's minuscule capitol, Carson City, with its fine courthouse and Victorian houses amidst the thrift shops and fast-food outlets.

"Is this the most direct route to Sparks, Paul?"

"Sandy give you another hard time, Nina? Not that I don't enjoy the pleasure of your company, but you are paying me to do this, so that, I assume, you can be doing something else."

"It's true I don't have time for this," she said, "but so much of this is new to me. I'm learning as we go."

That was the truth, but what Nina didn't tell Paul was that she couldn't help thinking he might have done a better job with the Tengstedts.

When they had gone about thirty miles farther, Reno appeared out of the dun-colored land surrounded by its desolate peaks. Past McCarran Airport, at the Sparks border, they found the trailer park on Kietzke Lane near the Hilton. The biggest casino in Reno, the Hilton was the only skyscraper for miles, surrounded by flat ranch-style houses on minilots and the air-cooled malls that had replaced Main Street in most desert communities.

"Misty and Anthony were married in the basement at the old Bally's. The Chapel o' Love, for ninety dollars," Nina told him as they parked in front of the manager's office just off Kietzke. "Her parents didn't come." A girl was watering a puny flower bed nearby, and when nobody answered the bell, Nina asked her if she knew which trailer belonged to the Otises. She pointed down the row to the fourth.

Many mobile homes here, stuck to concrete pads and decorated with desert plants and lawn furniture under umbrellaed patios, had achieved an air of permanence. Al and Sharon's trailer wobbled on blocks, huge tires propped against a makeshift concrete divider, still ready to roll at a moment's notice if the spirit moved them. No flowers or shrubs marred the dirt of their lot. Instead three freshly waxed motorcycles and a 1967 blue Mustang convertible heated up in the sun next to a hibachi and folding chairs. Paul walked over to have a look at the bikes.

Al Otis answered their knock. He was short, and his hair, thick and red with a lot of gray, was tied back in a ponytail.

A mustache shaded his face down to his chin, but his nose, cheeks, neck, and shoulders were burned a wicked scarlet. A baggy, sleeveless T-shirt sculpted folds over a museum-quality beer belly. Coconut suntan lotion competed with a liquid lunch in Nina's sniff test, with alcohol coming out champ. "Come on in, people," he said.

Inside, the trailer was surprisingly roomy. A deer's head, antlers tangling with a light fixture, adorned the far wall. A king-size water bed rocked invitingly beneath an Indian blanket. Underneath pervasive desert dust, the place had a tidy look and a homey feel.

"Have a drink," Al said, adjusting the temperature on the swamp cooler. "Scotch and soda is all I've got, but let me tell you, it's good Scotch. Which one of you is the lawyer?"

"I'm the lawyer. Nina Reilly," Nina said, nodding at the bottle. "And this is Paul van Wagoner. Where's Mrs. Otis today?"

"Who knows?" Al said vaguely, plunking the drinks down on a foldout table in the dining nook. "Sharon's got better things to do. I can tell you whatever you want. Here's to crime," he said, knocking back the entire glass. He got up from the edge of the bed again and fixed another one, not quite as lethal-looking.

When he was settled, Nina said, "We're here to find out about you and Anthony Patterson, Mr. Otis."

"Call me Al. How come the police haven't been over?"

"Unless you've told them, I don't think they know about you and Sharon and Anthony," Nina said.

"To old friends," Otis said, sipping. "Can you believe this? The casinos are on my case heavy. I may have to go back to linoleum laying, like I did for twenty years, only now it's mostly vinyl. I don't think my knees can take it anymore."

"You're lucky not to be in jail."

"I will say one thing for Prize's—they haven't dinged me for Gambling Code violations. Course, they'd have a tough time proving anything."

"Peter La Russa's still working there," Nina said.

"Your information's out-of-date. La Russa got fired last night."

"He called you?" Paul said. He had pulled out a folding chair, setting it up to give himself plenty of room, and he worked on a man-size Scotch.

"Could be," Otis said. "Now maybe you'd like to tell me where you heard all this good stuff."

"They have you on tape," Paul said. "The club knows all about the arrangement." His hands rested loosely on his legs, but his body looked alert.

The littler man reached over and plucked up a frayed deck of cards, looking more at ease, as if he felt not quite dressed without them. "My life," he said, "except for Sharon." He started to shuffle, his fingers and hands dancing the ballet.

"Nice ring," Nina said. "I like onyx."

"Yeah. I got it in Atlantic City. Lots of action in the clubs, but I like the country life. Give me the fresh air and the desert." He cleared a mountain of phlegm from his throat. "So what can I help you people with?"

Nina handed him Prize's report. "I brought a present for you," she said. She and Paul sat back and finished their drinks while Al read.

"Christ," he mumbled a few times, then he looked up. "So it was my lucky ring. And I'm offended. I made a lot more than twenty grand," he said.

"What was Anthony's cut?"

"Twenty percent. For doin' nothin'."

"He kept you in the club," Paul said.

"Nothing was gonna keep me in that club much longer.

They make you in a couple weeks, 'cause you win and everybody else loses. You attract attention." Al snickered.

"He did do one thing for you. He told you how the clubs made you," Nina said.

"He did do that for me." Al twisted the ring as he spoke.

"He wanted a bigger cut, though," Paul said.

"Hey, Anthony's old lady has got some good talent defending her," Al said. "I know you didn't hear that from Sharon. Okay, here's an early birthday gift for you too. Patterson wanted fifty percent, greedy bastard. Excuse the expression. He wasn't worth it. They were gonna catch us sooner or later."

"So how did you work it out with him?"

"I bet you'd love it if I told you we didn't, but we did. In our own way. We were square when he went fishin'."

"Was your way to pay him some extra in coke? Because some was found in his house."

"Now, that's a very personal question," Al said, smiling. "Here, let me get you a refill."

"Where were you and Sharon the night Anthony disappeared?" Nina asked. "The Thursday before he turned up dead. Night after your last party at Prize's."

"Oh, yeah. Home. Right here, hugging my honey, watching a James Bond flick on the VCR."

"So what was your reaction when you heard? Who do you think murdered Anthony Patterson?" asked Nina.

"First off, if it was anybody, I would have thought it would be Misty's toes put down permanent in the sand. I was truly amazed to hear Anthony was dead, because he was not a guy to let someone get the advantage. How that little babe put him out I don't know, but no doubt she had her reasons."

"He pissed off a few people, didn't he, Al? Including you."

He nodded agreement. "Right up to the end. You know, I was doing fine on my own. Now everybody's interested in my personal business. Any chance the casino's looking to charge me with conspiracy? What do you think? You're a lawyer."

Nina shrugged noncommittally.

"Anyhow, tell me this. Why'd Misty cop to tapping Anthony in the first place? And what's it got to do with me, huh? She pretty much wrote her own ticket to the pen. I'm nervous about all this attention I'm getting. Any kind of fame is a liability in my work. This kind is death."

He had a point.

"She has a problem," he went on, moving close, enveloping Nina in his fumes. "Because she cheats on her man. Now, that's not right, a woman behaving that way, although you gotta feel sorry for her, 'cause she's a looker, like my Sharon. She's got too many opportunities. Want another one?"

He got up and poured them all some more Scotch. The sun shot a warm glancing ray through the window onto Nina's hair. Al stared at it as if fascinated. Somewhere in back, a radio was playing a mournful country tune.

"How do you know about that, Al? Did Anthony tell you that?"

"He was always going on about it. I assumed he knew something. Maybe he didn't. She didn't make him feel real safe—bet on it." He laughed heartily.

"Did he say anything to you about his wife that last day you saw him?"

"Yeah. Said something to do with the advantages of the job. Said he was close to nailing her. We are not talking here about a happy man, I'm sorry to say."

So they had a confirmation of sorts. This could be bad news for Misty. If Anthony had seen the videos of Misty with Rossmoor during his last shift and had planned a show-down with his wife on Thursday, why did he end up dead? Did she kill him, defending herself? Like Paul, Nina wondered if Rossmoor did not consider earlier that Anthony would look at videos of the casino and see his wife entering and exiting his private rooms. Did he tell Misty? Or decide on his own to defend her from her husband's revenge?

"Me and La Russa really didn't want to hear, but he talked anyway. Last time he was in the dumps he went and talked with the wife of one of the guys he suspected of being after his wife. Now, that perked him up," Al said after a moment.

"Who was it?"

Al winked at her. "Janet. Jenny. Something along those lines."

Janine Clarke, thought Nina. So he told Clarke's wife.

"You'd think he'd go after his own wife," Paul said.

"She tell you he beat her? He was a forceful guy, yeah, but careful. He knew he was walkin' down a fine line with her and he didn't want to trip. Tell you something, Paul. Don't ever love anybody that hard. I should talk."

"Al," Nina said. "What's Sharon's reaction? To Anthony's death?"

Another hesitation. "She cried. They stayed friends, you know. She never liked Misty."

"Close friends?" Paul poured himself another slug.

Al laughed, a laugh that trailed into more coughing. "Sharon had enough of him when she was married to him, and nowadays, she likes younger guys. Anyhow, his wife had her claws curled in him."

"Which movie was it?" Paul said. "The James Bond one."

"Excuse me?" Otis said. "Oh. Who knows? They all run together, a baldy with a big gut, lots of skiing off cliffs and jumping outta airplanes and babes in bikinis. You tell me, you decide to check."

He looked at the antlers on the wall, then at Nina. For the first time she registered his eyes, amused and wary, unaffected by the liquor. "So . . . Nina, tell me—you do any Nevada work?"

"I'm not licensed in Nevada."

"I might need a lawyer," he said. "You decide to associate with somebody with a Nevada license, we'll do business together." He moved his eyes appreciatively over her body, and gave her another wide smile.

She straightened her back, setting off a minor cloud of dust. "It's not likely," she said.

"Huh? Oh. A shame. Have another drink," Otis said, blinking.

"Just soda," said Nina.

"You a swimmer, Al? Like to get out in the lake in the summer?" Paul said while his glass was refilled.

Otis said, "I'm from Tallahassee. Nearest I ever got to swimming in a large body of water was dipping my toes in Lake Okeechobee, and once or twice in the surf in Naples. After that warm gulf water, the lake could freeze off a guy's machinery. Why do you ask?"

"Just wondering about what people do for a good time here in Sparks, besides gamble. Ride any of those nice bikes parked outside?"

Otis flipped the cards out into the air and caught them neatly in his other hand. "Those belong to Sharon. She brings 'em home from the dealership, rides 'em a few days, then takes 'em back and sells 'em. I bought her a Honda motorcycle franchise when we got married. She don't make much, but it was always the only thing she wanted, and she's happy."

"You take good care of her," Paul said.

"The best. She's my baby," Otis said.

"So where'd you get all the money for a dealership? And who staked you on the playing at Prize's?"

"And how come I live in this funky dump, is that what you want to know? And where's the money I made? Now we come right down to it, don't we? Well, I got my up times and my down times. The money I made at Prize's went for back bills and some dinners with my wife."

"Gambler's ruin," Paul said. "Your stake had to be at least a hundred thousand dollars."

"It wasn't that much. I get by with a little help from my friends. And please don't bother asking for names." Al was having another drink, looking at Nina again, having a good time. Nina thought, life must get rather dull between junkets, so she and Paul were playtime. How much of what he said was true?

"Tell us about your system," Paul was saying in a friendly voice. "Is it the Thorp system?"

"Why not? It's public—I didn't invent it. Always a pleasure to be a mentor for an aspiring player. . . . No, Thorp is way too hard," he said, picking up his cards from the top of the small refrigerator beside the couch and shuffling again. "Only the Japanese are good enough at math to handle that ratio stuff. I learned my stuff from the Archer book."

"Archer?"

"The best. Simple. Elegant. You know the basic strategy for twenty-one?"

"Well," Paul said. "Hit a stiff hand against the dealer's seven through ace. Hit soft eighteen against the dealer's nine or ten. Stand on soft nineteen or above. Double on eleven and on ten against the dealer's two through nine. Split pairs of aces and eights, never split tens, fives, or fours. Split twos through sevens against the dealer's two through seven. Split pairs of nines against the dealer's two through six or eight or nine." He paused.

"Hey, you got the makings of a star, the way you reel that off." Otis dribbled fresh Scotch into his glass. The mostly empty bottle was now on the table. "Now I'm gonna take you further. Paul, you know we got 16 tens and 36 not-tens in the deck of fifty-two. The face cards count as tens."

Paul nodded. Nina couldn't follow, but knew there must be some reason Paul was egging Otis on about the cards. She let her attention direct itself to the way Paul was rubbing his knee. He looked absorbed, and maybe he was. You had to get to know him, to watch the hazel eyes close into slits, to realize how hard he worked to keep powerful impulses under wraps.

"It's a simple point-count method. Like an index to the Thorp ratios. The idea is, the more ten cards are left in the deck, the better your chance of getting an early bust out of the dealer. Count the tens and face cards as minus two. Count the other cards as plus one. Keep careful track during play.

"You got a net plus four in early play on a deck, you're getting favorable odds. You double your bet then, triple it at plus eight, quadruple at plus twelve. I seen plus sixteens plenty of times."

"You get bad minus scores, you know there's not many ten cards left. You bet the minimum, adapt your strategy, like you hit on twelve and don't double down. Things get seriously into the minus camp—minus eight—you hit all stiffs. It all makes perfect sense. Read the book."

"That's it?" Paul said, then took a long drink.

"It," Al agreed. "Everything flows from that." He poured another hefty straight shot into Paul's glass.

"Got to be getting back." Nina stood up, saying, "Thanks

for the lesson. Oh, by the way, tell Sharon I found the wings she dropped."

"Her silver . . ." Al threw his head back and snapped his mouth shut, aiming a frown at this new Nina, the one with horns who had just goosed him with a pitchfork.

"Her Harley wings," Nina said. "I'll be giving her a call."

"Sure," Otis said. He set his deck down carefully and followed them to the door, telling Paul to duck on his way out, "to keep the law offa me," he said, but his heart wasn't in it.

"How about this? Rossmoor had Anthony killed. He was disloyal, he had defrauded the club, and he was a threat to Misty." The van pulled hard up the steep grade back toward Tahoe.

"That type hires lawyers to fight their battles these days," Paul said. "But we can keep it in the possibility column."

"How about this? Anthony's ex, Sharon, and Al killed Anthony so they wouldn't have to give him a cut."

"Kill him over a few thousand dollars? Unlikely, but again there may be more to the story. I can think of several more," Paul said. "This is what I've been trying to tell you. Maybe somebody else did kill Anthony, and Misty's psyche really is irrelevant to this case."

"Maybe I can at least confuse a jury with this card-counting business."

"There you go. Keep her and her mental condition off the stand, let Hallowell put on his circumstantial evidence, and go for reasonable doubt," Paul said.

Nina looked down on the report again. "On the night of April twenty-sixth Al Otis was not playing cards, at least at Prize's, and Anthony wasn't on shift. I know Misty started work at four that afternoon. She thought Anthony just stayed home until she got home that night. But she said there was a full ashtray and several dishes."

"A man can generate a lot of dishes—but I follow, we're betting a visitor or two."

"Which brings up the police work, at least the way it shows up in those reports. They never looked into Patterson's last hours, satisfied the only important event occurred after midnight." A yellow pickup truck loomed behind them on the road, tailgating, then blinking its lights.

Paul's hands tightened on the wheel. Before he could pull over to let the truck pass, it roared across the double line on his left. A deafening bass line boomed from what must have been ten-inch woofers, and a boy of about eighteen leaned out the window, jabbing his middle finger into the wind. The truck pulled in ahead and out of sight around a curve, leaving a curl of oily smoke for a souvenir.

Paul sped up, his jaw muscles working. The van went from fifty to seventy on the next curve. "Hey, Paul," Nina said. "Down, boy."

"That punk needs a word of advice." Tires squealed as he hit the brake and skidded around a curve.

Nina had fallen against him in spite of her seat belt. "Don't force me to scream at you, you dumb cop," she said over the roar of the engine. "Slow the hell down."

He gave one last hard push, then slowly eased up on the accelerator.

Nina stopped clutching the handle on her side and breathed deeply. "What is your rush? We'll find him wrapped around a tree any minute now." But the kid and his rude manners did not reappear. Paul glued his eyes to the road. "You're angry now," she said, "but I'm alive, which makes me happy. Sometimes you forget—"

"I don't like to be talked to that way," Paul said.

"I said I was sorry," Nina said.

"You did not."

They settled back into their seats, Paul driving with perfect form.

"Hope you got all that," Nina finally ventured, trying to make peace. "Al had a lot to say."

Paul seemed to have calmed down. "Right here in my handy voice-activated recorder," Paul said. "Al's a bright fellow."

"Oh, I agree," Nina said.

"No formal education. He had to make his own career. A little card counting here and coke dealing there."

"What's the coke connection with Anthony?"

"Just like you suggested. Sweetened the deal. Misty say he used?"

"No. She says they both preferred booze. She says he just brought the coke out when people dropped by, or sold it. Why all the questions about card technique?"

"Oh, just a theory. I wondered at one point if the casino was trying to cover something up by shoving Al in our faces like a cheap trick, but there's no doubt. He's a card maestro. He's a king."

"You were listening hard."

"Hey, I lost a hundred bucks last night playing blackjack, an experience I don't care to repeat."

Nina snorted.

"What did you say?" Paul asked.

"I said, so is the Harley pin Sharon's?"

"Probably," Paul said. "That was a lucky break."

"Where's the luck come in there exactly?"

"Pretty crude tactic. Lulled him with the stockings and legs. My guess is, Al doesn't make too many mistakes. That one could have backfired on you."

"My decision to say something," Nina said, "and it worked. That's not luck."

"Once you get your teeth into something, you bite till it's dead, don't you?"

As they descended, Paul pulled over at a turnout overlooking the lake.

"You got a minute for this?" he asked.

"I guess I do."

They sat with open windows, enjoying the late afternoon breeze. Two girls were spread out on the rocks below in shorts and halters.

"Shouldn't have let Al get me likkered up," Paul said. "It brings out the beast—I mean the best in me." He put his arm around her and pulled her over aggressively. She could feel his heart beating fast, whether it was for her or the aborted drag race she couldn't tell. She started to laugh and, feeling softened by the booze, found herself leaning toward him.

"The beast and the boss," Paul said. His voice was husky. He kissed her thoroughly, hungrily, pulling her close with strong arms. Now his face was buried in her neck, kissing her there, and she was melting, melting. . . . His mouth roamed to hers and she let him bend her back onto the seat, settling his body on hers, while his hands moved possessively over her. She opened her mouth and sighed, and then his tongue was muscling down her throat, forcing her to open wide for him. Her skirt had shimmied up and if she didn't stop right now . . .

She pushed him back. "That's it. Enough."

He got out of the car and slammed the door, striding to the edge of the overlook. Nina shook herself mentally. When Paul returned, he flipped on the radio. Only when they were back in town did he say to her, "Who apologizes? Me?"

"Forget it," she said. She looked once more into the hazel

eyes, eyes she'd studied all day, and read his expression. "What, is this supposed to be my fault?"

"Don't mind me, Boss," Paul said. "I'm just the hired help."

15

SHE CHANGED HER name as she walked out the last jail door. No more Misty. That had been Anthony's name for her.

Her name was Michelle.

Nina had given her a twenty and the checkbook so she could get into Anthony's account at the B of A. A cab was waiting. She felt like she was returning from a foreign port, from far away, except there would be no greetings and no happy thoughts about returning home.

I'm back in the world, but not part of it, she thought, wondering if she would ever be anything like the girl who had gone into that jail. Tahoe looked like a stage set, the sky too blue, the sun artificially bright. Tourist couples walking the sidewalks in their baggy shorts grinned like extras. What truth did they know that she didn't know, that made them so pleased with themselves?

She didn't want to be out here yet. She wasn't sure her old smile, her old ways, fit the way she felt now. She wanted to hole up.

Business first.

At the bank she took out five hundred dollars. The teller just handed it over. Well, why not? It was all hers now. From the pay phone outside she made calls: Nina's office, her mother in Fresno. Nobody answered. Her mother must be at a Church meeting. She called Dr. Greenspan's office and left a message with the receptionist that she wanted an appointment. Nina wouldn't like it, but she needed the support. She climbed back into the cab.

The jail still had a hold on her, with Gordy and Delores and the overcooked spaghetti and the lights out and the feeling of always being watched. She sat up straight, looking out the window at the flowers and grass that had pushed up since she had gone to jail.

They pulled into the driveway of the house in the Keys. "I'll be about fifteen minutes," she said, aware that she was talking too softly, bending toward the driver so that he could hear.

"I'll be waiting," he said. "Clock's running."

She picked up some old yellow crime scene tape from the grass. Inside, a thick mustiness dried in her mouth. Dirty blinds filtered the light into a daylight dimness. She never even noticed they had any blinds. From the gloom of the entryway she could see the toaster on the kitchen counter. That's right, she had been looking for the portable phone, and then . . . she felt sleepy. Could gas be leaking? She checked the stove, but everything looked normal.

Dirty dishes and ashtrays lay abandoned in the sink. An inch of coffee in her favorite cup floated green mold on top. Time had stopped on a Thursday night in April in this house.

She had always liked the living room, with sliding doors opening onto a view of blue canal, but with the shades down its tawdriness jumped out at her. Where had they bought the furniture? Oh, the old Sears in Reno, the day after they got married. Anthony let her pick out the living room set.

She hated housekeeping, and they were both messy. Threadbare armrests recalled Anthony's many nights here, watching sports on television, waiting for her. Beer stains, coffee spills, and other old circles, small ones, mostly daubed at but still visible, dotted the rug she had bought from local Indians.

The missing glass coffee table she remembered cleaning up the day after Anthony disappeared, but where were the couch cushions? Evidence, of course. Anthony's head had fallen against the couch cushion, had been bleeding in back, and he was still conscious, she remembered now—have to tell Nina, he had touched it with his fingers, and looked at the blood on them so disbelievingly. That was when she ran into the kitchen. . . .

Looking at her living room, she felt ashamed of the dirt and disorder. Many people had invaded it. Unfriendly eyes had looked at the photo on the wall of her and Anthony, sitting on a verandah at the motel in Napa where they had spent their honeymoon. Anthony looked so much younger, and it had only been three years! How had his life with her become such a hell?

For a long second she considered and rejected the vacuum. She wasn't going to clean the place now, with Anthony's ghost dogging her every step.

Michelle hauled the empty suitcase into the bedroom and started pulling out her drawers. Anthony's dirty socks begged for intervention in the corner, and the untidy sheets took up the cry. The plants on the windowsill had turned to dry sticks long ago. His golf magazines fanned out in a pattern over the floor.

She stared at the bed. She could still see Anthony's body outlined on the right side. This small double bed held them both, with his feet sticking out past the bottom. She never told Nina or anyone about the good nights, the nights when he rubbed her feet and kissed her all over, when he told her he would love her forever and she wanted to hear it, nights songs on the radio would always remind her about.

Anthony would always be in her life. She might as well

resign herself to his presence, his heart beating forever and her trying to step out of its rhythm. He wanted only to be her husband, but she hadn't known how to be a wife. He had felt her contempt for herself and for him, even if he hadn't known the specifics. She had invited his cruelty, and then she had blamed him for everything.

Her drawers had been searched. She grabbed a handful of panties and mashed them into one suitcase, dumping in her T-shirts and jeans and the contents of her jewelry box. Opening the closet, she smelled Anthony in the stale cigarette scent of the clothes.

Turning around, she saw herself moving in the dresser mirror, a burglar caught in the act, wild-eyed and pinched in the face. She turned back and reached up for her lockbox of letters and mementos. Gone. Things just disappeared in this house, she found herself thinking, and had to quell a rising tide of laughter.

"Police," she said. Okay, she didn't need any of those things to remember. She could get back her old report cards and letters from her parents.

She took a last look around the kitchen and decided to take the coffeemaker and the juicer.

On the way back down the highway, she said to the driver, "You want to buy a houseful of furniture?"

"Moving sale?" he said. He looked like a college kid who could use some beat-up furniture. "I'm flat."

"Estate sale," Michelle said. "Free cab fare today? And tomorrow, until I pick up my car?"

"That's it?"

"Take everything. Here's the key. Only one thing. You'll have a big dump load. You have to take everything, I mean empty it out. Just make sure it's all gone by Friday."

She made him stop once more, at Cecil's just at the state line. Cecil's had everything, from sweatshirts with sailboats and key rings with dangling dice to groceries and every kind of liquor. She picked up a big bottle of Yukon Jack and some oranges and chips. She looked at the cigarettes, but she hadn't been smoking and the cartons made her think about Anthony's odor in the closet. She decided to pass.

The driver helped her unload into her ground-floor room at the Lucky Chip. "Looks like the makings of a party," he said. "If you want some company . . ."

She backed into the room saying thanks and shut the door and shot the bolt. Then she closed the curtains.

She was wearing the jeans they had picked her up in. She stripped and ran her fingers through her hair, feeling greasy and tangled. She had some bug bites and her legs needed shaving. Running the water in the tub until her fingers burned, she poured a tumblerful of sweet golden-brown liquid and put it on a shelf nearby, sinking slowly into the steam.

About an hour later, lying under the sheet in her clean bikini briefs and a soft T-shirt, she finished her third glass of Yukon. She flipped the channels on the remote control, finding almost nothing but talk shows and CNN.

In spite of the hour she was not hungry. A *Bonanza* rerun was on cable, so she watched Little Joe court a fragile blonde in pulled-back sixties hair, its long curly wisps arching in front of her ears, knowing the girl was doomed. All of Little Joe's women died at the end. She would be buried at the Ponderosa Ranch, right around the corner of the lake, head toward Reno, boots toward Mexico.

Turning over in bed, she killed the TV. She needed to think, but she was too drunk to think. Her stomach hurt and the way her brain swung when she closed her eyes made her nervous. What was the point of a drunk that didn't wipe out bad feelings? Falling back against the headrest, trying to hold her head still, she thought about the women's prison in

Santa Rita, as described by Delores. Okay, drink till it's all gone.

At two-thirty A.M. she was lying in bed wide awake, wishing she had some aspirin and wondering how much lower she was going to sink, when the doorknob turned softly. She stared right at the knob, willing it to move again, her sore eyes looking hard through the darkness. At first nothing happened, then the handle turned again. The door rattled, very quietly. A moment later she heard a scratch against the screen two feet from her.

Sc-rr-ape, the window said.

She was still drunk. She knew it. Her limbs swam spirals without moving.

A louder, sharper noise explained how the screen was being removed. Cold sweat stuck her T-shirt to her body. Evidence, plain as Michael Jackson's nose before he cut it, Anthony would say. We got ourselves an emergency. Slowly, slowly she lifted her head and pulled herself on her arms across the sheet toward the phone. She punched 0, despairing at the small sound of its tone. Nobody answered at the desk. With a discreet little screech behind her curtain, the window glass gave in.

The sound struck through her torpor, allowing all the fear to rush in at once. Unbalanced by terror, leaping up in a paroxysm of drunken heroism, she pounded at the unknown on the other side of the curtains, crying, "Get the fuck outta here! Get the fuck away!"

She beat and bellowed until her angry neighbors came knocking. Then she knew she was safe, because whoever had stood at her window would not be asking, "Hey! What you doing! You crazy?"

Somebody got Art Wong and they all stood outside, looking at the screen on the ground. "I told you, no boyfriend troubles," Mr. Wong said, pulling a windbreaker over sweatpants. "You have to pay for it."

The sight of her, bedraggled in her underpants and sticky shirt, shaking in the night air, cooled his anger. "Here, I'll fix it up for tonight. You going to make me call the police?"

"No. No police, Mr. Wong," Michelle said. "Just let me go back to bed."

"Sounds good," he said. "No need for everybody to get upset."

He took her back inside and she went back to hide under the thin covers. In a few minutes he had a piece of plywood nailed up. He knocked on the door and came in, walking into the bathroom and bringing back a plastic glass of water. "Go to sleep now. In the morning, things will be better," he said. She thanked him. "Liquor no good for a young lady," he said in reply, and he left with the empty bottle.

She rolled over on her stomach, her arm cradling her head. She would have to go to sleep unheld. She, Michelle, would wake up alone with a killer headache. She, Michelle, would cope alone, because she, Michelle, had no other choice.

Two days later, Michelle sat on Bruno Cervenka's office couch at the University of California Medical Center. Nina, who had driven her down to San Francisco, waited outside.

An old man, a Santa Claus type, he sat in a wheelchair, speaking in a deep, slightly accented voice. They talked for a few minutes about her treatments with Dr. Greenspan. She told him she felt ready to be hypnotized.

The office was so quiet, Michelle could hear the tape recorder whirr faintly on his desk. Dr. Cervenka edged up closer and said, "A few deeper breaths would feel good." Michelle breathed deeply, into her stomach, like Dr. Greenspan had taught her. A long sigh came out, and the doctor said, "Very good. Each time you breathe out, your eyelids feel heavier, a little heavier, till you just can't keep them open anymore, and you are beginning to relax now, feeling so peaceful, and now your eyes are closed and you are still breathing very slowly and deeply, and now, my dear, when I count backward from ten, you will find yourself going deeper and deeper into relaxation . . . just give me the slightest little nod when you are ready to go deeper, Michelle, I will see it. . . . Thank you. Ten . . ."

He counted her down ten steps and her feet numbed up, so they couldn't move even when she commanded them to move. She let her legs go to sleep, her belly, her back, each arm. His low, crooning voice suggested she let her scalp relax, her jaw, a big yawn here, her eyes. All the tension was gone, and she slumped down in the brown chair, her eyes closed. "Your breath wouldn't stir a feather," the doctor said, "but you hear me, and you want to answer my questions. Nod if you want to answer my questions, my dear."

She nodded. Her body slept, but her mind stayed awake.

"Let us go back now, to Subic Bay in the Philippines. You are living there, with your mother and father—"

She was breathing much faster now, much faster, and the cry erupted out of her very loudly in the office: "Oh no, oh no, oh no—"

"You are very calm, there is nothing to be afraid of. . . ."

Late at night, pulled from bed, rubbing her eyes, hot in the darkness, squeezed against her mother's body, her mother sobbing, and Michelle crying, and Daddy was back, walking toward them, drunk, his arms outstretched. . . .

"Relax, my dear, you are safe, tell me what you are seeing, what makes you cry. . . ."

" '*I'm taking her, Barbara. I'll keep my daughter. . . .*' "

"That's it, go ahead and tell me, Michelle," said the doctor.

" 'You can't have her! No matter what I've done! I won't let you!' but Daddy pulls me away, and I am screaming, pointing Mommy's car key—'Don't hurt her!'—Daddy and Mommy pull on me, smelling Daddy's sweat, the alcohol. . . .

" 'Daddy! Daddy!' " A cry sadder than tears spilled out. " 'Oh, Mommy, I can't breathe.' Mommy screams! And Daddy . . . !"

"And now you are forgetting again, the memory is growing dim, at the count of three you will be calm and peaceful again, One! Two! Three!"

Dr. Cervenka was talking to her, and she felt relaxed, a little sleepy. . . .

"Nod your head if you can hear me. Good. Your eyes are still so heavy, and you are so deeply asleep, but you can hear me, and you want to answer my questions. Nod your head yes, good girl. . . ."

She was nodding her head. . . .

And the doctor said, "All right now, Michelle, you're doing very well. Let's talk about the night Anthony disappeared. Would you like to do that?"

Michelle's head nodded slightly as she flowed through her memories to that night. There she was, bumping up into the driveway, snowflakes glimmering in the headlights.

"How do you feel when you see Anthony?"

"I'm hoping he's asleep. But he's been waiting up."

"Tell me, how do you feel?"

"I'm real worried. He's mad about something. He wants to make love to me. Oh, and I'm angry, too, because he's making me quit my therapy, but I don't show it. I've been thinking about leaving him but I don't say anything to get him going, I just want to ride the night out. He wants me to drink with him, and I do because it makes everything not so shitty. He's smiling and he lets me see him. Erect. You know." She could hear her voice. She sounded dead.

"He grabs me. He rubs his cheek against me and it's rough. I can smell him. Then he tries to pick me up, talking dirty. He's really strong, but my right arm is still free. I'm scareder than usual, and I don't know why. The way his arms are locked around me . . . I feel so trapped. I just want to break free. One hand is out, so I wave it around and grab what it touches. I swing up and hit him in the head. He slumps and lets go of me, so I hop down and get him onto the couch. He's bleeding and his eyes are closed. I'm shaking him, calling to him."

"How do you feel now?"

"I knew I would do something like this someday . . . something evil. Like a bad fortune," Michelle said, her eyes still open, downcast. "Oh, I get it."

"What do you get?"

"Why there's no escape for me. I—"

"Go ahead, Michelle."

"Hurt people.

"I go looking for the phone," she continued after a pause.

"Is he unconscious?"

"I don't think so. I hear a noise. I run back."

"And then?"

"I'm in black now. Am I dead?"

"No, you are leaving that room. Listen. You are very safe, very calm." She heard the doctor speak. It pulled her away from the room. She was panting. Her eyes were closed again.

"You are relaxing deeply, deeply," Doctor Cervenka said, but it wasn't true, her body was still and warm, but a terrible emotion was overwhelming her, traveling from her past to her present, filling her with pain. She couldn't move or cry out, she was paralyzed by the awful feeling. This was the feeling that made her want to die.

The doctor didn't know. "Good," he said. "If you feel comfortable and calm, you can tell me a little more about what happened after you came back into the living room."

Shame. She was so ashamed.

She started to cry. She was realizing how she had hurt Anthony. He had loved her.

He had been right about her. She was a slut. Years of shame and guilt oozed out of her.

"Tell me about it."

"I killed him," she said.

The doctor didn't say anything. She could hear him turn the pages of his notebook. Finally he said, "Was Anthony waking up? Were you afraid?"

"No."

"What else do you want to tell me?" he said, very quietly.

"That's it. That's what happened," she said. Her eyes were open, her body was still, silent, sleeping. Self-hatred burned within her.

"What are you feeling now, Michelle?"

"Hate," she said.

"Then what happened?"

"Nothing. I went to bed."

He snapped his fingers. "Come back, Michelle."

"I don't remember the session," Michelle said to Nina as they turned onto the Bay Bridge eastbound for Tahoe. "I never remembered my sessions with Dr. Greenspan either."

She didn't know what to say with Nina so silent.

"Hypnosis still isn't very well understood," Nina said. "The mind is tricky. Bruno is going to listen to the tape again and call me later."

"What I said on the tape, that stuff about Anthony? How I killed him? How can I believe that? Even now, in the car, I can't remember hitting him the second time. Everywhere I look inside I can't find that place where I believe I killed him, but that's the way it came out, isn't it? You probably think I've been lying to you or something. Believe me, Nina. I've never lied to you."

"You sure have confused the hell out of me." The lawyer put on her sunglasses as they merged onto the Berkeley freeway. Michelle had been shading her eyes to protect her big headache.

"But I do see now that somewhere way down deep I do remember my past, all of it. Something happened—but it makes no sense. I've never seen my parents fight. I've never seen my father drink. He's Dad, not Daddy."

"Maybe he reformed and you grew up. I'm just a lawyer, Misty . . . Michelle. I guess we should talk about your legal options."

Nina sounded so defeated.

They were embroiled in rush-hour gridlock on Interstate 80. In the BMW on the left a man was talking on the phone. Past him, Michelle could look across the sea of cars to the mudflats of the bay, decorated with whimsical contraptions made of driftwood.

"My head's cracking open, Nina. I have to rest for a few minutes."

When Michelle woke up her headache was gone. They were climbing the long hill east of Sacramento that marks the beginning of the Sierra. Sunset drew fiery stripes in the rearview mirrors. Nina probed a blue bag on the floor, unearthing some water and crackers. For a time neither woman spoke.

Finally Michelle was ready. "What do you think I should do?" she asked.

"I've been thinking about that. We have an offer from Collier Hallowell of voluntary manslaughter. Normally, you'd have to go to the women's prison for several years. I think we should agree to the plea bargain and try to get you into a psychiatric facility instead. You can get some therapy there."

"Maybe if we keep investigating—"

"Oh, Michelle. Let's not waste your money," Nina said. "Might as well hunt for grizzlies."

"I'm going to be locked up and tranked up and be known for the rest of my life as a murderer. Hearing that tape of my voice, saying I killed him . . . I can't believe my own mouth." She hit her hand against the side of her head. "I said it; I heard it, but I do not believe it."

Nina patted her hand.

"Time to move on to the next incarnation. I've wrecked this one," Michelle said, her voice trembling.

"It's a few years, Michelle. You are very young. You can come out of this and start over, stronger."

"I'm done with living in cells, Nina."

Sometime later, Michelle told Nina she needed to get something at the store. Nina stopped at the Apple Hill turn-off, and along with the thing she needed, Michelle picked up a fifth of Jim Beam, not wanting the sweetness of her usual choice. Her mood had changed. She figured she could stay drunk for a month and never feel a thing. Nina recognized the shape of the bag when she got back in.

"Why don't you skip it?"

"Why don't you give me a fucking break?"

"You need to make arrangements to get back to Fresno, Michelle. You can't stay at the Lucky Chip, not after what you told me."

"Think it was that cabdriver? Or a buddy he told about me? I must've struck him as a desperate woman. What did he think? He could just creep in and introduce himself?" She laughed a little. "Maybe he could've another time. Anyway, I scared him so bad he's not coming back."

"Look, if you're having a hard time going home, my sister-in-law, Andrea, runs a women's shelter here in town. Maybe your father would go for that. I told her about you—"

"Warned her about me, huh?"

"It might be a . . . refuge for you. Women and children with family problems stay there."

"I don't think so."

Nina looked at Michelle. She said, "You don't have to go there alone. I'll take you over. It's a room in a house just off Regan Beach. It's private and safe. Andrea is a counselor who would like to help you."

"Okay," Michelle decided suddenly. "I'll stay there for a few days at least. Here's to muddy waters." She opened the bottle and took a long drink, which was a mistake because it stung going down. Here she was, doing to Nina the same kind of BS she used to do to the folks. What was strange about this bad behavior was that, even while she was doing it, she hated herself, and that made her want to do it more. She should have laid that one on Dr. Greenspan while she had the chance.

Nina pulled the Bronco over and said, "When you're finished, I'll put the bottle in the trunk and we can get going again."

Michelle took another drink she didn't want before she handed it over.

As they came around the turn to the Twin Bridges cliffs the moon was rising. On the left Nina could see a sketching of immense granite boulders, and below, to the right, a void. The road here pitched them back and forth like a pendulum.

Some time passed before they both became aware of a car following. It had lingered behind for a long time and now it moved closer to the rear bumper.

Nina, sticking close to the speed limit, still had to slow to make the curves on the otherwise empty road.

The car behind flicked its lights.

"Another damn fool with a death wish. Where does he think I can turn off? This isn't San Francisco, Joe," she said. "Cool your jets." She slowed down.

The car dropped back a little, but Nina was uneasy. Maybe we should find a place to stop, she thought about saying. Before she could speak, the Bronco, rammed from behind, shot out of control. Her hand blew off the wheel with the shock of impact, in a bone-shaking rear-end collision that caromed them toward the cliff edge on the right.

Nina slammed her foot on the brake. The wheels froze, skidding along a black rubber trail.

She tried a quick correction, pumping gently on the pedal and steering into the swerve, wrestling to regain control, and praying out loud to every god she could remember. Well into a spin already, she hadn't moved quickly enough. She heard Michelle's cry as the Bronco leaped for the cliff, teetered there for a long moment, then fell forward into the sky.

They flipped into a long, silent somersault.

On the first big crash, upside down, Michelle jackknifed between the seats. Metal crunched. Nina shouted curses and imprecations between Michelle's high shrieks.

After the first surprise of falling, and the first crunching slam, Nina recognized the middle of her own death. In that instant, she bowed to the power of her terrible fear.

In the air again, they flew upside down, no pain yet. Oh, God, please let there be no pain. . . .

In another cracking bounce, metal squeezed and folded. They landed upside down again, the ceiling squashing to touch the tops of their heads.

No blood spurting. No terrible agony. Nina whispered, "Misty?" No answer.

The Bronco slid.

Sliding, bumping swiftly down the hill, the car traveled about forty feet until, to the blaring of a stuck horn, it slammed into a giant oak tree, movement halted, leaving the two women hanging sideways in their seat belts.

"Nobody move," Nina said. "Are you alive?" She had to shout above the horn's blare.

"I'm here," Michelle said weakly. She started wriggling out from between the seats.

Nina began to talk then, jabbering about the sleazeball who tried to run them off the road, her last wishes for her son, her thoughts about heaven, reincarnation, and dying, blasts at Detroit cheapskates and the antilock brake option she didn't have, her fear of fire, finally slowing down, exhausted, about two long minutes later. She felt around for Michelle's hand, squeezing hard. Then they both talked, simultaneously and incoherently.

And in the middle of that bedlam of the horn and their voices, the Bronco gave a final shudder, unstuck itself, and skied down the mountain on Michelle's door like a sled on a snowy hill. Down they slipped, screaming, past the shapes of trees, over low brush and rocky hillocks until a final thump stopped the horn and made Nina clamp down her teeth, drawing blood on the inside of her mouth. Nina opened her car door, climbing out, then sat on the back door and helped Michelle out of wreckage pocked like a fallen meteor.

They couldn't make it up the steep slope with the Bronco wedged above them, so they climbed down to a narrow ledge, eyeing the continuation of the cliff, imagining the rest of the long fall. The Bronco angled above them against a pitiful little tree, about twenty feet tall, growing on the ledge. Who would have believed that precarious, skinny tree could grow so strong! Nina stood beside Michelle, holding her arms around herself. All of a sudden, the violence arrested, there was no sound at all.

They both looked up. They were a few hundred feet below the summit of a mountain where the road ran between even higher peaks. Nina looked through big eyes at Michelle with her finger to her lips, trembling violently.

Then the quiet cracked as the small tree gave way to the enormous weight of the Bronco.

They scrambled along the ledge like goats, but the Bronco was directly above them, and as it roared by, Misty's skirt was caught by the broken side mirror.

Nina turned to her, grabbed her by her long Scandinavian hair as the girl fell, held on as she had never held anything, her back braced against the rock wall, her other arm locked around an outcropping. The arm that held Misty felt like it was dislocating, and she grunted with pain, but the Bronco was way below them now and she still held that hair, and Michelle hollered at her to let go, but her hand wouldn't open right away.

Nina helped the girl scramble back to the ledge. Her skirt had been ripped right off her. They clung to the rock face, breathless, Nina holding her arm gingerly, waiting. A very long time later they heard a distant crackling and then a soft thud as the Bronco sank into the forest.

Nina started up the hill first, climbing slowly and carefully, followed by Michelle. They were almost back up to the road when Michelle said, "He wouldn't be up there waiting for us?" They looked at each other, and tried to be quiet.

Nina lifted her eyes up over the edge first. All she saw was the road; and half a mile farther down, the curves, and the lights of Twin Bridges. No car and nobody. She pulled herself up. Michelle was right behind her. They didn't need to say it. If anybody came out of the bushes, they would fight, but nobody came.

Then they fell down in a heap at the edge of the blacktop.

Nina looked at the ragged pile that was Michelle. Michelle turned glassy eyes on the woman who was her attorney.

"You look like a semi rolled over you a coupla times and poured its load of cow shit on you for good measure," said Michelle, after a few more moments passed without incident, picking herself up and dusting herself off with those long fingers, now grubby and bruised.

"Oh, yeah?" Nina turned a cold eye on her companion. "Well, you look like you got cut up and reassembled by a three-year-old . . . lunatic." That made them both crack a smile. Nina, too, was trying to stand up but was having more trouble.

"Oh, yeah? How 'bout this? You"—Michelle pointed somberly at Nina, who had one hand on her knee and was trying to push herself into a stand—"you look like what the alley cat dragged in, ate, and threw up." By now they were laughing, tears smearing through the dirt on their faces.

"It was worth the whole thing just to get rid of that awful skirt of yours," Nina said unsteadily. Michelle laughed so hard she gave up and fell one more time onto the rocky, moonlit path.

16

"THE BRONCO'S TOTALED," Nina said. Following a long night and a long morning, she was telling Sandy about the accident. "There's a logging road down at the bottom. Matt's talking winches and derricks and heavy equipment. The insurance agent is out at Twin Bridges this afternoon to look at it with him."

"At least you're not totaled. You should go to the doctor," Sandy said. She sat behind her desk, majestic and implacable, a fixture already. Nina, sprawled in one of the reception chairs, could see why some of the clients preferred to wait out in the hall.

"Yeah. I live to fight again. Sore arm, bruised everywhere, but nothing broken. I never experienced a miracle before, Sandy. You can't imagine how great it felt to wake up this morning. Plus, the insurance company has already agreed to pay for the car this week."

"Now we are talking miracles. How's the client?"

"She's safe at the shelter. She was still asleep when I called. Andrea says her back hurt her this morning and she sprained a finger. Andrea's taking her to the doctor this afternoon."

"What do the cops say?"

"They say, without a better description of the car that rammed us, there's not much they can do. They say the curves at Twin Bridges are notorious for fatalities. They say it was dark and somebody came up on us too fast and then ran."

"But you say they're wrong," Sandy said.

"We were hit too hard. It was ferocious. It was deliberate. Somebody was trying to kill me or Michelle, or both of us."

"I didn't tell anybody where you were going," Sandy said. She looked ruffled.

"Bruno says nobody knew at his end either. I'll ask Michelle if she told her mother, Rossmoor, anybody."

"Why couldn't it just be a coincidence?" Sandy said. "I was in two accidents just last year. What with the wind, the mountains, the blizzards, and the drunks, you can't live up here without accidents."

"I was there, Sandy. I felt the . . . intent of the driver behind me. Oh, God."

"What?"

"I told Greenspan we were going to the City. What if he did it?"

"Why?"

"I don't know why, but he knew about the trip. Sandy, call Paul in Monterey. Ask him if he can check Greenspan out more thoroughly."

"Paul already called. He's sending his reports by overnight mail. He's coming back up next week. I can catch him if I call right away." Sandy flipped open her Rolodex and started punching the phone. Nina got up, massaging one arm, and went into her office. She had to proof her motions to suppress evidence, because the preliminary hearing was only one week away, and they would be heard at the same time. Then she would go home and lie down.

Calla lilies—how thoughtful of Paul or Sandy, she thought, greeted by a bold arrangement in the middle of her desk. Better tell them tactfully sometime that these alien-looking creatures belonged at funerals, not on a person's desk.

She plucked out a small envelope tucked into the bouquet with a plastic clip, opening the envelope and pulling out a card. As she read it, her legs wobbled, and she fell back in her chair.

Better luck next time, the card said. It had been printed with a felt pen. There was no signature.

The police would not be impressed, but she got it.

A message of malice and death.

She was still sitting there, not moving, when Sandy came in. "I got Paul," she said. "I forgot to tell you, Collier Hallowell made an appointment to see you after lunch. Says he has some papers for you." She looked at the flowers and back at Nina.

"How'd those get in here?" she said.

An old vacation home at the end of Ohlone Street, close to Regan Beach, the Tahoe Women's Shelter had been built by a lady named Annabella Wright. She had donated the building to South Tahoe when she died ten years ago, leaving a large private fund to keep things going there. The town used the building for the battered women's shelter, though you had to have a very good reason to know that. Because of the way the will was written, all the money went to maintenance, meaning there was limited funding for improvements, so the kitchen had no dishwasher or garbage disposal, but Andrea had talked an appliance shop into donating a heavy-duty clothes dryer two weeks before, assuring everyone that she would get everything they needed eventually, that private funding was out there to be tapped. Michelle believed if Andrea said she'd get it, she would. She was a woman who could quell a hurricane with a look.

If everybody doubled and tripled up, eight women and

twelve children could live there. People made an effort to get along, because they were all in trouble with the law or their husbands or their fathers, and they needed peace, although once in a while, Andrea said, somebody had to be calmed down. Nobody could stay more than thirty days, which was too bad, because Michelle woke up, had breakfast with Andrea, and realized how lonely and lost she had been, and how this place was perfect for her.

Her little finger hurt and she couldn't bend it. Andrea had wrapped it up and announced they would see the doctor at three o'clock. In spite of the pain Michelle felt issuing from her toes to her forehead, she concentrated her attention on her escape from death.

She kept going over the accident in her mind, especially that first moment when they rolled forward over the cliff. First she had thought, I'm going to die now. Part of her had said, about time; it's finally gonna be over; what a relief. When the car hit for the first time, in that loud moment, she understood what death meant—the end for Michelle, the extinguishing of everything—and another part of her said, I am not ready.

So today, walking around the shelter, she tiptoed through a different world, one richly magnified by the miracle of her survival. A table radio played a tune for two kids making dizzy belles, spinning with laughter and falling on the floor; a woman's necklace of glass beads glittered and breathed with the rising and falling of her chest. . . . Oh, she could think of so many happinesses here, and these soft tears she wiped away as she smiled were tears of thanksgiving, not fear and self-hate anymore.

There had to be a reason she was still around.

Michelle had never had much to do with kids, but on that wonderful morning in May, several of the ten children staying at the shelter pulled out an old Monopoly board in the living room and asked Michelle to play. Most of the houses and hotels were missing, but that didn't matter; they used poker chips for money and just rolled their way around the board, picking up properties and Chance and Community Chest cards.

After the board game they all went outside and walloped the ball against the garage door in a vicious game of dodgeball. Michelle watched the kids play tough, play mean, take care of each other, and make up again, better than miniature adults, nicer.

Everybody but Andrea and Michelle went to the movies to see the Disney dog flick after lunch. The tickets took a deep bite out of the weekly budget, but Andrea said, "Screw it. The whole idea at the shelter is to remind the mothers and children that life goes on and they can even have fun sometimes." Andrea went into the office to experience the unusual quiet and pay bills. Michelle lay down for a while.

She curled up in her bunk, not to sleep but to remember. She had so much to remember. She wasn't going to be afraid of her memories anymore.

Dr. Greenspan could help her. She got up again and called the number, which she had memorized, from the pay phone in the hall. She could tell it was Mrs. Greenspan who answered. The regular staff must be at lunch.

"It's me, Michelle Patterson. I've been trying to make an appointment," she said.

"Michelle Patterson," Mrs. Greenspan repeated.

"You know, Misty?"

"Your lawyer terminated you as a patient. The doctor cannot see you," she said.

"I'll talk to my lawyer. Meantime, please make me an appointment."

"You're terminated. Don't call again," the woman said.

The phone went dead.

* * *

Nina skipped lunch. When Sandy came back she said, "Good work. Fix these two typos in the Points and Authorities. Make four copies of each set of papers. Take the originals and two copies over to the county clerk before five. File the originals and have them conform the copies. Give me a set now and when Hallowell comes in I'll serve him personally. Know how to do a proof of personal service?"

She was showing Sandy a sample form when Collier Hallowell stuck his head through the door, saying, "Am I interrupting?"

"Oh. Hello, Collier. Come in."

The prosecutor walked in and sat down, setting his battered attaché on the rug. "Hi, Nina. Nice flowers," he said. "I heard about the accident. You ought to be in bed."

"I'm going there as soon as we're done, Collier. I mean, I'm not trying to chase you out or anything."

"Mind telling me about it?"

He sat across from her with his hands folded as she ran through her story. Andrea had filled her in on his private life, the adored wife now dead for two years, the dedication to work that got him through. Tahoe had all the gossip of a small town. Just the air was cosmopolitan. She recognized his expression right now, that of a man who had seen and heard everything without becoming jaded or cynical. Collier Hallowell was a man who seemed willing to consider alternative stories to fit the facts at hand. Too bad he hadn't applied that same open-mindedness she saw him use right now in the Patterson case.

She left out events that had to do with Bruno. When she finished, he was silent for a time. Finally he said, "It may be that someone was trying to kill you. Maybe it has to do with one of your cases. Maybe it has to do with your client. Maybe you cut someone off without noticing it just before

Twin Bridges. Maybe some mentally ill salesman had just decided to run somebody off the road last night. Remember the sniper who hid by Highway Fifty a few years ago and shot four drivers? There is always the possible random."

"What about this?" Nina handed him the card for the flowers.

He read it out loud, looking up at her with his eyebrows raised.

"Whoever tried to kill us isn't finished yet. That's what it means."

Pocketing the card and envelope, he said, "I'll ask one of the deputies to trace the florist shop and ask around."

"Thanks. Even if you don't believe me."

"Wouldn't want anything to happen to you," he said.

She felt so grateful, she forgot for a minute who he was.

"Look." He clicked open the attaché and broke the spell. "I wanted to come over personally with these papers. I didn't want you to get the wrong idea." He pulled out a thick manila envelope and handed it to her.

"I know. Today's the last day for filing motions. Here are the defense motions," Nina said absently, and gave him a set of copies that Sandy had just brought in. She was already reading. Initial disbelief quickly escalated into horror. This was no motion. It was a search warrant.

The warrant and supporting declarations were for all records of Bruno Cervenka, M.D., Ph.D., connected with examination and/or treatment of Michelle Patterson, and requested the cooperation of the San Francisco Sheriff's Office for the search. Attached to these papers was a court order setting an evidentiary hearing as to admissibility of any seized materials, to be held on June 10 in the El Dorado County Superior Court. Nina looked up at him, and he met her gaze steadily.

"Might as well read the declarations and the research," he

said, so she went on, her training allowing her to concentrate somewhere beyond the knife-strike music that filled her head. She read to the end and put the papers down.

He knew what he had done to her. Before she could speak, he said, "I'm sorry."

"How did you know about Dr. Cervenka?" Nina whispered. "Anyway, he's an independent consultant. You can't seize his records."

"I can't tell you how we learned about this, Nina. Our informant has requested anonymity. I couldn't let this go by. We have reason to believe the session included some therapy. His notes, tapes, anything he has is discoverable."

"I hired him," Nina said. "The session is privileged. It's work-product."

"File Dr. Cervenka's declaration, Nina. Make sure he swears he didn't do any hypnotic-regression therapy on your client. That would be therapy, not privileged under the attorney work-product doctrine."

"Even if it was therapy, you can't have it. That's still privileged under the physician-patient confidentiality doctrine."

"Not if you intend to put your client's mental state at issue. Remember the Menendez brothers? Their attorneys fought for three years to keep a tape of a session with their therapist out of the evidence. Eventually they lost, for that very reason."

"I noted your citation. You can bet I'll be able to distinguish that case," Nina said angrily. "And I've got another one for you. Attorney-client privilege. My client needed to communicate with me certain things, but could only do so under hypnosis. Dr. Cervenka was just the agent of that communication."

"I'll look forward to receiving your papers before the hearing on June tenth, Nina. Unless you're still too shook up and want to put it off a week or two . . ."

"I'm not as shook up as you'd like me to be, Collier."

"I mean, from the accident. For chrissake, Nina, I didn't come over here to watch you squirm. I want to play fair with you."

"When is this . . . search and seizure at Dr. Cervenka's office going to happen?"

"It's happening right now."

Nina nodded. Her hands were trembling, from rage or panic she couldn't tell. She wanted him to leave. She had liked Collier Hallowell, but this . . . betrayal felt so personal. But Nina knew he was just doing his job, same way she would, doing his best.

Then she thought of something else.

He saw the queer look on her face and said quickly, "What? What is it?"

"Your confidential informant," Nina said. "This mysterious person who told your office I was going to San Francisco with my client to see Dr. Cervenka yesterday. This person who knows so much about my movements . . ."

"You think . . ."

"That's the driver, Collier."

Hallowell's face changed as he seemed to wage an inner struggle. "I'm in a bind," he said. "I don't want to endanger you or Mrs. Patterson. I don't want you to think I would let anything happen to you. But I'm under an ethical obligation to keep the informant's name secret. That's the promise that's been made. If I had any hard evidence . . ."

Nina stood up. "If you won't give me the name, Collier, I think you'd better leave."

"I can't give you the name, Nina. But I promise you one thing. I will have that person watched."

As soon as he was gone, Nina got into her rental car outside and drove home. The house would be empty for another hour. She took three aspirin, went to her room, and turned on *Oprah*.

Michelle should be safe at the shelter with the alarm system, security patrol, and secret location to protect her for now.

Nina, however, hung out there in the wind, twisting, twisting.

Not happy to be a passenger in Andrea's car, Michelle sat back against the seat, belted tight, sweating where the heater blew on her feet, and wishing she could stop at Cecil's for a drink.

As if she were reading her mind, Andrea said, "Dr. Francis isn't far. She'll take a look at your bones. But you know there's more to you than flesh and blood. Tomorrow at noon there's a meeting over at the Episcopal Church I'd like to invite you to."

"Church? I had enough of that for my next eight lives."

"No, this is not religious."

"What is it, then?"

"An informal meeting of women who have decided they want to quit drinking. It's—"

"No, thanks," Michelle said quickly. "I don't have a drinking problem. It's just all this shit I'm going through, for God's sake."

Andrea let the words echo around the car, then said, "Ask, if you decide to go."

Several other people waited in a room that opened onto an atrium. A few kids bounced a ball away from the window. A nurse had Michelle pee into a cup and carry the unpleasantly warm liquid back to a counter. She thumbed through magazines for almost an hour after that before she was called in. Cheerful and brisk, Dr. Francis asked her a lot of questions and took shorthand notes, then gave her a quick physical.

"Your back pain is probably just a strain rather than something serious, but we should keep an eye on it. I have some nonprescription pain pills here." The woman reached into a drawer and scrabbled through dozens of tiny sample pill packets. "That's about it." Michelle put her clothes on to leave. The receptionist asked her to wait outside. Ten minutes later, she went back in.

Dr. Francis pushed her glasses back on her face, saying, "Well. A positive result on a standard test. Looks like we'll need to see you again, young lady."

"What's the matter? Do I have—"

"No, no. You're not sick. Healthy as a horse. Are you trying to tell me you haven't noticed some changes in your body over the past three months?" She was smiling, so it couldn't be too bad.

"Doctor. You have no idea. My life's been really crazy."

"It's about to become crazier. You're going to be a mother. Whoops!" She caught Michelle's shoulders and steadied her. "Are you all right?"

"Oh, I am in so much trouble. A baby . . ."

"Well, let's have you talk to one of our counselors tomorrow. Maybe I shouldn't congratulate you; I never know what to say these days."

That night, Michelle got into her car and drove to Tom Clarke's house. He walked his dogs every night about ten.

She hadn't told Andrea or anyone else. She wanted to tell Tom, see his reaction, see what he wanted to do. Of course, maybe this baby did not belong to Tom at all, but she wanted it to be Tom's baby.

Shouldn't the father hear the news first?

Tom had been avoiding her, not even trying to reach her. She wanted to see him and ask him to his face why he hadn't called.

She couldn't believe he would dump her, just like that, not after the way he had panted after her for months, made love to her in cars and motels and on the beach, all their secret places.

Michelle was lonely, and she had never been without a man since leaving her Fresno home. Wisdom said, don't go starting up something new at this point. She knew Tom. Steve had been nothing but a couple of quickies, a stranger.

She cruised by his house in Anthony's Subaru, which the police had finally released to her. Tom lived in a development called Montgomery Estates in a house that looked like a scale model of a castle. He complained enough about the mortgage that it should be full-size.

His kids would be in bed by now. His wife Janine would be in bed too. She had to get up at five to get to her job as a nurse at Boulder Hospital. Tom had talked about his family all the time.

Michelle parked the car down the street, rolled down the driver's-side window to let in the sweet smell of night-blooming jasmine, and settled back to wait, away from the light. After about fifteen minutes she tucked her head back against the headrest and closed her eyes. The pain pill had made her drowsy.

In what seemed like a moment, she opened them again to see Janine Clarke peering toward the driver's window, holding the two dogs. Wearing shorts and a sleeveless black T-shirt, her hair tied up in a ponytail, Tom's wife had the solid build and the pecs of a woman who lifted weights. Michelle had never seen her before, but she knew Tom's collie and the black Lab straining at the leash.

"Misty, right? The newspaper doesn't do you justice," Janine Clarke said. "No, don't start up the car. What are you doing here?"

"I came to see Tom," Michelle said.

"Oh. Dog walking. Usually his job. Do the two of you often meet this way?"

"No. Anyway, I gotta go."

"I guess Tom didn't know you were out here, or he wouldn't have made such a stink about me walking these guys tonight. So you're spying. Did you want to see if the kids and I were still around? Here we are."

"I never meant to hurt your family."

"Did you know we have three little children? Did you ever think while you two went about your business about the kind of pain you put us through? 'Daddy's gone again tonight'; me crying and the kids just frantic."

Michelle couldn't talk.

"Ruining his life, ruining his career. Yes, you had one prize bull working for you there."

"Who do you mean?" Michelle found her voice. Not Tom Clarke, because he might rate stud horse, but never bull status. "Anthony?"

"Paid me a special visit at the hospital. He wanted to make sure I broke as badly as he broke. He made sure I would walk out on Tom. You know he said he taped the two of you in bed? I ran. Missed the performance."

Michelle, thunderstruck, said nothing. She didn't believe it. Anthony must have made that up because he was in another jealous snit, to get Tom out of her life. He had suspected her, but he never knew.

"Leave us alone. Tom wants nothing to do with you." Janine looked hard at Michelle, then without warning raised a hand and punched her in the face. Michelle threw up her arm to protect herself, but the woman began walking down the street, the dogs pulling her forward.

Janine's knuckles had felt like concrete. Michelle put a hand to her numb cheek, watched the woman disappear into the night, and then started up the car and drove away.

17

❧

MICHELLE DECIDED NOT to try to tell anyone else about the baby until she was ready. She carried her secret around with the tiny spot of brightness she now knew was inside. The next day she went to the clinic counselor, who told her all about getting an abortion in the second trimester.

She should have known from losing her periods, but even before Anthony and jail, she had been so miserable and desperate she had paid no attention.

Now she felt the pregnancy enveloping her like soft baffling. That night she investigated her abdomen with her fingers. Deep inside there, just above the pelvic bone, she thought she could feel a spongy new lump right at her center, as alive in this moment as she herself felt. Her whole life had been concerned with death. Her childhood was dead to her, forgotten. Anthony's death had felt . . . expected, and her grief and guilt over that event, strangely familiar. She had almost died herself, the other day in Nina's Bronco. She had searched for death; for Anthony to kill her, for alcoholism, for AIDS. She had made friends with death. Now, at the last minute, this fragile new life had come to her, trailed by an insistent inner voice whispering all the excellent reasons to end it.

Her hands moved up and down her body, touching it as though they belonged to someone else. It was a healthy body, resilient, young and strong.

Just before Michelle fell asleep, the thought came to her that the case against her was all part of the same process she began with Dr. Greenspan. She needed to remove the darkness in her life, the mysteries, the accusations, the confession that made no sense. Nina could provide the muscle, but the spirit had to come from her, from inside, because she knew without her inspiration, whatever defense Nina cooked up would crumble. She, who avoided conflict. She, who played games with her husband so that he would never know the truth about her. She, who shielded herself from her own past. She would have to fight her old friend Death and welcome in a stranger.

The next day Nina came to the shelter. Michelle was peeling carrots into the sink in the kitchen, wearing sweats and a tank top spattered with ingredients for the chocolate cake she had just slipped into the oven.

"Nice to hear you whistling," Nina said. "I didn't know you could do that."

"There's a lot nobody knows about me." Michelle smiled. "Ain't that a shame." They sat down at the long kitchen table. "I feel happy today."

"How's your finger?"

Michelle held up the splint for inspection, a ragged bandage covered with cake mix. "It only hurts when I think about it. How about your arm?"

"Sore. I wake up when I roll over at night."

"It could be worse," they said at the same time. They looked at each other, two survivors.

"So," Nina said. "You decided to live."

"It could all be taken away tomorrow," Michelle said.

"I know what you mean."

"I've given up trying to control any of what's happening," Michelle said. "There's so much danger. It's like swirling around in a whirlpool, thinking each time I go around I'll get sucked down. But it doesn't happen. I could still come out of this somehow, Nina. I could!"

"Michelle, I really hope you do," Nina said.

She sounded funny, choked up, so Michelle, who was whipping icing, turned the mixer off and said, "What's wrong?"

"I have some very bad news, Michelle, and I don't quite know how to tell you about it. I'm just going to have to blurt it out. Somehow—I don't know how—Collier Hallowell learned about the session with Dr. Cervenka," Nina said, putting her head between her hands. "He obtained a search warrant for Dr. Cervenka's office. He has the tape of your hypnosis."

"But how could that happen? You said he would hide in the background and we wouldn't have to use him as a witness."

"The DA's office should never have found out. Someone knew about the session and talked to Hallowell."

"But who?"

"Did you tell anyone we were going to San Francisco, Michelle? Think hard."

"Nobody. Except Steve. He called me and wanted to see me. I said I had to go to San Francisco for an appointment. He said he would drive me, and I said I was going with you. Tell me it wasn't Steve."

"You shouldn't have told him that much," Nina said. "He has resources. He could have found out the rest. But don't feel too bad, Michelle. I told somebody myself, although I don't think I said the doctor's name. He could be tracked down, easily enough."

"Who did you tell?" Michelle could see Nina measuring her strength, wondering how much more she could take. Nina looked like she needed some support herself. Glasses perched on her nose made her look younger, like the smart little schoolgirl she must have been. "Go ahead, Nina," she said.

"Dr. Greenspan," Nina said.

"My doctor? You think he came after us and rammed the car? I don't believe it."

"You're in trouble, Michelle," Nina said. "I've seen it before. When somebody gets in trouble, the rats jump for safety. I know how much you trust Dr. Greenspan and feel you still need him. But you have to stay away from him."

Michelle got up and took her cake out of the oven, placing the hot pan carefully on top of the stove.

"I figured out what I want, Nina, because up until now I never knew."

"What's that?"

"A normal life. Like yours. A family, and work where I'm not required to entertain with a flash of skin."

Nina took a deep breath, which came out like a sigh.

"Chocolate cake and Christmas. Not killers and jail and traitors everywhere. You're the only one I can trust, Nina."

"I've betrayed you too. I've screwed up your defense. I should never have taken the risk of the hypnosis. I wanted to find the truth too fast, just mess with your brain and have it all come spilling out. I should have been more patient, and let the truth unfold. Now the prosecution has a confession."

"What do we do now?"

"I'm going to file another motion, to suppress the tape, anything to do with the session. There are powerful legal arguments on our side. I'm working on it. The search warrant was obtained under Penal Code Section 1524, which requires the tape be sealed and brought to court for an evidentiary hearing. At that hearing we will argue that the tape was protected by what we call a privilege, that is, a right to keep the tape confidential. The hearing is set for June tenth."

"Slow down. I don't get it. If the tape was sealed, doesn't that mean Hallowell doesn't know I said I killed Anthony?"

"He knows. Bruno told me the police played the tape at his office before they took it away. And . . ."

"That's not all?"

"Nope. It gets worse. Hallowell has withdrawn the plea-bargain offer. He's ready to try you for first-degree murder unless you'll plead to second-degree murder."

"What happens to me if I do that?"

"I would say you would be out in about ten to fifteen years. We've been putting off the prelim in hopes of resolving the case with a plea bargain. Now Hallowell says he wants to get that over with and get a trial date as soon as possible if we don't accept this new . . . offer by Wednesday." She looked up. "Michelle? Do you understand what I just said?"

"I get it," Michelle said. "It's okay."

"Then you definitely don't get it, Michelle. Let me explain again."

"No, Nina. Your turn to listen. If we lose on the tape, we'll have to have a trial. You almost had me convinced to plead guilty to . . . to . . ."

"Voluntary manslaughter."

"You're not going to tell me to plead guilty to second-degree murder, are you?"

"I might. If we lose this motion and I think you might be convicted of murder in the first degree. I've seen that happen, too, Michelle, a defense lawyer going for an acquittal instead of pleading to a lesser charge, only to find her client is off to San Quentin for twenty-five to life."

"Another twirl around the whirlpool coming up," Michelle said. "Let's have a piece of cake. And let's have a trial." She cut them two big pieces.

"Michelle . . ." Nina began.

"Nina, I never had a woman friend before. It's always been men for me. I don't know why. I guess I always competed with other women for men, some jungle thing. But I'm out of that, I'm changing. And I want to be your friend."

"Michelle . . . friendship doesn't enter into this. . . ."

"You're really on my side, Nina. So what if you made a mistake." Michelle had a big bite of the warm cake and put a piece in front of Nina.

"You nut. You ought to fire me," Nina said, scratching beside her eye with a newly minted fingernail. She lifted a fork and took a bite.

"Will you take it to trial if we lose on the motion, Nina? That's what I want."

"You could go to prison for life, Michelle. We have no defense. You've confessed, for God's sake."

"I've been rolling in garbage for a long time, hoping to get hit by something sharp, something that would do me some damage. Now I want to stand up for myself."

"I think I understand," Nina said quietly.

"There's something in what you say about the burglar at the Lucky Chip and the car accident. *One* bad thing, okay; I attract the wrong types. But two? Someone is out there, someone who did kill Anthony. You've got to keep looking."

"Oh, Michelle. I'm looking," Nina said.

"Because I only hit Anthony once. That's what I believe, no matter what I said in the doctor's office."

"Bruno didn't know what to make of your reactions at the end of the tape," Nina said. "He wanted to hypnotize you again. Of course, that's too dangerous now."

"You are going to figure this out, Nina." She licked icing off her bandage. "I want a trial, and I want it soon, because I need to clean up. We can beat them. All those good old boys, the ones who put me in a low-cut tux and then drool on me, are setting me up again, judging me before they even know me."

"They aren't the ones we have to convince."

"Oh, I disagree with you there. Did you see the head-lines? 'Barmaid Held in Husband's Murder'? Everyone assumes I'm this guilty, brazen tramp who should be punished. Everyone wants to believe I'm guilty because of what I am, what I've been. It's so simple. Well, that's not me, so they can kiss my fluffy ass. I'm innocent and I want you to prove it, in court, once and for all. Show 'em how wrong they are." Michelle yawned. "I could sleep for a year and wake up someplace else. It's almost exciting."

"You are one brave woman, Michelle Patterson." Nina took off her glasses and rubbed her eyes. "Okay, we'll do the prelim and set it for trial."

"You keep playing the cold deck, and eventually the dealer has to shuffle," Michelle said. "Even at Prize's."

Nina forced a small laugh, said, "All right, we go for the ace in the hole," and waved on the way out.

On May 24, the day set for the preliminary hearing and for hearing of her set of motions to suppress the physical evidence, Nina arrived at court at 8:00 A.M. exactly. Michelle went up to the counsel table with her and sat down. She wasn't nervous. Nina had told her that the results were a foregone conclusion.

Judge Flaherty's bailiff called the court to order.

Michelle watched Collier Hallowell, a few feet away from her at the other table, the man who was trying to send her to prison for the rest of her life. His hair was graying to match his eyes, but he had plenty of it, and he was tall, with a nice build. He smiled at her, as if to say, it's nothing personal, just my job. Michelle didn't think it would be easy to get past that smile to see the man underneath.

First, the court heard Nina's arguments that the police had no reason to search Rick Eich's boat or Michelle's house. In response, Collier Hallowell just said, "Submit it on the paperwork, Your Honor," like he knew he didn't have to argue it, and he was right, the judge ruled that all the evidence could come in. Nina didn't waste her energy. "Thank you, Your Honor," she said, sitting down. Courtroom manners could be pretty funny. The lawyer thanked the judge, even though the judge had just said "no way" to the lawyer, even though the lawyer might be steaming.

The preliminary hearing in Michelle's case passed without surprises and took less than the court day. Three police officers testified about finding Anthony's body and what she had told them about hitting Anthony. There was no jury, and Nina presented no witnesses, though she did cross-examine the officers on each point of their testimony. Nina and Mr. Hallowell then made short statements, but Michelle understood in advance that the Court would bind her over for trial. Nina had explained to her that the prelim in Municipal Court was a kind of formality, like her arraignment, and that the judge would find there was probable cause to believe a crime had been committed and she had committed the crime. The judge looked bored as he assigned the case to the Superior Court for trial-setting.

"How do you think it went?" Michelle asked Nina as they walked out.

"Textbook," Nina said. "We learned almost nothing new. Collier Hallowell is very, very good. He put on the minimum case to cause you to be bound over for trial and gave me very little. His burden of proof at this stage is much lower than it will be later. He's saving Bruno's tape for trial. He didn't have to use it in order to get you bound over."

"What happens now?"

"Well, we are now going to be kicked upstairs to the Superior Court's Judge Milne. The evidentiary hearing is set for June tenth on our motion to suppress the tape. If I lose, I'm going to file a special appeal called a Writ of Mandate before the trial. A trial date will be set next week. You won't have to come back to court for that. Judge Milne is very efficient, and there isn't much of a backlog of cases. The trial will probably get on the calendar for late September."

September was a long way away. Four months. By then she would be very pregnant, if—

Nina interrupted her thoughts. "Let's join the Reillys for an early supper at Sato's, Michelle."

Before driving to the Japanese restaurant, they walked out on the pier nearby and sat dangling their legs, ladylike shoes tossed aside. Down twenty feet through the transparent water they could see somebody's dilapidated "pump" athletic shoe and bottles shimmering brightly as a school of fish. Back at the beach a large family celebrated around a barbeque grill near one of the few picnic tables. The odor of mesquite chicken wafted their way, making Michelle hungry.

"Nina, I need to tell you something private."

Nina looked at her, brows arched behind the big sunglasses. She looked out of place in her white blouse and tight black skirt, though she had taken off her hot jacket. She noticed Michelle looking and said, "I feel like ripping the pantyhose off too. Ah, why not!" She lay down and hiked up her skirt, then swiftly rolled down the stockings and stuffed them in her jacket pocket. "Much better," she said. "What were you saying?" She straightened her legs out over the water and started rotating her ankles. Her toenails were painted pink.

That was Nina. So prim and proper and unemotional on the surface, with something wild and colorful struggling to burst out underneath.

"I'm pregnant," Michelle said.

"Whew, the sun's really beating down for so early in the summer. I thought you said—"

"I'm pregnant."

"Holy Christ."

"Three months along. I only found out for sure at the clinic a few weeks ago."

Nina kicked up some water. "Who's the father?" she asked.

"I don't know. Three months back means it could have been any of three guys. At least I know who they are. There've been other times . . ."

"Okay, okay," Nina interrupted. "Three men."

"Anthony's the most likely, you know, because of frequency. And next Tom. We were pretty heavy. And Steve Rossmoor."

"Didn't you use a condom?"

"Usually, with guys besides Anthony. Plus I had a Pill prescription, but I forgot to take 'em for a few days that month. Never was a problem before."

Nina touched her on the shoulder. "How do you feel about it?"

"The way things are going, I'll probably be in prison when I deliver. The baby will go into foster care. If I even keep it. It's not the best time to have a baby."

"That's an understatement," Nina said. "How long do you have to decide?"

"Not long. The sooner the better."

"If Clarke is the father, or Rossmoor . . ." Nina said.

"Tom already has three, and Steve is single."

"Still," Nina said, "maybe something could be worked out."

"I have to make the decision about an abortion all by myself. So for now, I've decided to go to AA meetings and keep the baby as healthy as I can while I make up my mind."

"I'm sure your baby would be beautiful, knowing its mother," Nina said.

"God, I worry about that. I mean, I got totally loaded those first two days right after I got out of jail. And what kind of life or family do I have to offer? I never even held a baby before."

"What about your parents?"

"No. What with my mom's arthritis—and they're getting old. They had enough trouble raising me. It wouldn't be fair."

"About the father," Nina said. "You could take a DNA test if the other two men will cooperate. We could even maybe get a sample of Anthony's blood from the police. Or we could file a paternity suit and force Rossmoor and Clarke to cooperate."

"Just what I need," Michelle said, "more court." She thought about Steve Rossmoor finding out he was the father. She knew almost nothing about him, except that Nina said he was rich and she knew he had a big-deal job. Or Tom. Tom and Janine. Janine would never take the baby. She said, "I dug me a hole and now I'm buried. I don't know what to do next."

"Look for the ace," Nina said. "And have a good dinner. Strange . . ."

"What?"

"With most of my clients, most of what happens in their lives is really irrelevant to my making a case. But with you, everything, even your pregnancy, seems linked to your case in my mind."

They put their shoes on and walked back to the highway. "When I first met you? You told me once that you have a son," Michelle said.

"I do. A great kid."

"You're a single mom now?"

"I guess I am. His stepfather still wants to see him. I'm going to try to work that out. Bobby misses Jack."

"What about you?"

"What do you mean?"

"Jack. Your husband. Do you miss him? Do you ever want him back?"

"Yeah, I do."

"Don't you wish sometimes you could go back to a certain day and start all over? Not, like, your whole life, but to a day you blew totally? Get a chance, maybe, to do something different? Turn everything around?"

"Sure, everybody has that fantasy sometimes."

"I'd like to go back to that Thursday, at work. Sometimes I think if I hadn't been in such a rotten mood that night . . . see, there was this guy pestering me all night, and I couldn't stop thinking about how bad I felt that Anthony controlled all the money and I couldn't even take a dime to save my life, because that's what Dr. Greenspan was doing. He was saving my life. I'd go back to that night and I'd change it. I'd do different things, you know?"

"You think if we could go back, we would change the way we behaved?"

"I do."

"I don't."

Once at Sato's, sitting at the long table with Nina and Andrea and her family, while Matt made fifteen pieces of

California maki disappear and the kids poured gallons of soy sauce on their rice, Michelle's hunger disappeared. Just the smell of sauce on fish was making her remember without pleasure her last trip on the Tilt-A-Whirl at the Modoc County Fair with Anthony. Nina offered to drive her back right away, but she said, "I'll just go breathe outside for five minutes."

"Keep your eyes open," Nina said, so she stood in the alleyway beside the restaurant, where she wasn't visible from the sidewalk.

A couple, man and woman, walked past her toward the Sato's entrance. The man, a suede jacket draped over one arm and the woman hanging on the other, was Tom. Janine walked on ahead without seeing her, but Tom had eyes like a cat and must have made some excuse, because in about a minute he was back there in the alleyway with her.

"Skulking in the dark," Tom said, not in a funny way. He leaned against the building with his arms crossed. "Where've you been? You dropped out of sight."

"And out of your mind. You could have called Nina."

"Misty, listen. Janine found out about us, and I've been making up for it ever since. If my wife sees you—"

"What about me, Tom? I've been so lonely."

"You know better than to look to me for emotional support. You came on so heavy, I couldn't resist. But no more. This mess, you killing Anthony—"

"I feel like killing you, right now."

Tom actually stepped back and looked at her hands. Was he afraid of her? "Don't joke about it," he said uneasily.

"Don't worry, your wife will probably kill me first," Michelle said. "Did she tell you she socked me the other night?"

"She told me. And told me and told me. It's been hell, what I've been going through."

"What about what I've been going through?"

"Try to understand, Misty. I have so much to lose, and you—"

"Just a stupid girl in spike heels. So who cares if I go to jail? Not you. Big relief for you, huh, Tom?"

"I don't expect you to understand. Just leave me alone in the future, okay, Misty? I have to go."

He turned toward the restaurant, his body stiff, his mouth a line in concrete.

"Just one more little thing, Tom."

"I really have to go." He paused, with his back still to her. She felt like throwing a rock at him. Make him turn around and face her.

"I'm pregnant."

She watched the shoulders hunch. He didn't move. With a kind of sad joy at her command of him and feeling overcome by a maniacal energy, she danced like a monkey around to the front of him, yelling, "Your baby! Remember that night you told me you loved babies, Tom? Remember that night? The one when you said you really, really, really loved me so much, more than anything or anybody? And I wouldn't believe you, so you tried to convince me?" He put his hands over his ears and strode away. "You weren't good enough. I never believed you! Never!"

She stopped and shook herself, trying to shake out the tears she felt inside. Then she slid down the wall and sat on the damp asphalt until Nina and the rest of them came out.

Delores moved into the shelter with her two kids on Friday. "The old man didn't want me back, and he was sick of taking care of the children," she told Michelle from the old sofa in the living room. "He let me know I wasn't welcome the day I got out of jail. With his fist. But this time I fixed him. I turned Philo's ass in to County Family Support. He makes good money trucking. The county's going to collect a thousand bucks a month for me. With that and a motel cleaning job we'll be just fine. First check they forward, we'll find us a little apartment and I'll pick up some fried chicken and ribs and we'll all have a big party."

It was good to see her. Del had three old suitcases and new hair, long skinny braids that she called "dreads." She and Michelle did the cooking that night and they went to bed late. Del put on what looked like a cotton shower cap, tucking her braids carefully inside. She lay down in her bunk and almost instantly Michelle heard her breath deepen.

"Del?"

"Mañana, girl."

"I'm going to have a baby." That got her up on her elbow.

"Well, well, well. I should have known when we were bunkmates, the way you slept and complained about the food all the time. The spaghetti wasn't *that* bad."

"I don't think I can keep it."

Del said, "Oh," then, "Well, what happened to that guy you were seeing? The school one?"

"I saw him yesterday. He's through with me. How can you blame him? He loves the family he already has."

"He just couldn't resist getting a little on the side. God save us from husbands."

"Have you ever had an abortion, Del?"

"Yeah," Del said. "Two."

"How come?"

"First one, I must have been about fourteen or fifteen years old. My mother never knew. My boyfriend took me to a clinic in Tijuana and it was all over in ten minutes. All over," she repeated thoughtfully. "Second one seems like yesterday. Rennie was three then and Sharille was only nine months. I was in my forties, workin' graveyard as a janitor in a downtown office building. How was I going to take care of another baby? I went to another clinic."

"Did it hurt?"

"Not if you don't mind a vacuum cleaner hose up your bazunga," Del said.

"Did you ever wish you hadn't?"

"Not for a long time. Then one day I said to myself, the oldest would be twenty-one today. Now, isn't that funny? That I had a birthday in mind? Same for the youngest. She's got a birthday, too, even if she never got born. Now when I think about it, I feel bad. I was meant to have four."

"You did what you had to do," Michelle said.

"I had my choices, the hard way and the easy way. I didn't realize something then that I know now."

"What?"

"When it all comes down, the years pass, you realize you're never gonna be rich and famous, enough men come and go, it comes to you—the children were the only thing that really mattered," Del said. "Listen to me, I sound like one of those guys with Deep South accents bangin' the Bible on the Christer station. Now, can I go to sleep?"

"Thanks," Michelle said.

"*De nada.* Say, Misty-Michelle. You still a boozer?"

"I quit. Because of the baby. I'm going to AA and I've been sober for sixteen days now."

"I told you you're a smart girl," Del said, her voice muffled in the pillow as she rolled over for good.

"Del."

"What?"

"You still a K mart shopper?"

Saturday morning dawned early and hot. Michelle put on her old Nikes and new big T -shirt and walked down to the beach. The north shore had mostly black-pebble beaches;

she liked the coarse, warm, yellow sand of the south shore better. She stood knee-high in the cool wavelets, looking out at the immense blueness of Lake Tahoe, thinking about Anthony.

Maybe someone would come and kill her right now. She wasn't supposed to sneak out alone. She scanned the beach, but except for a flock of gulls squawking their way toward Emerald Bay the beach was empty.

Bending down, cupping her hands, she splashed her face. It seemed to her that, though the doctor had told her it was too early, the baby fluttered inside her.

She had quit arguing with herself. She didn't deserve this baby; probably it would be taken away; but she already loved it. She would keep it. She was one with this child the way she should have been with Anthony.

18

AFTER A BAD night, Nina slept late and arrived at her office around nine-thirty.

Her recently improved nights had been blasted to hell on May eleventh, several weeks before, when Collier brought his ill tidings and Bruno called to tell her law enforcement was tossing his office. "I would have destroyed the tape if I had had any idea," he had told her in a low tone from his outer office at UCSF.

"Let's not compound the error, Bruno. Just do what they say and fax me whatever they served on you." She had sat at her desk, her brain clicking without progress, like stripped gears. No work-product privilege? How could it be? The affidavit for the warrant cited several cases. She had walked dully over to her California Reporters and started pulling out volumes, ignoring the pain in her arm. Her anxiety blinded her; the words in the cases swam before her eyes. This was it, the ruin that had been waiting for her.

How had she missed this? Looking back, she had simply assumed she knew the law. She had been sure she could deep-six Bruno and the hypnosis if she didn't like the result. She had never dreamed Collier would find out and pounce so immediately and effectively.

She had spent Saturday at the law library, looking up more cases. She had to file her Motion to Suppress for the June 10 hearing as soon as possible. She needed to reshape the case holdings Collier had cited, to draw distinctions, to find a critical dissent, anything she could use in her motion to suppress Michelle's statement under hypnosis.

Summary of Legal Arguments, she wrote now on her yellow pad. The phone was ringing in the outer office. Sandy fielded it. *There are at least five legal grounds for a finding that the seized material may not be considered at trial.* She sorted her research into five piles on the desk.

> *First.* The psychotherapist-patient privilege, codified in Evidence Code Section 1014, allows the defendant to refuse to disclose a confidential communication between a patient and her psychotherapist. This privilege supersedes the public policy and due process arguments advanced by the prosecution in its declarations supporting issuance of the warrant at issue herein. Menendez v. Superior Court, 3 Cal. 4th 435.

Sounded good. But this privilege was a trap. It had an exception, called the patient-litigant exception. Nina read the Menendez case again; two brothers from Beverly Hills, accused of killing their parents, had gone to a therapist and confessed on tape. The Menendez defense lawyers had raised some of the same arguments Nina would raise, but in the end the tape had been allowed in, because the boys' defense required some testimony about their emotional and mental states before and during the killings.

Unfortunately, Nina had the same problem. Michelle had told the police she couldn't remember what happened after she hit Anthony the first time. The jury would never believe that, unless Dr. Greenspan, Bruno, and perhaps Michelle herself testified about her previous amnesia.

Let Collier point out the exception to Judge Milne. She would deal with it after she saw his papers.

Second. Attorney work-product is confidential. The tape was a product of defendant's attorney's trial preparation.

Nina reread her research. Work-product included an attorney's impressions and conclusions and other material that was derivative or interpretative, like reports from consultants. But there was a case, cited in the leading case, Fellows v. Superior Court, 108 Cal. App. 3d 55, in which a private investigator's report of a witness interview had been kept out, while the tape of the actual interview with the witness came in. Not good. The tape itself, according to the Fellows case, was evidence, not work-product.

She would probably lose on the work-product argument. She hadn't known about the Fellows case. She hadn't done her homework before the fact, and there was no brilliant argument about attorney work-product to be conjured up after the fact.

There it was again, the sickening tide of anxiety rising from her stomach. She was disgusted with herself. She had made the decision to hypnotize Michelle without even cracking a law book.

She took a deep breath, pushed the feeling aside. She wasn't finished yet.

Third. The attorney-client privilege is applicable to any information that the client gives to a psychiatrist retained to assist the defense. People v. Lines, 13 Cal. 3d 500. In the instant case, the communication could be made only through a psychiatrist, as the information sought was not available in the client's conscious mind.

She underlined *only*. Nobody had ever made that argument before. But it was a good one.

Collier was arguing that the tape was not a confidential communication between a client and a lawyer, because it was derived from a therapeutic session between the client and the therapist as soon as hypnosis was used. Michelle's gasping sentences as she remembered the Philippines constituted hypnotic-regression therapy but were completely irrelevant to the case at hand.

Fine. Nina had her answer. If the Philippines portion of the tape was therapy, only that portion could be admitted. And it shouldn't be admitted, because it was irrelevant, as Collier conceded.

Her third point was her strongest. Judge Milne ought to buy it, keep the confession out as an attorney-client communication. It was the best chance they had.

> *Fourth.* The tape was made under hypnosis. It is unreliable as a matter of law and inadmissible for the same reasons posthypnotic testimony is rendered inadmissible, except under certain well-defined circumstances not present here. See Evidence Code Section 795.

Well, section 795 was not exactly on point, but it was close enough to control by analogy if Milne wanted it that way. Nina looked through the cases once more.

Uh-oh. *People v. Miller,* a recent California Supreme Court case, held that even if the hypnosis session was inadmissible, evidence discovered as a result of the session was admissible.

That case had to do with physical evidence, not a confession. It was distinguishable. Maybe.

Fifth. To the extent that statements by the defendant on the tape tend to inculpate (good word, that, stately and dignified) the defendant, they violate defendant's Fifth Amendment right against self-incrimination.

The Menendez lawyers had tried that one on for size also. Michelle had not been compelled to testify against her own interest in a criminal proceeding. It was mushy, very mushy.

Could she make any other arguments? She put her pen down and penciled in nine dots, doodling triangles, letting her mind meander through the information she had stuffed into it.

Nothing new came to mind. Nina picked up her microphone and began droning the details.

Michelle's parents arrived at the shelter on Monday afternoon. Her father's perfunctory kiss and her mother's apologetic air told her to be on guard—he had cooked something up and she was going to be invited to eat it. She took them out to the picnic table in back, glad to see them and as usual feeling a little sad there were so many shadows between them.

They seemed frightened by the shelter, the shabby furniture, the noisy kids running back and forth, the raucous laughter emanating from the kitchen as supper was prepared. Delores came over to be introduced and her father took in her old chenille robe and house slippers with astonishment. To Del, wearing the robe on Monday afternoon was a declaration of freedom. In jail she had to dress like they said, when they said. But Michelle's father, in his perfectly starched shirt from the French laundry down the street from his auto dealership, saw slovenly clothing and not what it stood for.

Michelle sat down on the bench, and her parents stood in

front of her, already anxious to leave. Seeing them like that, uncomprehending and judgmental, she felt her latest resolve weakening. But she needed their help, didn't she? Her time at the shelter was running out. For once she was going to be smart. Who could say? Maybe some time together would get them started on healing old wounds.

Before she could open her mouth to announce her good intentions, her father spoke.

"Michelle, we want you to come home now. But we want you to talk to Mr. Riesner first."

"Is that why you didn't come yesterday? You went to see him this morning?"

Her mother said, "We needed legal advice, Michelle, and while I know you like her very much, we have lost our confidence in Ms. Reilly. She had worked something out with the district attorney, where you could have gotten a light—a reasonable—sentence. But they withdrew the offer, and it's her fault."

"Mr. Riesner says hypnotizing you was a serious mistake, that Ms. Reilly is making a lot of mistakes. She should be replaced. You need somebody really good, now more than ever, and Jeffrey Riesner is known in this town. He's experienced and he is willing to represent you," her father said.

"Wait, slow down," Michelle said. "*She's* my attorney. I'm not saying she's perfect, but I'll decide if I'm going to ax her."

"I'm sorry, Michelle, but in this serious situation you are going to have to rely on our judgment. You're going home tonight, and we're hiring Mr. Riesner. Barbara, help Michelle pack her suitcase." He didn't know how to discuss anything. He seemed able only to issue commands. It was one reason she had needed to leave home. She saw him steel himself for the negative response he expected.

"Wait a second, Dad. I am coming home, but let me take

care of the packing. I'll drive down tomorrow in the Subaru, after I pick up my last paycheck and take care of some other important business. Nina got permission for me to leave the county to go home."

Her father blinked.

"I'll go talk to this guy you found in the morning. Believe me, I'm willing to listen to good advice. I'll listen, and then I'll decide about changing lawyers."

"Well, Michelle. I guess you always surprise us," her mother said. She came over and sat down on the bench next to her.

"Mom," she said, her voice cracking.

"What, dear?"

"I'm going to have a baby."

Her mom said nothing. Her mouth opened slightly, but she couldn't speak.

"Praise God," her father said, his voice hoarse. "Michelle, we've been praying for this day. And Anthony's poor baby is welcome in our house."

Michelle thought about clueing him in, but decided this was not the moment. It had eaten up her courage just to tell them she was pregnant. She needed time to build another brave face.

They sat there, too embarrassed to say what they were feeling for a minute or two. Her dad, still standing, was holding her mom's hand. Nobody was holding Michelle's hand, so she put it on her stomach.

Jeffrey Riesner's receptionist had a neat pageboy. She wore a sailor-style dress, complete with a long, white tie in front that was a little young for anybody to wear, but had the effect of making her look friendly yet formal. She was the same age as Michelle. Michelle looked down at herself, at her fuchsia socks and shorts, and thought she needed to go shopping. Now there was one thing she could do in Fresno.

Her feet sank into the rug as she entered Riesner's sanctum. She took care to duck the blast of arctic air-conditioning guarding the doorway. Riesner stood behind a wide desk in the middle of the office, surrounded by blue Japanese urns, Chinese curio cabinets, and African statues. She could have sworn his receptionist bowed slightly before she disappeared.

She recognized him right away. She knew him already, from Prize's. He used to come in on Tuesday afternoons to play high-stakes poker with three friends. A Jack Daniel's on the rocks man. As far as she recalled, he never drank much or lost much.

He recognized her too. A grin showed gums in his mouth. "I didn't know Michelle Patterson was my favorite barmaid," he said. "You look different without the black satin."

"I'm no different, just wearing more clothes."

She didn't like him. The decorator office told her he probably charged too much and she remembered how he looked at her at the club, that wolfish grin and those quick, groping hands. But she didn't have to like him. She was willing to listen; that's all she had promised.

He brought her a soda. She sat in an easy chair across from him. "What can I do for you?" he asked.

"My parents asked me to come, so I'm here."

"They consulted me about your situation. You understand I'm not your attorney, and I'm going to ask you to sign our form to that effect."

"I don't want to sign anything."

"Then I can't talk with you."

"Why not?"

"If you want me to help you, and it is perfectly within

your rights to consult me for a second opinion, you have to help me with this one little thing. Acknowledge on this form that I'm not your attorney on the murder charge."

She signed the form, but she didn't like the way he was pushing her around. He immediately said that he thought the district attorney could be approached again, that they didn't really want to try this case, that there was some sympathy out there. He said it would be a very bad idea to go to trial, as he didn't think she had much of a defense. He said in eighteen years of practicing criminal law he had never seen a lawyer make a more preventable and prejudicial error than Nina Reilly had, having her hypnotized under the circumstances. He said it wouldn't be easy, but he thought he could persuade the DA's office to reinstate the original offer of voluntary manslaughter. There would be a twenty-five-thousand-dollar initial retainer, plus costs.

She listened to everything he said, sipping her soda.

"Did you talk with Nina . . . my attorney, about this?" she said.

"Your parents asked that I wait, for now. They wanted to keep my opinion confidential, until a decision was made, and I respected that."

"Is that the way it is usually done?"

He didn't answer. They sat there. She could see the dirt ski trails at Heavenly out his window. She liked Nina's view of the lake better.

"Loyalty is all very well," Riesner said finally, "but you have to look out for yourself. Your lawyer is going to defend you right into the penitentiary."

"One thing I'm curious about, Mr. Riesner, is, how do you know all these things about my case? And why are you so interested?"

"The details I've just mentioned to you are all over town," Riesner said. "I hear things at the courthouse, at lunch, playing poker. I heard some things from your parents. Have I said anything inaccurate?"

"Not exactly."

"Why am I interested? Because I hate to see a case like this mishandled, Misty—"

"Michelle."

"It reflects badly on the criminal lawyers up here who are doing a good job for their clients."

"The thing is, I want a trial," Michelle said. "We're still investigating. I know how it sounds, when I told Dr. Cervenka under hypnosis I killed Anthony—"

"Precisely. I know half the cops in Tahoe. I know you confessed. That's just my point. Nina Reilly is gonna let you do anything you want. It doesn't matter that you don't know how dangerous it is. It doesn't matter that you're gonna get crushed by Collier Hallowell in a trial. All that matters to her is to grandstand, pick up some publicity, pick up some new clients—"

"You're wrong. She cares about what happens to me," Michelle said. "You don't."

"I know I won't be the only one to remind you what's at stake," Riesner said. "This isn't a decision to make based on how you feel about somebody. You like her, she's nice to you, she makes you feel good. So invite her over to dinner. But I'd be goddamned before I'd hire her to defend me on a murder charge."

Michelle got up to leave. "I'm not you," she said, unable to think of anything better.

"If you ever figure out which end is up, call me."

Out in the parking lot, Michelle moved her suitcases from the backseat into the trunk of the car, dawdling, not quite ready to drive away. Jeffrey Riesner made perfect sense, from a logical point of view. If the world really had been a logical place, she would have hired him. He could probably get the deal back, just like he said.

But what could you trust if you couldn't trust the way you felt about someone?

First off, if she hired Riesner, the baby would definitely be born in prison.

Second, it didn't matter what she'd said to Dr. Cervenka. She was mixed-up inside. She didn't believe herself. Period.

Third. Nina listened to her, and Jeffrey Riesner would not.

Okay, following her feelings had gotten her in trouble before, mostly with men, but Dr. Greenspan used to say that if you went down deep enough, that's where you could find the truth, and down to gut level she trusted Nina Reilly. Nina made a mistake and she would fix it somehow.

Wishing she could afford to skip her next chore, she drove off to Prize's to pick up her paycheck.

She didn't want to make the rounds and say good-bye, but she couldn't avoid it. She had to walk through the casino to get to the bookkeeping office. She hadn't been back since her arrest, but people all seemed happy to see her, and said encouraging things as she cleared out her locker. She couldn't help wondering what they would say when she was gone.

She passed the gift shop on her way out, the very same gift shop where she had picked out the polar bear a lifetime ago, a little gift from Steve, and far too expensive for her to explain to Anthony. She had told him it was a cheap imitation, and he believed it because he avoided shopping and didn't know better. She had lied to him about everything, hadn't she? While she was caught in the web of that thought, Steve Rossmoor came hurrying up, carrying a huge bouquet of flowers.

"I didn't want to miss you," he said. "I asked the clerk to give me a buzz if you came in."

"Well, here I am."

"Look, after we talked on the phone, and you couldn't see me, you said you would call You didn't return my calls to your lawyer; you left your house. . . . I've been worried. Oh. For you."

She took the bundle of flowers, all you could hold, purchased from the florist kiosk three doors down the hallway. "Thank you," she said. He took her elbow and steered her into the ice-cream parlor just past the gift shop.

"How about a cup of coffee?"

"Actually, a dish of strawberry ice cream sounds good."

He ordered two dishes. Then he tilted his head to the side, regarding her. "You're as lovely as always, but different," he said.

"I'm not blitzed," Michelle said. "And I've got my clothes on."

"I could say the same," Steve said. "How have you been?"

She shook her head. "Don't get me started. But I am glad you caught me before I left for Fresno. I wanted to say something to you, but I didn't know how, and there was so much else going on. . . ."

"Well, let's just eat ice cream, and maybe it'll come out naturally."

After a few bites, Michelle said, "I think what I want to say first is, I apologize."

"For what?"

"For being so afraid of you I slept with you so I wouldn't have to talk to you."

Steve Rossmoor sat back and looked at her.

"It's a bad habit of mine. I know you tried to make friends with me, but I couldn't understand why you would want to. So I—what's the word?—deflected you."

"I certainly enjoyed being deflected, if that's what it was. And it didn't work, because I still would like to know you better."

"Why?"

He took her hand in his. "Now you put me on the spot. I'll sound incredibly stupid, but let me just try to answer that question. Okay. Because I got hooked on watching you through the security mirrors. I liked watching you walk, and talk, and smile when you collected your tips. I got to meet you, and I liked your soft voice and the things you said. I got you into my bed, and we were good together, and I knew there was more, a lot more, inside your head I needed to find out about. And then all hell broke loose for you."

"Oh," Michelle said.

"And now you're leaving for Fresno. I have the worst timing in the world."

"Don't you feel a little bit worried about getting to know a girl who—"

"Not a bit. You forget, I knew Anthony. I watched him watching you, nights you were on shift together. I know things about Anthony you don't know. Someday you can tell me how you ever had the misfortune to marry him."

"That's not what I mean. I'm probably going to prison!"

He didn't seem to have an answer for that one.

Michelle looked at the young man opposite her at the rickety little iron table, licking his spoon.

"Steve . . ."

"Mmm-hmmm."

"Did you tell anyone I was going to San Francisco, that day we talked?"

"Of course not. Why?"

"Never mind. I guess I better tell you something."

"Anything."

"I'm going to have a baby. It's possible—"

But he was already rushing around the table. He pulled her up against him, her head against his chest, his heart beating fast. "Yes . . . it's possible you are the father," she finished breathlessly. He just held on to her, as though he would fall down himself if she were not now propping him up.

"How possible?" he said in a strangled voice.

"It could have been Anthony. Or one other guy. Or you."

"You weren't going to tell me?"

"It's so complicated. I really don't know what to say about it right now. We're sitting here eating ice cream and talking about making friends and then it's bombs away. Now we can't just be friends, can we?"

"I'm floored," Steve said. He loosened his hold on her, but touched her shoulders gently at arm's length.

"What if the baby isn't yours, for instance? Do you still want to get to know me better?" Michelle said. She looked searchingly into his eyes, and saw in them something she didn't understand, something dark. "I'm going to keep the baby," she went on.

"Don't go," he said. "Stay here with me. If you're sentenced to prison, we'll fly away somewhere and live happily ever after."

"My prince," she said, making fun of him, but liking what he had said. "Thanks. Really, thanks. But I have to go."

"Then let me see you in Fresno this weekend."

"Maybe. Here's my number and the address."

He walked her out to her car. Before he would let her shut the door, he picked up her hand and lowered his head and she felt his lips pressing against her palm. Then he closed her hand on the kiss and said, "Don't forget to wear your seat belt." She set the flowers on the passenger seat and headed for Fresno, watching Steve Rossmoor standing in the parking lot in the rearview mirror, looking like any man in a really expensive suit, a man used to getting his own way.

The Superior Court of the County of El Dorado, Tahoe Session, Curtis E. Milne presiding, heard law and motion on Monday morning, June 11, at 8:30 A.M. Collier Hallowell's hair was still wet from the shower.

"Motion to Suppress Tape Recording and for Disclosure of Confidential Informant," the judge said. He scanned papers as he spoke, peering down through reading glasses perched on his nose. He had the classic build of male judges; huge, leonine head, heavy brow ridge, puny body under the robes. Having already disposed of six other matters, he spoke to an almost empty courtroom. "People versus Michelle Tengstedt Patterson. I will hear the Motion to Suppress first."

"Nina Reilly, counsel for defendant. Good morning, Your Honor. We are relying on our declarations and we do not request an in camera evidentiary hearing. It is our understanding that the Court and both sides have heard the tape in question."

"Yes. You may proceed," Milne said calmly.

"As the Court can see from the declarations of Dr. Bruno Cervenka and myself, Dr. Cervenka was retained by me in a consulting capacity."

Milne broke in almost immediately. "No privilege there, Ms. Reilly. The work-product privilege clearly doesn't apply. The tape is evidence. Frankly, I see no basis for excluding the purported confession of your client. Your consultant ended up treating her. It's obvious from the People's Points and Authorities the session went beyond an examination. There's no question the evidence sought to be excluded is relevant. It's a confession. There's no question, despite the legal arguments attached to your Motion to Suppress, that the evidence falls within a well-recognized exception to the attorney work-product privilege. Anything else?"

"The psychotherapist-patient privilege also requires confidentiality. As stated in our brief—"

"Make up your mind, Ms. Reilly. Was Dr. Cervenka acting in a consulting capacity, or was he acting as a therapist?"

"For purposes of this particular argument he was a therapist," Nina said, not showing her anger. Judge Milne knew she had the right to argue in the alternative, to make arguments that were inconsistent.

"So he's a therapist now. What do you have to say about Mr. Hallowell's well-taken point that there will be no such privilege if you put your client's mental state in issue?"

"We haven't done that yet, Your Honor."

"Well, are you going to?"

Nina maintained her usual pleasant face. "As the Court knows, I am not required to reveal my entire trial strategy to Mr. Hallowell at this time."

Milne apparently decided not to bait her anymore.

"All right. Let's talk about the attorney-client privilege argument. You seem to be saying that Dr. Cervenka was merely a kind of translator for you. He elicited for you the language of the heart, so to speak, that the defendant could speak only while hypnotized."

"That's right. My client wasn't consciously aware at the time. I wasn't competent to access her buried memories. I turned to a psychiatrist. But the information was intended as a communication to me, for purposes of preparing the criminal defense."

"Mr. Hallowell?" Milne said, finally giving her a moment to breathe.

"It's simple," Collier said. He had been listening attentively. "You can make all the convoluted arguments you want, Judge, but that tape is evidence. The prosecution can't be foreclosed from using it if counsel for the defense tries to explain why the defendant struck her husband and claims not to remember what happened next. We all agree Dr. Cervenka was trying to help the defendant remember some things. He wasn't a translator, he was a therapist helping a patient. It wasn't a communication, it was a therapy session."

Nina said evenly, "I hired Dr. Cervenka. I set up the meeting. I drove the defendant to the meeting. Attorney-client privilege, Your Honor."

"Converted into a therapeutic session, Judge," Collier said.

"We're starting to repeat ourselves," Judge Milne said, turning his head to the calendar tacked to the wall. "I'll take it under submission. I'll try to let you know within ten days. I see we need to set a trial date. Shall we take care of that today? September twenty-fourth? Ms. Reilly?"

"Fine, Your Honor."

"Mr. Hallowell?"

"Okay by me."

"Anything else?"

"The defense requests that the Court order the district attorney's office to reveal the source of its information leading to seizure of the tape."

Hallowell said, "Excuse me, Your Honor."

"Go ahead."

"The district attorney's office has promised to keep the name of the person providing this information confidential. That person's identity is of no relevance to the question of whether the confession should come in."

"We need to know who is so interested in getting the defendant convicted, Your Honor. The defense contends the confession under hypnosis is completely unreliable as evidence. The plea is not guilty. That information might lead to important admissible evidence," Nina said.

"I'm afraid the word *might* is the operative word in your argument, Counselor. Conjecture and speculation of this sort is not sufficient to persuade me that I must compel the deputy district attorney to disclose his source. The motion that the prosecution divulge its source of information is denied. Anything further?"

"Nothing further, Your Honor. Thank you, Your Honor," Nina said. Up yours, Your Honor, she added to herself.

The clerks gathered up their papers and the lawyers filed out. Nina hoped Collier was just as puzzled as she was as to how the judge would rule on her Motion to Suppress.

Jack called that night, late.

At first, they discussed the case, a neutral enough topic, Nina thought, wrongly. When it became clear that he had far too much advice and criticism for her to accept, she clammed up. He invited Bobby for a week, and she readily assented. And finally, when he couldn't stand it any longer, he asked her when she would be returning the divorce papers.

"We're not going to talk about it, are we, Jack? I don't know if I can stand to have it end this way. You won't even let me apologize."

"Don't apologize, Nina."

"There isn't any hope for us, is there? I can't believe I make one mistake, even a big *wow* of a mistake, and that's the end of Nina and Jack." She was as unsure of her feelings as ever, but the thought that Jack wasn't calling in the hopes of mending fences made her frantic.

"It isn't that simple. It isn't all your fault."

His words hung there. In the silence that followed, she

allowed her mind to drift back to that wet March, all the fights about his long hours, and her terrible loneliness of spirit.

"It's not all my fault." She said it the way he had said it, in a bald statement. She needed to buy herself some time to react to words that held such unpleasant promise. "Are you planning to expand on that?" she asked when his silence became painful, and her initial shock at his meaning had finished its assault on her.

"I admit I haven't been a very good husband. I loved you, Nina. You should know that." He laughed nervously. "I can't think of anything to say that doesn't have a hackneyed ring to it."

However he said it, she knew she didn't want to hear what was coming. "You want me to make it easy on you, don't you, Jack? Maybe that's my biggest fault. I made it easy. Now are you going to tell me who she is, or just keep me in suspense?"

"Are you sure you want to hear this?"

She thought. She assumed the name would be familiar, some mutual acquaintance. Better to face the whole story now, instead of constructing a fantasy that might be more bitter than the truth.

"First I want to know, how long? How long before you left?" she said.

"About a year. I hated lying to you, Nina. I still wanted to be with you. I couldn't make a decision."

She drew a deep breath. Would it be Francie, her friend, whom she had trusted? Or someone else she had eaten lunch with, gone to the movies with, some friend? "Yeah, I want to know, Jack."

"Evanelle Cherry."

Ms. Cherry! She started laughing, quickly revising her picture of Jack's lawyer. "Let me guess. Age around twenty-nine. The totally successful woman. Victoria's Secret lingerie. An uncle at city hall. How practical of you to pick another divorce lawyer."

"Come on, Nina, we're all pros. You don't have any problem with the settlement, do you? Please don't hold it up. Eva and I want to get married. Soon. Why are you laughing?"

"I keep thinking you're one of my clients, or I'm talking to opposing counsel just before the hearing, and Ms. Cherry is a fellow woman lawyer, my husband's mistress, and definitely opposing counsel. You talk to me like your colleague, not your wife. This is all bathos, not pathos. Lawyers in love. What a contradiction in terms."

"It was hard, seeing you like that with someone else," Jack said.

"What? Did I hear something real just then, rising out of the dump of BS that constitutes Jack McIntyre?"

"You're hurt, Nina," Jack said, "but don't get like that. It doesn't get us anywhere. I don't want an argument."

"I don't care what you want," Nina said. "Bobby wants to see you, so he can go see you. As for the settlement agreement, I'll have my counsel review it and get back to you some month."

"I'll take you to court if you try delaying tactics," Jack said.

"You'd better consult with your lawyer first," Nina said. "You could try a Motion to Bifurcate Marital Status from Property Issues. San Francisco County's running about four months behind for setting those hearings. See you in October."

"I never thought of you as vindictive, Nina," Jack said. "What's the point? It's all over now."

"You let me wallow in guilt all these months, Jack. Your turn to cry." She hung up slowly.

Finally she knew what she'd seen in him that day at the

condo when he found her with the plumber, had seen but had not understood. It was relief she had seen on his face, relief at having an easy out. He was that shambler Mr. Hyde, faking Dr. Jekyll, all along.

So in their last conversation as husband and wife, she had lied. She had signed the agreement and put it in the mail yesterday.

Wasn't it Nietzsche who said no one was such a liar as the indignant woman? Let him sweat tonight. She only wished it was for longer.

19

JULY CAME, BRINGING with it a plague of tourists. Judge Milne had left for a holiday in Barbados with his wife, his mother, his two grown children, and their families. His clerk was sure that as soon as he came back he would get right to his decision on the motion.

Michelle called regularly from Fresno. She was working in her father's car dealership. The district attorney's office had made no move to revoke bail. Nina believed it must be because Collier was fully aware that a first-degree murder conviction was unlikely.

Nina had turned to her Theory Two, the idea that someone else had killed Anthony. Paul had been looking for motives and methods. He had sent workups on Frederick and Ericka Greenspan, Tom and Janine Clarke, Al and Sharon Otis, Peter La Russa, Stephen Rossmoor, and the Tengstedts: alibis for the evening of April 26 and early morning of the 27th, swimming abilities, Harley-Davidson affiliations, familiarity with boats, past brushes with authority, tax problems, family complexities.

The material was fascinating, though mostly old or irrelevant. Janine Clarke had tried out for the Olympics in the 200-meter butterfly ten years before. Sharon Otis belonged to a Reno Harley Club, was a known drug dealer, and had done time in the Nevada state prison system. Tom Clarke had lied on his résumé; he had been fired from his previous position as assistant principal of an elementary school in southern California. Steve Rossmoor owned both a catamaran and a water-ski boat, and his father owned a number of brownstones on Riverside Drive in New York City. The IRS had recorded a lien against Peter La Russa's home, and his wife was about to leave him.

Information on the Tengstedts remained scanty. Sandy had written again to her Aunt Alice at Subic.

No one had a perfect alibi.

Paul's report on Anthony Patterson was the most surprising. Originally from Philadelphia, Anthony had been born illegitimate to an Italian girl who later married a butcher. She never told him the name of his real father. His mother and stepfather were dead, killed in a car accident when he was sixteen. His half sister had been paralyzed from the waist down in the same accident. Anthony had sent her money every month. Nina supposed the wreath at his funeral must have come from her.

He had drifted around after high school, eventually hitchhiking to California and a job parking cars at a Fresno garage. He lived with an aunt in Fresno, as Michelle had mentioned. At the age of twenty he applied to the police academy. By all accounts he had been a model police officer for two years. Paul had an old friend from the SFPD who had transferred to Fresno. He checked around on Carl Tengstedt's statement that while in Fresno, Anthony had been involved in strong-arming and extortion.

According to Paul's friend, Anthony had once been an honest cop. He had been cleared of serious charges made against him by a local appliance-store owner with a grudge. But after that he had known there would be no more promotions. He had gotten lazy and began taking shortcuts and got caught and reprimanded several times. After a final, larger-scale event a few years back, he had quit under duress, moving on to Tahoe and Prize's, taking Michelle with him.

Had he become bitter? Cynical? Had he felt like a failure? He hadn't confided much in Michelle. Had he talked to his ex-wife, Sharon Otis? Nina decided to set up a time to see Sharon when she couldn't slip away and let Al handle the questions. The silver Harley pin was Sharon's. Maybe those had been her footsteps in the snow.

Just after the Fourth of July holiday, Nina put Bobby on Amtrak at the rail station in Truckee, on the north side of the lake.

"Can I call you anytime I want, Mom?" he asked as they unloaded his backpack and luggage.

"Of course you can, honey pie."

"Are you mad that I want to go back to San Francisco and see my friends?"

She knew what he wanted to know. Was she mad that he wanted to see Jack? "Of course not. Now that summer's here, you can get Jack to take you to the Exploratorium and the park. I want you to have a great time and write me some letters too."

"It feels funny to be going back."

She didn't know what that felt like. She could not go back.

He was so thrilled to be going to San Francisco and so agonized about leaving her behind, he burst into tears just as the train pulled out of the station, so her last sight of him was a tear-stained face pressed forlornly to the Amtrak window. She was glad to see him whisked away before her own eyes blurred.

A hot mountain sun beat down. A crafts fair was in progress in the Old West part of downtown, the storefronts decked with flags, vacationers thronging the sidewalks. Nina strolled around, wishing she hadn't allowed the trip, already feeling lost without him. Bobby was her bedrock, her purpose. Why had she let him go?

Bobby had wanted to see Jack. She loved her son, so she had let him. What bothered her was the feeling that when he came back he would be that much older, that much more experienced. He was not such a little boy anymore. He was ready to cross a line, a line she wished she could keep him from crossing.

Someone was watching her from across the street. A chill went up her spine. She stopped dead and looked directly back at him.

He was wearing Bermuda shorts and a baseball cap. When he saw her looking back, he doffed his cap and smiled, and started across the street toward her. Now she could see through the sea of traffic that his shoulders were peeling and he was carrying a shopping bag.

It was a pickup, not a murder attempt. Relax, Nina! she said to herself angrily, ducking into a nearby clothes shop to escape her harmless admirer.

Stephen Rossmoor came to the office the following week. Paul had described him, but Nina wasn't prepared for the deep tan, the white teeth, or his youth. He was supposed to be about thirty-four but the male-model looks were deceiving. He seemed abstracted, and neglected to turn on the charm Paul had encountered. He refused her offer of a chair and Sandy's offer of a soft drink, and stood there in front of her desk, so her eyes were even with the gold belt buckle she suspected was real.

"I need your help," he said without preliminaries. "I'm worried about Michelle."

"You understand I can't talk about her case with you?" Nina said.

"Whatever the rules are. We have to talk."

The lawyer waited.

"I've been seeing her down in Fresno. I've asked her to take a DNA test so I can find out if I'm the father. She won't do it."

So Michelle was seeing Rossmoor again? She shouldn't. She had told him about the trip to San Francisco. What if he was the driver of the car at Twin Bridges? Nina would call Michelle as soon as Rossmoor left.

Ask him. Watch his reactions.

"She shouldn't be seeing you. Only two people knew Michelle and I were going to San Francisco last month. Someone ran us off the road. You were one of the people who knew."

He looked shocked, then hurt as the meaning of what she had said sank in. "You think I . . . But why?"

"Patterson knew too much about club operations. You couldn't just fire him for the scam with Al Otis. You had to get rid of him another way. And Michelle was a scapegoat, but now she's fighting the charges, and you're afraid we will learn too much about you and the club."

"Paranoid fantasy," Rossmoor said. He was angry. He looked ready to walk out.

"You were making love to her. You came to the house in the Keys. You saw Patterson get off the couch and you figured he was going to hurt her. You came in while she was in the kitchen and—"

"That's a little more plausible, but still untrue," Rossmoor said. "It's much more likely Michelle killed him and is blotting it out. And I don't care if she did."

"If you want some help from me, convince me that I'm wrong," Nina said.

"I'm in love with her!" Rossmoor burst out. "Please, don't poison her against me. I understand you can't trust anyone, but don't destroy what is happening between her and me." Now he did sit down, as though his legs had decided not to hold him up any longer.

"You want a DNA test. What happens if she agrees and the baby isn't yours?"

"Doesn't matter," he said. "But, my God, wouldn't you want to know?"

"Not necessarily." There were many reasons for Michelle to decide the baby's father should not be known.

"Ms. Reilly, you have very great influence in Michelle's life right now. You can choose not to believe me, and Michelle will probably not see me again. Please believe me. I mean you and Michelle no harm. I didn't tell anyone about your trip."

"I'll give it some thought," Nina said. "Tell me about Peter La Russa."

Rossmoor seemed confused by her sudden change of subject. "I'm not sure—"

"I heard he was fired."

"He was fired. He retained an attorney in Carson City. We're talking. We don't want publicity about the card counting. We were supposed to report it. We didn't."

"That's of no interest to me," Nina said. "What I want to know is, did he kill Anthony Patterson? Did he receive his share of the profits? He needed the money."

"I know he needed money. I know he was involved. I'll try to check further for you," Rossmoor said.

"You do that," Nina said. "I'm going to let Michelle make up her own mind about you. But if anything happens to her, anything close to you, I'll find you and I'll nail you, Mr. Rossmoor."

"Fair enough," Rossmoor said. "But I ask you to remember this: If you make any more stupid mistakes in Michelle's criminal defense, I'm going to see to it that she retains an outstanding and experienced criminal counsel, and you are going to be finished in this town."

Then he walked out.

Nina didn't have to call Anthony's ex-wife to set up an appointment. Sharon Otis herself called the office and spoke with Sandy about a time she could meet Nina in Reno.

"Did she say why?" Nina asked Sandy when she saw the appointment in her book.

"She said she wanted to make a deal with you," Sandy said. "No details."

"All right. Don't plan on seeing me tomorrow."

Nina drove her new Bronco. She wished Paul were with her, just to have a reassuring figure next to her on the seat. She kept looking through her rearview mirror, checking out the cars. At one point, going over Spooner Pass, she was sure she was being followed. An old blue Chevy stayed a couple of cars behind all the way down the mountain, through Carson City and into Reno. But she lost sight of it in the city traffic.

Paranoid fantasy? She looked over her shoulder all the time now.

Sharon Otis Honda sat on a good commercial corner on South Virginia, between two auto dealers and not far from the University of Nevada campus, providing an alternative to cars for people who fancied themselves invulnerable to the high desert heat and snow. Instead of neat rows of Preludes and Accords, the cement drive was filled with motorcycles, Hondas, Kawasakis, and a few Harleys.

In back by the offices, her sales force, all young men, patrolled the lot. Sharon apparently liked her employees beefy and long-haired. Two of them turned to watch Nina work her way past the bikes. She had an impression as she hurried along of piranhas massing for a strike, but no one caught up with her by the time she turned into the main office.

She wasn't sure why she was there, or what Al's wife could possibly say that would change the depressing facts.

Sharon Otis opened the door. Her fringed black leather jacket had seen some action, and her hair was big. Under the hair her face was small, hard, and thin, her eyes encircled in black. Lines around her eyes put her at about forty, with some tough years behind her. She went around a utilitarian desk and sat down, her hands behind her head, clearly the boss. "Take a load off," she said.

A metal folding chair sat in front of the desk. Nina took it, noting no shelves, just a big table covered with paperwork, a phone, and a computer. A fifties' table radio played Garth Brooks. Posters of brightly chromed motorcycles and a rather frightening rear view of a male Italian bodybuilder in a G-string decorated the dingy wall. A job ad for a motorcycle salesperson was Scotch-taped to the desk. LONG HOURS, LOW PAY, MEAN BOSS said the ad.

"So you're Misty's lawyer. I hate lawyers."

"Then why am I here?"

"I have something to tell you, maybe. Want some coffee?"

The coffeemaker on the desk showed a half cup of what might have been coffee yesterday. "No, thanks. Let's get on with it."

Sharon Otis's line buzzed. "No. Tell him he has to put five hundred down or get a cosigner. Best we can do. Don't pass me any calls for a while, okay, Gene?" She talked, waving her hands, while Nina stared in horrified fascination at the woman's nails, an inch long, deep red, weapons of war.

"So, okay, here it is, Counselor. You met Al. He's a babe in the woods, a genius at cards and no damn good at anything else. He told you about the setup at Prize's. You gave him the report; so, okay, he can't go there anymore. But they're coming after him now. The Nevada Gaming Commission paid us a visit yesterday. La Russa went to them with his story. I guess Prize's didn't offer enough to shut him up. Anyway, they want Al to talk about La Russa and Anthony. That could be dangerous to his health, you know what I'm sayin'? The clubs already hate him. Add a fink reputation and he won't be safe anywhere."

She reached for a cigarette, which she stuck unlit between her lips. "These state guys are leaning hard on him. They're telling him, either he helps nail Prize's or they arrest him for conspiracy."

"He ought to move on, to the Bahamas or something, if he wants to play blackjack," Nina said. "Everybody knows him now anyway."

"He really likes it here. Can you believe it? That tin can we live in. He's quitting. He's retiring. He's got enough socked away and he's fifty-five, he wants to write up his memoirs. But first he has to get rid of this hassle." She inserted a nail into her hair and scratched thoughtfully. "We figure you could handle it. Get the point across to the State of Nevada that Al can't help and they should leave him alone."

Sharon the loyal wife? Nina could go along with that, but she had a feeling Sharon Otis wanted more.

"Is that Al's only legal problem?" she asked.

"Al? Yeah, he's clean otherwise. But I have a problem or two."

"And you want me to represent you too?"

"Lawyers cost a lot. I don't want Al to find out about all my business. He doesn't need the stress. He has high blood pressure. You help me out, I'll fix you on your case."

"What kind of problems are we talking about?"

"Some grand larceny, some drugs. Major bad guys are mad at me right now. So, are you in?"

"I'm thinking. While I'm thinking, tell me about your marriage to Anthony," Nina said.

"Married to him for about six months in Fresno eight years ago. He was a hot-blooded dude, no mistake, cop to the max. Left him first time he laid a hand on me. Don't get me wrong, he never had a chance to beat me. But you know, we had a lot in common." She laughed. "That's why we got married. And that's how we got involved later. 'Cause he worked at Prize's and I knew he'd go for a deal."

"How long have you been married to Al?" Nina said.

"Two years," Sharon Otis said. "I sold a little meth about five years ago. In Nevada, that means a year in the women's pen. A very bad year. Al picked me up hustlin' downtown at the Glass Slipper. He took me back to the trailer and I've been there ever since. He set me up here and gave me a half interest in the business. He gives me space, he doesn't give a damn when I ride my new bike with the club. . . ."

"Your new Harley?"

"Business is good," Sharon said, tapping the cigarette on the desk.

"You ride one," Nina said, "but you don't wear the wings."

Sharon looked down at her jacket. "Oh, you mean my pretty silver Harley wings. Al told me you had them."

"In a police evidence storage locker at South Lake Tahoe. Found right outside the bedroom at Anthony's house. When were you there?"

"The answer to that question is your retainer when you agree to represent Al and me, Counselor." Sharon smiled. Red lips, a flash of gold in her mouth. A real rough rider.

"Let me make sure I understand. You want me to perform legal services for you, and in exchange, you will give me some information that you say will help my client. Look, Ms. Otis—"

"Missus," Sharon Otis said. "It'll pop the DA's case like a bullet in a bald tire."

"You need a Nevada attorney. I only have a California license. I don't know the Nevada gaming or criminal laws. It's not that I don't want to help, it's a question of competence."

"Okay, you bring in the Nevada mouthpiece and cover the cost, make sure he handles it right."

"I can't pay you for providing information. It would make your information valueless, and it would violate legal ethics."

"Far be it . . ." was all Sharon Otis said. "But I really have no particular reason to tell you anything, otherwise. This may surprise you, but no matter what your client has told you, Anthony was a good guy. He'd had a rocky life, like me, took it in the gut a few times. When he met Misty, he still had it in him to love her, deep, deeper than I'll ever get. And she took away every shred of dignity he had left. Pisses me off. I ain't helpin' her for nothin'."

"Maybe you don't know nothin'," Nina said.

"Maybe you're full of it," Sharon said. "Let me try again with you. Maybe I went to see my ex-husband while little Misty was at work. Maybe we talked money and a few other things. Maybe Misty came home and walked through the front door while I was moving out the back. Maybe I stuck around and saw something very, very interesting. Something that will clear the little brat, not that she deserves my help."

She shrugged. "You're not the only one I've talked to. But I'd rather give you the exclusive, 'cause you can do more for me." The phone buzzed again. She ignored it. "So you better decide quick, Counselor."

"I advise you to tell me now. Obstruction of justice is a crime."

"Listen, you want me to help you, you help us. I only do favors when I get favors in return." She finally lit the cigarette. She leaned her head back and opened her mouth with an odd little pop. Out floated a series of perfect smoke rings. Nina didn't know anyone could do that anymore.

"Mrs. Otis, it's dangerous to withhold information about a crime," Nina said.

"Ooh, you're scarin' me. Call me when you decide." Sharon got up, giving Nina her card, trailing the odor of hair spray and smoke through the room. She picked up a gold-glittered, lacquered helmet off the table with the name *Sharon* emblazoned in flame lettering on the way out. When she saw Nina looking at it, she tucked her hair underneath, saying, "I've been in trouble too much to get picked up in California for some jack-shit violation of the helmet laws."

"Tell Gene to lock up, baby cakes," she sang to a salesman as they walked out to the bikes, then she swung up into the saddle of a black-and-purple Harley Sportster. She pulled goggles out of the saddlebag, kicked the kick-starter a few times, and the machine roared to life. "Take it easy, Counselor," she called to Nina, working the throttle a little. She gunned it and roared out the driveway, then quickly pulled over a few feet down the street.

"Hey! Counselor! C'mere!"

Nina walked over, admiring her style, the way her slim legs straddled the bike, the wrist tattoo, the way she acted like she owned the road. The traffic whizzed by the Harley at the curb. Sharon seemed to pay no attention. "I'll give you a clue, so you know I'm not kidding," she said, still working the throttle. "Check the brand of ciggies in Anthony's pocket, if you can. Virginia Slims. He had to borrow mine."

Nina knew it was no accident, because she was turning back toward the lot and saw the car hurtling up the road, veering toward the sidewalk and the Harley and the two of them, speeding up even more as she dove for cover into the bushes, crashing with terrific force into the Harley from behind.

Time stopped after the crash, and the small figure in the gold helmet flew up and slammed into another moving car. Even on hands and knees from the bushes Nina could see the blood leaking out of the helmet as Sharon Otis slid slowly to the curb. Then Nina was scrambling, shouting, and a crowd was gathering. The car backed away from the bike and tore off, its muddy license plate illegible.

An old Chevy with fins. Was it the one that had been behind her? Sharon Otis lay bleeding in the road, her shiny Harley a few feet away as spattered and torn as she was, spectators blocking out her blue sky, one praying, a lone child crying. She died before the ambulance shrieked around the corner.

20

❦

AT FOUR O'CLOCK on the day after Sharon Otis's death, Nina found Collier Hallowell chatting with the county clerks in their big second-floor office across from Judge Milne's courtroom. "Could we talk in the law library?" Nina asked. Piling a load of papers into his arms, he followed her next door. In the small library, empty except for them, they looked out the windows toward the new community college campus across Al Tahoe and the cumulating clouds.

The room's incandescents glowed in a feeble protection against swiftly descending blackness. Windowpanes rattled and trees writhed in the gale winds outside. Nina was tired. Her night had been haunted by the small figure in the golden helmet slamming with bone-crunching force into the car windshield, over and over. "Sharon Otis," she said. "She was murdered."

"Go ahead," Collier replied. His thoughtful face showed the strains of the day. He had already spent several hours at his desk, she knew, lining up witnesses, and several hours in court, and he had probably missed lunch.

"Do you know who I'm talking about?"

"Sharon Otis," Collier said. "Hit and run during rush hour last night on Reno's busiest boulevard. Anthony Patterson's ex-wife, ex-inmate at Carson City Women's Correctional Center, ex-hooker and meth addict, wife of a card sharp, suspected current meth dealer. . . . Yeah, I know."

"I saw it," Nina said.

"I heard. Was it bad?"

"I had just finished talking to her. She was going to provide me with important exculpatory evidence in the Patterson case. She told me she was at the Keys place and saw something. We were standing together at the curb. I saw the car coming, but she couldn't see behind her. She never had a chance. I told the Reno police everything."

"What did she see?"

"I don't know. She insisted I do some legal work or pay her off before she would tell me."

"She said specifically she was there?"

"She said maybe she was there. She played with me."

"Why would she be there?"

"I can't go into any details of the defense that you don't have to know now," Nina said. "You understand my position."

"Well, but you have to understand mine, too, Nina. Think about it. Sharon Otis had plenty of enemies. Hard-driving boss who cut deals off the back of her bike."

"She was Patterson's ex-wife. She was still friendly with him. They did some business together."

"If she was killed so she wouldn't tell you something," Collier went on inexorably, "why was she killed *after* she talked to you, not before?"

"Maybe the car was aimed at me, not her."

"I see."

"It could have been the same car that pushed me off the road with my client in May."

"Can you swear it was the same car?"

Nina didn't answer.

Collier spread working hands with square fingers and calluses. "Suggestive, but I don't understand what you want from me."

"I want the name of the person that told you about Dr. Cervenka. I want protection for myself and Michelle Patterson. I want you to reopen the investigation."

The storm struck.

Collier's teeth gleamed in the flash of lightning, disappeared, and showed again as a second bolt slashed through the trees. All of Tahoe, whipped first by wind, now beaten by rain, ran for cover.

"Makes me feel small," he said loudly, his words fighting the thunder. "Scares me. I want to go home, batten down the hatches. This work I do, the files, the people, the whole thing, doesn't seem important when the sky is falling."

She understood what he felt perfectly. "We're so exposed up so high in the mountains," said Nina. Matt and Andrea would be scurrying to bring in the patio mats and settling the kids in front of a fire. She wished she could be there. She wished Bobby were back from Jack's. "The weather. The people. It's so raw." She turned to look at him. "How do you handle all the suffering you see?"

"Bad things happen, sometimes to people I've tried to protect. I lost a witness a year ago. I almost quit. Dangerous people stay out in the streets. Things happen that would tear me apart if I let them."

"By all accounts you're the best, Collier," she said.

"I'll call the Fresno police and ask them to watch out for your client, Nina. I'll send patrol cars by your office and home. Here's my home phone number. Call me if you need me, and I'll be there. But—"

"I won't make you promise everything will be all right. I know I have to look out for myself. Thanks."

"You could just drop the case, Nina. You could go back to appellate work, writing those fine briefs you write."

"Run scared, you mean," she said. "Believe me, I think about that whenever it's dark outside. At this point sometimes I wish I'd never met Michelle Patterson. But she depends on me. She needs me. She's so vulnerable. You know she's going to have a baby?"

He didn't say anything. He didn't have to.

"Collier. Tell me the name of your informant."

"I already checked," he said. "The informant was sixty miles away from Reno when Sharon Otis was killed. That information is reliable. You can trust me on this."

"But—"

He held up his hand. "Wait. We never know enough to protect ourselves completely. The person who told us about Dr. Cervenka, who you think might have attempted to enter your client's room at the Lucky Chip, who you think ran you off the road, is not the person who killed Sharon Otis. She could have been killed for some reason totally unrelated to this case. The same is true for all these events.

"Maybe Michelle Patterson's burglar was a late-night drunk who thought he was locked out of his room," he went on. "It happens. Maybe the car that ran you off the road was another jerk driver who went too far. You said in your report that the car behind you blinked its headlights. Assassin or road hog?"

Nina swallowed. Another flash cut through the clouds of rain.

"Or maybe you are right, you and your client are being pursued. Assume the worst, Nina. Take precautions."

Nina reached in her purse and took out the tape she had made during her conversation with Sharon Otis. "I'm going to go ahead and give you this, Collier. Listen to it. I want to persuade you to look at this case another way, to consider for a minute that Michelle is telling the truth."

"The investigation is open until trial. I'm always happy to learn additional facts that help us get closer to the truth. No offense, Nina, but you seem to be in a tough situation with your client confessing and yet not willing to take the only fair offer I can make. . . ."

"You know this isn't a first-degree murder case. Even if she's lying, there was no premeditation."

"Premeditation can occur in a very short period of time. She had time to take him out on a boat. She struck him a second time when he was probably helpless. She threw him overboard. She cleaned up the mess afterward, at home and on the boat."

"You know this is a voluntary manslaughter case. You know if she killed him, he drove her to it. But I don't think she did it."

"I'm sorry, Nina. We have the three factors listed in *People v. Anderson* that add up to premeditation." He listed them on his fingers. "*One:* Evidence of planning activity just prior to the homicide. *Two:* Motive to kill based on the prior relationship. *Three:* Manner of killing, from which it can be inferred that there was a preconceived design."

He fleshed out the threat of life in prison for Michelle Patterson.

"Think about the offer of a plea to second-degree murder, Nina."

"Not with somebody out there trying to end the case another way, Collier. And Judge Milne hasn't ruled on my motion to suppress the tape."

"He got back yesterday."

"And?"

The expression on his face said everything. She ran for the clerk's office and read through the single sheet of pink paper with fury.

Collier had won. If she put Michelle's mental state at issue in the trial, the confession would be allowed.

★   ★   ★

"We call that thing propped over by the door there an umbrella," said Sandy when Nina dripped into the office. "You might want to take it next time they tell us there's a one hundred percent chance of rain." Nina hung her jacket on the bentwood rack and sipped from hot coffee Sandy handed her. "Jeffrey Riesner is in the library. Chose not to wait in here."

Riesner stood up when she entered the room, but he didn't extend his hand. "I have coffee," he indicated. "And," he said, nodding his head toward the door behind which Sandy sat, "I wouldn't dare ask her, if I didn't. You can spare a couple of minutes before you go home, I take it?" No one waited in the waiting room, they both knew.

"A couple of minutes."

"You know that the Tengstedts consulted me about your case?" he said.

"Yes."

"Maybe you don't know that after I talked with Michelle, I was ready to file a complaint against you with the bar association."

"No. I didn't know that."

"The way you've handled this case . . . well, I probably don't need to go into the fact that mistakes have been made. The kind of mistakes you might expect of a rank beginner."

She waited, standing, arms folded.

"No. A beginner would have taken the original plea. That makes everything you've done even harder to buy. After I finished thinking about the hellish mistakes you've made, it occurred to me that it might help if I—"

"I don't need your help, Mr. Riesner."

"Wait a minute. Let me finish. Michelle is so . . . young. I would like some assurance that you're planning to proceed with more prudence than you've used so far."

"You are not working for the Tengstedts now, are you?"

He shook his head.

"You may disagree with the risks I've taken. My client doesn't." Since she didn't drop me for you, Nina didn't say.

His face reddened slightly.

"I'm confident I can defend my handling of the case, if necessary. When we go to trial—"

"Don't go to trial. I don't want to see you . . . your client crucified."

"Plead her out."

"Exactly."

"Look, nobody's willing to make any deals that are remotely favorable to my client at this time. Unless you have heard something different?" He said nothing. "You like to win, don't you?"

"Of course."

"So do I. I don't plan to lose."

"You don't plan," he amended. "You compel me to give you some information that I hoped would be unnecessary. My firm represents Dr. Frederick Greenspan. We have handled his legal work for some time. He is concerned that, in your flailing about for some distraction from your client's guilt, you will attempt to harm his reputation in the community."

"What does he think I'm going to do, accuse him of the crime?"

"Even you would hardly go that far. However, I think you would go so far as to suggest that he was somehow professionally negligent in his treatment, such that your client became unhinged. Even if that is not your idea, he is not going to become involved in some flimflam defense. If you subpoena him, one might assume his testimony will not be favorable."

"One might wonder what he is trying to cover up," Nina said.

"Dr. Greenspan has helped many people in the community over many years. He has a sterling reputation, unlike you. He won't be slandered by some fly-by-night. Before I came here, I asked around town about you. Since nobody knew much, I called San Francisco. Not Jack McIntyre. My friends in the City."

"You have friends?"

"You've never handled a felony trial on your own until this one. You're an appellate attorney. That's something I haven't given the press, yet. So before you gratuitously attack my client, do me the courtesy of thinking very carefully about alternatives that might serve you better at trial."

"I'll certainly remember what you've said. And now I'm sure you have better things to do," Nina said. "I know I do."

"Nice to see you working hard for a change, Sandy," Riesner said as he left the reception area. He didn't see the jutting finger with which she bade him adieu.

When he was gone, Nina flopped down into her office chair. Sandy came in and settled herself across the desk.

"A prick," she said. "Told you."

"We lost the motion, Sandy," Nina said.

"Too bad."

"We have to file a writ of mandate in the Court of Appeals in Sacramento, right away."

"Can we go home and get some dinner first?"

"We'll start on it tomorrow," Nina said.

When the dark came, the Reillys splashed through the streets to Pizza Hut.

Contrary to her intention, Nina unloaded her day. Matt and Andrea listened in dismal silence. Sharon Otis's death had frightened them. Matt had spent the day installing better locks at the house. Brianna and Troy, adopting their mood, occupied their parents in disputes over crayons, napkins, and each other's ugly face.

Just as the waiter set their hot pizzas on the table, the lights of the restaurant went out.

"It was a dark and stormy night," Matt said. They waited for light, drumming on the table. "Remember what Dad used to sing when he wanted to cheer us up, Nina? About Brian O'Linn?"

"You mean when he had a snort too many," Nina said, but was drowned out by the kids shouting, "Sing! Sing!" The waiter lit candles in red glass holders covered with netting and went back to the kitchen, where the cook could faintly be heard banging pots and pans and cursing in Spanish.

Matt sang:

> *"Brian O'Linn was a gentleman born,*
> *His hair it was long and his beard unshorn,*
> *His teeth were out and his eyes far in—*
> *'I'm a wonderful beauty,' says Brian O'Linn!*

"Aye, and he always made the best of things," Matt said in his best brogue.

Nina sang:

> *"Brian O'Linn had no watch for to wear,*
> *He bought a fine turnip and scooped it out fair,*
> *He slipped a live cricket right under the skin—*
> *'They'll think it is ticking,' says Brian O'Linn!"*

Troy and Brianna giggled and threw pepperoni slices. Andrea smiled into her glass of burgundy. Matt and Nina went on together:

"Brian O'Linn was hard up for a coat,
He borrowed the skin of a neighboring goat,
He buckled the horns right under his chin,
'They'll answer for pistols,' says Brian O'Linn!

"Brian O'Linn and his wife and wife's mother,
They all crossed over the bridge together,
The bridge broke down and they all tumbled in—
'We'll go home by water,' says Brian O'Linn!"

Their fellow patrons clapped; the lights blazed; Matt and Nina bowed.

The doorway greeted them with a torrent.

"Tonight it's 'by water,' " said Nina Reilly.

21

⪦⪧

AUGUST, THE HEIGHT of summer, passed, bringing still, hot air and swimming in the lake. Even more people poured in from all over the world, heading for the yellow beaches to bake under the high-altitude vault of blue sky. In the crowded grocery store Nina heard as much French and Japanese as English. The casinos hummed day and night.

Hikers jammed the trails, sending the prudent coyotes, jackrabbits, and mountain lions up toward the windswept granite pinnacles, up higher to where the pika played outside their rocky dens. Close to the ground, yellow cinquefoil, yarrow and wild onion, and red Indian paintbrush blew in the warm winds. Aspen leaves fluttered among the lodgepoles and red fir.

Nina worked. As the weeks passed without a recurrence of violence, she had stopped looking over her shoulder all the time, though she and Matt and Andrea stayed on guard. She had begun seeing a tall, very big, dark young man now and then as she went in and out of the office. "That's my son, Willis," Sandy said when she mentioned it. "We call him Wish. He's watching."

"It's nice of him, Sandy. It's nice of you."

Sandy ducked her head behind her computer. In a gruff voice she said, "Jobs are hard to find," but Nina was getting to know her now. She knew what Sandy meant.

Now and then at night, looking out her bedroom window, Nina would see a patrol car glide by noiselessly. Collier was being true to his promise.

She filed her writ of mandate in the Third District Court of Appeals in Sacramento in mid-August. She knew the arguments could go either way. If the judges agreed Bruno's hypnosis had been converted to a therapeutic session, Judge Milne's decision would stand. She began a period of worry and waiting.

Riesner wouldn't be sitting at his desk biting the skin where his fingernails used to be. He'd take Collier to lunch, badger him, complain a lot, and then tell his client it was too risky to go to trial, and Michelle would be whisked off to Santa Rita on a second-degree murder conviction quicker than you could say "Cocktails?"

In the first week of September, on a hot Tuesday morning, Nina called Michelle in Fresno. Michelle talked about how the baby kicked sometimes. She couldn't sit at a desk filling out forms for her dad with her "whale belly." The mind-bendingly hot weather in the Central Valley reminded her every day about how much she liked Tahoe. Nina asked her to run through Anthony's last few days one more time, and Michelle obliged, speckling her commentary with complaints.

"What's this for?" she asked again.

"You know something about what happened, Michelle. I'm just going to dig until I do too." Nina told Michelle they should be hearing soon on the writ.

"I've been thinking," Michelle said. "I want to know who the baby's father is, just for my own sake. I can pay for DNA tests."

"I'm relieved, Michelle. You should know. The information could be useful to you, your baby, even our case. I wish going into this trial all mysteries could be put to rest. At least this one will be."

"I should get a blood test."

"I can help you with that. There's a lab in Sacramento."

"Can you get Tom and Steve to give a sample?"

"I don't think Steve's a problem. We'll handle Tom for you. And I'll have a sample of Anthony's blood analyzed. The police have samples," Nina said.

"Poor kid," Michelle said, and hung up.

Nina buzzed Sandy. "Sandy, what are you working on?"

"Your responsive declaration on the Airleigh divorce."

"When's it due?"

"Tomorrow."

"Good. All the time in the world. Call Sacramento information for a lab called, I think, Cytograph. I used them once before. Ask them to set up a DNA analysis for a paternity case. The mom's sample will be coming in from Fresno. Find out what they need from Tom Clarke and Steve Rossmoor. Then call those two and ask them to give a sample. If Clarke says no, tell me right away."

"Oh, he'll love this," Sandy said.

"Now, here's the hard part. Tell Cytograph we have some tissue coming in from a man who is deceased, and find out if any special arrangements are needed. Then call the morgue in Placerville. Ask for a Dr. Clauson. Find out where he sent a cancerous tumor from the body of Anthony Patterson. You need to get a sample from it."

Silence at the other end of the line. Nina thought, this is too hard for her, I should do this myself.

"Ten bucks an hour, starting today," Sandy said over the com line.

Nina thought. She should have done it long ago.

"Okay, on one condition. Fax your Aunt Alice. Find out if she's dead. If she isn't, make her get what we need."

"Done," Sandy said.

After lunch, Nina went down the hall and put on her new blue maillot bathing suit under a robe.

She had been wondering for a long time how, on the night of April twenty-six or, to be more accurate, in the early morning of the twenty-seventh, her client dragged Anthony's body onto Rick Eich's sailboat, chugged out half a mile, dumped the body, and then jumped out of the boat and swam back.

The killer abandoned the boat for the simple reason that the gas ran out, but there was a limit as to how far anyone could swim in icy-cold water without a wet suit. Half a mile was close to that limit.

How—now, this was the question—how had the killer survived the swim in the freezing cold? Maximum survival time at the water temperature on the night of April twenty-sixth through the twenty-seventh, Paul had checked with the Coast Guard and told her, was thirty-five to forty-five minutes. Nina had seen Michelle and Tom Clarke a few days later in her office, looking relatively healthy.

How long would it take to swim the distance today?

Nina rented a motorboat and persuaded, with a twenty-dollar bill, one of the boys hanging around the dock to come out with her. They headed directly out to the wide expanse of Lake Tahoe. Dotted with sailboats and picnic cruisers, as beautiful as the ocean Nina loved, the lake looked as pristine and impressive from here as it had when Mark Twain saw it. At half a mile on the odometer she cut the engine and sat there, looking back toward the shore a very long way away.

"Out here, the lake's cold," the kid said. He pulled off his baseball cap and wiped sweat off his forehead. "It's not like near the beach, where the sun warms it up. I hope you're a good swimmer." A lantern jaw and prominent Adam's apple were all she could see under the Giants baseball cap. He seemed to be staring through her bathing suit.

"I'm good," Nina said. "You just follow along behind me about a hundred feet. If I get in any trouble, just toss me that life preserver and haul me in."

"Okay," he said.

The sun picked this moment to disappear behind a large cloud. The temperature dropped palpably. Nina debated one last time whether to allow herself her goggles, and decided in favor of them. The killer hadn't had goggles, but there were limits. She stood up a little shakily and said, "What time is it exactly?"

"Two thirty-three," he said. "Don't drown or anything."

"Bottoms up!" She dove in.

Two seconds later she popped up. She began swimming in a slow crawl toward the distant shore.

It took a few minutes to find her rhythm. The water, swooping into crests, was not as smooth as it looked from the boat. Turning her head and opening her mouth to breathe challenged her, as unexpected small waves slapped her in the face. Nina, who loved swimming in the ocean, found Lake Tahoe similar. She matched the cold vigor of the water with her own energy.

Somewhere near this spot Anthony had sunk, slowly, and sat upon the sandy bottom. This late in the season, in summer's shallower water, she caught glimpses of the bottom. What a strange place to try to hide a body permanently. Farther out made more sense, because most of the last decade had been so dry the water was invariably shallow close to the Keys. Now, had the murderer headed straight out, instead of to the right like this, he or she would have hit very deep water more quickly. So, the killer showed lack of foresight at the very least. If this was premeditated, someone didn't think too clearly.

What if Anthony had just disappeared into the lake? Who would have cared? Michelle would have continued crashing through her life, wondering for a short while what had happened, but forgetting as new men and adventures intervened. No one else would care except maybe his sister in Philadelphia. But Anthony had not cooperated. That was not his style.

She lifted her head to have a look. The shoreline appeared no closer. She swam steadily on. There would have been lights, far away, that the killer swam toward that night, indistinct in the snow flurry.

The cold was an old enemy. Back in Monterey she had taken a freezing ocean swim one night, a dangerous swim. She had not gone in the ocean since, five—or was it six?—years later. Her mind flowed back to that other time, and she remembered how it felt to be drowning. . . . She took a huge gasp of air and stopped, treading water.

"Doin' okay?" she heard from behind her. She raised her hand and began stroking through the water again.

She had expected silence, but she had forgotten about the boat motor. Its low drone blocked out all other sound. The killer would have heard only the sliding water of the lake and hard breathing.

Paul had collected some swimming histories for her. Michelle, to make things difficult, had won medals on her high school swim team. Tom Clarke took swimming lessons for eight summers as a child. Steve Rossmoor could do anything physical. Al swore he couldn't swim. Sharon? Hard to imagine that hair ever wet.

For a long time she stopped thinking. Stroke, stroke, breathe. Stroke, stroke, breathe. She paused again. She couldn't feel her chin and her toes ached. She tried swimming harder to generate heat.

Toward the end, she called up all her endurance. The

water was too cold. She started to suck it in now and then, coughed, and lost her rhythm. She fought her way back. Without waiting to touch bottom as she finally came to the shore, she let her boatman come up alongside and pull her, breathless, into the boat.

"What time?" she said, spitting out water and huddling under a blanket.

"Three-fifteen," the kid said. Forty-two minutes. The swimmer in April must have been near drowning or death from hypothermia. What a miraculous performance.

How could Michelle have done such a thing? How could anybody, with the possible exception of Carl Tengstedt?

22

◈

RICK EICH MET her at his house, next door to Michelle's former residence, the next day. The Patterson house was rented to a couple with several children. A silver tricycle and red skates littered the driveway. Dad wasn't going to be happy about that.

"Come on out back," Eich said. He wore nothing but a pair of red trunks that said LAKE TAHOE RESCUE TEAM in small white letters on the side, a pair of mirrored sunglasses, and sandals. He had a neat beard and well-cut hair in a dark shade of brown.

Behind his house a small dock extended out over the water, the white Catalina moored securely at the end, its sails furled.

"It's a good-looking boat," Nina said. A breeze over the lake ruffled her hair and eased the heat.

"Take a look." They climbed onto the deck, then down narrow steps to a small cabin with a booth and table. Eich sat across from her, their knees almost touching. Through the porthole Nina could see the deck and the slope of grass to his house. The boat didn't rock; it jerked from trough to trough with the slap of the water.

"What else is down here?"

He showed her. An enclosed cubicle held the toilet. Behind it, on a shelf with high sides, the bed rested. A tiny galley with stove, sink, and fridge built into the wall by the booth completed the picture of a compact human habitat.

"Shipshape. I've taken her all the way to Hawaii and back."

Nina looked at the fresh red upholstery in the booth. "Had that redone," Eich said. "The police cut out the bloodstains." He indicated the side on which she was sitting.

"Were there any on the bed?" Nina asked.

"No. Just here and up on deck."

Why hadn't Anthony's body been kept up on deck? It would be very difficult to get him down the narrow stairs and prop him in a booth. He must have regained consciousness at some point. These events just got more mysterious, layering infinitely.

"Did you notice anything broken?"

"Not a thing. Of course, everything's tied down or bolted down on deck. With nothing loose lying around, it might be hard to tell."

"I'd appreciate it if you would show me how to start up the motor," Nina said. They went on deck to the steerage and Eich showed her how very simple it was; insert the key and turn it, start up, and start steering.

"Where did you keep the key?"

"I left it with Misty and Anthony while I was gone," he said. "I remember handing it to Misty. She set it on the kitchen counter." Nina examined this key. On the key ring dangled a transparent plastic boat. Anyone who looked around Anthony's house would have found it and known what it was.

"This is your original key?"

"Found in the boat motor."

"Did Michelle know how to take the boat out?"

"In a way. She loved to sit there and make like a captain. Steering is half the fun. Of course, at night, with visibility down, you have to keep a sharp eye out until you get to the open water."

"Does she know how to sail?" That would have done her dubious good in the dead calm of that night anyway. Nina didn't suspect Eich was involved, for the simple reason that this smitten boat owner would know better than to head out on a night without wind in a sailboat without carrying extra gas. She waited for his answer.

"That's much more complicated," he said. "They helped me with the sails a few times. Anthony might have been able to, but Misty's not into boats. She just came out to keep us company." He took a rag from under a minisink and swiped at the counters. "Say, Nina, I'd like you to give Misty my best. Whatever happened between them, I don't hold it against her."

"How well did you know them?"

"Just neighbor stuff. They went out a few times with me and my girlfriend. The summer before, Anthony and I sat out on his deck a few times and drank beer. He was a beer aficionado. He always had something different for me to try—Sam Adams, Anchor Steam, Sierra Nevada Pale Ale. . . ." Eich was far away, in beer land. Nina had seen that happen with Jack now and then.

"Did you like him?" she asked.

"Sure. He liked football, baseball, any kind of spectator sport. He liked to throw darts. He played golf. We were gonna have a game. When I saw him, he was hangin' around his house on a Saturday, puttering around in flip-flops."

It was hard to incorporate this picture of Anthony.

"What about Michelle? How did you get along with her?"

"She's a nice girl, Nina. But . . . she's a teaser. She used to wear this bikini out on the boat . . ."

"Did she seem interested in you?"

"Not really," Eich said. "Not with her husband there. She'd try to drive me crazy, though, the way she sat, touching me accidentally. I had a hard time keeping my hands off her, to tell you the truth."

"What about the two of them?"

"She stayed quiet around him. He kept his hand on her all the time, like he was afraid she was going to get away. He didn't like her to go out alone. It must have been hard, living with a woman like that."

Nina sat on the railing. It was about eighteen inches higher than the deck, about ten inches wide. Lifting an unconscious man that far would have been easy for just about anybody.

After a nap at home, Nina felt recovered enough to dispatch herself to the grocery store for swordfish steaks and salad fixings. She picked up hot dogs for the kids and a large bottle of champagne, which she put in the refrigerator immediately. The day's heat lingered in the kitchen.

Matt arrived home first, disgusted with one of his parasailing customers. "This guy just couldn't get off the ground, because he was scared to death to lift off in the harness. Ever heard of a deadweight? Lead, this guy. He took a couple of dunkings when the boat couldn't stop in time and ran him right off the beach into the water. We finally got him flying and he had a good ride up there. Then it was time to come down and land in the lake and he started twisting and turning as he came down. The harness wrapped around his legs and we had to hustle over in the boat before he swallowed too much water." Matt popped a beer.

"He doesn't sound like someone who would go parasailing in the first place."

"He told me it was a gift from a customer. An unsatisfied

one, I'll bet. He said he's going to talk to his lawyer about negligent infliction of mental distress."

"At least your insurance company will have to handle it, not you," Nina said, plopping the swordfish into a big bowl of marinade.

"What insurance company?" Matt said. "For a parasailing business? The premiums would leave me with a net loss. Should have let the sucker drown." He went outside and she heard his ax splintering wood. He must be sweating.

Andrea came in with her arms full of groceries. "Oh," she said. "I never dreamed you'd make it to the store."

"Special feast tonight. Paul's driving up with Bobby. He stopped in San Francisco and picked him up."

"Do I detect a certain enthusiasm that goes beyond the return of the prodigal son?"

"Go read a magazine." Nina pulled out the lettuce to shred.

"Matt said," Andrea began, "you told him once you were afraid of Paul van Wagoner. That he was out of control."

"Matt has a long memory!" Nina said, showing her exasperation. "But for Matt's information, I'm five years older now. So's Paul. We have graduate degrees in controlling our antisocial impulses."

Andrea sat herself on a stool and tidied lettuce leaves from the counter. "Do you think that his being one of Jack's friends has anything to do with your . . . hiring him?"

Nina, aware of the real concern behind Andrea's words, relented. "Nothing more than a sneaking thought that I might be able to get through to Jack via Paul. He disabused me of that notion right quick. Refused to act the intermediary. And now he's turning out to be a fantastic help to me on this case. Believe me, we have very little else in common. He's a womanizer and a hard ex-cop, and that makes him mud in my book."

"But you like him," Andrea said.

Nina laughed. "Yes, I do."

By the time Paul pulled up in his van she was out on the front lawn in her shorts basting swordfish with marinade.

Bobby ran to her, his hair flying. Then she was holding him to her, smelling the familiar smell of her son. She clung to him for a long time, feeling whole again.

Within five minutes he took off to play with his cousins, showing them a handheld video game Jack had bought him.

Two hours later the adults sprawled out on the lawn, watching the sun's shadows grow long. The kids had gone in to watch TV. Lying on the warm grass with the last of the champagne, Nina could hardly believe in a few months the whole place would be under six feet of snow. She found herself talking about the case again.

"I talked to Al Otis yesterday, Paul," she said. "He really loved that woman, his wife. Called me yesterday to grieve and carry on, saying how she was the best."

"The best what?" Matt asked, dangling a marshmallow over the coals.

"The best motorcycle mama in Reno," Nina said. "What she saw at the Keys that night may never be known. I believe she could have cleared Michelle."

Matt gathered up plates.

"Let's take the last tram up to the restaurant at Heavenly," Paul said. "We can just make the sunset."

"Not me, thanks," Andrea said. "Time to put the small ones in bed." Matt shook his head, carrying empty platters into the house.

Paul looked inquiringly at Nina. "Let me get a jacket," she said.

They stood in a short tram line, whispering about their fellow passengers. Paul bought the tickets. They climbed into the lurching car, rising rapidly from the lake level along the Gunbarrel, a black-diamond run at Heavenly. At this time of year the steep slope showed only beaten-down dirt, flanked by the dark forest. Stepping out onto the platform several thousand feet up the mountain, they walked to the deck of the Top of the Tram, which maintained a year-round bar on top of the world for tourists seeking memorable photographs. Chairs and tables with Cinzano umbrellas oriented themselves toward the edge of the deck, which dropped off precipitously. They put elbows on the railing, admiring the last glow of sun on the lake, Nina acutely sensitive to Paul's hulking presence beside her.

"Now this . . . this feels like a date," Paul said. He put his arm lightly around her. "About time we went on a date, don't you agree?"

"I never liked dating. That's something you have to go through with people you don't know."

He studied her. "And you think you know me?"

She shrugged, remaining silent, enjoying the feel of his arm around her.

After a moment, he said, "Say something."

"There's so much I know and so much I don't know about you. Jack envied you, I think, and that colors my feelings, you could say."

Paul shook his head.

"Secretly, he did. Life was fairly easy for him. He saw you struggling and fighting against your nature and the status quo all the time. That's what he expected, even wanted to do all his life, but his kind of WASP always flies through a golden field."

"If Jack envied me, it was only in the way everyone has a yen to be something they aren't once in a while. Didn't you ever want to be a ballerina? Or a king?" He grinned.

"You're getting to know me, at least!"

"I'd like you to know me, too, Nina."

"You know what I need, Paul? I need to keep things clean. I need to focus on the Patterson case. I don't want to get . . . swept up. You're my friend now, and a colleague. That can last. Anything beyond that right now I can't face."

"Commitment, Reilly style?"

"Anything, anybody that relates to work, *that* I can get serious about."

"Sexy."

Nina found she was not ready to let it rest quite yet. "Paul? I'm not your usual type. Is Marilyn?"

"I wanted to talk to you about that, Nina." They started walking.

"You're living with her?"

"I was. Not anymore."

"Since when?"

"Since yesterday. A showdown that ended with her throwing all my stuff out the window. Defenestration, I believe it's called." He didn't laugh. "She was ready to settle down."

"And you're not?"

"Not with her." He removed the arm from around her that had been a warm link to him. Facing her, without touching her, he said, "Don't believe everything about me you heard from Jack."

"Which part shouldn't I believe?"

"Anything at all unflattering." They both laughed.

"You saw Jack today. How is he?"

"You sure you want to know?"

"I do."

"He seems okay. He's living with Evanelle Cherry, light-haired, too skinny, tall. Late thirties."

The words made her shiver. "Like someone we knew once." The woman Jack had loved before Nina looked like that.

"I prefer a woman who dances and spills wine on her clothes, myself," Paul said, smiling.

"I miss him terribly. I . . ." Now she was ready to bawl on his shoulder.

"Jack's an idiot. And I told him so."

"Oh, Paul. Thanks." The sun faded behind the mountain, a still, orange landscape.

"Did you ever wonder, how much who you are had to do with who Jack wanted you to be?"

"Every day," said Nina. "Every single day."

"Almost forgot," Paul said as they got off the tram in the dark below the mountain. "Stopped by the office and Sandy foisted this on me."

She tore open the big envelope and read the fax inside.

"It's from Sandy's Aunt Alice." Under a light in the parking lot she studied it. "Payroll records for Carl Tengstedt, from Subic." They walked a few steps.

Nina read out loud. " 'Dear Sandy, glad I can help you with this. How's your ma? And did you grow up half as wild as your daddy? Does he still trap rabbits in the Pine Nut Mountains? Write soon, love, A.A.' "

"What else is there?"

She leafed through a messy sheaf of copies in various sizes. "We've got his pay records here, nothing too exciting. His pay went up as he was promoted, whoopee. Hardly seems like he made enough to live on. Got his insurance benefits records, W4's. Just a bunch of nothing. Shoot. Personnel files might've done us better."

Paul drove her home and walked her to the porch. Reaching beyond her to push open the door, his hand brushed against her soft blouse and the nipples unprotected as rosebuds under a spiderweb. Nina froze, feeling the blood rush to her throat. He pulled his hand slowly back, and then, carefully, delicately, he took both breasts in his hands, looking into her eyes as his fingers lingered, exploring her. Gathering her to him, pressing his body against her, he blistered her neck and breasts with the heat of his kisses, never once raising himself up to kiss her on the lips, concentrating himself over her heart. Nina closed her eyes and absorbed him. When they finally parted, she took both his hands and said good night. Paul said nothing, just turned and ran down the driveway to the van.

Stumbling just inside the door, drowning in confusion and lust, she managed to get to her room without seeing anyone.

She threw Aunt Alice's envelope on top of the teetering stack beside her bed, threw off her clothes, and climbed between the covers, every small hair on her body alive.

Okay, so she told him what she wanted. She hadn't asked him what he wanted. He had his own goals. She could accept that. Paul was not going to be easy for her. He wouldn't be controlled by her, she could see that now. And what about controlling herself? Why were her mind and body so often at odds? Though these thoughts usually left her numb, tonight she let the physical shock waves his touch left behind course through her body, this traitor to her mind that had its own desires and needs, this neglected waif of a body that cried for attention when she gave it none. Face it. She needed to forge peace between these warring selves before another plumber was required.

After a long time, unable to sleep, she picked up the envelope, rereading the letter, imagining Sandy's father hunting in the mountains, a long time ago.

Going through the material again, forcing her way to the bottom, she waded through the incremental financial changes in the life of Carl Tengstedt. Yawning, she stacked the old W4's, and read the last form, Form C360, "Notification of Change in Beneficiary." She read it again. She hunted for another form. She read it again.

She reached for the phone.

"My God, Paul."

"What?" When she didn't answer, he repeated, "What?"

"Form C360, change of beneficiary, and Form 61936-872, number of dependents claimed. Michelle and Barbara Tengstedt were added."

"So? They met and married in the Philippines right? He was already there, right?"

"No!" she replied, the springs under her mattress creaking as she jumped off the bed, still holding the phone. "The dates! He added them on when Michelle was ten years old!"

"Meaning?"

"Meaning, she's adopted. Meaning, Barbara was married before. Meaning Carl Tengstedt is not Michelle Patterson's biological father."

23

IF CARL TENGSTEDT was not Michelle's father, then who was? Should she tell Michelle? What would be the psychological consequences?

Michelle would want to know. Maybe she would remember her past, and in so doing, recollect that Thursday night as well.

On Sunday Nina called the Tengstedts, finding no one home. On Monday morning, first thing, she called Bruno's office. She needed his advice on how to break this to Michelle, but she called too late; he was on another line and just about to leave. After setting up a telephone conference for three that afternoon, she called the Tengstedts again.

Barbara Tengstedt answered. She had that gravelly just-woke-up voice. Nina apologized for calling so early and said, "I'd like to talk to Michelle, but first, I'd like to talk to you, Mrs. Tengstedt."

"Michelle's still in bed."

"Could you give her a message, then? I'd like her to drive up here on Thursday to prepare her for the trial. We'll need most of the day, so can you ask her to be here by ten in the morning?"

"I'll tell her. I guess that means Mr. Hallowell isn't going to change his position."

"No. I'm sorry."

"Have you heard from the Court of Appeals? Carl was

talking about that last night at dinner, about how important it is."

"No, but I expect to hear by the end of today or tomorrow. I'll call you then."

There was a pause. "What did you want to talk to me about?" Barbara Tengstedt said.

"About Michelle's father," Nina said. She couldn't think of a graceful way to lead into it, so she just said it.

"Carl? What about him?"

"No, not Carl. Her natural father. I've learned that you and Mr. Tengstedt married when Michelle was ten years old. I haven't said anything to Michelle yet."

Barbara Tengstedt hung up on her, the grating finality of her response lodging like shrapnel in Nina's ear. Nina called back.

No answer.

"A fine way to start the day," she muttered. She began working on jury instructions, but one part of her mind concentrated on Barbara Tengstedt.

Why couldn't Michelle's parents cooperate? Nina could tell how much they loved Michelle and wanted to help her. Now, with a trial in one week, she needed to have everything in command, anything significant to the case, anything, however irrelevantly deemed, that might cast some light on Michelle's actions that night.

Sandy typed subpoenas and answered the phone. In the juggling act of trial preparation, many balls flew through the air that had to be caught and tossed back up at precise intervals.

Sandy buzzed. "Cytograph."

"Dr. Carlos, here," the woman on the phone began, without preamble. "We have the results on those DNA tests you sent to us. None of the samples you sent us match for the fetal DNA. Guess you didn't have enough of a pool," she said with a muffled sound that could be a laugh.

"There must be some mistake. Anthony Patterson's tissue . . . it's almost six months old . . ."

"It was admirably preserved," Dr. Carlos said. "Though I have to admit I have never looked for paternity using that type of tissue before. In death there is life, as they say. All we can do is test what you sent us. We tested the tissue sample from the decedent, Mr. Patterson, and the blood samples from the labs of, uh, Thomas Clarke and Stephen Rossmoor against the mom and fetus. No match, sorry."

Nina hung up. Tengstedt wasn't Michelle's father. And nobody was Michelle's baby's father. She fielded an ache in her chest. Michelle had to be lying.

Paul took out the stack of subpoenas and directions Sandy had given him in his van. He disliked process serving for the low-class, unpleasant work it often was. No one welcomed a subpoena. The best you could hope for was a reaction of polite distaste, so you could crawl away like some banana slug partially squashed under a shoe, still alive, if not respectable.

That was what he missed about police work—respect. He sure didn't miss the pay scale. He looked at the first subpoena. Dr. Frederick Greenspan. Nina still hadn't made up her mind whether he should testify or not, but she had to go ahead with the subpoena.

She had described the bungalow and its location, so he had no trouble finding it.

Inside, the air-conditioning was on the blink. Elderly parties perspired into magazines. From behind a frosty window a frostier receptionist slammed the window shut between them when he explained he needed to see the doctor personally. "Just a moment," she said, muffled by the glass.

Watching her for several minutes while she shuffled papers, he knocked again, and she opened two inches of access. While she glared, he rolled up the subpoena and pushed it through the crack. "Substitute service," he said. "Just in case Doctor isn't in. But I think he'll want to see me." Once again he was shut out. Deciding somebody would have to march out sooner or later to get rid of him, he picked a comfortable chair and immersed himself in a *Reader's Digest*.

He read one joke before a woman opened the inner door and motioned to him. Following her into a cramped office with a computer and files, he sat down when she indicated a chair with a "Please." She studied him, and he studied her. What he saw was a handsome middle-aged woman, slim, with an austere expression. She looked smart and capable. She had to be Mrs. Greenspan. He said as much, and she nodded her head. The subpoena lay on her desk.

"I take it the doctor won't see me?" Paul said.

"He has far too many patients this morning," Ericka Greenspan said. "I can handle this business."

"I've just subpoenaed your husband to testify as a witness in the Patterson trial. Normally, when a physician is going to testify, we try to make whatever special accommodations that might be needed. For instance, if he can only come one morning that week, we can ask the judge to put him on the stand out of the usual witness order."

"How nice," Mrs. Greenspan said. "But Mr. Riesner told us my husband would not be testifying. I believe he talked to Mrs. Reilly."

"Yes. Your husband seems to think Mrs. Reilly intends to attack his professionalism at this trial. That's one reason I'm here, to assure him again, that is not her intention. His testimony, as I'm sure you'll understand, is necessary to show Michelle Patterson's emotional problems and state of mind just before the incident."

"So you say," Mrs. Greenspan said.

"He has to come to court. He would find it much more tolerable if he talked to Mrs. Reilly about the areas she will ask him to testify about."

"He doesn't intend to talk to her. Why does Mrs. Reilly think he will say anything that will help her case?"

"Why would he want to harm his patient?" Paul said, and caught a flicker of uneasiness in her eyes as her self-possession abandoned her momentarily.

"He doesn't want to harm her," she said finally. "But he can't help her. He might be compelled to allude to certain violent fantasies Mrs. Patterson had about her husband."

"Fantasies he neglected to mention in his notes, or in his conversation with Ms. Reilly? Not very wise, Mrs. Greenspan. Even people who testify frequently have trouble lying in court. It usually rebounds in an unanticipated way."

"I never said he would lie," Mrs. Greenspan said, satisfied with the veiled threat. "You can go now," she went on, the queen dismissing her courtier.

"Did you ever meet Anthony Patterson, Mrs. Greenspan?" Paul said.

Again she wavered. "We are finished," she said.

"Dr. Greenspan does a good business. Mostly elderly people, it looks like. Probably doesn't get too many as knockdown pretty as Michelle Patterson, does he, Mrs. Greenspan? Young too."

"What's your point?"

"I have to wonder what your role is in protecting your husband. It all comes down to what you find to hate about Michelle Patterson."

She rose to evict him, but she couldn't let that one go by. He had fired the starting shot and she was out the gate and running.

"You're full of slimy insinuations, aren't you? Just like the bitch you work for . . ."

She had leaned forward and was now in his face. He put his big hand up, the heel of his hand under her chin, and pushed her hard back into her chair, knocking the breath out of her.

As he got up, Paul said easily, "You open that mouth before I leave, I'll have to wash it out with Lysol." He picked up the subpoena, placed it between her nerveless hands, and said, "Tell the doctor—he's been served."

After lunch, Nina received more bad news to cap a black day. The Wall Street brokers must have felt like this, hunching over their ticker tapes as the stock market toppled in 1929.

The latest came in the form of a too-light letter from the Court of Appeals. Nina didn't have to open it to know she had lost on the writ. If she had won, the letter would have been thick, weighty with an opinion and instructions for the next step. She had the urge to ask Sandy to read it to her. No. She opened it quickly. *Writ denied as to all arguments. Copies sent to opposing counsel and Superior Court. Proceed to trial.*

Go directly to jail. She looked out her window, at the clarity and simplicity of Mt. Tallac, as distant from her now as Pluto.

Her San Francisco call came in at three-thirty. "Sorry, my dear, I was talking to the president when you called."

"You mean . . ."

Dr. Cervenka laughed, a deep ho-ho-ho. "My superior, the president. He's offering me the gold watch, the golden handshake, an appreciation dinner, and a swift kick out the door again. He does this every year."

"Bruno, how old are you?" Nina said.

"Methuselah was my younger brother, that's all I'm going to tell you," he said. "I'll think about it, as I do every year. I do not wish to retire and have him bring in some snot-nosed behaviorist who delights in torturing rodents. If the school becomes too vigorous in its efforts, it will be your turn to give advice."

"How's your hip?"

"I'm still in this damn wheelchair," Bruno said. "But let's not talk about me. Let's talk about your case. Have you had an epiphany?"

"It sounds exciting, Bruno, but I don't know what that is."

"I am surprised. I mean, have you reached an understanding in this case? Have the facts unfolded into a complete and compelling truth?"

"Not exactly. I'd say the facts have unfolded into complete and total chaos, Professor," Nina said. "Listen to this. Michelle told me there were only three men who could possibly have fathered her baby. She claims the only men she had intercourse with are Tom Clarke, Stephen Rossmoor, and her husband. We tested tissue from all three, including Anthony Patterson. The lab called this morning and told me none of the samples match. So who got her pregnant, huh? She's lying."

"Lying? Perhaps."

"Come on, Bruno, this all happened only seven months ago. She can't have forgotten. She's keeping the information from us that she had another lover. She's lying to her own lawyer. I should drop the case."

"You're distressed," Bruno said. "You like your client very much."

"I believed her, Bruno. I trusted her. I'm sick about it, and angry."

"If she is repressing it . . . why?" Bruno said.

"Her story has never made much sense, Bruno. The DA is just going to keep on saying, 'You left your husband bleeding on the couch and went to bed? You didn't remember him until morning?' I believed her, in spite of everything. But now . . . Bruno, you taped her confession right there at UC. Please . . . don't try to soften anything for me. Did she kill her husband, or not?"

"There are some inconsistencies in that confession, as you know, Nina, and the young lady is suffering from strong underlying guilt, some of which arises out of old events in her past. These feelings are enough, I believe, given her current vulnerability and the sensitive nature of her therapy, which was left hanging, to make it possible that she is accepting blame in some symbolic, not literal sense."

"Well, how about this new convenient memory loss? She denies that she had sexual relations with someone other than the men she has named. That's a lie. The DNA tests prove she was with someone."

"If you want to believe her, you could think like this: Maybe one of the DNA tests is incorrect. Then she would not be lying," Bruno said. Nina leaned back in her chair, holding the cordless phone against her cheek, feeling like Bruno had handed her a good idea.

"You mean one of them was faked? Not Anthony's sample, unless the El Dorado County sheriff's department was involved. So . . . how do you fake a DNA analysis, Bruno?"

"I can do it the layman's way," Bruno said. "I can send in someone else's skin or hair or whatever they used as the sample."

"Blood in these cases, but that does sound like a small possibility. Thanks for this idea, Bruno. Now I'll have to get another sample from Tom Clarke and Stephen Rossmoor. I expect Clarke will refuse, and it will take ages to get a court order. So I'll get Paul to help. And this time I'm going to collect samples from every male connected with this case. Paul can go down to Fresno and get something from Mr. Tengstedt just to remove the possibility of an ugly surprise there."

"You mean you will obtain samples surreptitiously? How?"

"Let me see, it says right here in my bedside reading, almost anything will do as a test sample: skin, blood, hair, saliva, semen. . . ."

"I hope you realize that this could be a rather dangerous undertaking. Have you learned who told the authorities about my session with Michelle?"

"No. It could have been Jeffrey Riesner. He's a lawyer up here who represents Dr. Greenspan. I told Dr. Greenspan about the session. He might have passed the news on to Riesner. Or it could have been Stephen Rossmoor, the manager at Prize's. I just can't see any of them trying to kill us, running us off the road, maybe killing the wrong person in Reno."

"You are being careful?"

Nina thought gratefully about the people who were watching out for her: Matt, Andrea, and Collier, even Sandy's son Wish, whom she still glimpsed now and then as she went about her business. "Yes. I have help. And Michelle seems safe at home. Speaking of home, I seem to have almost forgotten the reason I called you."

"I often have that effect on lawyers," Bruno said. "Excuse me a moment. I'll be back."

"I'll be here." He was gone for several minutes. Nina doodled a picture of Michelle, dream lady, liar, trouble following her around like a monkey on a chain.

"Sorry. Intermission for my pills," Bruno said into the phone. "Why did you call, then, my dear?"

Nina explained about Aunt Alice, the fax to Subic, and the payroll records. She told Bruno about her phone call that morning to Barbara Tengstedt, and the reaction.

"Here's how I feel, Bruno. I want to tell Michelle. The Tengstedts won't take the responsibility. If she knows this much, she'll force the rest out of them."

"You'd like to do that," Bruno said. "You can't tolerate the ambiguity. You want to charge into the field of defenses and secrets and lay about you with your lance of truth."

Feeling slightly foolish, Nina said, "Yes, but I did have sense enough to call you first. I know she's got a psychiatric problem, though God knows nobody seems to be able to put a nice, clean label on it. I know she's under tremendous stress from the coming trial and the uncertainty of the future, and worrying about the baby. That's why I'm calling you."

"For absolution," Bruno said softly.

"How's that?"

"So you can tell yourself you asked me. It doesn't matter what my advice is, Nina. You will not be able to keep this to yourself."

"I do want to know what you think, Bruno."

"I think you are right to tell her," Bruno said.

"I want to do more than that," Nina said. "If her parents won't tell her the rest, and she doesn't remember after learning this, I want to call Barbara Tengstedt to testify at the trial. And I am going to ask her under oath about Michelle's past, make her tell her secret in open court."

"I admire your courage," Bruno said. "But please, don't do that until you have obtained Michelle's permission."

Nina thought about this. He was absolutely right.

"Bruno . . ."

"Yes, my dear," he said with that unfailing patience the university would never find in a younger replacement.

"Do you suspect what happened to Michelle? When she was a child?"

"If you don't mind a wild stab."

"Please."

"She hurt her daddy, Nina, and he never came back."

"But how?" Nina asked, hiding her frustration. "Emotionally or physically? With a polar bear statue to the head?"

"That doesn't matter. Don't ask how. Ask why he never came back."

24

⚜

THE TRIAL LOOMED. Jury selection would commence the following Monday. In the midst of the long hours of preparation, Nina thought about Bruno's words. She read Freud and Jung each night after she climbed wearily into her bed, falling asleep to Kafkaesque dreams of trials, castles, and imprisonment.

After five months of activity into every nook of fact, she knew little more than she had when Michelle first told her the story of the night Anthony disappeared. She reread the reports, drawing diagrams of the living room and the boat. She drew her nine dots in three rows and tried a new series of triangles.

Nothing new came to mind.

Paul was busy all Tuesday. He ran into Sandy on her way out at five. "Don't do nothing I wouldn't do," Sandy said. She punched him on the arm as he passed.

"She likes you. Did you have good luck?" Nina greeted him smoothly. Only an intimacy of eyes passed between them in reference to their last informal meeting.

"If accumulating locks of men's hair is good luck. Played dodgeball with the janitor and snagged some of Tom Clarke's off his chair in the principal's office and ran into Rossmoor at the casino. Knocked him down in the hall.

Think he appreciated it when I helped him up and brushed off his collar for him, although his security guards didn't."

"What about Tengstedt?"

"Yeah. Fresno at 109 degrees. I finally met our client, the famous Misty. She was propped under a tree in the front yard with an icy drink, long legs under the sprinklers, a chrysanthemum, lush and summery. I now get it about Tom Clarke and that noodle Rossmoor. I had to restrain the impulse to suck her toes. Her mother gave me a glass of lemonade and disappeared. I made up some news about the case for Misty, used the facilities, and ripped hair off the male comb." He handed her a brown paper sack, which crinkled as she set it on the table. "The whole world in a drop of water, or in this case, a strand of hair. Everything's labeled. I hope it's not the father, I mean, Carl Tengstedt. That's a gruesome thought you have there."

"Can you take the samples to Sacramento Wednesday?" said Nina. "I've got a sample or two of my own to add."

He nodded, picked up his tennis bag, and said, "Interested in a game before dinner?"

"No," said Nina. "I can't."

"You need to do something physical or you'll seize up like an old car engine out of oil."

"After the trial," Nina said, meaning it, hoping he understood.

"One more thing," Paul said. "I ran by the sheriff's office on my way in and looked at the physical evidence again. Virginia Slims. The wrapper had been in his robe pocket. Sharon Otis was there."

Janine Clarke came to the office on Wednesday, looking like she'd won at keno, acting like she knew Nina well. Evidently her husband hadn't mentioned that he had been subpoenaed. "Tom asked me to stop by, believe it or not. Things have been going so great with us lately. . . ."

"Glad to hear it," Nina said. "What can I do for you today?"

"He wants to get a written copy of the DNA results. Guess he doesn't want Misty changing her mind later about who's responsible for her little bastard."

"I don't have them here," Nina replied, wincing for the sake of Michelle's child and her own illegitimate son. "And the lab is taking a second look at those tests. Once those results are in, I'll send out a copy to your husband."

"Just what the hell is going on here?"

"There's just some doubt that needs to be cleared up on the results," Nina said firmly. "And that's all I can say about that."

"I don't believe this. You're saying there is still some possibility that Tom is the father, and that's just a damned lie. The test came back negative. This is some kind of sick frame-up. Misty . . . oh, hell, this is all her fault."

"Mrs. Clarke, I—"

"Why did he get involved with that witch? He's broken my heart. . . ." The woman had begun to weep uncontrollably. "This has all been such torture. He was so cruel, coming to the hospital to tell me his ugly suspicions. . . . We used to be so happy, and now we look at each other and wonder . . . He did the right thing, I guess, the only thing a man can do. . . ."

"Who?" Nina was almost shouting to be heard over the wails. "Who do you mean?"

Janine Clarke looked up from her hands and frowned. "He'd throw it all away, just to sleep with that face. . . ."

Nina tried to sort out the referents and failed. Janine

Clarke gave her one more tear-streaked, bitter look and ran out of the office.

She pitied her. Tom Clarke she did not pity.

Sandy came in at twelve. "You have to go out today. No more sandwiches on call."

The floor was stacked with law books, files, and papers. Nina searched furiously for a case opinion.

"Three Cal. 3d 82," she said. "Sandy, help me."

"I am helping you," Sandy said. She hung Nina's purse off her shoulder and walked her out.

In the oven of the Bronco's interior, Nina started up and drove down Highway 50. She would go for a walk by the lake, fix a salad at Safeway, and get back to the office in half an hour.

Her replacement Bronco proved as rebellious as the old Bronco had been. It drove itself to Caesar's, parked itself in the parking lot, then ejected her. She walked in, digging into her purse for a couple of twenties.

On her way to the slots she had to pass the blackjack tables. She pulled out a chair at a table and passed over her twenties to the dealer.

A ten and an ace for her first hand, not bad, thought Nina, ignoring the catcalls from her stomach. A white-haired lady close by stacked a tower of chips. Her suffocating perfume warred with the cloud of smoke on Nina's left. The lady won a hundred bucks while the smoker went down. Nina watched her hands fly, flashing a tight cocktail ring. A very good player, the woman continued to stockpile chips. Nina started betting with her, putting out ten dollars whenever the lady put out a hundred. In a short time, Nina was up three hundred dollars. She tipped the dealer ten dollars as another dealer came in, a young man with a distant expression. All the players felt the change of atmosphere, and the table emptied.

As she wandered toward the slots, her blazer pocket heavy with chips, the lady came up beside her and said, "Nice going, Counselor," in a Southern-inflected bass voice.

"I like what you've done with your ring, Al," Nina said. "Doesn't fit as well as on your pinky, of course. Diamond surround?"

Al Otis smiled under his makeup. "Cubic zirconia. Still brings me luck. The dealers haven't caught on yet. I'm cleanin' up. Can't talk long, though, because they're gonna know who you are, and they might be watchin' you out of curiosity."

"Why would they care about me?"

"They keep track," Al said. "Well, got to get back while the lunch crowd is still in. I get too conspicuous after one-thirty." He was turning to go, his skirt brushing against her, when she said, "Al . . ."

"Hmmm?" he said in a ridiculous falsetto.

"Did Sharon tell you she was at Anthony's the night he died?"

"Sharon didn't have to tell me squat. She was the best thing that ever happened to me," he went on, his eyes inscrutable. "The sharpest babe that ever wore trick leather underwear. And the cops don't care who offed her, any more than Misty cared about Anthony. So long, Counselor."

On her way back to the office, Nina tried to sort out what Al had really said. Translated: Even if he did know something, he wasn't going to talk about it, because Misty didn't deserve it? Was that it?

It hardly mattered. Whatever he had heard was hearsay, and inadmissible as evidence.

When Paul dropped by for last-minute instructions on his

way to Sacramento, he found her on the floor, 3 Cal. 3d 82 heavy in her lap.

Driving with both eyes glued to the rearview mirror, Paul breezed down the mountain, making good time until he hit road work after Folsom.

When he got into Sacramento, he lost himself getting off on the Sixty-fifth Street exit, fumed in the early rush-hour traffic, circled around a green park with an inviting swimming pool, and was pleased to finally find himself on the right side street. He slid into a parking space just that moment left empty by an aging red Camaro. Leaping from his seat, he collected the paper bag, ran for the entryway, and got there just in time to hear someone bolting the door from the inside.

"Hello? Hello!" he called. The door opened and a young, dark-haired woman looked out.

"We close the doors at five," she said.

"I have to drop this off." He handed the bag over. The girl took it.

"What is this?"

"Oh, they're expecting it. They know what to do with it."

"Tahoe paternity case?" The girl's head came out farther and she looked inside the bag. She had red, Kewpie doll–shaped lips and curly black hair tied back with a shoelace. Noting the hands, and their chewed-off fingernails, and looking more closely at her face, Paul could see that she was in her late thirties at least. "More hair samples?" asked the woman.

"Yeah."

"Every baby's got a father," the woman said.

"Till they figure out some new way," Paul said.

"Personally, I think in vitro's as far as they're taking it."

She started to close the door. "Most scientists are still men and they aren't going to make themselves obsolete." She opened it again, looking at Paul. "You drove all the way from Tahoe just now? In a real hurry."

"I'm the investigator for the attorney for the woman . . . involved in this. My name's Paul van Wagoner." They shook hands.

"I'm Emilia Carlos. Listen. I'm going to break for dinner. Why don't you join me? Afterward, maybe I can show you the lab."

She took him past an empty reception area. They ate microwaved dinners in a lunchroom in the basement, burritos smothered with ketchup. Fluorescent light bounced brightly off cinder-block walls and acoustic ceilings. "Timelessness," Dr. Carlos said when she noticed Paul blinking in the glare. Men and women in lab coats, jeans, and athletic shoes bustled through the halls, passing the door to the room they sat in, greeting the doctor, spilling coffee from a badly adjusted vending machine. "I like days. Swing shift people have the weirdest hours to adjust to, if you want to talk a normal life, I mean."

"Worse than graveyard?"

"Yeah, for some reason the body can adapt to 180-degree switches better."

"It's a much bigger operation than I expected."

"I founded Cytograph with my husband about five years ago. When he died, I took over. This is our only child. I've been up plenty of nights with it."

Still admiring the Betty Boop lips, Paul couldn't help thinking she might be squandering her native gifts. He would never get over these women, her, Nina, all these women wanting to be more than they already were. Wasn't goddess enough? Why were they so anxious to sink to being lawyers and scientists?

Thoughts of Nina going about her business today, somehow planning to win this trial with horrible odds against her, assailed him suddenly. He wished he could protect her from the blows to come, not that she didn't deserve them. Was there a nasty desire in there, a wish that she would be taken down a peg or two in all this? A wish that she would fall into his arms at the end and be his love toy?

He stifled a laugh that would have bounced around the hard room.

Painted Sheetrock walls surrounded the shining lab equipment, which on closer inspection yielded the marks of hard use. Tubes, rubber hoses, metal gadgets, wires twisting from multiple outlets; there were shelves full of equipment whose purpose would forever remain murky to Paul. The room rumbled with machinery, down to its vinyl floor.

Two techies, one wearing a woolly beard and white coat and one decked out in what must be the uniform, jeans and a dress shirt, filtered unknown substances through a fine sieve. The bearded one set down a porcelain cylinder.

Dr. Carlos showed Paul the original results on the first set of DNA tests that had been made, raising her voice above the man-made din, pointing to what looked like photographic prints with variegated strips of gray, white, and black on them. "Electrophoresis," she said. Paul wished that Mrs. Garrigues had done a better job teaching him chemistry. Or was this biology? "This is the fingerprint."

She pulled up some charts on a computer. "We use just a fragment, and count repetitions. Or rather, have the computer do the count and comparison." Paul double-checked that his recorder was on, and adopted an intelligent expression. The doctor went on. "First we extract the DNA from the sample by adding a series of chemicals and doing a series of extractions. Then we add primers: nucleotides; enzyme buffer. Then we take the tube and carry out PCR, by heating and cooling the sample."

"PCR?" asked Paul, contemplating his intellectual blind spots.

"Polymerase chain reaction." The doctor, who had covered her hands with gloves, pulled a hair from one of the sample bags with tweezers, moving it slowly to a glass tube. "Then we load what came out of the PCR into the well of the electrophoresis gel. We apply high-voltage electric current to the gel and make an autoradiograph. That's what you're looking at. Nothing to it, really. Of course, you've brought us five samples this time. The pool is expanding, I see."

Paul rustled the paper. "Sounds like a long process."

"Not always. It depends. We're ordering a beta scanner next month. Then we'll be able to have answers in about half an hour."

"We need the second set of results as quickly as possible," he said.

"Three weeks would be the earliest. We'll fax the results."

Michelle arrived at Nina's office promptly at ten o'clock the next day. She wore shorts, a sleeveless overblouse, a sun visor, and a deep tan to set off a blinding smile.

Nina had never seen her so happy before. It must be the baby.

"I brought you a present," she said, handing Nina a basket wrapped in pink cellophane. Inside, fruits and vegetables from the San Joaquin valley nested: dates, walnuts, figs, grapes, asparagus, a head of garlic, and deep-green broccoli. "For your family."

"Thanks." Nina picked up a walnut.

"See, you hold two of them in your hand like this and squeeze." A crack and Michelle opened her hand, handing

Nina a chunk of the walnut meat. "It was so hot coming up the valley," Michelle said. "I'm going to go swimming when we're done."

"How are you feeling?" Nina said.

"Healthy. I'm seven months now. See how big?" She lifted her shirt, the same way she had that day in the office to show Nina her bruises. "Being at home helps. The folks keep to a routine. Boring but peaceful. I'm still off the booze."

"Good. Good."

"Tell me how it's going."

"We'll be ready, but we had bad news on the writ." Nina explained about how the confession would come in, and how they were going to have to get into Michelle's problems. "Has your mother told you about the phone call I made to her earlier this week?"

"About me coming up?"

"About something else, as well."

"She's been awfully busy. She's been out of the house a lot." Michelle finally seemed to catch Nina's mood. "What's up?"

"We have a lot to talk about, Michelle. Some of it's going to be hard for both of us. There's plenty of time. Let's go over your testimony first."

Nina took Michelle through her rehearsal. She had a transcription of her first interview with Michelle, and she had drafted her questions from it. There was a lot to cover, Michelle's background, her amnesia, her marriage to Anthony, her depression, her affairs, her drinking, her decision to go to Dr. Greenspan, her job, the night of April twenty-sixth, the morning of the twenty-seventh. They broke for lunch at twelve and started again at twelve-thirty. By four Nina was satisfied that Michelle would know how to answer her questions.

Michelle was tired when they finished. She was planning to drive back to Fresno, and it would be a long three hours with what Nina had to say now.

Nina started with the DNA. She was tired too. "We got the results from the lab."

"Oh. I'm not sure I want to know."

"I'm going to tell you anyway. Michelle, we tested for a match with Anthony, Tom, and Steve. None of them matched. Now, who did you forget to mention?"

Michelle put her hand on her stomach and started rubbing it. "How weird. They made a mistake. There's nobody else."

"You know, it hurt me, Michelle," Nina said, "to think you were lying to me. And if you were lying about this, you could be lying about everything." The Vesuvius inside her shot up clouds of smoke and superheated ash.

"Nina—"

Nina erupted. "Let me get this out," she said, standing up and walking around the littered office. "I should have known better. I've been in this business long enough to know better. I trusted you, even though my common sense said you sounded like a liar. Maybe I should have been harder on you, confronted you, laughed at you until the truth came pouring out. Maybe the simple truth is, Michelle, that you had a fight, and you won; that you took Anthony out on the boat and dropped him off the side, figuring his body wouldn't be found. Maybe we could even have made a self-defense argument. Well, it's too late now. You've outsmarted yourself, thinking I could win you an acquittal."

Michelle was shaking her head, her eyes filling with tears.

"How about you let me in on it at this late date? I'm thinking maybe you need a new lawyer. Riesner. A guy as slick as—"

"Nina, don't talk that way. We're friends."

"You're making a fool out of me, Michelle. I'm new in this town, and I'm trying to establish a practice, and you're going to hurt me just like you seem to hurt everyone else."

When Nina finished her tirade, Michelle said, "Nina, sit down and listen to me."

Nina sat. Her angry energy had evaporated. She had said what she had to say, not very gracefully, as always.

"I didn't lie to you, Nina. I swear."

"Yeah, right," Nina said.

"The lab made a mistake."

"We're double-checking that now."

"They'll catch it this time. Can't you give me the benefit of the doubt, just a little while longer?"

Nina shook her head and turned her eyes to the desk.

"We almost died together. I trust you, Nina. You can trust me."

Nina didn't look up for a long time. She scratched out a picture of a Bronco falling down a hill, two figures inside, their mouths stretched wide in a Munchian O.

"We're giving the test one more try. Then we'll see."

"Thank you," the girl said gravely. "And now, what about my mother?"

Michelle finally came home to Fresno at midnight. Her mother was waiting up for her, sitting in her recliner with the red afghan over her legs, reading *Ladies' Home Journal*, the lamp on the table beside her shedding the only glow in the living room. She looked up and smiled, but Michelle wasn't fooled.

"Where's Dad?"

"Gone to bed."

"Get him up," Michelle said. When her mother wouldn't

budge, Michelle went into the bedroom and woke him up herself.

When they were both sitting there, faces riddled with guilt, Michelle said to Carl Tengstedt, "You're not my father."

"Oh, yes, I am," he said. "A good father."

"A liar," Michelle said. "Don't lie to me anymore."

"We never lied, Michelle," her mother interjected. "A long time ago, it seemed like you forgot. And we were grateful to God."

"I want to remember now. Tell me about my real father. Tell me!"

"Don't shout," her mother said. She moved close to Carl Tengstedt on the couch, adjusting first her pink curlers and then her glasses, still holding the afghan around her knees. He wore the threadbare plaid robe Michelle had bought for him out of her allowance, for his birthday, when she was fifteen. His unshaven cheeks looked sunken into the square, military face. He was looking back at her, with that same shamefaced, defiant look she recognized from her own face.

"I make no apologies, Michelle. And I don't intend to go into it at this time. Your mother and I feel that the Lord took the memory from you in His infinite grace, to spare you. It is not our place to interfere."

"Don't you realize, until I remember, I can never get well?" Michelle said, her voice shaking.

They didn't move or talk. They adopted a defensive pose, huddling together like mice on the couch.

They looked old, so old! How had she not seen how old they were getting?

"Listen to this," Michelle continued in a low voice. "He's Death, and he's coming toward us. . . . We'll never stop him, Mommy, he's too strong. . . . He's taking us to Hell with him, you said so. . . ." She closed her eyes and lived it. But her mother came forward to hold her. And Carl Tengstedt broke the spell with his arms around them both.

"Tell . . . me . . . the . . . rest."

Still infected by the horrible vision, she heard her mother singing and felt cold hands smoothing her forehead as they had when she was a little girl, but the touch scared her, and the voice aroused a wild fear. " 'Hush, little baby, don't say a word . . .' "

Michelle broke the vise and ran, crying, "You will tell me."

Carl Tengstedt held his wife back with strong, muscled arms.

A few minutes later he knocked on Michelle's door, the weak sobbing of his wife far behind him.

Michelle didn't answer.

He opened the door a crack and kept his hand on the knob. "Michelle," he said in a voice so low she had to strain to hear him, but she could smell the familiar, safe smell of him, this man she had trusted to love her and take care of her for so many years. "You are my daughter and I tell you now, this will stop before you kill your mother."

She heard him like she had a thousand times before, the demand for respect backed up by the threat of his power over her, his physical strength and his fatherhood.

"You understand me?"

Inside the room, she sat down on a chair, her arms folded. "I won't ask her again if you tell me."

He shook his head, sagging, and pulled the door shut in her face. She heard the key turn in the lock. She threw herself at the door, pounding and yelling, but no one came.

25

SIX-THIRTY A.M. Monday morning, on the first day of the trial, Nina took a long shower and dressed in the usual getup, a navy blue suit with a silky white blouse, her mother's gold earrings, black stockings, and heels. She ate a plain bagel cold, drank some milk, looked through the stacks of paperwork, the motions *in limine,* the statement of case, the proposed jury instructions, the trial brief, the evidence file, the research file, the pleadings, the witness files . . . everything was still there. She loaded them into the Bronco in two trips.

Eighty-six prospective jurors in varying moods of boredom and curiosity milled around the hall in front of the large main Superior Court courtroom. They turned to watch as Nina walked by, pulling her wheeled cart of briefcases and books, her posture erect, her expression resolute, her knees knocking together.

Inside, under the bright lights, another crowd thronged; the media, the courthouse cronies, some police, and the players. Up front, looking calm and confident in dress grays at the table on the right, Collier Hallowell and his paralegal pitched their tent of files and papers with the ease of nomads. Michelle sat with Paul at the table to the left, her hair spotlighted, wearing a beige maternity jumper. They both looked relieved to see Nina rolling her cart up the aisle.

The bailiff, a smiling, older Japanese man whose uniform

had grown too tight around the middle, chatted with the judge's clerk at her desk just under Judge Milne's dais. The court stenographer had already set up her curious machine on its tripod and was threading her paper through it.

At nine o'clock precisely, the bailiff went to his desk at the left wall under the clock, the clerk looked sharply around, and the stenographer straightened her back. "All rise," the bailiff intoned, and Judge Milne appeared in full black regalia, seating himself upon his sparse throne with the ceremony of a pharaoh. "Be seated." Murmurs and rustling, coughing and half-suppressed laughter stirred as they all sat down. Milne frowned slightly; a hush fell.

"People of the State of California versus Michelle Tengstedt Patterson," the clerk read.

"Counsel?"

"Ready for the prosecution."

"Ready for the defense, Your Honor."

"Let the record show the defendant is present and we have a jury roster of eighty-six. Counsel, I'm hoping that will be enough. I'll be asking the jurors the basic information. Then you can ask the questions we've already gone over. Deputy Kimura, bring in the jurors."

The bailiff returned with the jury panel, who took the vacant seats reserved for them in the courtroom. Milne's usually sour visage took on a warm and friendly cast as they came in. He sounded downright avuncular. "Good morning, ladies and gentlemen," he said with a smile. "Thank you for doing your duty and appearing here today."

He made a few more introductory remarks, and introduced the attorneys, then said, "This is a case in which the defendant has been charged with the crime of murder. She is charged with the death of her husband, Anthony DiNatale Patterson."

Fourteen men and women were called to the jury box on

a random basis and took their turns answering the questions
Milne read to them, then the lawyers' questions. Milne never
lost his courteous attitude, but he moved them along remarkably quickly.

Michelle, sitting next to Nina at the counsel table, leaned
over and said in a low voice, "How can you tell who to
pick?"

"Inspired guessing is the biggest part of it," Nina told her
lightly under her breath. She was tapping her pen on the
diagram in front of her, a seating chart that contained fourteen numbered boxes. She had written the name of the person sitting in each box. The bailiff had also handed her ques-
tionnaires that had been filled out by each of the people in
the seats.

Some big law firms conducted background investigations
on the entire jury panel, spending tens of thousands of dollars to find out political leanings, financial status, and many
other interesting tidbits that could not easily be asked in
court. These facts were then compared to an ideal-juror pro-
file prepared specifically for the case by a highly paid consultant. A number of expensive and authoritative-sounding
books had been written on the subject of juror selection.
The way Nina saw it, they made dandy paperweights.

A few of the stereotypes did seem to make sense. Conven-
tional wisdom held that women judged women defendants
more harshly, especially if the defendants were young and
good-looking; that members of minority racial groups went
easy on each other, as well as members of the same occupa-
tional group; that young people tended to be broader-
minded. There were supposedly "defense" occupations—
teaching, publishing, anyone in the arts, athletes, the unem-
ployed. The "prosecution" jobs included engineers, medical
workers, anyone who wore a uniform at work. But these
notions were changing rapidly too. A black accountant

might judge a black man who had stolen money sternly, but feel sympathetic toward a young white single mother who had done the same.

Nina had her own set of standards for judging the jurors, gleaned from many sources. She wanted jurors who could stay alert and not be put off by the sometimes lurid details of Michelle's recent life. She wanted skeptics with some life experience who would not be swayed from their own convictions. Most important, she intended to send on their way all the opinionated blowhards, usually male. These folks made up their minds early and pestered weaker-minded jurors into going along with them. The point was to try to have twelve independent-minded people available to weigh the facts.

Some jurors were excused simply because they worked at Prize's. Some had pressing obligations elsewhere, which hadn't amounted to an automatic exemption. Some felt prejudiced by newspaper accounts they had read. One man in his twenties kept staring at Michelle, broke into a broad smile, and finally said, "I know her. That's Misty. Listen, you don't want me on this jury." Michelle looked down at Nina's nine-dot doodles.

He joined the others excused for cause. Another member of the panel heard her name called and made her way to the box for questioning.

The peremptory challenges went faster. Hallowell, looking earnest and morally upright, excused the young women. Nina excused the older, conservative types, who might be too tempted to make moral, not legal judgments. Both of them courted the jurors with their questions. They remembered names and occupations, they made harmless jokes, and they began the job of influencing the jury.

One boy hardly looked old enough to be there and didn't seem able to comprehend what was going on; Nina did the honors and thanked and excused him. Another joker enjoyed all the attention, displaying an offhand regard for the issues. Hallowell excused him.

They did not finish that day, or Tuesday. Milne stopped allowing even good excuses, apparently worried that he would run out of juror candidates. Finally, on Wednesday at four o'clock, Milne dismissed the lucky chosen twelve, along with the two alternates, and the remaining half dozen who had not been chosen, and called the lawyers into chambers. Hallowell opened the door for Nina, and she went in first. Milne said, "Hey, Collier," giving her only a curt nod.

Milne's chamber, the closely guarded inner room of the pyramid, accessible only by invitation, was filled with personal treasures: family photos, certificates, golf clubs, a thank-you poster from a third-grade class, and a collection of pipes on the bookshelf. A wide window overlooked the forest. His bird's-eye maple desk gave off the smell of furniture polish. In this serene room, he signed orders that changed lives. Protected from all disturbance, flanked by his staff, comfortable as Cheops, he had only one duty, to decide. Most of the time his decisions would be carried out. Few jobs in American society created so much respect and fear; few wielded such power. Small wonder Milne treated the jurors, his voters, so kindly.

"I asked you this Friday, when we were going over some other matters, and I'm going to try one more time. I want to know why this case is going forward," Milne said to Nina from his high-backed red leather chair. "I read the trial briefs over the weekend. There's a confession. No amount of hocus-pocus psychiatric testimony is going to take that away. And if you don't put up a defense, just to keep that confession out, Collier's going to run away with the case. Not that I have any preconceived ideas, here. I'm just going by what I see in the briefs."

"We offered a second-degree, Judge," Hallowell said. "She has no prior record. She'll get fifteen years with the mitigating circumstances and be out in ten." He didn't look at Nina.

"This can't be good for your client's health," Milne said coldly. "She'd better not go into labor in my courtroom."

"She wants a trial, Your Honor. That's what we're going to have," Nina said. "The baby's coming whether we like it or not and she wants to take her chances. She knows what she is up against. The district attorney hasn't made an acceptable plea bargain offer. This woman was in an abusive marriage. There's no evidence of premeditation."

"He was hit twice," Hallowell said. "She neutralized him with the first blow. She could have left the house, called the police. She had time to think about it, and she decided to kill him. That's premeditation."

"At the very least, there was a fight. She has psychiatric problems. The so-called confession on tape is unreliable as evidence." She resisted the disapproving judgment emanating from the two men. Milne thought she was showing off. He looked at Hallowell and shrugged his shoulders.

"Mizz Reilly," the judge said, his drawl of the word implying disrespect, "don't misunderstand me. You're the lawyer; you think you have some kind of Twinkie defense, try it. But, in the interests of all concerned, including the interests of judicial administration and the interests of your client, I think you ought to take Collier's offer seriously."

Nina considered all the responses she would like to make, and discarded them. Nothing she could say would change Milne's ideas about the case, or his opinion of her, at this point. "Mmmm," she said. Mel Akers had taught her that. When in doubt, mumble.

"All right, then, let's not waste any more time. We'll start with opening statements at nine A.M. tomorrow. If you people reach a plea bargain before that time, call my clerk immediately." Milne picked up a letter.

She followed Hallowell into the hall, glad to exit the room.

"I believe my client might still be willing to accept voluntary manslaughter," she said stiffly.

"I'll talk to my boss again, Nina," Hallowell said. "But don't expect miracles." They were shoulder to shoulder, his up higher, moving down the empty hall behind the courtrooms. Nina spun around and faced him. The tension, anxiety, and paranoia of the preceding months disintegrated the last tatter of her self-control.

"You know, Collier, I have an unpleasant thought that I want to share with you today: You would offer Riesner that plea. He told Michelle you would. So why not me?"

Hallowell said nothing.

"Riesner, who told you about Dr. Cervenka, handed over this live torpedo, all to blow up my defense. A real guy thing, right? A trade, a deal. He saves your office an intensive-care headache, grabs my client, pleads her out quickly, and everyone goes home early to eat meat."

He regarded her calmly. Up close, he was still unreadable. His steady eyes and firm mouth, his damnable composure, infuriated her even more.

"Tell me who told you about the hypnosis," she demanded.

"Not Riesner."

"Prove it."

"I don't have to prove it."

"You and Riesner gonna go get drunk, after; share a few jokes about the trial, pat each other on the ass?"

"Don't look too far for someone to blame for how you're handling this case," he said easily, but he was breathing harder, letting her feel his scorn.

"Who withdrew a decent plea bargain? Who's wasting state time prosecuting an innocent pregnant girl who had an abusive husband? Who's got a lot of jive and no real evidence of premeditation, or for that matter murder in any degree?"

"Careful, Nina," Hallowell said. "You attack me personally, you'll wish you hadn't."

"You can't put this case into a tight professional compartment in your mind, Collier," Nina said. "I won't let you. She's a human being, not a case file."

"Save it for your fans on the jury," he said.

Andrea made supper, but Nina couldn't eat. She struggled with Bobby over some long-division homework. They finished late, both tired and strained. Outside, an enormous yellow harvest moon floated in the sky. She pulled on Matt's warm leather jacket and followed it. Leaving the street, she walked off into the woods to a ghostly white-speckled boulder not far from the house. Up at the top was a flat place covered with pine needles, just wide enough so that she could lie down. Heat from the still-warm granite flowed through her bones as she stretched out, staring up through the dark branches into the brilliant night.

She allowed her mind to drift through the mistakes of the day. She had let the pressure get to her. She had lost her temper and blurted out some half-baked thoughts she only half believed, because Milne's attitude stung her and Collier's refusal to offer her a better plea bargain at this last moment scared her.

In the court hallway Collier had bested her. He had shown his strengths; he was more confident, more experienced, and cooler under fire than she. Very well. She would learn from her formidable opponent. She would maintain her self-possession; she would be more discreet; and she would outwork him to compensate for her relative lack of trial experience. Determination flowed through her body, strengthening her.

Though the treetops rustled intimately above her, the cool air around her had stilled. Moonlight fell like weightless, shimmering veils over her. She seemed to float among the trees, her thoughts fluid and bold.

In this quiet mood, she reached again for the truth of the Patterson case.

She knew the facts. She knew more than Collier, Paul, or Michelle. She had the facts memorized, organized, consolidated, and analyzed, but she still didn't know the truth.

The truth about Anthony Patterson's death lay beyond intellectual analysis, in the realm of emotion and impulse; she could see that now. Her training had led her astray. She would have to look to her own heart, her own impulses, her instinctive reactions to the people in the case.

The Patterson case had its own mood, its own emotion, coloring the motives of so many of the people she had met. What was that emotion? She had felt it often, but she had pushed it away because she thought the irrational could not be valuable.

Oh, yes, she knew that feeling. "Jealous love," she whispered, and the wind in the pines seemed to whisper it back. "Jealous love, jealous love . . ."

Anthony Patterson had lived and died by it. Ericka Greenspan and Janine Clark were consumed by it.

What about the men in the case? Tom Clarke wanted Patterson dead. He had said so at that first interview. He had been protective of Michelle, until her arrest. Then he had run for his wife. Now he was protecting himself. From what?

Al had loved Sharon. Had Anthony resurrected the old relationship?

Stephen Rossmoor, wrapped up in Michelle's magic, had been haunted by her. For how long? Long enough to hate her husband?

The dangerous current between Anthony and Michelle had shifted that night, and brought one of them death and the other a nightmare.

Jealousy . . . the icy water . . . the second strike of the polar bear.

Harley wings. A crumpled pack of cigarettes. A bottle of Yukon Jack.

A sailboat, bobbing serenely in snowflakes, a drowned man, his eyes wide open, all his meanness gone . . .

Jack, the plumber boy, and Ms. Cherry . . .

She sat up with a start. Yes, she knew where to find the truth.

Find the jealous love at the heart of the case.

Find the jealous lover.

26

❦

"As you have heard, I'm Collier Hallowell. I've been with the office of the District Attorney of the County of El Dorado for more years than you want to know. Before we start, I just want to thank you myself for the important work you are about to undertake.

"It won't be easy. At times you will feel very frustrated with having to sit and listen, and not ask questions yourselves. At times I or perhaps Ms. Reilly will neglect to cover some point with a witness that you feel you need to hear. It's also hard to take several weeks out of your life for this trial. Believe me, I appreciate how difficult it can be. But with all the difficulties, I know you will carry out your responsibility conscientiously."

Hallowell paused, while several of the jurors nodded encouragingly.

"Sometimes people feel confused in a criminal case about who the prosecution represents. We like to think we represent the victim."

"Objection," Nina said. "Improper argument." Hallowell was supposed to be telling the jury about the evidence he intended to present.

"Overruled."

Ignoring the interruption, Hallowell went on, "Technically, we represent the People of the State of California. It is the People who are bringing this case to you for trial—"

A jet roared overhead, drowning him out. He smiled slightly, not missing a beat, and continued.

"And it is my duty to present evidence that will prove to you, beyond a reasonable doubt, that Michelle Tengstedt Patterson murdered her husband, Anthony Patterson, on the night of April twenty-sixth and the morning of April twenty-seventh of this year.

"We will show you why and how she committed that crime. We will take you every step of the way through the investigation carried out by the authorities. And we will, I believe, convince you beyond a reasonable doubt that this is a case of premeditated murder, not a crime of passion, not self-defense, not a crime with any mitigating circumstance.

"You will hear how Michelle Patterson, a cocktail waitress at Prize's, known in this town as Misty, struck her husband with a large, heavy object during an argument. He was wounded, he was bleeding. She laid him down on a couch in their living room.

"You will hear testimony that Misty Patterson then dragged her husband to their neighbor's boat and drove out into the night. At some time, she struck him again. But he still did not die. So she threw him overboard, into Lake Tahoe, still alive, and she finally accomplished her purpose.

"But in her haste to kill her husband and hide his body forever, she made a mistake. We will show you that the boat ran out of gas about half a mile from shore, where the depth was only thirty-five feet. And we will show you that she was forced to abandon the boat and swim ashore, leaving it to mark the spot where she had dumped the body of her husband. A cold night, ladies and gentlemen, and a cold-blooded act of murder."

"Objection!" Nina said, standing. "Beyond the scope of an opening statement."

"Approach the bench, Counsel," Milne said.

The lawyers walked up to the sidebar, where Milne could lean down and whisper off the record.

"Sorry, Judge. I got a little carried away," Hallowell said.

"You never get carried away. Cool it," Milne said.

As Nina returned to her seat, she saw some of the jurors looking curiously at Michelle in her big white blouse with the soft bow. She knew they were registering the cold fact of a dead husband. Although they knew Hallowell's statement was not part of the evidence, they were taking it in along with the flood of facts that would come next, as the lawyer for the prosecution knew they would.

"At this point my job is to try to give you an overview of the evidence that we are about to produce, a kind of road map. That way you'll be able to see where I'm going even if the questioning gets confusing." The jury's little helper, Nina thought.

Hallowell began to summarize the expected testimony of each prosecution witness. He used plain, direct language, staying in his role of helper, never lecturer.

Hallowell did not refer to the tape. He could not anticipate the defense, and would be able to bring it in during rebuttal only if the defense put in evidence that Michelle's mental state on April 26 had direct bearing on the case.

"I trust you will do the right thing," he said. "Thank you very much."

Smiles of approval. Good, honest man, that lawyer. Works for the County, doesn't make much money. Looks like he's worn out with too many cases, better make allowances if he makes any mistakes. Now here comes the defense lawyer, youngish woman, hair kind of shaggy, no wedding ring, nice suit, private attorney—so big bucks, wants to be called Ms., her client has a lot to lose, defense is going to be looser in the ethics department, the Misty girl probably got pregnant for sympathy. Well, don't expect any favors from here. . . .

"Anthony Patterson," Nina began. The jurors waited, polite but skeptical. "A man who made enemies. A man who cheated his employer, took revenge when he felt slighted, abused his wife physically and emotionally. An ex-cop with grudges so deep they poisoned his entire life. And, on an early Friday morning in April, his life was taken, but not by the young woman who sits here today, knowing her life is in your hands."

"Counsel," Milne warned, letting her off easy because she hadn't added the tempting but implied: "and her baby's."

"Let me tell you what you won't hear in this case. You won't hear any evidence placing Mrs. Patterson on that boat. You won't be shown evidence that she went outside at all after she returned home. You won't see any witness testifying that she dragged her husband, who weighed about two hundred and twenty pounds, several hundred feet through the snow, loaded him into a boat, struck him a second time, dumped him overboard, and swam back half a mile in freezing-cold water at night."

A few glances at Michelle. Good. She looked small, frightened, and handicapped today, nothing like the requisite amazon.

"Apparently *somebody* did those things, somebody who came to the house after Mrs. Patterson had gone to sleep, to find Anthony Patterson on his couch in the living room. An hour earlier he had argued with his wife. He had been drinking. He had left bruises on her. And at last, to keep him away, you will indeed hear that she struck him one time, which she freely admits—one time, ladies and gentlemen, at least an hour before his death. Dr. Clauson will tell you that the first strike did no serious harm.

"During this trial you will get to know the defendant, Michelle Patterson. You will learn that Michelle is a well-liked employee who came to Tahoe with all the hopes and dreams of any young new bride, some three years ago. You will learn that she has never before been accused of any criminal or violent act.

"You will also hear from Dr. Greenspan and Dr. Cervenka that Michelle had entered therapy because she wanted to understand why she couldn't remember her childhood. She suffers from a type of amnesia. You will hear that while she was seeing Dr. Greenspan, her husband died. And this will help you understand why she told the police that she could not remember what occurred after she struck her husband that one time, except that she woke up in bed. I know you will pay careful attention to Dr. Cervenka's testimony in this regard."

A juror in the back row—Bill Whittaker—stopped just short of rolling his eyes. Nina forged on.

"You will also meet some of the other people in Anthony Patterson's life. You will discover that the police haven't asked any of them what they were doing that night. The police are as eager as the prosecution to accept pat answers. The police are busy and, like the prosecution, would like to wrap up this case."

"Your Honor, I hate to interrupt Counsel's statement with an objection, but—"

"Approach," Milne said.

When they stood at the sidebar, Milne said in a low voice to Nina, "That's improper argument, and you know it's improper. Cut the crap. I mean it."

She turned back to the jury, who responded to Milne's tone with some glances at each other, some small smiles.

"You will hear of several reasons other people had for wanting Mr. Patterson to go away. And, as the judge will tell you in his closing instructions to you, it is not the burden of the defense to prove to you another person killed Mr. Patterson. All that is required for you to acquit Mrs. Patterson of this charge is for us to raise in your minds a reasonable doubt as to whether someone else was involved." Hallowell started to stand up, but to her relief sat down again. She had misstated the law slightly to suit her purposes.

"I believe that upon hearing all the evidence you will find that the prosecution has failed to carry its burden. You've all heard it, and I know you'll remember it: Michelle Patterson is innocent until proven guilty."

Nina gave the jurors a friendly nod and returned to her seat. Paul drew a happy face on the legal pad, and Michelle smiled at her. Milne announced a break for lunch.

Then she eyed the jury for a reaction, but none of them returned her look.

They stood up, collecting their jackets, eager to get out and make calls, hit the bathroom, and gulp down a Coke and hamburger.

"Call your first witness," Milne said at one-thirty.

"Officer Robert Tomlinson," Hallowell said.

Officer Tomlinson was sworn, spelled his name, and adjusted himself comfortably in the witness chair.

"You are a police officer for the South Lake Tahoe Police Department?"

"Yes, sir."

"On April thirtieth, a Monday morning, were you on duty at the main office, located right across the street from this courthouse?"

"That's right, on desk duty."

"Did you at some point that morning take a missing property report from a man named Rick Eich?"

"Yes, about eight A.M."

"And is this the report?" Tomlinson looked over People's Exhibit 1.

"That's it."

"Mr. Eich signed it?"

"Then and there."

"Request the report be admitted into evidence."

"No objection," Nina said.

"What did Mr. Eich say had been stolen?"

"Objection. Hearsay."

"Sustained."

"Did you note in your report the object that was supposed to have been stolen?"

"Objection. Lack of foundation. Best-evidence rule."

"Sustained on both grounds."

Hallowell looked a little surprised. "Your witness," he said, marching back to his side of the room.

Without getting up from her table, Nina asked her first question. "Officer, didn't you go out to Mr. Eich's home to take the report?"

"No."

"Directing your attention to People's 1, do you see on line thirty a statement regarding where you took the report?"

"It says I was dispatched and prepared the report."

"Does that change your testimony?"

"Guess that's right, then. I do seem to remember being there."

"Do you remember going out on the dock behind Mr. Eich's house?"

"Now you say it, I do."

"You might recall snow on the ground?"

"Yes, there was some. It was slippery out there."

"When you checked the area for footprints, what did you find?"

"I didn't."

"You didn't? Why not?"

"Well, Mr. Eich said he'd been gone a week. I didn't

expect to see any footprints. Besides, they're of very limited value in an investigation, what with snow melt and all. You don't get a definite impression like, say, with mud."

Nina gave the court a moment to digest the weak excuse. "You did check the mooring lines?"

"Yes, they were thrown down at the edge like you'd expect." He looked relieved.

"Did you notice if any were cut?"

Officer Tomlinson propped his fingers against his forehead and closed his eyes. "I don't recollect."

"Did you in fact perform *any* investigation?"

"Listen, I was just there to take the report," Tomlinson said. "I got the numbers on the boat and I got the right people looking, and they found it quick enough."

"The right people?" she asked, with another pause. "And who were the right people?"

"The Coast Guard's in charge of Lake Tahoe. Interstate passageway."

"Call Rick Eich." Hallowell examined a paper on the table and moved back toward center court.

Rick Eich strolled up, natty in a light brown sport jacket.

"Where did you reside in April, Mr. Eich?"

"Two twenty-four Tahoe Vista Lane. In the Tahoe Keys."

"And did you know your neighbors at number 226 Tahoe Vista Lane?"

"Uh-huh. Anthony and Misty."

"Patterson?"

"Correct."

"For the benefit of any jurors who are not familiar with the Keys area, will you describe it?"

"Most of the houses down there back onto little canals. Like Venice, maybe, minus the filthy water. They've got small docks. Almost everyone living there has a boat of some kind."

"Did you own a boat at that time?"

"Oh, a beauty. Had her for a couple of years. A Catalina, sailboat, twenty-two-footer."

"Is a boat that size tough for a single man to handle?"

"For sailing, it's better to have two on the boat. But I can rig the sails alone. Just got to know how."

"In April did your boat have any other source of power?"

"A small motor."

"So you could go out on the lake without using the sails?"

"If you wanted. I mainly use motor power to control the boat in and out of the Keys area, where you got to go slow to avoid the traffic. Of course, you get out on the lake on some days, the wind's unholy. Then the motor comes in handy."

"The week you were in Hawaii, was the boat to your knowledge equipped with a dinghy or other type of life-boat?"

Eich laughed. "That would take up half the space on board. I used to have an inflatable. Now I just go with jackets. You capsize, you hang on or swim for it. Take your pick."

"Prior to April, had either Mr. or Mrs. Patterson gone out in the boat?"

"Several times with me, and a couple times without me."

"Both of them?"

"Correct."

"And how did they come to go out on the boat without you?"

"Well, Anthony would ask to borrow it. I had insurance, and he knew how to work the motor."

"What about Mrs. Patterson? Did she know how to take the boat out?"

"I guess. I never saw her at the rudder without Anthony standing there, telling her where to go and so on."

"But you did observe her steering the boat?"

"Yes."

"More than once?"

"Yes."

"Now, sometime in April, Mr. Eich, did you go out of town?"

"Yes. The last week of April, I went to Hawaii to do some windsurfing. Oahu."

"Where was your boat at the time?"

"Well, I covered it good, and the forecast said calm weather ahead, so I left it out on the dock behind my house." He added, "Anthony had asked to borrow it."

"And how did that come about?"

"Well, actually, Misty came over and asked me while I was packing."

"Mrs. Patterson asked to borrow the boat? Why did you say Anthony wanted to borrow it?"

"He sent her to ask."

"How do you know that?"

"It was the way they were together. You know. Anthony made the decisions. She wouldn't borrow that boat on her own."

"But you didn't really know, did you?"

"Objection. Argumentative."

"Overruled."

"She didn't specifically say one way or the other, if that's what you mean." Eich put his hands together in a small clap.

"Can you say from your own personal knowledge that Anthony even knew his wife had come over and asked to borrow the boat?"

"Of course he knew!" Michelle whispered to Nina at the counsel table. Nina nodded.

"I guess not," Eich said. "But—"

"How did you arrange for Mrs. Patterson to get the keys?"

"I gave her the key. There's only the one."

"Did you get it back?"

"The Coast Guard gave it back when they found the boat."

"And they found it where? On the boat or at the house next door?"

"Objection. Calls for speculation," Nina said quickly.

"Do you know where they found it? Don't make any assumptions," Milne said.

"No." Eich said.

"Objection sustained."

"So, when you returned from your trip on Sunday, April twenty-ninth, your boat was not tied to the dock in the usual way?"

"No."

"When did you notice?"

"Oh, right away. I went straight down to the dock. I love her, you know? Wanted to see how she fared."

"What did you do when you couldn't find your boat?"

"First I went next door—"

"To the Patterson residence?

"I figured Anthony and Misty must know something, but the place was deserted. Nobody home. Now, one thing is, when they went out in the boat, they always took the life jackets stored on the dock. When I went back again, I found the jackets. That freaked me. So when I still hadn't seen them by early the next morning, I called the cops."

"Officer Tomlinson came and took a report?"

"Yes. I never said the boat was stolen, only that it was missing. He just nodded his head and said somebody would be out looking and I said, hey, man, call the Coast Guard, you know?"

"Did you at some point ask the Coast Guard to search for your boat out on the lake?"

"Yeah, sometime later. Somebody needed me to say it again. I could just picture somebody lying out there injured on my boat. That would mean flak for me, you know?"

"Did you then, or do you now, have any objection to the search made of your boat by the Coast Guard on April thirtieth?"

"No, that was fine. They found her for me; I owed them. Wasn't even too excited when they found blood."

"Objection, Request that the last line be stricken. Hearsay."

"Sustained."

"Thank you, Mr. Eich. Nothing further," said Hallowell pleasantly.

Nina had watched Hallowell's show with one eye on the jury. The prosecution went first. In effect, the prosecution attempted to give the jury a road map with just one road, the road to a guilty verdict. Hallowell had surprised her in his opening statement with that hackneyed metaphor, but Nina appreciated its simple virtue. For Hallowell's true purposes, a railroad track would have said it even better.

This jury, she thought, would not be railroaded, because Tahoe souls were independent souls. She had watched for the smile on one side and the reproving stare from the other, and saw them both.

She rose. "Good afternoon, Mr. Eich."

"Good afternoon."

"You testified that you saw Mrs. Patterson steer the boat, more than once."

"Yes."

"Did she ever start up the motor?"

Eich snorted. "No way."

"Why do you say 'no way'?"

"She's used to having men do for her, you know? And because Anthony or I always did it. It's man stuff." Juror number five, a young mother in the front row, looked affronted.

"So you never showed her how to start it up?"

"She didn't need to know."

Nina let that sink in.

"Did you show her how to sail?"

"Don't you get it? I mean, excuse me, but she wasn't interested. She was too busy laying on a tan."

"Did Mrs. Patterson ever swim in front of you?"

"Yeah." Rick Eich looked at Michelle, his face grateful.

"Would you describe her as a good swimmer?"

"She mostly liked to float around on an air mattress. She could swim, I guess. I wasn't worried about her out there, but she wasn't *into* swimming, if you know what I mean."

"Did you ever see her swim as much as half a mile."

"No. That's a long way."

"You say you observed Mr. and Mrs. Patterson together on a number of occasions?"

"Mostly on the boat."

"How would you describe their relationship?"

"Objection," Hallowell said matter-of-factly. "Vague, calls for speculation, lack of foundation, beyond the scope of direct examination."

Milne pursed his lips, said, "Overruled."

"Go ahead, Mr. Eich," Nina tried not to let her pleasure at Milne's ruling show.

"Okay. Anthony bossed her. He told her what to do. Used to sing an old Rolling Stones song about it, how he had her under his thumb."

"Who else knew how to start up the motor on your boat?"

"Friends. People I took out over the years. Anyone who's started a similar one."

"Lots of people?"

"Objection," Hallowell said, but Eich was already saying, "Lots of people."

The prosecutor smiled, shrugged, sat down. "Withdrawn," he said.

Another pause. "When she was on your boat, did Mrs. Patterson go down in the cabin?"

"Sure she did."

Having primed him, Nina asked, "Would it surprise you to learn that Mrs. Patterson's fingerprints were found in the cabin?"

"Of course not. The head's down there, for one thing." He grinned broadly. "You know women."

Somebody tittered.

"One more question, Mr. Eich. Did you wash down your boat, or even just the cabin thoroughly, including walls, floors, and fixtures, before you left Tahoe in April?"

"She coulda used a scrubbing, but no."

"Mr. Eich, we've been talking about starting up this motor of yours. Why don't you help the jury out and explain how you do start it up?" Hallowell, patient and kind, began his rebuttal.

"Sure. You turn the key. Then you pull on the starter rope, you know, like for a lawn mower or a motorcycle, so it goes *vroom-vroom,* then you adjust it to the speed you want to go, and then you start steering her out using the rudder handle."

"Doesn't sound too hard."

"Objection. Not a question."

"Withdrawn. You start it up like a lawn mower, eh? So anybody with enough brains to turn the key and pull the starter rope can get the boat going?"

"Objection," Nina said at the same time Eich said, "Sure."

"Overruled. Too late, Counsel," Milne said.

"You said you gave Mrs. Patterson the key when you left for Hawaii, is that correct?"

"Correct."

"You testified that lots of people could start up the boat?"

"Yes."

"Could they start up the boat without a key?"

Rick Eich was rubbing his jaw. "You're not supposed to be able to. I guess you can hot-wire a boat, or get a key made."

"Could you start up your boat without a key, Mr. Eich?"

"Not me."

"Nothing further."

"The witness is excused." Eich smiled at Michelle as he passed, and she smiled back. The jury watched.

"Court is adjourned until nine o'clock Friday morning. Counsel, make sure you have sufficient witnesses available for next week. We're going to work hard. Thank you, ladies and gentlemen. You're excused." Milne admonished the jurors and witnesses not to discuss the case, or read or watch the news, and vanished.

Nina made notes on a pad as Paul escorted Michelle out of the courtroom. Hammer on the amazon aspect. Be amazed at the fantastic suggestion that little Misty could ever physically commit the deed. Laugh at the fingerprints. Make the police look as if they'd conducted a shoddy investigation. Remind the jury, however she could, not to be led down Hallowell's road without questions.

She packed up her files and left the courtroom, alone.

27

❧

On Friday morning, Collier called in the Coast Guard.

Captain Frank Buell stepped up, sharp and smart in his uniform. He spoke carefully, hoarding his words.

"Were you the commanding officer of the Coast Guard cutter U.S.S. *Emerald Bay* on Monday, April thirtieth of this year?"

"Yes, sir."

"What was your duty assignment at that time?"

"General patrol duty on the lake."

"What were the weather conditions at that time?"

Captain Buell pulled out a notebook and flipped some pages. "According to my log, about forty-eight degrees Fahrenheit at dawn. Windless conditions had persisted for several days."

"Did you at some time during that day receive a ship-to-shore communication regarding a missing boat?"

"Yes, sir. A Catalina sailboat owned by a gentleman named Richard Eich was missing."

"And in response to that communication did you begin to search the lake for the boat?"

"Yes, sir."

"Describe your search efforts, please."

"The owner indicated the boat had been low on gas. He thought it might have somehow torn loose from its mooring. We searched the Keys waterways first, although it was unlikely a drifting boat could have gone unnoticed in that area. When we found nothing, we commenced a sweep of the lake in a roughly triangular pattern extending out from the Keys outlet to the lake. After searching the triangle perimeter and lines parallel to shore at a quarter mile and a half mile out, we located the boat at approximately a half mile out, drifting."

"What did you do then?"

"We had telephone permission to board from the owner. I sent two men over to investigate. They reported what looked like blood spots on the inside flooring and outside deck."

"I presume there were no people on board?"

"No, sir."

"Any sign of a struggle?"

"Other than the blood, none, sir."

"What, if anything, did your men discover regarding the condition of the motor?"

"The key was still in. The motor appeared to have run out of gas."

"What did you do then?"

"Notified the land authorities we had a problem out there. And I sent down our chief diver, Ensign Pepper, for a preliminary search."

"Did your diver locate anything?"

"Yes, sir, a body on the sand about thirty-five feet down."

"Anything else?"

"Not at that time."

"The diver went down again at another time?"

"In the evening, after we winched up the body. He requested permission to cover the immediate area, since the water was relatively shallow and clear and we had good night-lighting equipment."

"And was anything else discovered, to your knowledge?"

"Only one thing, I believe. A statue. Looked like soapstone. Eskimo, maybe. A polar bear statue."

"Located where?"

"About two hundred feet in a direct line from the sailboat."

"What occurred then?"

"We secured the vessel with a towline and towed it to the Ski Run Dock. The Tahoe police met us. They have jurisdiction up to a mile out on the lake in the Keys area. They received the vessel, body, and statue and took reports. We moved out again at 0100 hours."

"Thank you, Captain. Your witness." Collier nodded at the jury from his table. Open and shut, his kind face said. Just a matter of getting straight facts out to you folks.

Captain Buell expelled a long breath and turned slightly in his seat as Nina began her cross-examination.

"Captain, can you tell us the water temperature of the lake in the area the boat was found drifting that night?"

He opened up his book again. "Fifty to fifty-two degrees Fahrenheit. That's a few degrees warmer than usual at that time of year."

"That notebook is your daily log for April?"

"Yes, sir." A couple of jurors smiled, but the captain was oblivious.

"Can you tell us the air temperature in Fahrenheit about midnight on April twenty-sixth?"

More page flipping. Nina waited impatiently, praying that Collier would not object that she was going beyond the scope of his direct examination. She stole a glance at him and with relief observed him in conference with his paralegal. Their heads almost touched.

"Cold, snow flurries, high thirties about that time of

night. Again, no wind. Hardly any wind between the twenty-sixth and thirtieth."

"And the water temperature on the twenty-sixth?"

"About fifty to fifty-two."

"Now. You testified there was spotting that appeared to be blood both on the deck and in the galley portion of the Catalina." Nina showed him some blurry photos of the boat deck and galley areas. Hallowell had provided her with the shots and they had been marked for identification, but he had not used them, probably because all you could see were some blackish marks that could have been anything. "Have you seen these photographs, marked as People's 7?"

"I took the photos," Buell said.

"Are these all the spots you suspected to be blood, which you and your men noted that night on the Catalina?"

Buell held the photos up. His lips moved. He was counting spots. "Seems to be."

"How many spots are there?"

"Four on the outer decking. Two on the stairs leading down into the galley. Two on the padded bench. A smear on the table."

The jurors listened intently. Why had the body been brought down into the galley? So it wouldn't be seen as the boat slipped out of the Keys?

"He wasn't exactly bleeding to death, was he, Captain?"

"Objection. Calls for speculation. Lack of foundation. The captain hasn't been qualified as a medical expert."

"Withdrawn, Your Honor," Nina said. "Captain, can you tell from the photos or any observation you made whether the decedent, Mr. Patterson, was bleeding at the time he was brought aboard the boat?"

"I would say yes. The droplets appear at the edge of the decking and head in toward the stairs to the galley."

"Can you tell if he was bleeding from one head wound or two at the time he was brought aboard?"

Buell thought. So did Hallowell, and before Buell could open his mouth to answer, he said, "Objection. Again, this is a subject for expert testimony."

"Do you wish to approach the bench?" Milne said, looking up from his note taking.

"It's a proper subject for lay opinion," Nina said.

"Objection sustained," Milne said, his voice tight. Maybe the coroner could answer her question. She was ready to move on. According to her notes, she had nothing further to ask. But she didn't want to let him go. He had seen the blood, seen the body. He could help her, if only she could think of the right question. It was on the tip of her tongue, then she lost it. She stared at the witness, her mind a blank.

"Thank you, Captain."

They took a break. Nina and Michelle and Paul convened at the courthouse coffee shop. Paul said, "Feeling all right?" to Michelle.

"Hangin' in there." Michelle nudged Nina with her arm. "Since the trial started, you're so distant, like I'm just another job for you."

Nina, hearing the hurt in her voice, resisted the surge of annoyance she felt. "Sorry, Michelle. Right now, it's my job to be obsessed and professional. Only way to win." What had Michelle expected? What did they all expect from her? If she cared any more, she'd be incapacitated.

In this court, in front of these jurors, she knew the outcome depended on many factors Hallowell did not have to consider—a run in her stockings, too much or too little makeup, hair in her eyes, the cut of her clothes, the amount of emotion she allowed herself, even the loudness of her voice, because in spite of the fiction she read, where there was this suspension of reality, where women lawyers acted like and were treated exactly like men lawyers, she had not gotten the same comfortable, instant credibility with the jury Hallowell got.

You take the situation as you find it. She would earn their respect. Some of them would start to root for her, and by extension, for Michelle, if she showed she warranted their trust.

Now that she was in the middle of the trial, she knew she would provide Michelle a good defense. Collier's workman-like approach had its drawbacks. He got the job done. But she could do more than that. She could turn it around. She could make them care about the case and about Michelle. But she couldn't do that and be a friend, and mother, and sister all at the same time. Some things had to suffer.

"Thinking about the guy who's up next? The scuba diver?" Paul said. He looked uncomfortable in his suit; his tie was too wide: Nina recognized it as a derelict from the seventies.

"Easy pickings," Nina said. "I only want one thing from him."

"And what's that?"

"A shiver," she said. Paul laughed.

"I called Cytograph today. They're talking next week sometime for the results of our second DNA go-round."

"What difference does it make?" Michelle asked. She was resting her legs across another of the hard chairs.

"You never know," Nina said.

"There are so many things against us," Michelle said. "I don't know where I'm winning or where I'm losing. The only thing I'm sure about is, I'm scared to death."

"Courage," Nina said. "If our bridges tumble down, we're out of here via the waterways."

* * *

Back in court, it was Ensign Pepper's turn. Sandy-haired and freckle-faced, he displayed an incongruous Howdy Doody overbite over a prime V-shaped physique. He went over the same ground as his captain, outlining his dives and how he had located Anthony's body and the statue. He discussed the underwater photographs, high-tech infrared, of the body before it was moved. Anthony sat in ghastly twilight, about to say something, his face indistinct, his torso naked and undefended. "Nothing further," Collier Hallowell said.

"Ensign Pepper, you observed the body after it was brought on board?" Nina asked.

"Yes, ma'am."

"Did you observe any fish bites or other evidence the body had been disturbed underwater?"

"No, ma'am. Not many fish swimming around."

"Did the body appear to have decomposed in any manner?"

"Not that I saw. That's your basic deep freeze down there. I've picked up bodies off the bottom that sat there for a year, fresh as the day they sunk. A couple of years ago, another patrol vessel picked up a Chinese man who probably worked on the railroad decades ago. They used to dump troublemakers in the lake. He must've been buried in the sand. Looked like a guy I know. We call them lake mummies."

A ripple of laughter passed over the court. "When you went down in that icy water on April twenty-ninth, were you wearing any protective gear?"

Ensign Pepper frowned, disappointed at this show of ignorance. "Subfreezing wet suit and mask designed for frigid conditions. You can dive under ice in the rig I wore. Even so, my lips got so stiff the regulator fell out of my mouth."

"Have you ever been for a swim in water the temperature of the lake that night without such protective gear?"

"One night," Ensign Pepper said slowly. "We picked up a drunk gentleman and we were towing his boat. He fell overboard, and I didn't have time to suit up."

"How long were you in the water?"

"About five minutes."

"Did you experience any discomfort due to the temperature?"

Ensign Pepper wrapped his arms around himself, torturing his young features into a rigor of intense pain. Nina cast a sidelong glance at the jury. They got it.

"Now I ask you, based on your experience as a Coast Guard diver, do you think an average swimmer could swim unprotected in that water for a half mile?"

"Objection! Calls for speculation. Incomplete hypothetical. The witness hasn't been qualified as an expert witness. Lack of foundation."

"Overruled," Milne said, looking at Nina with . . . no, could that be a twinkle?

"Not a chance," the witness said with finality. "Or if this swimmer somehow made it, he'd better crawl himself straight to a phone for an ambulance."

Several jurors gave Michelle their attention. Nina urged them on in her mind. Yes, imagine that girl, the one that liked to loll around on a sailboat tanning, the one that relied on men to pull a motor to life. Picture her on a freezing night like that, swimming mightily away from her dead husband. Michelle was leaning back in her chair to make room for her belly, her figure buried and her physical grace obscured. See her like that, flailing in the water.

"No further questions," Nina said.

Dr. Clauson, after the lunch recess, faced sleepy jurors fighting carbo overload. The court provided the jury lunches, which today must have been heavy on dessert.

A pack of cigarettes nested in Clauson's shirt pocket. His thick glasses kept his eyes mysterious. Soft, bloodless, hairless hands held his brown briefcase close to his body as he sat down.

Hallowell took him through the autopsy report, which was introduced into evidence. The details of the contents of Anthony's stomach, the wounds, and the changes associated with drowning took Nina back to the morgue. The jurors looked at their fingernails, lighting fixtures, or stared intently at Michelle, wishing to skip this part of the trial, please, Judge.

"You also have the laboratory results?"

The witness pulled out a sheaf of papers. Nina already had copies, and the lab reports had become part of the evidence in the case by stipulation.

"What were the significant findings?"

"Depends on what you mean by significant."

"Findings possibly related to the death of Mr. Patterson."

"Well, the blood alcohol showed up at .15."

"Indicating the level at the time of his death?"

"We make adjustments, so this figure gives our best estimate of the level at time of death," Dr. Clauson said.

Juror number eight, a lady in a gaudy knit dress, had surrendered to a postprandial doze. Nina hoped her neighbors would jog her awake before she had to say something. You couldn't let sleeping jurors lie.

"Based on your experience, does this result indicate Mr. Patterson was unconscious at that time?"

"No. Not just the drinking. If that was all that was wrong with him, he would have been somewhat intoxicated, but not staggering drunk."

"What else do you note on the lab reports?"

"Traces of cocaine."

"Why don't you go ahead and summarize the other findings."

"All right. He had the beginnings of arteriosclerosis. No evidence of other drugs, or poisons. And he had a small carcinoma on the right lobe of the lung. Probably symptomless, but malignant."

"Curable?"

"That's not my area," Clauson said. "All I can say is, small and nasty."

"Okay. Let's return to the autopsy, because I know the jury wants to be very clear on the cause of death of Mr. Patterson. What was the immediate cause of death?"

"The man drowned," Dr. Clauson said.

"And in what manner, if at all, did the two blows to the head contribute to his death?"

"Right. Based on the edematous changes and other evidence, the first blow, the one in the back of the skull, occurred at least an hour prior to the second blow. That one, first blow, she knocked him out, probably just for a few—"

"Objection!" Nina said, rising and leaning over the table to emphasize that the witness was way out of line. Clauson knew better than that. She would have to be very careful examining him.

"Sustained. The jury will disregard the last sentence of the witness."

Oh, that helps, Nina thought. Here the medical examiner had carefully let slip that he thought Michelle was guilty. Talk about small and nasty.

"So the first blow would have knocked him out?"

"Certainly for a few seconds, maybe longer."

"Could it have killed him?"

"Didn't do enough damage. No fracture, just superficial bleeding."

"And the second blow? In the frontotemporal region?"

"Harder, stronger, caused a linear two-inch fracture from point of impact toward the base of the skull."

"Would it have knocked him unconscious?"

"Almost definitely."

"Can you give us an estimate as to how long before he drowned that Mr. Patterson was struck the second time?"

"He hit the water within seconds after . . ." Clauson paused, looked meaningfully at the jury, and shut his mouth.

"Was he alive at that time?"

"Yes. He breathed in water. Alive, but probably unconscious."

"And your comparison of the wounds with People's 14"—the polar bear—"leads to what conclusion, if any?"

"The statue caused his head wounds. He was struck with the same statue twice, an hour or so apart."

"Good afternoon, Dr. Clauson," Nina said.

The physician nodded. Careful now.

"You testified that the first blow didn't do much damage."

"Well, it probably knocked him out for a second or two. That's damage. But concussions, the brain knocking around in the skull, come easy in higher primates. Now, billy goats, rams, woodpeckers, can tolerate impact velocity and deceleration a hundred times greater than humans."

"Based on your experience, could the first blow alone have killed Mr. Patterson?"

Clauson thought. He didn't want to give Nina anything, but he wasn't going to lie.

"Probably not."

Nina wanted better. But Clauson was leaning forward, a hungry vulture eager for something to scavenge.

"Question, Counsel?" Milne said.

"Nothing further of this witness, Your Honor." Clauson, reaching into his pocket for a cigarette, stepped down with his briefcase and left the court, an unlit butt pressed between his lips, talking softly to himself all the way out.

Another break. The jurors filed out. The lawyers stood to show respect as they walked by. Nina tried to find a smile that did not presume, but suggested, a warm, delightful person anyone would find an irresistible dinner companion.

The final session of the day began. Collier called Lt. Julian Oskel, who strode up in uniform, hat off and holster empty. Under the regulation haircut Nina saw intelligent eyes, a strong nose, full lips. He flashed a killer smile at the jury. The women jurors sat up in their chairs, except for the sleepy lady in back, whose eyes were open but who had turned off for the day. Jack always said out of the twelve, you were lucky to get eleven live bodies.

"Lt. Oskel, you are employed by the South Lake Tahoe Police Department?"

"Yes. I've been there ten years," Oskel said in a deep, manly baritone.

"In what capacity?"

"I started as a patrol officer, then was assigned to major crimes investigations, and I've been there ever since."

"You handle homicide investigations?"

"Some of them, yes."

"On April thirtieth, did you perform any investigative work regarding discovery of a body in Lake Tahoe?"

"Yes." Oskel pulled out his own report. "White male, apparent drowning, head injuries, reported by the Coast Guard."

"And did you proceed to investigate the incident?"

"Yes."

"Describe the scope of your investigation, please."

"I wasn't the only one working on the call that night. Do

you want to hear what the department was doing, or just me? I wouldn't want to steer you wrong."

"What was the department doing, to your knowledge?"

"When the call came in, Sgt. Higuera and two officers were dispatched to the Ski Run Dock. They performed an initial investigation—"

"Please describe the investigation."

"The team at the dock took photographs. They made a preliminary examination of the body and called Dr. Clauson up to take charge of it. They took the decedent's fingerprints and also dusted the statue and boat for prints.

"We have a new, computerized system for comparing prints. I made the comparison with prints on file and was able to determine that they corresponded with those of the decedent. I obtained his address and at 2200 hours went to the residence on Tahoe Vista to inform the wife and continue the investigation. Prior to that time, I obtained a search warrant to search the residence."

After more formalities, the warrant and accompanying affidavit came into evidence.

Nina's shoulder ached with weariness. At four forty-five, court adjourned, Judge Milne's robes rustling the whisper of good night.

"Oskel will be back on Monday," Nina told Michelle as they walked to the parking lot. "We're doing fine. Go home and try not to worry. Get some rest."

"I'm not going home," Michelle said. "I guess you noticed, my parents haven't been here."

"Yes. But I didn't have a chance to ask about it."

"I can't stand to be there anymore, Nina. They're lying to me. I'm too tense. I'm too pissed off."

"Your parents probably weren't too happy, either, when

your mother was served with my subpoena," Nina said. "Do you still want to go through with it?"

"God, yes. Put her on the stand. Make her squirm if you have to. She's a lot stronger than she gets credit for. Just make her talk."

"That's exactly what we'll do." Her shoulder was killing her. She needed to get home and lie down. "Meantime, Michelle, where are you staying?"

"The shelter. I'm safe and comfortable there."

Nina nodded. "Call me at home if you need to talk."

"Sorry I was such a baby today. You don't need to hold my hand, and anyway, I can see your hands are already full."

"Forget it," said Nina. Michelle hugged her briefly, then opened the car door and jumped in. She drove slowly out of the lot.

Paul had come out with them. "Tiring work," he said.

"But you're your own boss," Nina said. They walked toward the Bronco. "Going back to Monterey?"

"I've got a new place down there. Need to get myself organized. Catch up on other work." He looked unhappy.

"But you can't possibly get back before ten. You should stay."

"Not unless I have some pressing business in Tahoe tonight," he said meaningfully.

Nina frowned at the asphalt. "But you'll be back."

"Next week."

"We're a good team, aren't we?" asked Nina, stopping by her car. "It's good . . . working with you."

Paul put his hand on her arm and swung her into a kiss deep enough to snake through to her toes. "I don't have to leave," he whispered into her hair.

"Oh, yes you do," she said when she recovered her breath. "Because I do have pressing business. Just don't forget . . ." She turned to her car and jumped in, slamming the door behind her.

"What?"

Holding tightly to her steering wheel, she spoke through the glass.

He pounded on the window and she rolled it down. "Don't forget what?"

"I need you, Paul."

"At last," he said, "we agree, Nina."

Driving home, Nina looked at herself in the rearview mirror. No lipstick, hair needing surgery—so what? What she felt inside, beyond the warm flood of feelings for Paul and underneath that, the clicking technology of her intelligence, was a surge of confidence that made her thankful.

And she saw something else. Now that she wasn't smiling, now that she was alone, thinking about the trial, still hearing Jack's voice but over him, no longer subject to his interpretations, out of his orbit, she saw the eyes narrow and bright, the clamped jaw and cheekbones in high relief. She saw passionate conviction and courage in the face.

"Billy goats, rams, and woodpeckers," she said, and that lean, mean reflection laughed.

28

MONDAY MORNING, PREDAWN. New day, new suit. Nina's contacts refused to go in for a long time. The cream curdled as soon as she poured it in her coffee, standing in the kitchen looking out at the stars.

Just before she left, she tiptoed into the kids' room and over to Bobby's bed. He clutched his stuffed purple dragon even in sleep. He liked to use his sleeping bag as a cover, and two pillows. Dipping her head toward his sweet-smelling hair, moist from the heat, she examined the curve of his cheek for traces of her baby. She kissed his cheek softly. He stirred, then sleepily put his arms around her. "Love you," she murmured, but he was already asleep again.

She drove to the office at dawn, the dark sky gradually paling to gray, taking her place on the highway with the delivery trucks, late-night revelers and casino workers. A blinking sign and yeasty warm aroma announced a doughnut shop. She stopped and had a cop's breakfast.

By six A.M. she was at her desk, slogging through correspondence and rummaging through files, trying to catch up on her other cases. Some things could not be put off. She had no interest in any of it at the moment, which made the dictating that much harder. At six-thirty Sandy came in, looking surprised, and introduced a black woman with a crocheted cap over long red hair.

"This is my friend Albertine. She's tutoring me with the word processing."

"I thought you knew all that already."

"I had to say that. Would you have hired me if you knew I didn't?" They settled into the reception area. The three of them worked concentratedly until eight-thirty. Nina stood up to leave. "Hold the fort," she said to Sandy.

"Keep those pesky Indians out," Sandy answered smartly.

"You know what I mean." She was shoveling papers into her briefcase, her jacket half on, and walking out the door at the same time.

"Nina."

Nina stopped in surprise. Sandy had never addressed her by her first name before.

"Go get 'em."

The participants took their places in the Superior Courtroom. Nina, Paul, and Michelle had no time to talk. Michelle seemed to have expanded an inch or two over the weekend. She looked endearingly clumsy.

Tahoe had entered Indian summer. The temperature would hit the nineties. Paul had reverted to shirtsleeves, worn with a new-looking Hermès tie. Nina reviewed her notes. She had no intention of discrediting Oskel. He was too popular with the jury, and she thought she could turn their approval into an advantage. Use him, don't abuse him, she told herself.

She checked the things she needed from Oskel one more time. She needed acknowledgment that the police had focused only on Michelle, not investigating other possibilities. She wanted him to tell the jury about Anthony's old arrests. She had to deal with the cocaine problem. And she had to make Michelle's statements at the time of arrest, and her disposal of the broken coffee table, look innocent.

The long day began. Hallowell spoke from his table, and Julian Oskel answered.

"You are still under oath, Lieutenant," Hallowell said.

"I understand."

"Directing your attention now to your search of the Patterson residence on Monday night at ten P.M . . ."

Oskel nodded. He looked eager to help.

"What, if anything, did you seize at the residence pursuant to the warrant?"

Oskel pulled out a list of items, a copy of which Nina was already studying. The list went into evidence, and Oskel summarized it.

"We noted no sign of a struggle. We saw stains on both couch pillows, which someone had evidently unsuccessfully tried to clean—"

"Objection. Speculation, as to the last sentence of the testimony," Nina said. Oskel made it sound like a cover-up.

"Sustained."

"Based upon your careful inspection of the stains you noted, did you observe anything unusual about them?"

"Objection, vague and ambiguous," Nina said.

"Overruled."

Oskel said, "Yes, they appeared to have been tampered with. Parts of the stains were much fainter than others and could be seen only with difficulty." Okay, Hallowell had made his point.

"And are these the couch pillows you seized?" Hallowell pulled out a big Raley's shopping bag and presented Oskel with Michelle's couch pillows after showing them to Nina. The pillows went into evidence. Nina chose not to waste time with technical objections.

"And it was later determined that these were indeed bloodstains?"

"Yes. Type A negative, kind of unusual."

"Did your laboratory compare these bloodstains to the blood of anyone else?"

"Yes, tissue taken from the body of the victim. Anthony Patterson."

"And did you determine—"

"It was a match," Oskel said.

Hallowell moved on to his next point. "What else did you seize?"

Oskel looked down the list. "Pay stubs from Prize's, showing Michelle Patterson was employed there."

"Anything else?"

"Cocaine," Julian Oskel said, giving the jury a rueful shake of the head. Michelle received some disapproving stares. Hallowell did not dilute the impact of the word by going into any more detail. He moved on.

"Anything else?"

"We went through the garbage pail set out on the street for pickup. We found pieces of a coffee table, a lot of broken glass that looked like part of it. We saw what appeared to be blood on several of the glass shards."

"And what did you find, if anything, regarding this blood?" Hallowell had examined so many witnesses for so many years he didn't make mistakes in the form of his questions. On his direct examination, he was not allowed to lead the witness. Adding the tag, "if anything" allowed him to lead the witness while complying with the technicalities.

"A match. With the victim."

"The blood on the glass you found hidden in the garbage bag—"

"Objection!" Nina said. "Mischaracterizes the testimony." She couldn't let the word *hidden* insinuate itself into the jury's collective mind without a fight. Hallowell was subtly reinforcing the idea that Michelle had gone around hiding evidence.

Hallowell didn't wait to be called to the bench and chastised. "Withdrawn, Your Honor." Once again, his point was made. He turned the page of his tablet and started on Michelle's statements the night of her arrest.

"Did you on Tuesday night, May first, contact the defendant, Michelle Patterson?"

"Yes. I received word from the Douglas County sheriff's office that Mrs. Patterson was located at the Lucky Chip Motel, on the California side, which brought her back into our jurisdiction. Sgt. Higuera and I waited in the parking lot and she arrived there not long after midnight. I guess that made it May second."

"What occurred then?"

"I asked her, 'When's the last time you saw your husband?' She said, 'Thursday night' and that they had a bad fight on that occasion. Then I informed her that the victim was dead. She asked me, 'Where'd you find him?' I told her and then she took off across the parking lot."

"What happened then?"

"Sgt. Higuera called for backup and we went looking for her. We found her about two tenths of a mile away, sitting on the ground on a wooded slope south of Pioneer Trail, just before it runs into Lake Tahoe Boulevard. At that point we considered her a suspect. Sgt. Higuera read her her rights."

"Did she say anything after that time?"

"Yes. She was pretty hysterical, and I didn't catch everything. But she did say clearly . . . uh . . . 'I didn't mean to kill him. I didn't think I hit him that hard. I can't believe he's dead.' Then, in the car on the way to the station, she said, 'We had a million other fights like that.' Then she mumbled something else, but I couldn't catch it."

"Anything else?"

"Not that I recall."

"Did she request a lawyer?"

"Not at that time."

"Did you have any further contact with the defendant?"

"On the way to the station, she said she went to a lawyer on Monday and the lawyer told her to move to the Lucky Chip."

"Did she give the name of the lawyer?"

"Nina Reilly." The jurors' eyes focused on Nina. That hurt. They would assume she had been up to something underhanded. Even the name *Lucky Chip* sounded shabby.

"What else did she say, if anything?"

"She said words to the effect that during that violent argument she hit the victim on the head with an Eskimo statue. She also said after she hit him, she got him onto the couch and then she couldn't remember what happened next."

"She said she couldn't remember?" Hallowell said, looking surprised, and repeating the statement so the jury couldn't miss it.

"That's it. She said she didn't know what happened next. One minute the victim was lying on the couch and the next minute she was waking up the following morning in her bed."

"Did she offer any explanation for her inability to remember what she did after striking her husband?"

"She just said she couldn't remember, so she must have just gone to bed."

"She said she left her bleeding husband in the middle of a violent argument to go in and go to bed, and she doesn't even remember doing that?"

"Objection," Nina said. "Asked and answered."

"I'm just trying to get these statements as clear as possible for the jury," Hallowell said.

"Approach the bench," Milne responded. At the sidebar he said in a low voice, "Collier, you've rammed it home. Now move on."

"Okay," Hallowell said. He stood next to Nina, confident, in control, everything going his way. She was close enough to kill him, but Milne wouldn't like that. The lawyers sat down again.

"Did she say anything else at the time she was booked?"

"Later on she asked to call her lawyer."

"Nothing further," Hallowell said.

They took the morning break. Michelle and Paul made small talk. Nina drank a carton of milk. She checked the things she needed from Oskel one more time.

"Okay, Lt. Oskel . . ."

He beamed at her from the witness stand.

"Who else did you interview in connection with this case?"

"We interviewed Brenda Angelis, a cocktail waitress at Prize's. We interviewed Art Wong, the owner of the Lucky Chip Motel where the defendant was staying. And Mrs. Patterson's supervisor at Prize's. We took the reports from the Coast Guard and the Douglas County sheriff's department. We checked with the garbage company to see when it was supposed to be picked up. Rick Eich . . ."

"Anybody else?"

"Her doctor, Frederick Greenspan. Also, we traced the statue of the bear to the Prize's gift shop. She bought it."

Nina shouldn't have given him that opening. She would keep her questions narrow.

"Did you at any time investigate the possibility that someone besides Mrs. Patterson might have committed this crime?"

"No evidence popped up that implicated anyone else."

"Did you talk to any of Anthony Patterson's fellow employees at Prize's?"

"No. We didn't have the need."

"Did you talk to his supervisor?"

"No."

"Now, among the evidence that did pop up was a small silver pin found outside the bedroom window at the Patterson residence. Did your department attempt to trace that?"

"It could have been there forever."

"Do you recall if you had to dig for it?"

"N-no. It was right there on top."

"On top of what?"

"There was still some snow."

"It was right on top of the snow?"

"Yeah."

"Indicating it had fallen there very recently?"

"Yeah."

"So, in fact, it couldn't have been there forever. In fact, it could have fallen there on the night of Anthony Patterson's death?"

"Could have."

"So why didn't you check it out?"

The jury waited. Oskel sat there like a handsome mannikin.

"Well, Lieutenant?"

"It didn't seem important," he mumbled.

"It was too much trouble, when you already had your mind made up—"

"Objection!"

"Sustained."

"Also in the physical evidence was a package of Virginia Slims cigarettes found in the pocket of Anthony Patterson's robe, the robe he was wearing when he was discovered. Did you check to see what brand of cigarettes Anthony Patterson smoked, Lieutenant?"

"No." Oskel was not looking so helpful anymore.

"What if I told you he only smoked Camels? Would you

then have made some effort to find out who gave him those cigarettes?"

"Objection," Hallowell interjected quickly. "Presumes a fact not in evidence."

"I can make an offer of proof, Your Honor," Nina said. An offer of proof had to be heard outside the presence of the jury. Nina could then explain, on the record, how she would be able to put that fact into evidence at a later time.

"Approach the bench," Milne ordered, and up they came again. "Do we have to go through this long, involved process? I hate to send the jury out. They'll get lost in the bathrooms and it takes fifteen minutes just to round them up."

"Mr. Hallowell could stipulate that Mr. Patterson smoked Camels," Nina said.

"I don't know that," Collier said.

"So who's going to prove it for you? The defendant?" Milne asked.

"No. Peter La Russa. Mr. Hallowell's witness back there in the second row."

"Do you want to stand on ceremony, Collier?" Milne said.

"Oh, let it come in. Subject to a motion to strike if La Russa doesn't back her up."

Nina and Hallowell walked back, Nina holding her head high.

"The witness will answer the question, subject to a later motion to strike," Milne said.

"Uh, what was the question?" Oskel said.

"For purposes of this question, Lieutenant, I want you to assume that Mr. Patterson smoked only Camels. I also ask you to remember your testimony that a pack of Virginia Slims was found in the robe Mr. Patterson was found wearing underwater. Now, if you had known he only smoked

Camels, what conclusions, if any, would you draw as an experienced homicide investigator upon finding the Virginia Slims?"

The jury waited intently for his answer.

The lieutenant came through. "I would assume he ran out of cigarettes and somebody gave them to him," he said simply.

"Now, we know he smoked, and we know that package and no other was found in his pocket. What conclusion would you draw from that?"

"That he was smoking those cigarettes the night he died," Oskel said. It was a wonderful answer.

"Wouldn't you also investigate whether someone who smoked Virginia Slims was with him the night he died?"

"I suppose."

"You're the investigator, Lt. Oskel. What would you do?"

"If the defendant also did not smoke that brand, I'd look into it."

Nina moved to close that particular loophole.

"Then why didn't you? You had all the information readily available. Why didn't you draw those conclusions and make that further investigation?"

"Because we already had the perp," Oskel blurted.

"You had already decided to concentrate your efforts on convicting Mrs. Patterson?"

"Objection!" Hallowell sounded troubled. "Misstates the testimony."

"Overruled."

Oskel didn't answer.

"Answer the question," Milne told him.

"I guess so," he said. Nina wanted to throw her arms around him.

"Let's move on," Nina said. "I believe you found Mr. Patterson's fingerprints on file."

"Yes."

"Why were they on file?"

"Well, he was a security guard, so he had registered. And once upon a time he had been with the Fresno police."

"Any other reason? Take a look at your report if you wish to refresh your recollection."

Oskel didn't need to do that. "He had a couple of prior arrests. But no convictions."

"Move to strike the preceding question and answer as irrelevant," Collier said.

Milne thought about it. "Overruled," he said. "Too late."

"What were the charges?"

"Objection. Irrelevant."

"Sustained."

"In your experience as a homicide investigator, would the fact that the decedent had been charged with at least two crimes have indicated the possibility that his death might be related to criminal activities in which he was involved?"

"Maybe." It was all she was going to get.

"Then why didn't you look into that possibility?"

Oskel didn't have to answer. The jury understood. To keep on with this line of questioning would be overkill.

"Okay, let's talk about this cocaine you found."

"Objection. Not a question." Hallowell was going to cut her no slack.

"You testified you found cocaine at the Patterson residence?"

"Yes."

"How much cocaine?"

"An eighth of an ounce."

"Did you find any evidence that this was for sale, rather than for personal use? Scales, other paraphernalia?"

"Not that I noted here on the report."

"Would you have noted it on the report?"

"Yes."

"Where did you find the cocaine?"

"In a sock drawer."

"Men's socks, or women's socks?"

"Men's socks."

"Anything in Mrs. Patterson's sock drawer?"

"Socks and some very sexy underwear."

"Your Honor . . ." began Nina.

"Please refrain from characterizing the evidence, Lt. Oskel," said Milne with a slight smile.

"Did the location of the cocaine in the man's sock drawer indicate anything to you, as an experienced homicide investigator, about who possessed the cocaine?"

The way she had phrased the question, there was no real out for Oskel. Hallowell had his hand to his forehead, apparently trying to think up an objection. "That the man possessed the cocaine," Oskel said reluctantly. "But that doesn't mean she wasn't using it too."

"Move to strike the last sentence as nonresponsive," Nina said.

"The sentence is stricken. The jury will disregard the statement."

"Did you also check to see if Mrs. Patterson had a criminal record?"

"Yes."

"Was there any indication whatsoever that she had ever been connected with the use or sale of cocaine?"

"Not in the criminal records check."

"Anywhere else at all? Any indication in your investigation that Mrs. Patterson even knew her husband had that cocaine?"

"No." Lt. Oskel now looked resigned. He knew she wasn't going to maul him, just nip him a little here and there.

Nina paused. There were several more points to make. She glanced at the clock. Eleven-thirty. She would try to finish by twelve, keep the judge and jury fed and happy.

"By the way, you said Mrs. Patterson became almost hysterical when you started asking her questions."

"Yes."

"Did you take this as an indication of possible guilty knowledge?"

"Well, it could be."

"Lt. Oskel, isn't it true that this was the first time this lady had learned of her husband's death, so far as you know?"

"I suppose."

"Are you married, Lieutenant?"

"Objection!"

"Would you think it evidence of guilty knowledge if a woman became hysterical on hearing suddenly that her husband had been murdered?"

"No."

"Did you take this into account in considering whether Mrs. Patterson's reactions looked guilty to you?"

"Objection! Misstates the testimony."

"He may not have said it, but he implied it, Your Honor," Nina said.

"Approach," Milne said. Now it was Nina's turn. "If you want to argue an objection, you bring it to the sidebar, Counsel. If you do that again I'm going to see that you regret it."

"Sorry, Your Honor," Nina said, without looking sorry.

When she was seated again at the counsel table, Nina said, "You also testified as to certain statements allegedly made voluntarily by Mrs. Patterson before and after her arrest."

"Right."

"How many times did she say she struck her husband?"

Nina turned and looked intently at the jury, and they obligingly listened closely to the answer.

"Once."

"Only one time?"

"That's right."

"Did she indicate she had been out on a boat that Thursday night?"

"No. I wrote down what she said."

"Did she say anything that might indicate she had knowledge of any events that night after striking her husband that one time?"

"It's what she didn't say that was the problem, ma'am. She had no story at all."

That hurt. Nina moved hastily on to her last point. "Regarding the coffee table in the garbage, and the stains on the sofa . . ."

"Uh-huh."

"What conclusions did you draw from those facts?"

"Looked like she was trying to get rid of evidence, rub out the stains and get rid of the garbage."

"Why would she wait for five days, from Thursday night to Tuesday, when the trash was picked up, to get rid of that evidence?"

"I have no idea."

"Isn't that delay more indicative of a housewife cleaning up a mess than a murderer covering up evidence of her crime?"

"I have no idea," Oskel said, looking to Hallowell for help. The jury saw the look. They were now clear that he was a far from neutral witness.

"Nothing further. Thank you, Lt. Oskel."

"Any rebuttal?"

"No, Your Honor," Hallowell said. He wanted Oskel to

go away. Oskel climbed down. He didn't look at the jurors
as he left.

"Counsel, I understand you have stipulated all the physical
evidence on the list may be admitted."

"Correct, Your Honor."

"Right, Judge."

"We'll recess for lunch," Milne said. "Please be back in
court at one-thirty."

"Call Art Wong," Hallowell said. He had three witnesses
set for the afternoon. Besides Art Wong there were Brenda
Angelis and Peter La Russa. The trial was taking on momen-
tum, gathering speed. The official witnesses were finished.
The rest of the witnesses knew Michelle and Anthony. Their
testimony could cut deeper.

Art Wong, the motel manager Sandy had recommended
so long ago to Michelle, took the stand in a seersucker suit,
hardly seeming tall enough to peer over the witness box.

"Mr. Wong, you are and have been for twenty years the
owner of the Lucky Chip Motel, correct?"

"Mmm-hmmm."

"Please say yes or no."

"Yes."

"Located in Stateline, near Harvey's Casino?"

Mr. Wong nodded. "You have to speak out loud, please,"
Hallowell added.

"Yes." A soft, shy, high voice. He twisted a handkerchief
in his hands.

"On April thirtieth, a Monday, were you on duty at the
motel?"

"Yes."

"Did you have contact that night with the defendant, Michelle Patterson?"

Mr. Wong tipped his head and stared at Michelle. "She looks a lot different," he said. "Yes."

"Please describe that contact." Hallowell was looking for a narrative answer. Good luck, Nina thought.

"She booked a room." Hallowell waited, but nothing more was forthcoming.

"Did she book the room in her own name?"

"No."

"What name?"

"Iris Summers."

"But you're sure it's the same woman."

"Yes."

"Do you know why she used a false name?"

"No."

"Did she appear distressed in any way?"

"No." What was he looking for from Mr. Wong?

"Who made the reservation for her?"

"The lawyer's office."

"What lawyer?"

"That lady over there," he said softly.

"Nothing further." Big deal, Nina thought.

"Hello, Mr. Wong," she said.

His eyes brightened a little. He had realized the worst was over.

"Do you know why my office made the reservation?"

"No."

"Did anything Mrs. Patterson do suggest to you she was trying to hide from the authorities?"

"No."

"How often do people register under false names at your motel, and you later learn the names were false?"

"I never know all," he said. "But many."

"And what are some of the many reasons somebody might use a false name?"

"Objection. Calls for speculation."

"Sustained."

"Did Mrs. Patterson return to your motel on May eighth?"

"Yes."

"Did she have a peaceful sleep that night?"

Mr. Wong looked up at the ceiling for information. "No."

"What happened?"

"Somebody tried to break into her room."

"How do you know that?"

"She was screeching and the other people got woken up, so I came outside."

"Then what happened?"

"She calmed down. I fixed her screen and window so she could go back to sleep."

"What was wrong with her window?"

"Somebody used a knife to cut the screen. The window was broken, too, but it was still locked."

"So it appeared someone was attempting to get in her room?"

"Like I said." He appeared annoyed at having to say it twice.

"And she was very frightened?"

"Very loud screaming. And running around in cold night with only underpants."

"So she was in danger?"

"Objection," Hallowell said as expected. "Calls for a conclusion."

"Withdrawn," Nina said. Mr. Wong waited, expressionless, for the next question. "Nothing further."

Hallowell stood. "Just a couple of questions on rebuttal."

"Proceed."

"For all you know, Mrs. Patterson could have engineered

that whole incident herself, couldn't she?" he asked. It seemed like a foolproof question, but Mr. Wong was a smart man.

"No," he said.

"Why not?"

"Too scared. And no reason to."

"Did you see the intruder?"

"No."

"All you saw was the defendant dancing around in her underwear, right?"

"Objection. Leading the witness."

"Sustained."

"Nothing further." Hallowell sat down again, looking disgusted. Nina thought he had not gotten far.

"Call your next witness."

"Brenda Angelis." A tall, thin girl with a gamine haircut and deep red lips took the stand. She wore a tight jacket and skirt of blue denim, black stockings, and black high heels.

"Is it Miss Angelis?"

"Yeah."

"Where are you employed?"

"Prize's. I'm a cocktail waitress."

"And did you know the defendant in April?"

"Sure. We worked together." Miss Angelis was looking around, enjoying the attention.

"On Monday evening, April thirtieth, were you and Mrs. Patterson working at Prize's?"

"You got it."

"What, if anything, did Mrs. Patterson tell you about her husband?"

"She said they had a helluva fight the Thursday before. She said he was trying to rape her, and beating on her, and she went nuts and bonked him over the head with a statue.

And then she said he disappeared and she thought he was going to ambush her or that he was dead or something. And she was moving to a motel till things cooled down."

It was a sensational statement. Brenda Angelis knew it, and she basked in the limelight.

"Did she give any details?"

"She said he was drunk, and he smelled bad."

"Anything else?"

She thought, then shrugged.

"No?"

"No."

"Did she state anything about the reason for the fight with her husband?"

"Oh, yeah. Right. Uh, he wasn't going to spring for her therapy anymore. She was seeing a shrink—we should all be so lucky—and she didn't want to quit."

"Thank you, Miss Angelis." The witness looked disappointed. Hallowell turned to Nina, muted triumph in his eyes. "Your witness."

Nina had decided to be very careful with this girl. "You say Mrs. Patterson beat her husband over the head?"

"Yeah."

"How many times?"

"Excuse me?"

"Did she tell you how many times she hit him?"

"No. I got the impression once was enough. Now I come to find out—"

"So she never stated she hit him more than once?"

The witness thought for a minute, then said, "I guess not."

"And then she said he disappeared?"

"Yeah."

"Anything about taking him out on a boat?"

"No, nothing like that."

"Did she seem to think he was alive?"

"She was scared shitless he was. Excuse me."

"Nothing further," Nina said. She hoped she had contained some of the damage, but Brenda had hurt more than any of the previous witnesses. Her testimony had a vitality and immediacy that let the jury see Michelle striking Anthony. The barmaid, wearing something similar to Miss Angelis's outfit today, something tight and cheap, came home, picked a fight, and hefted that bear to sculpt Anthony Patterson's skull. Anyone could now see that.

After the mid-afternoon break, Peter La Russa, Anthony's friend and coconspirator, took the stand, but he wasn't alone. Jeffrey Riesner walked up the aisle with him. "I represent Mr. La Russa," he said. "I request to stay by the witness box in the event my counsel is needed."

So La Russa might take the Fifth! And Riesner had insinuated himself into the trial after all.

"Any objection, Counsel?" Milne asked her and Hallowell. They shook their heads. Riesner had a right to be there.

"Mr. La Russa, during April you were a pit supervisor, commonly known as a pit boss, at Prize's, is that correct?" Hallowell asked.

"Yes." La Russa sounded nervous, torn away from his stomping grounds.

"Did you know Anthony Patterson?"

"Yes."

"Were you friendly with him?"

"Somewhat."

"And you worked with him?"

"He worked Security. He was around."

"And did you know the defendant?"

"She brought drinks to the tables."

"Did Mr. Patterson ever discuss his marriage?"

"Objection, calls for hearsay," Nina said. Where was this going?

"Overruled."

"Yes, he did."

"Did you ever watch the two of them together?"

"Many times."

"And what, if anything, did you observe with regard to their relationship?"

"She hated the guy," La Russa said.

"What specifically did you observe in that regard?"

"She avoided him. Whenever he touched her, she looked disgusted. She never smiled at him or showed him any respect or love. She slept around on him."

"Thank you, Mr. La Russa," Hallowell said, showing his happiness with the testimony in a smug smile.

Up to this point Riesner hadn't made a peep. He just stood there. Nina hoped she could get through her cross-exam without setting him off.

"You don't like the defendant, do you, Mr. La Russa?"

"No. I don't like her."

"Would you like to see her convicted of killing your buddy?"

"If she did it."

"You were fired from Prize's, is that right?"

"That is under litigation," La Russa said. Riesner began to uncoil.

"Why were you fired?" Nina asked.

"Objection. Irrelevant," Hallowell said.

Milne didn't seem to know what to do with the objection. He, too, was watching Riesner. "Overruled," he said finally. "You may answer."

La Russa nodded. "I refuse to answer on grounds that it may tend to incriminate me."

"You're taking the Fifth Amendment?"

"That's what he said," Riesner interposed.

"Okay, Mr. La Russa, isn't it true that you and Mr. Patterson had a business relationship independent of the casino?"

"I refuse to answer on grounds it may tend to criminate— I mean *in*criminate me."

"And wasn't your business to conspire to defraud the casino by permitting a known card counter to gamble there, against policy, and then splitting the profits?"

"I refuse to answer on grounds it may incriminate me."

Nina was enjoying herself. "And didn't you yourself have a falling out with Mr. Patterson because he wanted a larger share of the profits?"

La Russa wanted to say no, but Riesner was shaking his head. "I refuse to answer on grounds it may tend to incriminate me."

"Perhaps you murdered him?" Nina said. She felt possessed by some wicked force that was saying, push it to the limit. Riesner glared at her.

"Hey, wait a second! Not me," La Russa said loudly.

"How can we know that, if you won't even talk about the deal?"

"Objection. Counsel's arguing with the witness."

"Sustained."

"Anthony was jealous of his wife's relationships, isn't that so?"

"Very jealous. He had reason."

"Did he threaten or harm any of the men he was jealous of?"

"I wouldn't know about that," La Russa said.

"Isn't it true that on the day Anthony Patterson died, you presented him with a Security videotape taken when he was off shift?"

La Russa knew exactly what she was talking about. "Yes."

"And what was on that tape?"

"The casino boss, Stephen Rossmoor, and her saying good-bye in front of his suite, that's what."

"She was coming out of the suite?"

"Yes."

"And she was showing some affection?"

"She had her hand clamped on his balls and her tongue down his throat," La Russa said loudly, looking pleased with himself.

"What was Mr. Patterson's reaction?"

La Russa gave a small laugh. "I didn't stay for the whole show."

"Did he threaten Mr. Rossmoor?"

La Russa had finally seen where she was going. He made haste to head her off. "Not really."

"Did you consider, when you gave him that tape, that you might be putting Mr. Patterson's life in danger?"

"No! It was the other way around. Rossmoor's, maybe."

"You mean Mr. Patterson might go after Mr. Rossmoor? Did you stop to think Mr. Rossmoor might then decide to remove Mr. Patterson as a threat?" She waited for the objection.

"Calls for speculation," Collier said. "There's no evidence . . ."

"Counsel, do you want to approach the bench?"

"It's all right, Your Honor. I withdraw the question," Nina said, leaving the jury with rich new lines of thought to ponder that evening.

"Oh. By the way, Mr. La Russa. What kind of cigarettes did Mr. Patterson smoke, if any?"

"Camels. No filter."

"Thank you, sir."

La Russa and Jeffrey Riesner walked down the aisle together in their suits like ushers at a wedding, Riesner casting a condescending look at Nina as he walked by, a look that said, you can't even keep me out of your trial.

"It's drawing near the close of the day," Milne said. "I'd like to meet with counsel at eight-thirty tomorrow. Court is adjourned until nine o'clock tomorrow."

Nina gathered up her papers. The adrenaline stopped propping her up and she felt faint with exhaustion. Paul and Michelle helped her pack up and carry her files to the Bronco.

"See you tonight?" Paul said.

"I'm sorry. . . ."

"Okay, get your rest," he said. "It only gets harder. I enjoyed the show today."

"How'm I doing, Paul?"

"Hallowell's case is a mess," Paul said.

"Yeah, but the confession's going to come in tomorrow."

"You'll think of something," he said, hopping in his van and taking off.

Michelle was fitting herself stomach-first into her own car. "This baby wants to go beddy-bye," she said. "So I'll be getting on back to the shelter."

"See you tomorrow," Nina said.

Michelle spoke over her shoulder. "I wish you hadn't trashed Steve like that."

"I had to."

Michelle drove away.

29

NINA WOKE UP slowly. Pressure and lack of sleep had saddled her with a massive headache. Three aspirins and a cup of coffee later, she trundled her files through the courtroom halls.

Until now, she had not carried the burden of going forward in the trial. Hallowell had set the scenes, built the framework, taken all the responsibility. Her job had been merely to limit the damage.

Today Collier Hallowell would rest his case.

Now the defense would step forward to persuade the jury not to convict. She was going to give Hallowell the confession.

The prosecution already had enough evidence to take the case to a jury with a good chance of a murder conviction. Dr. Clauson's testimony that an hour had elapsed before the second blow was struck added up to a possible verdict of premeditated murder—life in prison for Michelle.

Michelle had told Oskel and Higuera that she couldn't remember what happened after going into the kitchen. The jury was unlikely to buy this statement.

Yet Nina could not explain Michelle's statement without going into Michelle's mental state that night. And the Court of Appeals had ruled that Bruno's tape could then be used by the prosecution to rebut her explanation.

If Michelle was convicted of murder after Nina allowed

the tape to come in, Nina knew she would be publicly condemned as completely incompetent. She would have to pack up and skulk away; she wouldn't be able to pay somebody to be her client. The prudent thing to do was not to make a bad situation worse.

But she had decided to take the risk. There was no other way to introduce doubt into the minds of the jurors. Maybe if the jury knew everything she had learned, they would believe Michelle. If not, maybe they would decide Anthony had been killed in the heat of passion, and Michelle would then be convicted of manslaughter, not murder.

The defense strategy was so dicey, Nina wished with all her heart she had not had to make the choice. But Michelle agreed with it. "Let it all come out," she had said. So they would embrace the facts, not hide them; trust the jurors, and hope they would be just.

Milne had called the lawyers in early. The only people in the courtroom were Milne, the clerk and stenographer, the bailiff, Hallowell, herself, and oh, she had hoped yesterday was his last day here, Jeffrey Riesner, bathed in musky aftershave. She would gag for the rest of her life whenever she smelled it. What was he up to now? She didn't think she could handle one more complication.

Riesner was staring at her again. He was like the school bully who comes right up to the new kid and pokes him in the eye. He couldn't leave her alone.

Some people she liked on sight. Some she had to get to know first. A few, like Jeffrey Riesner, aroused a chemical antipathy in her. It wasn't just the physical intimidation of his big, ropy body, his coarse-featured face and heavy jaw. No, he riled the primitive female in her just by being him. Strange how the same chemistry that repelled her seemed to arouse an irresistible need in him to engage and defeat her. He would have hit on her, crudely, if she met him in a bar, and would have called her a bad name when she rejected him. Here in the courtroom, hemmed in by the rules, unable to approach her directly, he still sent out waves of hostile aggression.

Milne was talking. She focused her thoughts on him with difficulty.

"All right, Counsel, we have several matters on the record before the jury comes in this morning. Ms. Reilly, I understand you have a motion to dismiss this case. We have to talk about how this confession will be brought in. We should go over the witnesses the defense now knows it intends to produce. That's if you still intend to rest your case, Collier."

Hallowell nodded. "As soon as the jury comes in." He looked fresh and confident. It was his turn to take potshots.

"Let's do the motion to dismiss. Ms. Reilly?"

Nina made her pitch. When the prosecution rested its case, the defense could ask that the case be thrown out on grounds that, as a matter of law, there was so little evidence that the case should not go to the jury. It was a formal motion, for the record on appeal. Milne was not going to take it upon himself to wrest this case from the jury. Ample evidence to convict Michelle existed, even without the confession. "Request the Court grant defendant's motion. Thank you, Your Honor."

Hallowell stood up and ran through the main points he had made; Michelle had motive, opportunity, and means to commit the crime. Milne nodded his head.

"Motion denied," he announced in a perfunctory voice. "Now, Ms. Reilly, you have said in your opening statement that you are going to explain your client's mental state at or near the time of the murder. As we all know, that opens the door to the taped statement. Have the two of you worked out when and how that's going to come in? I don't want any wrangling in front of the jury."

"We haven't talked about it, Judge," Hallowell said. "I could wait until Ms. Reilly has put on all her witnesses and rested for the defense, make it part of my rebuttal. But it seems to me the easiest way to bring it in is on my cross-examination of Dr. Cervenka. I see he is listed as the first witness for the defense. He can authenticate the tape." His look at her was too personal, maybe hinting just slightly at pity. She faced the judge.

"Any problem with that?" Milne said.

"What about this? I'll bring it in in my direct examination of Dr. Cervenka," Nina said.

"You're willing to bring in your client's confession as part of your case?" Milne said. He seemed to be trying to give her a chance to back away.

"Yes."

Hallowell gave her a quick, incredulous glance. Riesner smirked.

Milne pushed his glasses up on his nose and said, "So be it."

"Regarding defense witnesses, Your Honor, the Court and Counsel have our list, subject to rebuttal or some special circumstance," Nina said. The list wasn't very long. Bruno, Barbara Tengstedt, and Dr. Greenspan, today and continuing into tomorrow; then Tom Clarke, Janine Clarke, Steve Rossmoor, Carl Tengstedt, and Al Otis. She had not yet decided whether to put Michelle on the stand. "They have all been subpoenaed and told to report to court this morning. I expect I will ask some of them to be denominated hostile witnesses."

"You think you can get through your psychiatric expert today?" Hallowell asked.

"If your cross-examination is reasonable," she told him. "But it will be tight. We may well go into tomorrow with Dr. Greenspan."

"Very well," Milne said. "Now, Mr. Riesner, I see you have brought us some papers."

"Yes, Your Honor. I represent Dr. Frederick Greenspan, who is under subpoena to appear today. While I realize that because he is the treating doctor of the defendant, his testimony may be needed, I request that his testimony be strictly limited."

"In what manner?"

"Ms. Reilly's defense is going to consist of slandering as many of these witnesses as possible. It is my information that she is going to attempt to impeach her own witness, Dr. Greenspan. She is going to accuse him of malpractice. That may or may not be actionable in a civil suit, since the testimony will be taken in court, but it is certainly preventable by the protective order we request."

"It wouldn't be the first time that defense has been used," Milne said. "So. Ms. Reilly, do you intend to imply that Dr. Greenspan drove her to it? You wouldn't be thinking he hypnotized her into murder?"

"No. I only ask that Dr. Greenspan tell the jury about her problems and how he attempted to treat them. I do intend to point out that he is not a qualified psychotherapist."

"See, Judge?" Riesner said. "She's going to try to drag this respected physician through the dirt. She doesn't care who she hurts so long as she gets the jury confused. If she goes after my client, she should know I'm going to go after her."

Milne looked unimpressed. He scanned the papers again, then said, "Okay. I'm going to order, Ms. Reilly, that you ask no question and elicit no answer that would tend to indicate some kind of malpractice by Dr. Greenspan. That includes implying things. You say you have no evidence, so no innuendos, is that understood?"

"Yes, Your Honor."

"However, I see no reason why the jury should not understand the doctor's qualifications fully and fairly. I am not going to order that you refrain from discussing his qualifications."

"Thank you, Your Honor."

"All right. Let's get moving."

The court doors opened and the people took their seats. Andrea had taken the day off and sat in the front row near the counsel table. She gave Michelle's arm an encouraging squeeze as she passed. Nina's witnesses sat in various parts of the audience, looking uniformly glum.

The Tengstedts sat in the last row. Mrs. Tengstedt looked like she had been crying. Carl Tengstedt had his arm around her, his angry face turned toward Nina. Al Otis sat right up front, in a plaid sport coat with a white carnation. Today his hair was brown, combed straight back and he wore heavy horn-rims. Must have made a quick stop at the casino on his way over.

The Clarkes sat together near the main aisle, not touching, Tom Clarke looking as worried as if he were on trial himself. His wife sat stone-faced, her arms folded.

Steve Rossmoor had come in with Michelle attached to one arm, a laptop computer at the end of the other.

Early bird arrivees, the Greenspans, flanked by Riesner, had avoided Nina. Ericka Greenspan appeared to be arguing with the lawyer. Maybe she didn't feel the protective order had gone far enough.

At last, just before the doors closed, Bruno Cervenka came rolling in in his motorized wheelchair. He was accompanied by a student who must have been his designated driver. His white hair had been neatly pasted down, and his attaché hung off the pushing handle. He parked in a corner in back.

Nina looked back at him and smiled gratefully. She knew how hard it had been for him to come.

Today would make or break Michelle. The spectators seemed to sense it. Even the jurors were particularly restive this morning. The emotions in the room created an atmosphere of rushing toward a finish. The trial had become an entity in itself, and it had seized them all.

"Mr. Hallowell?"

"The prosecution rests its case-in-chief, subject, of course, to rebuttal, Your Honor."

"Very well. Ms. Reilly, are you ready to proceed for the defense?"

"Yes, Your Honor. The defense calls Bruno Cervenka." At this signal Bruno wheeled down the main aisle, letting the jury have a good look at him. Bruno had never been handsome. Now that he was old, the bulbous nose, prominent ears, and shaggy brows had resolved into a quite respectable picture, Jack Klugman mixed with Albert Einstein. He stopped beside the witness box and placed his case in his lap.

"Good morning, Dr. Cervenka," Nina said, as soon as he was sworn in.

"Good morning." The deep, rumbling voice she was depending on held out a morsel of comfort to her.

"You are a medical doctor who is a psychiatrist and a professor of psychiatry at the University of California Medical School in San Francisco, is that correct?"

"Yes. I received my medical degree from UCLA in 1946. I completed my residency at—"

"The People will stipulate that Dr. Cervenka qualifies as an expert witness in the field of psychiatry," Hallowell interrupted. This prevented Nina from going into great detail about Bruno's past, his awards, his writings, his professorships. But the jury seemed adequately impressed.

"How long have you been practicing psychiatry?"

"Forty-two years."

"And during this time have you had an opportunity to diagnose or treat patients with amnesia?"

"Oh, yes. In my work, I see it often. I have had hundreds of such opportunities."

"Were you contacted by me at the beginning of May of this year regarding acting as an independent consultant in this case?"

"Yes."

"What did I ask you to do?"

"You asked me to review the medical records of Michelle Patterson, especially the records of her current treating doctor. You asked me to interview Mrs. Patterson and perhaps hynotize her. You asked me to provide you with a diagnosis of her psychiatric problem, and to try to recover lost memories."

"And did you carry out those requests?"

"Yes. I did all that. I read the records, and Mrs. Patterson came to San Francisco for evaluation in May."

"And did you prepare a written report for me at any time regarding this work?"

"No. You did not request it."

"You mentioned possible hypnosis. Do you use hypnotherapy in your practice, Professor?"

"Yes. It has a limited use, however."

"And how is it limited?"

"Hypnosis is not used in classic psychoanalysis at all. Freud found that the improvement in patients using hypnosis was always temporary. He discovered that hypnosis actually prevented the patient from expressing his resistances and working through his problems."

"How else is it limited?" Bruno was so smooth. His answers meshed effortlessly with the points she was trying to make.

"At present, reputable practitioners of hypnotherapy use it for only a few purposes. To put it simply, it can help a tense or anxious person relax. It is sometimes helpful in treating some addictions, such as tobacco smoking or compulsive eating. And, occasionally, it is helpful for patients who have amnesia due to some mental or physical trauma."

"You say it is only sometimes helpful. Why is that, Professor?"

"You have touched on the main problem with hypnosis, which is its lack of reliability. This is especially true when it is used to attempt to uncover matters that have been repressed, that is, pushed into the unconscious."

"In what specific respects is hypnosis not reliable for patients with amnesia?"

Bruno talked to the jury as if they were students in one of his seminars, casual, at ease. "Well, first you have to realize that hypnosis is merely putting the body and mind into a relaxed state in which suggestibility is enhanced. This may affect the accuracy of the memory that is recovered.

"For example, some patients have a strong desire to please the therapist. This may distort the memory. The patient may add in fictional details, or invent a memory that he cannot uncover. There is a word for this: *confabulating*.

"Also, other material from the patient's unconscious—guilts, fears, other repressed matter from the patient's childhood—may leak through when the patient is in this state. The patient's memory may be colored by this material. The result may be a memory of something that never, in the patient's life, occurred." Bruno was gesticulating as he talked. The jury appeared appropriately mesmerized. Bruno stopped talking, to cement the mood.

"Let me back up a little now, Professor, and ask you . . . what is amnesia?"

"It is a mental condition in which the patient is unable to bring to his or her conscious mind an event that has been personally experienced."

"So the phrase *loss of memory* is a reasonable description?"

"Yes."

"What causes amnesia?"

"Objection. Relevance."

Milne agreed that Nina was generalizing too much with that question. "Why don't you ask about the amnesia in this case, if that's what you're driving at, Counsel," he said.

"Certainly, Your Honor. I will return to that in a moment." Nina paused to gather her thoughts now that her rhythm with Bruno had been broken. Her back was to the audience. She felt the pricking of a hundred pairs of eyes.

"Returning to the work that I asked you to perform, Professor, can you give the jury a summary of the treatment Mrs. Patterson received from Dr. Frederick Greenspan here in Lake Tahoe?"

Bruno pulled out Greenspan's notes. They had already been admitted by stipulation, so Nina was able to avoid that group of questions and answers. "He saw her for ten sessions, between January and April of this year. She was hypnotized at all but the first session. She terminated the therapy rather than completing it."

"And what do you understand were her presenting symptoms, based on the notes?"

"She came to this doctor primarily due to anxiety and depression. At the first session she also discussed certain compulsions that were bothering her. She compulsively acted out sexually. Dr. Greenspan noted possible alcoholism."

"Anything else?"

"She also discussed in the first session that she could not remember her childhood before the tenth year. This was causing her some suffering, as though she required a great deal of energy to keep these memories suppressed."

"Do the notes indicate any diagnosis was made?"

"No. The doctor was not a psychiatrist, he was a physician with some training in hypnotic techniques."

Riesner stood up in back and said, "Your Honor . . ."

"You will remember the matters we discussed this morning?" Milne said in a warning tone to Nina.

"Yes, Your Honor."

"Continue."

"Your Honor," Riesner said again.

"Sit down, Mr. Riesner," Milne said.

"Please describe the therapy undertaken with Dr. Greenspan, if you would," Nina said. The jury turned its collective head back to Bruno.

"I really can't do so. The notes are rather sketchy, and there are no tapes. It appears the doctor would put Mrs. Patterson into a deep hypnotic state to remove anxiety and depression. After a few sessions he apparently made various suggestions to help her cease her compulsive sexual activity. In the ninth and tenth sessions he appears to have been trying a technique called hypnotic regression."

"And that is?"

"Trying to access the lost childhood memories."

"And was he successful in this regard?"

"Not that I could tell."

"Let's turn now to the evaluation of Mrs. Patterson you made in San Francisco." Nina was feeling nervous. She missed Hallowell's objections. He was biding his time.

"Yes. I talked with Mrs. Patterson for some time. Then I put her under."

"You hypnotized her?"

"Yes. An excellent subject, she was extremely receptive."

"What happened next?"

"I had two objectives. The first was to try to evaluate the extent of resistance of her unconscious to releasing her childhood memories."

"By using the technique of hypnotic regression?"

"Precisely. My second objective was to try to evaluate her more recent loss of memory."

"Referring now to a memory loss on the night her husband was killed?"

"Yes, her inability to remember what occurred after she struck her husband the single time."

"All right. You made a tape of the entire session, is that correct, Professor?"

"Yes."

"Do you have it with you today?"

"No. It was taken from my office by the police."

"Showing you this tape now, which has been in the custody of the Lake Tahoe Police Department since its transfer by the San Francisco authorities . . ." She handed the tape to Bruno. At her counsel table, the clerk was setting up a tape recorder.

"I can tell if it's the same tape that I made, if I can hear the first sentence or two," Bruno said.

Nina turned on the tape. Bruno and Michelle talked, her voice floating above his. The jury was hearing Michelle for the first time.

"Yes, that's the tape," Bruno said.

"All right, let's listen to the section regarding Mrs. Patterson's childhood loss of memory. Unless you have some objection, Counsel?"

"Be my guest," Hallowell said.

The courtroom hushed. Breathing fast, Nina turned on the tape again.

And they all heard Michelle, talking about the Philippines, then seeming to go back in time, her voice higher, her speech immature. There was foreboding in the voice, then quickly came the explosion of fear and horror, her thin voice crying "Daddy!" They heard wild weeping and sobbing, then Bruno's soothing words, pulling Michelle into another place. Nina turned off the tape.

The Tengstedts left the room, Barbara Tengstedt's face buried in her husband's shoulder, their departure followed by curious glances.

Silence. Michelle's hand covered her mouth, and her head was down. Paul whispered, "Are you all right?" and she nodded, looking back at where her parents had sat.

Nina said in a quiet voice, "Did this portion of the hypnotic session, along with your review of Dr. Greenspan's notes and your interview with the defendant, allow you to arrive at any conclusions regarding the childhood amnesia?"

"Oh, yes."

"What were those conclusions?"

"First, I would say there is obviously a traumatic memory locked up in this lady's brain, a single devastating event with great emotional content. It is buried so deeply that even after the session was over she could not remember even saying these things. In other words, she still could not access the memory consciously. Second, I would say this memory blocks all the other childhood memories, and they could easily be brought back if she consciously remembered this thing on the tape.

"Third, the regression itself is suspect. You can hear on the tape that it is piecemeal, incomprehensible to the child experiencing it. It is impossible to tell what is actually occurring. It is only a beginning. Mrs. Patterson would need several more sessions to try to bring this memory into a place where she herself could explain it."

Bruno was performing brilliantly. The jury remained in thrall.

"All right, Professor, let me ask you this: Is there a tendency for such an amnesia to recur if another traumatic event occurs later in life?"

"Exactly. Each person has his or her own way of reacting to overwhelming emotion. The brain follows the path of least resistance. If the brain has managed to contain the first event by amnesia, it will tend to take the same defensive action when a second traumatic event occurs."

His statement sounded dry, not as significant as some of the other things he had been saying, but Hallowell was sure to understand the impact of what Bruno had just said. He had presented the jury with a bona fide explanation for Michelle's amnesia on the night of the killing. Nina glanced over and saw that Hallowell was writing notes frantically.

"Could a violent struggle with her husband have provoked another attack of amnesia?"

"If there was sufficient emotional content," Bruno said.

"All right, Professor . . ."

"Let's take the mid-morning break," Milne said.

When the jurors returned, Nina thought she saw a new openness in their faces, as if they were now willing to consider the possibility that there was indeed a doubt that Michelle had committed the murder. She had her chance.

"Professor, I am now going to play the remainder of the tape, the portion in which you have said you were trying to determine what happened on the night of Anthony Patterson's death, and then I will ask you some questions."

She pushed *Play* and the tape turned.

When Michelle said, "I killed him," there was a general gasp. And then Bruno asked, "What are you feeling now?" and she said, "Hate."

The tape ended. Nina stole a look at the jury. They all looked appalled.

She hadn't realized how damning the tape would sound, no matter what background she provided. Michelle had confessed. The words, indelibly etched on the minds of the jury, hung there. She felt the shaky structure she had worked so hard to build wobbling.

"Uh, Professor. You, uh . . ."

"Ms. Reilly?" Milne said.

She took a long breath. "Professor, can you conclude from this tape whether or not Michelle Patterson killed her husband?"

"No," Bruno said equably. He seemed the only one unaffected by hearing the tape.

"How can you say that, when the defendant uses the words, *I killed him*, and apparently says she hated her husband?"

"I simply don't draw that connection. Let me explain. These statements are not reliable. It is more than possible that the previous trauma has leaked into these statements. The statement, 'I killed him,' may be more metaphorical than real."

The jury seemed to be lost. What Bruno was saying went against the evidence of their own ears.

Bruno said, "A few years ago another patient said that to me, a charming lady whose elderly mother was dying of Alzheimer's disease in a nursing home. When she died, this lady came to me and told me under hypnosis that she had killed her mother. She said the same thing. 'I killed her.' She had great guilt from her inability to keep her mother at home. She truly believed she had murdered her mother, though all she had really done was put her in a nursing home."

"Why do you say that the previous trauma may have somehow distorted this confession?"

"Ten minutes before, I had seen Mrs. Patterson go through a powerful emotional experience. Those emotions may have still been alive. In my opinion, the second portion of the tape was tainted by the first."

"Thank you, Professor. Your witness," Nina said. She had done her best.

They broke for lunch before Hallowell's cross-examination. Paul, Nina, and Michelle took their usual cramped table in the coffee shop. Paul was the only one who could eat anything. He shoveled down two tuna sandwiches and a pint of orange juice while Nina and Michelle sat there, not talking.

"That's what I call proactive lawyering," Paul said. "You took control of the tape and dressed it up before and after with all the reasons why it shouldn't be believed. You showed you weren't afraid of it. You took it away from Hallowell. Nice going!"

When Nina did not reply, Paul asked what the matter was, but Nina couldn't explain. She was numb. There were no words for what she was feeling. "Don't lose it now," Paul said as Nina got up and trailed after them into the courtroom.

Now Hallowell had his turn. He was ready.

Nina could see Bruno was tiring, but he still looked game. She wondered how long he would last.

"Professor Cervenka, how many times have you testified for the defense in a criminal case?" It was a marvelous opening question, zeroing in on Bruno's weakness as a witness.

"I couldn't count."

"More than a hundred times?"

"Possibly."

Hallowell turned and faced the jury as he asked the next question.

"And how many times have you testified for the prosecution?"

"That hasn't come up."

"Never?"

"Never."

"You're not a neutral witness at all, are you?"

"What do you mean?"

"Isn't it true that you have a strong bias against the prosecution?"

Bruno hesitated. In view of his record, if he said no, he would lose all credibility.

"My consulting work—"

"You're a defense consultant, aren't you?"

"You might say that."

"A paid consultant, at that. How much are you being paid to be here today?"

The answer would come in. Nina didn't bother to object. She squirmed instead.

"Three hundred dollars an hour."

"Three hundred dollars an hour! Well, for that you'll explain away anything, won't you?"

"Objection! Move to strike counsel's comment!"

"Sustained."

"You told us all about amnesia in your testimony."

"I discussed it briefly."

"You explained that the defendant's amnesia about the events on April twenty-sixth through twenty-seventh could be a reaction to the trauma she experienced?"

"Yes."

"Then let me ask you this. How do you know she has amnesia?"

Bruno said, "Because . . . because she told me."

"In fact, you're relying totally on her self-serving statement to you that she has amnesia?"

"I have to," Bruno said.

"What if she's lying about that?"

"Well, I have to assume—"

"And for three hundred bucks an hour, you'll make any assumption, won't you—"

"Objection!" Nina said indignantly. "Counsel is trying to—"

"Sustained."

Mid-afternoon break. Bruno spent the whole time in the bathroom. Back at the witness stand, his face seemed washed out. The pain pills for his hip must not be working.

"Now, you've tried to explain away this confession—"

"Objection! Approach the bench?" Nina said. She went to the sidebar with Hallowell.

"Your Honor," she whispered fiercely, "Mr. Hallowell is making far too many editorial comments in his questioning. I ask that he be admonished."

"She can dish it out, but she can't take it, Judge," Hallowell said. He tried to catch her eye. She ignored him.

"He's right," Milne said to Nina. "Deal with it."

Nina returned to the table, her cheeks flaming.

"Rephrase the question, please, Counsel," Milne said.

"The defendant said, 'I killed him,' right?" Hallowell went on.

"Yes."

"And that doesn't indicate to you that she killed her husband?"

"No. As I explained—"

"If I tell you under hypnosis, 'The sky is blue,' does that indicate to you that the sky is not blue?" One of the jurors giggled. Hallowell looked at Nina, his face dark with concentration.

"No, it is just not evidence either way that the sky is
blue."

"The sky could still be blue?"

"Yes."

"Thank goodness," Hallowell said, and the whole courtroom enjoyed a chuckle.

"As you sit here today, Professor, do you have any idea
whether this woman murdered her husband?"

"No."

"Now, she said on the tape, 'Hate,' when you asked her,
'What are you feeling now?' Doesn't that indicate that she
hated her husband?"

"Not necessarily."

"Why would she lie?"

"I don't say she was lying."

"Then what was she doing? She wasn't telling the truth,
and she wasn't lying? You're not earning your fee, Professor." More laughter.

"Objection! Argumentative! Not a question!"

"Sustained."

"She confessed to murdering her husband on this tape,
didn't she?"

"Objection. Calls for a conclusion."

"Overruled."

"It wasn't necessarily a confession, I'm telling you."

"Okay, now let's talk about the defendant's other problems besides this so-called amnesia. She was depressed?"

"Yes."

"How did she feel about her husband? When she wasn't
in a trance?"

"She expressed some fear and some anger," Bruno said.

"Did you ever figure out why she sleeps around?"

"Objection! Vague and ambiguous."

"Rephrase the question, Counsel."

"Why does she go looking for sex?"

"It's probably part of the symptomatology, connected with the original trauma."

"And why does she get drunk? Excuse me, drink excessively?"

"My understanding is she no longer drinks alcohol."

"How long did your evaluation of this young lady last?"

"If you mean the session in my office, one hour."

"That cost another three hundred?"

"Yes."

"So you've known her for one hour, and you've read some notes secondhand from some other doctor, and you think you know all about her psyche?"

"Objection. Argumentative."

"Overruled."

"Not at all. That I would never presume. But I have reached some conclusions."

"Like when she says, 'I killed him,' she may not really mean it?"

"Yes."

"And when she says she hates her husband, you can tell after one hour she doesn't mean that either?"

"She may not mean it in the sense you imply . . ."

"After this one-hour session, do you think you can tell when this lady's lying?"

It was the best question of all. Bruno couldn't think of a way to field it.

"As a trained psychiatrist, I can probably tell a lie more easily than a layperson," he said finally.

"I'm not asking for a generality. I want to know if you can tell if this lady, the one who's on trial for murder, is a liar or not?"

"Perhaps not in every instance."

"How about a yes or no for us laypeople?"

"No."

"Nothing further."

"We will resume with the testimony of Barbara Tengstedt at nine o'clock tomorrow," Milne ordered. They all headed for the doors. Nina went up to Bruno and said, "Can I walk with you to your car?"

She pushed his chair out into the parking lot. His driver had been waiting, leaning against Bruno's specially equipped van.

The cool air sent a chill through Nina. "I hope I didn't let you down, my dear," Bruno said.

"You were wonderful."

"Call me when you have your verdict." They drove away.

Nina stood there, wishing she could hit the road with them and head out over the mountains.

30

On Wednesday, Barbara Tengstedt came out of the shadows.

Michelle had not even spoken to her parents since returning to the shelter in Tahoe. The Tengstedts refused to speak to Nina about Mrs. Tengstedt's subpoena. They had avoided the trial until required to appear on the day before, and they had not approached Michelle.

Their estrangement seemed complete. Nina believed Carl Tengstedt would never forgive Michelle for forcing his wife to testify. Up there on the stand, he would not be able to protect her, hush her, direct her. To compel her, in this rude and public way, to speak of matters so private, must seem to the Tengstedts like a betrayal of the most vicious kind.

Barbara Tengstedt would be a marginal witness. Her contribution would be tangential, even confusing to the jury. At most, she would be able to corroborate Bruno's theory that a past trauma had led to amnesia, and that when faced with a new trauma, Michelle had used the same psychological defense.

But Michelle wanted it, and Nina wanted it. She had decided that ultimately it might serve the Kitchen Sink defense well, casting doubts all around. Nina would take that past and see if she couldn't make it work for Michelle for a change.

In examining Mrs. Tengstedt, Nina would have to violate

her main rule, to know the answer to any question she asked. And at the back of her mind she replayed Bruno's suggestion over and over.

Why did Michelle's father disappear? Was he dead? Her efforts to track down further information about him through Sandy hadn't netted anything. Maybe he would show up today. Or maybe he couldn't. Maybe Michelle . . . She turned her mind away. They would find out, wouldn't they?

The jury filed in, chatting with each other, comfortable at last after a week and a half in this important new role.

Nina had half expected that Barbara Tengstedt would not appear that morning. If she did not, Nina had decided to tell Michelle she would do no more. The idea of asking Milne for a bench warrant to chase down the people who had paid her attorney's fee was just too ludicrous.

But she had come, a wraith in a black suit, a white blouse, and a brave little scarf that matched perfectly.

"Call Barbara Tengstedt," Nina said. Michelle's mother took the stand.

She was a woman whom others never noticed, the invisible matron who took up no space in the store, the church, or the living room she inhabited. She would never have raised her voice in a public place or quarreled loudly with her husband. She had eluded the attention of others all these years.

Now the court took her in: the hair a nondescript blond, the features fine once but now blurred by time, the faded blue eyes, anxious and embarrassed. She was a camouflaged creature, put brutally on display outside her habitat. Nina felt a pang of compassion.

In the back row, Carl Tengstedt seethed.

"Please state your full name," Nina said from the counsel table.

"Barbara Tengstedt."

"Your full name. Including your middle name and maiden name."

Mrs. Tengstedt said something inaudible. "You have to speak into the microphone," Milne told her.

"Barbara Elaine Underhill Tengstedt."

"You are the mother of the defendant?"

"Yes."

"And you live in Fresno with your husband, Carl Tengstedt?"

"Yes."

"Do you work outside the home?"

"No."

"Does Mrs. Patterson still live with you?"

"No."

"When did she cease living with you?"

"Three years ago."

"When she married Anthony Patterson and moved to Lake Tahoe?"

"Yes."

"Prior to that time, had she always lived with you?"

"Yes."

"Where did she live from infancy to age ten?" Nina could see Hallowell at his table. Jump right in and hang yourself, his grim mouth said.

"In the Philippines."

"Where in the Philippines?"

"At the naval air base at Subic Bay."

So far, so good.

"Who is Mrs. Patterson's father?"

"Carl Tengstedt."

"Is Mr. Tengstedt her natural father?"

A long pause. "I don't care to discuss that."

"Please answer the question."

"Do I have to?" Mrs. Tengstedt said, tilting her head up to Milne, who was jerked out of his reverie.

"Yes, you do," Milne said.

"What will happen to me if I don't?"

"I will have to order you to answer. If you don't answer then, you will be in contempt of the court."

"What would happen then?"

"I would have to jail you," Milne said shortly.

"All right, send me to jail."

"Barbara!" Carl Tengstedt cried despairingly from in back.

"Bailiff, make that man sit down," Milne said.

Nina thought, this was definitely not a good direction. "Your Honor, if I may . . . I am willing to withdraw the question at this time," she said.

Milne looked relieved. "Proceed," he said.

"Mrs. Tengstedt, do you love your daughter?"

"Yes."

"You are not here today of your own free will, is that right?"

"Yes."

"But you understand you must answer my questions truthfully?"

"Yes. Or go to jail."

"You were in court yesterday?"

"Yes."

"Do you remember Dr. Cervenka's testimony that your daughter may have suffered an episode of amnesia on the night of her husband's death?"

"I remember."

"And that he based his conclusion primarily on your daughter's statements to him and Dr. Greenspan that she suffered from amnesia about her childhood?"

"Yes."

"Did she, in fact, tell you that she could remember nothing about her past to the age of ten?"

"Objection. Hearsay."

"Sustained."

"Did you observe any memory problem with your daughter during her years with you in Fresno?"   •

"Objection. Vague and ambiguous."

"Approach the bench?" Nina said.

Milne was not in a good mood. Hallowell lounged to the side as Nina argued.

"The answers to this line of questions are relevant to our defense, Your Honor. They explain the tape and they explain the memory lapse. I didn't just drag this lady up here for laughs."

"Keep your voice down. I don't want the jury hearing this. You're asking for hearsay."

"I've put the defendant's mental state in issue. The answers aren't offered for the truth of the matters stated. They are offered to show her mental condition, and therefore they fall under an exception to the hearsay rule."

"Well, Collier?" Milne said, looking at his watch.

"Sure, there's an exception to show mental state. But we have a unique situation here. Nina's trying to show the defendant's mental state thirteen years or more ago, not her mental state the night of the murder. She's going too far afield, and the exception can't apply with that lapse of time."

"Does anybody around here have any legal authority?" Milne said. "I'm not interested in making new law."

"You're going to have to, Your Honor," Nina said. "Look. She was undergoing hypnotic-regression therapy when she made this so-called confession. She was in the present physically, but she was in the past mentally. Her mental state at the time she spoke those words is clearly relevant. Furthermore, on the night in question, it is our contention that the defendant experienced the same psychiatric problem. That's why she can't remember—"

"I don't even want to think about this," Milne said. "You're the defense, you have wide latitude; I'll let it in. But I'm not here to act as a foil for your creative lawyering, Ms. Reilly. Don't do this to me again."

After Nina and Hallowell had sat down again, Milne said, "Objection overruled."

"Did your daughter tell you she couldn't remember anything about her childhood before the age of ten years?" Nina asked Barbara Tengstedt, rephrasing the question they had all forgotten by then.

"The jury is instructed that this testimony is offered to show the mental state of the defendant at the time of the tape you have heard and on the night of April twenty-sixth and morning of April twenty-seventh. It is not offered to show the truth of the matter stated," Milne said. Several of the jury members were waiting for more, but Milne apparently had decided not to wade into deeper waters with more comments.

"You may answer the question," Nina said.

"Yes, she talked about it," Barbara Tengstedt said.

"Did you refuse to discuss her past with her?"

"There was nothing to discuss."

"Request this witness be considered an adverse witness, pursuant to Evidence Code section 776," Nina said. As an adverse witness, Barbara Tengstedt could be impeached, even though technically she was Nina's witness.

"No objection," Hallowell said.

"I show you now this certified form entitled Notification of Change of Beneficiary, stamped United States Naval Station, Subic Bay, the Philippines, marked for identification as Defendant's Exhibit 36. The form is a summary of benefits provided to Major Carl Tengstedt." She handed it to Mrs. Tengstedt, who almost dropped it.

"Yes."

"That form indicates that Mr. Tengstedt's marital status changed on the date given, and that two dependants were added for benefits purposes on the same date. Will you please read for the jury the names of those new dependants?"

"Barbara Tengstedt and Michelle Tengstedt."

"And your daughter's age is stated to be what?"

"Age ten."

"Now, Mrs. Tengstedt, why didn't you discuss with your daughter that you married Mr. Tengstedt when she was ten years old?"

"I . . . I . . ."

"Mrs. Tengstedt?"

"Leave me alone!" Mrs. Tengstedt cried.

Nina readied her next sally, but Milne had had enough. "We'll take the mid-morning recess," he announced.

Out in the hall, Nina hurried after Carl Tengstedt. "Please let me talk with you for a minute," she said. He turned pink eyes on her and fiddled with a mangled necktie. "Please," she said. "It can't hurt."

He did not reply, but followed her down the hall to a quiet corner near the wall. "I'm sorry to put your wife through this."

"It's my daughter, not you, doing this. But you have the power to let my wife go." Up close, Tengstedt looked close to collapse, a fine stubble of beard rimming his round face, his scanty reddish hair uncombed, his tie knotted crookedly.

"I can't do that. I'm going to press her and press her, Mr. Tengstedt, until she answers."

"God knows we made a mistake paying you to hurt us."

"You're so busy protecting your wife and yourself. Don't

you see your daughter's liberty is in danger? Don't you see she has to know? Can't you think about her for once?"

"You are a kind of slaughterhouse technician, aren't you, Miss Reilly? You smile, you keep your hands clean, you dismember people without a thought. What does making my wife suffer have to do with Michelle and Anthony? Nothing, except to help you to confuse those people out there who have been called to judge my daughter."

"Mr. Tengstedt—"

"After this is over you hang up your bloody apron and go home. What about us?"

"I don't like you, either, Mr. Tengstedt," Nina said. "You think you have the right to keep your daughter ignorant and suffering. You aren't sparing her, you're torturing her."

Tengstedt covered his face in his hands. "You don't know what you're asking!" he said, his voice muffled.

"Whatever it is, it happened a long time ago. Please . . . ask your wife to answer my questions."

"I'll talk to her," Carl Tengstedt said wearily.

"Michelle . . ." Nina whispered. Michelle turned her head. Her eyes were the summer sky her mother's must have been, once long ago. Paul sat at her left at the counsel table, listening.

"I'm not afraid," the girl said. She squeezed Nina's hand. Barbara Tengstedt had mounted the witness stand without looking at her. She sat waiting for court to resume, while the public eye she detested came back to rest upon her.

"Remain seated," Deputy Kimura said.

Nina got up and walked around the table. Her feet felt encased in concrete. She faced the witness.

Something was wrong with Mrs. Tengstedt's expression. She didn't look resigned, or tearful, or nervous, or hostile, or even detached, all moods Nina might have anticipated. Her eyes shone, her lower lip trembled, and she leaned forward, catching Nina's eyes.

She was eager. Chilling, that eagerness.

Nina thought, confession is good for the soul. But I wish I were behind a grille, invisible. I'm going to exhume something old and frightful, something that maybe should stay buried. Ah, look at her, she wants to tell us, she wants to say it out loud. It's been choking her for thirteen years.

Nina looked back at Paul. He was watching Barbara Tengstedt, his expression sharp, professional, and inquisitive.

"Mrs. Tengstedt, there was a question pending when we took a recess—"

"I don't remember it."

"Let's start over, then. Why didn't you tell your daughter Carl Tengstedt was not her natural father?"

"When we realized Michelle had forgotten him, we thanked Jesus for removing it from her memory. We felt it was a miracle. We didn't have the right to undo His act of grace."

"But you are willing to answer my questions at this time?"

"I am willing to confess."

That word. Nina's spine was ice. She shuddered.

"Who is the defendant's natural father?"

"Was. He's dead now, he can't hurt us anymore."

"All right. Who was he?"

"His name was Larry Stokes."

"Michelle was born—"

"Michelle Stokes." Mrs. Tengstedt smiled at Michelle. "She was such a lively little girl. She takes after me. You can't see Larry in her face at all."

"You and Mr. Stokes were married?"

"Oh, yes. He married me in Fresno. He joined the navy and was posted to Subic. We flew there when Michelle was two years old."

Come on, her eyes said. The words were tumbling out of her mouth.

Nina wondered what to ask next. The courtroom had quieted. Even the clerk had stopped shuffling her papers and was listening. The stenographer's fingers rested uneasily in the air above her keys.

"Did . . . did problems develop in your marriage?"

"Problems. Yes. Problems. Drinking problems. You know—liquor."

"Go on."

"He had been drinking since he was twelve years old. At first it was a friend, it helped him sleep, be sociable—Larry Stokes was a shy, miserable man—and so he drank more and more, till alcohol was his only friend, and it grew stronger and stronger. And one day I saw his sickness, peeking out of Larry's face. Alcoholism, not Larry, dislocated my shoulder that day."

"Your husband was an alcoholic?"

"No. That doesn't say it right. My husband was possessed by alcohol. They call it a demon. That says it right . . . a living, raging disease in him, with its own personality. And I never—never—knew how it happened, but one day I was living with both of them."

"How did Mr. Stokes's alcoholism affect your family?"

"We became slaves. . . . Larry got drunk two or three times a week, and if we were lucky, he disappeared. . . ."

"And if you were unlucky?" Nina said gently.

"He went to war on us. He found all the ways to hurt us. When his sickness made him hit me, late at night, I could always see Larry in there, screaming and suffering, but he didn't have the strength to save us anymore." She turned to the jury, raising her chin. "I used up my tears. You won't see me cry."

"What did you do? About protecting yourself and Michelle?"

"What did I do? What did I do? I knew you would ask that, because you can't understand, no matter what I say. I did nothing. I endured it. I prayed. I was living off base—because he insisted—with a little girl in a foreign country, and I had no money, and he wouldn't allow me to leave. You can't imagine."

Nina glanced quickly at Michelle. Her hands covered her mouth as if she were trying to prevent herself from crying out.

"Why didn't you go to a superior officer, a chaplain, someone for help?"

"Larry would have been court-martialed. We would have starved. And . . . I was ashamed. Larry's shame was my shame. And Larry loved us. When he was sober he promised he could still win, and he wouldn't drink for a couple of days, but then I would watch the pressure rising in him, the demon eating him from inside, and he would try to hide it; we would pretend he could hang on. . . ."

"What about Michelle?"

"I'm weak, Ms. Reilly. I need someone to take care of me. Michelle and I—we had no one else."

The jury had gone from puzzlement to embarrassed attention. They still didn't know why Mrs. Tengstedt had been brought up there to make her pathetic revelations. Milne had stopped taking notes. Nina knew her time was running out.

"Mrs. Tengstedt—"

"He got worse. He brought women home, bar girls he paid. He broke my jaw when Michelle was eight. When she was nine, he was driving her in a car, very drunk, and ran it into a ditch. Michelle had a concussion. She was sick for a long time. She started to block out everything around her. She went around in a daze. She still does."

"Go ahead."

"Only Carl knows these things," the witness said. "We have never spoken of these things, even between ourselves."

"What happened then?"

"I started going to church, the Science of Mind Church. There were meetings on Saturday night, when Larry was never home. I met Carl." Her head lifted as she looked for the balding, puffy-eyed man in the back row. "He was kind. He helped me find God. I realized"—she blinked several times—"I had come to love Carl. I told him about my life. We decided that I would pack our clothes and leave. He had found us a place to stay until we could be married."

"Do you need a break, Mrs. Tengstedt?" Milne asked her. She shook her head and ran her hand across her forehead. Her pale skin had blotched with crimson. Strands of hair fell across her face, but she did not try to brush them away. She stared above the audience, working up to something.

A darkness had entered the courtroom, almost as if her memories had grown so real twisting inside her they would materialize any moment.

"Of course, that day Larry came home early. He had just learned he was going to be thrown into the brig for assaulting a woman in the village. He had stopped at a bar and gotten drunk. He came to the bedroom door. Michelle and I were standing by the bed. The suitcases were half full."

"How did Michelle react to seeing her father?"

"Crying, crying, crying. Scared, but she still loved her father."

"Then what happened?"

"He stood in the doorway, watching us. It was raining outside, pounding the tin roof, and he was dripping and muddy. He looked from me to the suitcases, then from the suitcases to me. Like that." She moved her head back and forth.

"What did Michelle do?"

"She ran to me and held on to my dress. She stopped crying and watched him. She could see it wasn't her daddy. The sickness had taken over."

"It was Larry Stokes, but he was drunk?"

Mrs. Tengstedt nodded, her chest heaving, watching the air. Several jurors were watching the same spot. "Yes or no?" Milne said.

"Yes," she breathed.

"And then . . ." Nina's voice had constricted.

" 'Leave me alone, Larry! Please!' That's what I said."

"It's clear in your mind?"

"It's burned into my mind. And he shouted, 'You go, and you'll never see Michelle again.' . . . His voice was so thick and ugly. I fell down on my knees, praying, 'Larry, Larry, please stop and save us all.' . . . He started toward us, staggering, his face not human anymore, his arms out for balance, dripping, like something from outside that didn't belong in there. And I thought . . ."

"Yes?"

"And I thought, I'll never leave here. Never . . . leave here." Barbara Tengstedt couldn't seem to catch her breath. Her mouth was open, her eyes squeezed shut. "Michelle, she started screaming something, and she tore over to the table and picked up a bottle, a full bottle of whiskey. Then . . . it was like he jumped at me, or maybe he just tripped, but while he was in midair she swung that bottle. . . ." She stopped, panting, kneading her hands, eyes still closed.

"Go on."

"I can't go on. Don't make me."

"You came here to confess it all. Go on. Make your confession." Nina heard cruelty in her own voice.

Loud breathing for a minute, then: "She hit him with it."

Nina spoke quickly to quell the sounds rising from the

courtroom, and to stifle her own frantic despair. What had she done here? What had she done to Michelle? "What happened then?" she said, with as much calm as she could fake.

"He ended up on top of Michelle . . . dead . . . his blood everywhere. . . ." Mrs. Tengstedt slumped down in her chair.

Milne turned and said softly, "Ms. Reilly? How much longer?"

Nina, watching her case crash around her, said, "Just a moment, Your Honor." The facts might still save her client. And nothing could be worse than what had already been said. "Mrs. Tengstedt, continue."

"I called Carl. He put Larry in the trunk of his car and dumped him in the jungle by the village. They found him the next day. I believe they thought someone from the village killed him, but they never charged anyone. We moved in with Carl, and he took care of us. After a while, I married Carl. . . . There were too many memories, so Carl decided to leave the navy."

"What did you tell Michelle? How did she deal with it?"

"She wouldn't speak for a month. We kept her out of school. We prayed she would forget. And God granted our prayers. She had forgotten until this day, in which I confess my sin and accept my punishment." She turned to the judge, as though expecting to be arrested on the spot.

"But . . . why do you feel you must be punished, Mrs. Tengstedt? If your daughter killed her father—"

"Oh! No, no, no! Michelle, listen now," her mother said, focusing at last on her daughter, her eyes alive again, full of love and pain. "You never killed him. When the bottle didn't stop him, I'm the one stabbed your daddy with a butcher knife."

31

HALLOWELL JUST SHRUGGED when Milne asked for any cross-examination of Mrs. Tengstedt, so Milne adjourned for lunch. Michelle ran to her mother, and Carl Tengstedt got there at the same time. They huddled together, looking at no one as they left the courtroom.

"And they say 'kill all the lawyers,' " a reporter from the *Mirror* called out. "Where else would we get stories that make your eyes pop out into your breakfast cereal! Watch for mine on the front page tomorrow."

"Let's get out of here," Paul said. He took Nina's arm firmly and led her through the crush. They drove out on the highway to the town of Meyers, where the restaurants were few, pulling into the parking lot of the Freel Peak Saloon. Inside, regulars occupied themselves peaceably watching a game of eight-ball at the pool table. Paul sat Nina down in a corner and brought two brandies.

"Drink up," he said. "So. What now?"

"I can't go on with it. I'm too shook. I'm going to ask Milne to adjourn until Monday. That woman. What I'm doing to that family. I never should have let Michelle talk me into this. I woke up this morning feeling today would be the day I was going to lose control of my case. That's exactly what's happening."

Paul shook his head. "Don't stop now, Nina. Hang on a little longer. Don't lose your impetus. The case goes by itself;

that's good as long as it goes your way. Just open your mouth and the right words will come out. You're a natural."

"What's happening today, Paul? What is the jury thinking?"

"Some of them are thinking that Michelle is a very sick girl who reenacted her father's death. Some of them are thinking there was no confession, just like you said. I think you've got a hung jury at the moment. The thing is, there's a favorable atmosphere right now. You've got the tiger by the tail, not the DA. That can only help Michelle."

"What about the Tengstedts? Milne didn't even stop her to tell her she was confessing to a crime and she could take the Fifth."

"He was as slack-jawed as the rest of us." A couple of skinny hot dogs with plastic bags of chips were delivered to the table. "Yum." He opened the bag and crunched away. After a minute he said, "Don't worry. Stokes died a long time ago. It's so close to self-defense, I can't imagine they'd ever be charged."

"You know, I never could have gotten this far without your help, Paul. Your notes were great on the police witnesses. You saw holes I never would have seen. But what I appreciate most is, you put things into perspective. I was so horrified when we left court. Now I'm fitting it into the evidence, thinking about what to do next."

"The next thing is, eat your hot dog. Keep up your strength for the afternoon." At least there was plenty of mustard. Nina was as hungry as if she had just climbed Tallac.

"Okay, I'm up and going again," she said when she finished.

"Who's the next witness?" Paul said, while she neatly stacked all the refuse onto the two paper plates.

"Frederick Greenspan. And his cuddly attorney."

"What's Riesner doing here?"

"It's within the judge's discretion to let him stand around and tell Greenspan not to answer if I violate the protective order."

"What do you want from Greenspan?"

"That Michelle never threatened Anthony. That she repeated the childhood amnesia story to him. That she had problems, but she was rational. That she wasn't worked up enough to kill her husband in cold blood."

"You have to watch out for him," Paul said. "I think he doesn't care what happens to her. Plus he's hiding something."

"I think so too. But I don't have anything on him."

Paul wasn't listening anymore. He had glanced at his watch. Court resumed in fifteen minutes. "Nina, I have to go back right after the trial, you know. Marilyn quit. My business needs my attention. But as soon as I can I'm coming up here to do some hiking and camping in the Desolation Wilderness and I want you to go with me."

"We're a bad fit, Paul," Nina said. "You know it." Paul's sudden change of subject had left her breathless.

He motioned for the bill. "You're low because of the trial. And the divorce. I'm going to ask you again in a few weeks. And I bet you five to one you'll come."

Nina smiled her first real smile of the day.

Michelle came in and sat down at the counsel table at the last minute. Her parents took their seats in back. "Michelle, if you want—"

"I'm with you, Nina, whatever you want to do."

"Let's just get through the afternoon."

Michelle nodded, resting her arms on her stomach. She looked calm enough to complete the day's work.

"Call Frederick Greenspan," Nina said. The tall, hollow-cheeked physician stood and made his way to the stand to be sworn. Jeffrey Riesner approached and stood at his side, wearing a double-breasted suit and looking smug.

Nina took the physician through his education and experience, eliciting nothing she did not already know. Greenspan appeared rested and relaxed. He knew she would not attack his competence. Milne's protective order would stop her.

"You treated the defendant over a period of months?"

"Three and a half months," Greenspan said.

"How many sessions?"

"Ten."

"And why was treatment terminated after ten sessions?"

"You advised me that my notes of sessions might be used against your client."

Nina tried to think of a way to get the answer stricken and decided to say nothing.

"Are these the complete and original notes of your sessions with Mrs. Patterson?"

Greenspan looked carefully through the group exhibit. "It looks complete, yes."

Nina asked a few more questions, then had the exhibit entered into evidence.

"Now, Dr. Greenspan, what were the presenting symptoms of this patient?" she continued.

"Well, she was experiencing a mild to moderate depression. She had some compulsive feelings, which bothered her. She felt she was drinking too much. She had marital problems."

"Did any other symptoms or problems become apparent after treatment was initiated?"

"She claimed that she was suffering from a type of amnesia. She couldn't remember her childhood, basically."

"And what was the course of treatment for these symptoms?"

"We tried hypnotherapy, for stress reduction, to see if we could elevate her mood without chemicals, and in an attempt to access the blocked memories."

"Was the treatment successful as to each of these three goals you've identified, Doctor?"

"I'm afraid I couldn't describe it that way, no. We had hardly started when my patient was arrested and we had to abruptly terminate treatment. Perhaps she had some help with the stress—it was really too soon to tell."

"Did she discuss her marital relationship with you?"

"At length," Greenspan said. He was beginning to look unhappy up there. Riesner stood bristling, waiting for a misstep.

"How did she describe it?"

"Objection, vague and ambiguous."

"Rephrase the question, Counsel."

"Did she express any feelings of unhappiness in her marriage?"

"Yes. She was . . . ambivalent, I would say."

"Did she describe to you any instances in which her husband, Anthony Patterson, physically injured her?"

"I would say so, though I understand her injuries were not severe enough to cause her to seek medical treatment," Greenspan answered.

"Did she describe any emotional abuse?"

"Objection, ambiguous. Lack of foundation. The witness is an M.D. He hasn't qualified as an expert in psychiatric disorders," Hallowell said.

Milne thought it over, said, "Overruled."

"Yes, she felt intimidated by her husband. She wanted to leave him." His answers were pat. Nina decided to try to knock him off balance.

"Have you ever been analyzed, Dr. Greenspan?" Nina asked.

"No. Perhaps someday," he said.

"And you have no degree in psychology, right?" Riesner took a breath. Greenspan held his hand up as if to stave him off, his eyes never leaving Nina.

"No, not formally. It's an interest of mine."

"How did you come to practice hypnotherapy?"

"After many years of general practice I had come to the conclusion that many physical diseases originate in the mind. I learned of a certificate program in hypnotherapy that appeared to be quite complete. I finished the program in 1987. I consider it a very useful skill for certain types of common problems not amenable to drug therapy, for example."

"Such as stress reduction?"

"Yes."

"How about alcoholism?"

"Perhaps. In conjunction with other therapeutic measures."

"How about the compulsive problem you say my client had—what's the psychiatric term for that?"

"Uh, I believe it's called erotomania. Well, if the compulsion was mild, yes, I believe the patient could be given some relief. Hypnosis can be a very valuable tool."

"That's what Freud said, at first, didn't he, Dr. Greenspan? Do you happen to know why Freud turned away from hypnosis and developed the tools of psychoanalysis instead?"

"Objection," Hallowell said. "Irrelevant. Where is this lecture going?"

"I would appreciate some latitude, Your Honor."

Milne creased his forehead, but said, "Go ahead."

"Just a moment, Your Honor," Nina said. Paul had swept into the courtroom and motioned to her from the counsel table.

"Two minutes," Milne said. Nina and Paul put their heads together. Greenspan took a drink of water. Behind them, the spectators took advantage of the moment to talk. Under cover of the general buzz, Paul murmured in her ear, "The DNA results from Cytograph came in. Take a look." He passed over a sheaf of test result reports.

Five tests. Five sets of results. She tried to read, but the words merged into technical gobbledygook.

"Are you ready to proceed, Counsel?"

Paul pointed. "Right there," he mouthed.

And then she saw it. She froze in the chair.

"What's wrong?" Michelle whispered.

"I'll tell her. You go ahead," Paul said from behind his hand.

"Ms. Reilly!" Milne, after almost two weeks of trial, had reached a heightened state of irritation that meant she would have no time to prepare her next questions.

Nina rose, smoothing her gray linen jacket.

"I've forgotten the question. Sorry," Greenspan said.

"Why did Freud stop hypnotizing his patients, Dr. Greenspan?"

"I believe Freud decided the results of hypnosis were too unreliable," Greenspan said.

"Freud had some concerns about unanalyzed therapists treating patients, too, didn't he, Doctor?" Nina asked. A wild tide of excitement filled her, making it hard to choke out the words.

Greenspan looked puzzled. "Yes, but the hypnotherapy I practice is for mild difficulties only. I am not trying to psychoanalyze patients."

"Yet you have just discussed Mrs. Patterson's ambivalence toward her marriage, depression, stress, alcoholism, erotomania, and amnesia—"

"Only up to a point. It is true that I was considering referring Mrs. Patterson to a psychiatrist."

"In fact, she had some rather complex psychological problems. Didn't you know that after, say, five sessions?"

"Perhaps," Greenspan said.

"Why didn't you refer her?"

"I thought I was helping her."

Nina watched as Paul showed the DNA results to Michelle. She let out a small sound, like a kitten crushed by a car.

"Did Mrs. Patterson develop transference toward you?"

"I beg your pardon?"

"Transference—you know, did she fall in love with you?"

"Objection!"

"Overruled."

"I should say not," Greenspan said. "As I said, I was merely undertaking a short course of hypnotherapy."

"Was she a good hypnotic subject?"

"Excellent. She was able to achieve a very deep state of trance."

"Did she ever express to you that she could not remember the contents of her hypnotic sessions with you?"

"Yes. It's rather common. It's called posthypnotic amnesia. Not surprising, considering her history of memory loss."

"Not surprising at all," Nina said. "And you didn't tape any of the sessions?"

"As I told you, that's not my practice. I take notes. I'm old-fashioned in that respect."

"Have you ever heard of countertransference, Doctor?"

For the first time, the doctor hesitated. "Yes. That goes back to the psychoanalytic situation."

"Describe your understanding of that term, if you would."

"Objection! This has gone on too long. Counsel is wasting the jury's time with this irrelevant line of questioning!"

"Approach the bench."

When Nina came up, Milne leaned over and said in a very low voice, "Are you by any chance stalling for time, Counsel?"

"No, Your Honor. Just give me a few more questions."

"Make it snappy," Milne said.

As she walked back to the counsel table, Nina took a quick survey of her audience. In the back row she spotted Al Otis, dressed up today to look like a businessman; Mrs. Greenspan with a bag of knitting right up front; and there sat Tom and Janine Clark, right next to Mrs. Greenspan. The Tengstedts kept close together in a middle row, holding hands. Stephen Rossmoor had placed himself right behind Michelle, behind the railing. The gang's all here, she thought.

"Okay. You can answer the question, Doctor."

"I'm sorry, I don't remember it," Greenspan said.

"What is countertransference, Doctor? Not *trans*ference. Tell us about *counter*transference."

"Right. Countertransference has to do with our previous, ah, discussion. About unanalyzed therapists."

"Go on."

"Well, the idea is that the therapist may have some psychological needs or problems that obtrude into the therapeutic relationship. . . ."

"For example, the therapist falls in love with his patient?"

"Objection!" Hallowell roared.

"Did you have sexual intercourse with Mrs. Patterson while she was under hypnosis?"

"What?" Greenspan cried. "Never!" He had unfurled his long arms and spread his hands, like a bat.

"How dare you!" came a female voice from the audience.

"Your Honor, I must protest!" Riesner said. "She's doing exactly what you—"

"Just a couple more questions, Your Honor," Nina said.

Milne gave her his careful regard, clearly unsettled. She challenged him with her eyes.

"Proceed," Milne said. "All objections are overruled."

"You did take advantage of her sexually while she was your patient, did you not?"

"No!" Greenspan had sat down again, but his hands squeezed the railing.

Nina said directly to the jury, "Suppose I told you I have here the results of a DNA test comparing samples of hair taken from Dr. Greenspan's lab coat by me personally with the DNA of the unborn child Mrs. Patterson is carrying. . . ." She turned back to the witness. "Congratulations. You're going to be a father."

Michelle Patterson stood up. For a moment they all paid respectful silence to her swaying, ghostly figure, all in white. She started to open her mouth, then covered it in a familiar gesture. She moved her hands into a praying position, pressing them hard against her lips. Paul put an arm around her and pulled her to her seat.

"I demand the Court put a stop to this!" Riesner shouted, but nobody was listening. Hallowell stared at the physician, his eyes blank as a video screen without power. They all watched Dr. Greenspan's face crumple and his body shrink in his suit.

A wail came from somewhere in the audience, starting small and swelling until everyone in the courtroom was looking at Ericka Greenspan.

Face haggard, she had risen, her hands clenched around her knitting bag.

Milne said, not unkindly, "Now, ma'am. Court's in session. Please take your seat."

The words had no effect. "Frederick, look at me."

The only person in the courtroom not already looking

heard her. His wire-rimmed glasses glinted as he turned his long torso slowly toward his wife.

"I would have been a better doctor than you," she said. "I covered for you so many years. It was my life too. Our good reputation. Our good name. We helped people together. I was so proud."

No response.

"Then the dead man came to me. He wasn't dead then, though, was he?" A sound like a small laugh escaped. "A man like that, pretty as his wife. Oh, he was nasty. He hinted about things. I didn't believe him at first. He told me to watch out for you and her. He said, 'You don't put Misty on a couch and just talk to her.' How could I believe him? You and that cheap tart? But the things he said stayed in my mind, driving me crazy. I started having these terrible doubts. About us. About what I gave up so that you could be an important man. The world's better off without people like him. He was a malignancy."

"You, Ericka?" Greenspan whispered.

Milne opened his mouth, closed it. The bailiff waited alertly for instructions. In the silent courtroom, nobody breathed. The lights glared down on Ericka Greenspan's straight back and superbly cut suit. People in the seats beside her stared up at her.

"You always did underestimate me," she said. "I listened at your door the day the lawyer came. I learned the girl was going to go to a psychiatrist in San Francisco to be hypnotized, and I told the police. That lady lawyer told you, when you were talking to her. Didn't you stop to think that she might destroy us? At the very least, she was bound to dream up some malpractice. Never thought of that, did you? You're actually a very stupid man, Frederick."

"Ericka, don't say any more," Greenspan said in a low voice.

"Right, don't talk," Riesner echoed, edging away from the witness box toward the wall.

Ericka Greenspan stood there, swaying, her chest heaving, working herself up to some fresh disclosure. Her presence now, at first a minor disruption in the long proceedings, had continued far too long without containment. The witnesses to the trial's disintegration looked to Milne for leadership. But he was sitting there, a fascinated expression on his face.

"I drove them off the road, and I tried to get into the girl's room while she was dead drunk. To smother her. Just taking care of you, darling." Her mouth was a snarl now. "You make a mess; I clean up, just like always. But now—"

"Ericka, please stop!" Greenspan cried. He looked ready to leap over the witness stand.

"I hate you! And her! And that lawyer! All of you make a joke of my whole life!" Her head bobbed, and her mouth kept moving jerkily, as though she was going to retch.

Milne found his voice. "Bailiff, take that woman into custody!" he ordered.

Before the bailiff had even begun to move, Ericka Greenspan pulled a heavy gun from her knitting bag. She aimed at Greenspan, holding it in both hands, her face wild and determined.

The people in front of her began to scream and scramble for the exits.

"You make . . ."

Blam!

". . . me sick!"

Blam!

The blasts slammed Greenspan back into the witness chair, echoing off the wooden benches. The bailiff had pulled his revolver, but in the confusion of screams and bodies rushing to get out, he couldn't stop her.

Nina, amazed and unbelieving, watched as Mrs. Greenspan, seeming to have all the time in the world, turned and pointed the gun at Michelle. Unable to move fast, fingers spread over her belly, her eyes wide with terror, Michelle cowered in her seat for what seemed like minutes before Paul hurled his big body against her, pushing her below the counsel table. The gun moved uncertainly like a black snake until Nina was watching blackness inside the barrel. Then its tongue licked toward her brightly.

A cannonball thudded into her chest, knocking her flat against the witness box. She went deaf from the roaring in her ears, and she couldn't raise her hands or breathe or feel a thing. Most of her had fled deep inside at the awful shock, but her eyes stayed open wide, dispassionately witnessing the shiny black gun. It had searched out Paul and Michelle tangled on the floor. Nina waited for the next lick of fire.

When it finally came, the boom came from a different direction as Deputy Kimura shot Ericka Greenspan in the chest. Blood blossomed in a grisly bouquet over her elegant suit. She emitted a grunt of surprise and fell backward over the bench, hard, the gun firing again and again and again.

32

LIGHTS. VOICES. SHE had heard those voices before. She opened her eyes.

"Easy there," Matt said. He stroked her forehead. Andrea stood beside him, her somber face glinting with tears.

She was on a gurney, in a hospital corridor, eyes momentarily blinded by the snowstorm of light surrounding her. Closing her eyes, she disappeared into a disorienting half-dream where pain hid and emerged.

She floated on the drugs, listening detachedly to her own voice moan. At some point Matt shouted. As the gurney jolted forward, she caved in to the pain in her chest and prayed for a quick death.

A *Bonanza* rerun. The theme song was playing, so Hoss and Adam and the other cowboys must be riding their Tahoe ranch, tall in the saddle. Adam would be looking around, holding the reins firmly, steely-eyed and twinkly at the same time. He had a dimple and she had such a crush on him. What a shame when Hoss died. Everybody loved him. The TV watchers were sad for such a long time.

The TV hung from the ceiling in the corner of her hospital room. Hoss was dead, but Nina discovered herself to be alive, though the drugs and TV had pushed her into a 1972 flashback. Her mother might come in at any moment and catch her curled up on a monumental bad trip.

Hoss met some mean shooters on the way to Virginia City. But Nina was comforted, knowing he would escape due to the perfect and just rules of television land. There were gunshots, but she wasn't afraid. Buddhist monks could only yearn for such a transcendent state of acceptance. She would have to tell the holy men. Bonanza *was the short cut*. Eyes closed and ears listening, medicated into the metaconscious, she achieved egolessness and merged with the TV program.

Days went by, and the medicine took her from daffy to dazed. Memories surfaced gently and faded away. She thought a lot about her mother, and cried now and then. Paul came to see her and hold her hand. Bobby came every day, pressing his sweet cheek against hers, careful not to disturb the IV drip. Other faces came too . . . her dad. Was that Jack? Slowly, reluctantly, she woke up again.

"What day is it?" she asked the nurse.

"Tuesday. A good day," the nurse said. She was writing something on a chart. "You're looking chipper." She had short, frizzy red hair and thick, curly eyelashes, freckled hands, and a tattoo of pink-and-blue flowers peeking out from the neck of her sedate white uniform.

"My chest hurts," Nina said.

"It should. You were shot in the lung. Broke a couple of ribs. Came out your back. You're going to hurt for a while, but you're going to be fine."

"Really?"

"I swear," the nurse said, holding her hand to her heart. "Couple battle scars to tell your grandchildren about. Now eat your breakfast." She pressed a button and the top of the bed creaked upward. Nina drank some orange juice and ate some toast, getting used to the tight wrapping around the upper part of her body. She breathed shallowly, blunting the cudgel of pain that pounded at each ebb and flow.

Andrea brought Bobby over after school. He had made her a cartoon in his computer lab at school, showing a funny bunny with a balloon that said, I LOVE YOU, MOM. She held him close, kissing the top of his head until he begged her to stop.

"I have a question for you, kiddo," she said. "One I've been dying to ask."

He laughed nervously. "Is this about Troy's skateboard? Because I already explained to Uncle Matt—"

"Don't worry," she said, taking a pencil from her bedside. "It's this darn puzzle." She drew nine dots in three rows. "Four connecting lines, right?"

Bobby took the pencil from her, drew a triangle with a line through the middle, and showed it to his mother. "It's kind of a trick, see? You have to be willing to go outside the dots to make it work. I thought it'd be easy for you."

He hustled down to the lobby to buy himself a treat, while she threw her hands up in a despairing gesture. "I like to think I'm a creative person," she said to Andrea.

"But you are, Nina. Really, everyone's just flabbergasted at what you pulled off in that courtroom."

"Flabbergasted must be an understatement." She punched her pillow weakly and lay back.

Andrea stood by the bed, trim in her neat jeans. "We're glad it's over. You want to know what's happened, don't you? Curiosity is a good sign. It means you're better. They say they're going to let you out of here in a few days, but you'll have to take it easy for at least six weeks after that. Your chaise will be waiting."

"It punctured my lung," Nina said. "Andrea, she almost killed me."

"I know, sweetie. But she missed the aorta by a centimeter. A little less air won't hurt your law practice. One centi-meter." She frowned. "Don't cut it so close next time."

"What happened to the trial?"

"I don't know where to start, except to tell you how happy we are you made it."

"Mrs. Greenspan shot her husband," Nina said.

"She killed him. He died on the witness stand. Then she shot you. Then the bailiff shot her. She didn't make it."

"Michelle?"

"The judge declared a mistrial. I understand the DA isn't going to refile charges against Michelle. No jury is going to convict her now. Talk about reasonable doubt. The consensus seems to be that Mrs. Greenspan went to the house that night, saw the fight, and killed Anthony after Michelle was out of commission, hoping Michelle would be blamed."

Nina was quiet.

"Well, aren't you glad?"

"Did she say anything after she shot me?" Nina said.

"Not a word."

Nina sighed, resting her hand on her bandaged chest. "I wish she had confessed to killing Anthony."

"Oh, come on, Nina. What's your problem? She came close enough. She said Anthony came to her with his suspicions. She said she protected her husband. She said she tried to kill you and Michelle. She told Collier Hallowell about the San Francisco session."

"Yes, she confessed to plenty, but not that."

"You are the most obdurate, the most exasperating, the most long-eared mule who ever dug her heels in and wouldn't go," Andrea said. "Let's talk about something else."

"How's Michelle?"

"Back in Fresno. She starts Lamaze classes next week with Steve Rossmoor as her partner. Isn't that a kick?"

"He'll want to marry her. Don't think she's ready, do you?"

"She's been calling every day. She's found a woman therapist. Her parents had a rough week. They came through the bad time. You know, I think they were half dead before. Hiding Stokes's death took so much energy. I think their lives will be better now. The baby's coming soon, so they'll be busy. Nobody talks much about Greenspan being the father. I wonder what Michelle will tell her child about the father."

"The baby will inherit Greenspan's estate," Nina said. "They had no children."

"Ohmigod. Only a lawyer could think about something like that."

"I'll never forget Greenspan's expression when I told him about the baby. He had Michelle's medical chart. He knew she was on the Pill. He didn't know she'd missed a few that month."

"That disgusting pervert, giving good therapists a bad name," Andrea said firmly. "They were both twisted." She turned her wedding ring around on her finger for emphasis. "After what he did to Michelle . . ."

"I'll call her tomorrow," Nina said. She wanted to say to her, thank you for your faith. Michelle had been the only one to trust Nina unflaggingly, and she had had the most to lose. And Michelle would say, thank you for believing in me. Nina had been the only one.

They were so different, but shared so much, bad and good. Now Michelle, too, had a child to tell some difficult truths to. What about my father, Mom? Nina was waiting for Bobby to ask that question. Maybe Michelle would do better. Did these events drop rotten burdens through the generations, fruits of poisonous trees? They would talk about it.

"Jack came up to see you, but you were out of it," Andrea went on. "He brought the divorce decree. You're single again."

"Ouch," Nina said. She had jerked involuntarily.

"He cried right here in this chair, if that's any consolation to you. Here, let me fix your pillow. Other news: You're famous, at least for a few miles around. Sandy is collecting the appointment requests. According to the *Mirror*, you rode in here on a big white horse and ran the bad guys out of town. Saved an innocent girl when no one else believed in her. . . . You'll be embarrassed when you read the articles. They even reported the shootings on CNN. Matt saved the tape."

"Me? What'd I do? I muddled around, making mistakes, until I got shot."

Andrea grinned. "You never learned how to pat yourself on the back, did you? I'm going to have to do it for you." She leaned close to Nina's pillow and patted her softly on the shoulder. "Congratulations, Nina. We're all proud of you."

But when she had gone, leaving behind a novel about sleazy lawyers involved in big-firm chicanery, Nina lay there, troubled. The Greenspans were dead. She could never ask Ericka Greenspan exactly how Anthony Patterson died. Okay, she had found him wounded, lying on the couch. Okay, she was strong, she had seen the keys on the kitchen counter and hauled him to the boat. Somehow, she had swum back.

But why go to all that trouble? Why not just hit Anthony again, and leave Michelle to face a murder charge?

She shook her head and reached out painfully for the cards stacked on the nightstand. Judge Milne had sent her a Hallmark get-well card. She last remembered him scurrying off to his chambers like a panicky weasel to its burrow. She would never be afraid of him again.

Collier's card played "You Only Live Twice" in tinkly computer music when she opened it. Inside was a folded copy of the mistrial order. "Congratulations, Counselor!" the card said.

Smiling a little, she looked around. Silver Mylar balloons from Paul flew above a champagne bottle with a note that made her laugh and blush at the same time. Flowers from Michelle, chocolate-covered macadamia nuts from Nina's father in Monterey, a soft wool blanket covered with bird designs from Sandy. A scribble from Bruno: "Classic countertransference. An intriguing footnote to Freud. I'll send you my first draft."

She found the Judgment of Final Dissolution of Marriage at the bottom of the card pile. The effective date was the same day she had been shot. Ultraprofessional Ms. Cherry had written a cover letter regarding the details.

Clipped to the top of that letter was a note from Jack saying he knew she'd be out there again soon, persevering until even the impossible gave way, and wishing her luck. She stared at the note a long time, till the nurse came in with a cupful of pills that erased all her pain.

On October 13, the morning before she left the hospital, Nina's doctor came in to give her discharge instructions. To him she was nothing but a right lung. Take this and this and this, he said in the excessively cheerful bedside manner affected by the medical profession, and come into the office in a couple of days.

A *couple of days*. Those were Michelle's words, the first time she came into the office. Anthony Patterson, too, had seen his doctor a few days before his death.

Nina dialed the phone.

"Sandy, it's me."

"Well, I'll be."

Hearing that familiar flat voice on the phone actually choked Nina up. "How's it going? Are you hanging in there?"

"It's a barrel of laughs," Sandy said. "I'll come see you tomorrow with a U-Haul full of new files. You are still going home tomorrow?"

"I'll be there. See you after lunch."

"With pen in hand."

"Listen, Sandy. I have a chore for you. Could you find out the name of Anthony Patterson's regular doc? It must be somewhere in the case files. Right away."

"That's what you pay me for," Sandy said. She called back ten minutes later with the name, and Nina thanked her. "Sure," she said. "By the way, there's a powwow at the Washoe Center all this week."

"And?"

"I took down those awful gray photographs. Got tired of staring at 'em all day long. Those things took all the life and color and drained it right out of the landscape. What we need's a couple of bright Washoe wall hangings in here."

"You took down my Ansel Adams prints?"

"You're gonna love it," said Sandy.

33

HER HEART POUNDING, Nina called Anthony Patterson's doctor with her question. He was in and talked to her. Lunch came, something pinkish and something greenish and something whitish.

While a nurse organized medicine on a tray, she called Al Otis in Sparks. He asked no questions, just said he'd be glad to stop in. He couldn't come until later.

Otis poked his head around the door late in the afternoon and tiptoed in as if she had died after all. A red-haired man in a ponytail once more, he must be running out of disguises.

"Brought you a little something, Counselor," he said, reaching into his vest pocket and pulling out a tiny silver flask. "Hair of the litter. Go ahead, the nurse is down the hall."

She shouldn't. She really shouldn't. It was very good Scotch, about an inch, which made her cough, which in turn made her groan, but it was worth it.

"You're lookin' good, considering," he said, pulling up a folding chair. "It happened to me in Nam. See my leg?" He pulled up his trouser leg and she inspected the puckered white scar. "Worse things happened to my buddies. Goin' home soon?"

"Tomorrow."

"Good, good." He seemed lost in thought. "Did you hear

they caught the sumbitch that rammed my baby?" he asked suddenly.

"You mean . . . Sharon?"

"My baby," he said, and began to cry. "Love is cruel," he continued after a while, blowing his nose loudly. "I'll never love like that again. It was a geek named Blackie she met at a bar. She had some friends of hers rip off his bike, and she sold it to one of her best customers. Blackie saw the customer riding the highway out in the desert, by Pyramid Lake, took it back and beat up the rider. Then he got loaded and wiped Sharon out, there at the side of the road. She was only forty-three. Forty-seven if you believe her driver's license." He wiped his eyes.

"I'm sorry," Nina said. She really was sorry.

"She loved me, and she let me try out anything on her," Al said in a melancholy tone. "And she was loyal to her friends."

"Anthony was her friend. Was she loyal to him?" Nina said.

"If you only knew," Al said. He snuffled into his tissue and drank some Scotch.

"But I do know, Al."

His eyes grew big and wide. "About the night Anthony bought it?"

"I know, and you know. It wasn't Ericka Greenspan. Sharon told you about him, didn't she, Al?"

"Sharon told me what happened, and Sharon never lied. Steal, yes, beat up on somebody, yes, but she had a strong moral compunction about lying. She told me."

Nina sat up, repressing another groan. "Al, Michelle Patterson was on trial for murder. You had crucial information. Why didn't you call me?"

"I did, once. Right before the trial. But your secretary put me on hold for so long I changed my mind. And Sharon wouldn't have wanted me to tell you. She lived outside the law.

"And we never owed pretty Misty anything, that little stinker. She was out of control. She showed her husband no respect. She was drivin' that man nutso, cheatin' and lyin'. . . ." Al pulled at his ring, which was again missing its bright zircons. "Besides, I knew you'd get her off. I trusted you from the minute I seen you step into my trailer. Great legs."

"Thanks," Nina said weakly. "So . . ."

"And you paid your dues, and took care of business, so I didn't have to be a witness and blow my cover."

"Al, I suspect that I've got the story in substance. Now I want to know what Sharon said."

"Promise you won't hold it against her? She was a very moral girl, in her way. She was just carrying out Anthony's last wishes."

"I won't hold it against Sharon," Nina said. "Al, please."

Al Otis smiled. "I like to get 'em begging," he said. If she'd had the strength to reach him she would have shaken him. He put up his hand as if to fend her off, saying, "Relax. I'm harmless."

"Al."

"You don't want to play no more?" He drained the last of his flask, cleared his throat interminably, and finally said, "All right. Here's how it went down.

"Sharon rode up the hill to see Anthony about ten. We owed him a few grand from the week's take. Don't ask me what else they did, I never asked myself. They were friends. That was her business. So she gets there, and she's half frozen, and she has to haul in some logs and get a fire going because Anthony's lyin' there on the couch in his robe, and at first he won't even talk to her.

"So she gets a fire blazin' and strips off her leathers. The guy has hardly moved, and she keeps askin' him what's wrong. She fixes some drinks and gets him talking, and he tells her two bad things have happened. I mean bad with a capital B."

"Go on."

"His doc has just confirmed that day he has lung cancer. He's been smoking for twenty-five, thirty years, what did he expect? It's advanced, there are a few cells here and there, he's got about six months. He cries on Sharon's shoulder for a few minutes, they have some more drinks. Then he tells her—"

"How are we doing?" said the nurse, sweetly. Pill time. Al watched sympathetically while Nina swallowed and swallowed.

"What did he tell her then?" Nina said as the nurse bounded out in her springy white shoes.

"Anthony had been puttin' out Misty's fires all over town. He was shuttin' down that schoolteacher guy, Tom, by talkin' to his wife. And he thought there was some hanky-panky with the doc whose wife blew him away at your trial, so he talked to the wife there. The thing is, he really didn't know what to do about Misty, because he knew if he bitched at her like he wanted to, she'd move out for good.

"That day, right after he saw the doc, his snake-eyed compadre Peter La Russa came by and handed him a security video of the fourth-floor hallway, trained on the general manager's apartment up there. It showed Misty leaving, maybe the day before, maybe that very day, with heavy smooches and gropes all around. It's a wonder she ever got any sleep."

"How did he react?"

"I'm telling you. Sharon had never seen him like that. She said he was in black despair. He was a hard man, but even the hard ones have a soft spot, and Misty was his. All those suspicions, and he never really believed she was cheatin' until that day. He was too quiet, then he'd start raving. She calmed him down some, put him to bed. She hoped he'd stay there until morning, maybe wake up thinking straight. Those were some bad knocks he'd taken.

"Then it was after midnight, and Sharon knew Misty'd be coming in from the night shift. Sharon didn't want to be there. Anthony was snoring away, but she was worried Misty would wake him up. She heard the Subaru in the driveway and she slipped out back and looked into the living room from outside. She'd parked the bike down the street."

Al paused. "No reason for me or Sharon to invent this shit, right?" he said.

"No," Nina said. She was rubbing her forehead, rerunning scenes in her head. Dr. Clauson in Placerville, smoking stoically next to Anthony's body, telling her and Paul about the cancer; La Russa, testifying about the videotape he had given Anthony; Steve Rossmoor, telling Paul he had videotapes of his hallway that would prove he'd never gone out the night Anthony died.

Here, right here, was where Michelle Patterson had come in. And, according to Al, it all happened just as she had told Nina, eons ago in her office.

"After the fight Misty ran into the kitchen. Sharon was thinking Anthony must be hurt bad. She could see he was bleeding. She was going to come around and see if she could help. But then she saw Anthony get up. He was moving okay. He stood by the kitchen door. And when Misty came back out, he clipped her. Sharon said it looked like he was being careful to do it so he would just knock her out.

"He carried her into the bedroom. Then he went into the kitchen, and he picked up the bear statue Misty had hit him with, and he went outside. No coat, no shoes, just holding that red robe of his closed in front.

"Sharon came around the side of the house to meet him, but he was already crossing the snow, heading toward the neighbor's boat. There was plenty of moon and the snow had slowed down to a sprinkle. She called to him but he didn't pay no attention. By the time she got over there he was cast off and a hundred feet out.

"Then she hollered across the water, 'Come back, you crazy motherfucker!' "

"And he yelled back, 'Don't let on!'

"Those were his last words. He disappeared out there in the dark with a wave, and Sharon watched for him a long time, but he didn't come back."

Al's voice trailed off.

"He framed his own wife," Nina said. She had been sure, but hearing Al tell the story she still felt a kind of awe. She slumped back in the bed.

"Give me a call when you get back on your feet, Counselor," Al said, rising. "We'll talk some more. I'll teach you some cards." Then he was gone.

Sometime later, the nurse brought her a heavy brown package. Nina broke the twine with her teeth and let the paper fall to the floor.

"The police gave this back, but it's a bad memory for me. Keep it, Nina, and think of me and all the good you did by believing in me and trusting yourself." The card was signed by Michelle. Inside white tissue, she found the polar bear statue. She placed it next to her bed, on the table in front of the window.

She closed her eyes, allowing herself to appreciate fully that she had come at last to the heart of her case, the heart of a dead man. She felt she had known Anthony all these months. All the emotions had begun with him. He had made everyone in the case into unwitting instruments of his revenge.

For a moment, she hated him. She had almost been killed. Because of him.

But this feeling was replaced by a grudging sympathy. Now that she understood him, she could not hate him. His suicide had been his declaration that he would die his own death, his own way. He had defied the fate that awaited him: divorce, illness, and loneliness. He had placed his faith in love, and avenged himself when his love was betrayed. In the midst of his brutality and the limitations of his personal history, she could not help seeing a thumb-your-nose kind of bravery in his actions.

She understood him at last. And at last she believed she knew his story. Exhausted with her thoughts, aching with cold in the chilly room, she lay back against her pillows. She lay back to dream the story of the jealous lover. She heard the song Michelle hated. She saw him waving back to Sharon on the dock, shivering, going down to the galley where it was warmer. She imagined him thinking of Misty, wanting her never to forget. He was halfway drunk already. All it would take would be one firm blow and he would sink below the cold, black surface. The moon had even sent a trail along the water for him; the lake would do the rest. She could see him close his eyes, lean out, bring the statue up hard . . .

The nurse was shaking her shoulder gently. "Dinner," she said. "Are you cold? You're shaking." Something bluish had been added tonight, in a plastic bowl. Must be dessert. "Yum," Nina said, thinking of Paul wolfing his food at the Freel Peak Saloon. She missed him.

After she ate, she dialed Michelle's number in Fresno. While the phone rang, she considered whether to tell Michelle what she knew, a simple tale that went beyond the facts and connected all the dots. Knowing what happened the night Anthony died might burden her with new guilt, but protecting her wasn't respecting her for the woman she had become, a person who played the hand she was dealt.

Should she suppress this final truth?

She hung up. There was no rush.

She was tired again. The last thing she saw shaping itself on the inside of her eyelids as she drifted off to a dreamless sleep was the same thing she saw every day now: the familiar window of her office, her porthole on the world, the zigzag of Mt. Tallac looming outside, purple and magnificent, waiting patiently for her.

ABOUT THE AUTHOR

PERRI O'SHAUGHNESSY is the pen name for two sisters, Pamela and Mary O'Shaughnessy, who live in California and at Lake Tahoe. Pamela graduated from Harvard Law School and was a trial lawyer for sixteen years. Mary is a former editor and writer for multimedia projects. They are the authors of eleven Nina Reilly novels: *Case of Lies, Unlucky in Law, Presumption of Death, Unfit to Practice, Writ of Execution, Move to Strike, Acts of Malice, Breach of Promise, Obstruction of Justice, Invasion of Privacy,* and *Motion to Suppress.*

Don't miss the newest thrilling novel
featuring Nina Reilly

CASE OF LIES

Now available in hardcover from
Delacorte Press

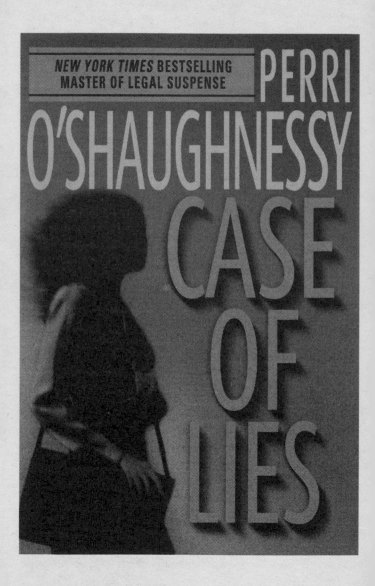

NEW YORK TIMES BESTSELLING
MASTER OF LEGAL SUSPENSE

PERRI
O'SHAUGHNESSY

CASE
OF
LIES

CASE OF LIES

A fresh mug of Italian espresso in hand, stockinged heels riding the edge of her desk, Nina stole a moment to reflect.

The long workday had begun. On the drive down Pioneer Trail that morning toward the office, Nina had watched the bicyclists and joggers with even more than her usual envy. They were out grabbing the last glories of fall, so damn happy, smelling the fresh tang of high snows and watching fluttering dry leaves while she contemplated her day, the bitter child-custody battle coming up, along with two grisly settlement conferences, all to be conducted in the windowless courtroom of the irascible Judge Flaherty.

Long ago, when law began, the advocates and judges must have met in tree-shaded glades, toga-clad, birdsong the accompaniment to their work, courtesy and dignity their style, and—

—And of course, as a woman, she would have been pouring the wine from the ewer, not arguing the case. But one could fantasize at seven forty-five in the morning while watching birds and squirrels chase around the autumnal marsh that rolled out toward a distant, twinkling Lake Tahoe.

After several months in Monterey, she and her son Bob had returned to Tahoe. Sandy Whitefeather had returned to her domain in Nina's office in the Starlake Building and was drumming up business before Nina had time to put her cup down on the desk. The young woman lawyer who had been handling Nina's cases found a job in Reno, and left open files and a busy calendar of court appearances.

In spite of the time crunch, Nina found just enough space in the morning to pour Hitchcock's kibble and Bob's cereal, and to enjoy the short trip up Pioneer Trail to her law office.

When evening came, after she and Sandy locked up, Nina would drive home through the forest to the cabin on Kulow Street, noting hints of the winter to come in the dry pines and parched streams. The cabin still basked in early evening sun. Inside, she would kick off her shoes, pour herself a glass of Clos du Bois and watch the world news, make dinner and dog Bob into finishing his homework and bath. Once a week she called her father, and once or twice a week she and Bob went to her brother Matt's house for dinner.

September and October passed in a flurry while she reestablished her routines. The fees rolled in and she paid off her debts.

The judges accepted her back. She had a pretty good working relationship with most of the local lawyers, and she finally knew what she was doing.

The small office suite in the Starlake Building on Lake Tahoe Boulevard, right in the heart of town and less than five miles from the Nevada state line, now felt like home, but some part of her was still restless. She had gone from Carmel to San Francisco, to Tahoe and back to Carmel and then back to Tahoe again in the past few years. She was beginning to ask herself, uncomfortably, if she would ever settle down. Bob deserved stability, and she was going to have to stay put for a while.

She wasn't even sure why she had returned to Tahoe. She might just as well have stayed in Carmel and joined the Pohlmann firm, which had made her a very good offer.

And she had made one other uncomfortable discovery since returning to Tahoe.

Her ex-lover, Paul van Wagoner, and his new flame, Susan Misumi, had quickly moved in together down in Carmel. Fair enough, since Nina had ended it. The why of Susan Misumi, her black bangs, her humorlessness, escaped Nina, but it wasn't her business anymore. Nina and Paul still checked in on each other. They managed to stay friendly because they had been friends before they became lovers.

Nina had moved on. She went out, danced, ate good food, had a few unexpectedly intimate conversations. But she had discovered that she didn't expect much from men anymore. She didn't want to try for love.

That feeling had been growing in her for a long time, and she sometimes wondered if it even had something to do with the breakup with Paul. Finding a partner seemed impossible, based on her experiences, so she put it out of her mind.

Men and places. The restlessness would come over her, and she'd feel a need for another place and another man. Other people followed their life lines. She careened along too fast, not able to see her own.

But she would always have two constants to ground her: Bob and her work.

Today, we persevere, she thought. With the last gulp of coffee, she threw two ibuprofen down her throat.

The phone buzzed. Nina swung her legs down, sighed, and picked up the phone. Sandy must have come in. Her desk was only ten feet away, through the closed door, but Sandy didn't like getting up.

"He's here, and so's she. Your eight o'clocks," Sandy said.

"And a fine morning it is."

"Hmph. You have half an hour."

The man stood with his back to her, hands in his pockets, looking at one of Sandy's decorations, a Washoe Indian basket on the shelf. He wore a green and black plaid lumberjack shirt tucked into a well-broken-in pair of jeans. The belt, a leather craft affair, must have dated from the sixties. Work boots, a body used to physical work.

A conservative local, Nina thought, pegging him almost before he turned around. Nice wrinkled tan face. Grim expression. Plenty of gray-brown hair on both head and chin. A belly, that was a surprise.

Behind him, clearly trying to fade into the white wall, pretty Chelsi nodded. She was taller than her uncle. She wore her hair down today and it fell straight and satiny. Something had turned off the smile.

"Hi. I'm Nina Reilly," Nina said, looking the man in the eye, holding out her hand.

"David Hanna."

"Please come in." After ushering Chelsi in too, Nina glanced toward Sandy, resplendent this morning in a heavy turquoise necklace and a denim jumper, who seemed to be writing something in the appointment book. Sandy gave Nina a swift look back, one eyebrow cocked.

Look out.

Now, that was an interesting take, since Uncle Dave looked harmless, but Sandy's first impressions had to be taken seriously. Sandy knew where clients hid their guns and buck knives; she knew if the Rolex was real or faux; a few words to her in the reception area revealed if a new client was resentful, desperate, or suicidal. Recently they had installed an emergency button hooked up to the local police under her desk, and a thick, intricately carved walking stick propped behind her desk only doubled as a decoration.

Such is solo law office life in a gambling town. Prepare for Uzis, Sandy frequently said.

Nina closed the door and Hanna pulled an orange client chair away from the wide desk. He sat, crossing one leg at the ankle, stroking his beard, looking out the window behind her desk toward the steel-gray lake, but not focusing, just gazing. Chelsi sat in the chair next to his, back straight.

Nina took her time getting comfortable, arranging a few papers on her desk, adjusting her chair. Let them get used to her.

"I don't know why I'm here," David Hanna said finally.

"Because you need to be," Chelsi said.

"I'm not working much. Money's tight. Chelsi and her dad, they've offered to pay for your services, but I just don't know. It doesn't seem right. I hear Chelsi's already told you about the case."

"A little," Nina said.

"Rog was Sarah's brother. I know he can't help wanting to do something. What I can't figure out, what I haven't been able to get my head around all along, is what good it does, suing someone. My wife is gone."

"What's your brother-in-law's name again?"

"Roger Freeman." While Nina made a note on her yellow pad, Hanna watched, squinting. The tops of his ears were flushed red, like raw meat, and looked sunburned too. Either he spent a lot of time outside, or, as Chelsi had suggested, less healthy indoor pursuits heightened his natural color. "What's your usual line of work, Mr. Hanna?"

"I'm a carpenter. Used to be a firefighter."

Nina looked at her Client Interview Sheet. "Placerville's a great town."

"It's a long drive up Fifty to get here. I don't come up the Hill much anymore since it happened. Chelsi said this conversation right now isn't going to cost us anything?"

"Free consultation," Nina said. "We have half an hour and you came a long way, so how can I help you?"

Hanna shrugged and said, "That's the point. I haven't got a fucking clue."

When Nina didn't bridle at that, he added, "Like I said, talk won't bring her back."

"But you'r e already involved in a lawsuit. Isn't that right?"

"There's this lawyer in Placerville? Name's Bruce Bennett. Two years ago, after Sarah died, Roger contacted him and had this lawyer file a civil suit against the motel where it all happened. I wasn't sure about the whole thing, but Bennett got us in his office and oh, he talked it up, how much money we were going to hit them up for, how they were negligent. They let the bastard onto the property. No video camera and the clerk off somewhere. The lawyer talked us into suing the motel. Why, he practically had us convinced that the motel owner, who by the way wasn't even around that night, did the shooting."

"Sounds like he was trying to put on a very aggressive case on your behalf."

"I guess." He shook his head. "It never sat right with me, blaming the motel, but Roger was so gung-ho. We used up some of Sarah's life insurance to pay Bennett, but when the money ran out he filed a substitution of attorney form and left us flat."

"I guess that didn't leave you with a very high opinion of lawyers. I know Bruce. The lawsuit stayed active?"

He shook his head. "I really don't know where things stand with it."

"You couldn't pay Bruce Bennett, so he quit?"

"Basically."

"I would think carpenters were in big demand around here. I can never get anyone to come out and fix my porch," Nina said.

"I don't work much lately." He sighed. "I have problems."

"Problems?"

He chewed on a thumb, as if the question demanded

arduous consideration that was beyond him. Scanning the room as if he might locate a swift escape route that wouldn't require him to pass Sandy, his eyes landed on Chelsi.

"Uncle Dave's been sick," Chelsi said, taking her cue. "Like I told you."

"Hmm," Nina said. "Well, I understand you were going to bring me the court papers to look at," she went on neutrally.

"Right." He reached inside his wool shirt and pulled out a battered envelope. He set it on the desk, the hand revealing a slight tremor. Nina looked at him carefully, noting the thin burst of broken capillaries in his ruddy cheeks, the tangle of red veins around the edges of his eyes.

He hasn't had the hair of the dog this morning, she thought, and he misses it. No wonder Sandy had given her a warning eyebrow. Sandy didn't like drinkers.

On the other hand, wasn't it a positive sign that he had held off to talk with her? Maybe there was still hope for him.

She opened the envelope and pulled out several legal documents in the Wrongful Death and Negligence case of *Hanna vs. Ace High Lodge and Does I-X.*

The complaint Bruce Bennett had drafted was on top, followed by some unserved summonses, an answer filed by the Ace High Lodge, and a set of pleadings filed recently by the Lodge's attorney, Betty Jo Puckett of South Lake Tahoe. While Nina skimmed through the pleadings, Dave Hanna slumped in his chair, never taking his eyes off her.

Chelsi had displayed a good grasp of her uncle's legal

situation. He was about to have his case dismissed on the motion of the Ace High Lodge, because he had done nothing to bring the matter to trial for almost two years.

Bennett had done a workmanlike job laying out the facts in the complaint. The Hannas had been celebrating their tenth wedding anniversary by spending the weekend at Lake Tahoe, at the Ace High Lodge, one block from Harveys and the other Stateline casinos. They had gone to a show at Prizes and walked back, then stepped out to the second-floor balcony of their room.

There, according to the dry legalese of the complaint, "They observed an armed robbery in progress." And, in what seemed to be a case of being in the wrong place at the wrong time, at thirty-nine, third-grade teacher Sarah Hanna had been shot once through the heart. She was three months pregnant.

There were few traces of the gunman or other witnesses. The motel clerk, Meredith Assawaroj, had heard the shots from an adjoining property. She had missed seeing the killer, but had provided the South Lake Tahoe police with a fair description of the three motel guests who had been held up, young people who had packed up and left before the police arrived.

The clerk's descriptions of these three led nowhere. The gun hadn't been left at the scene.

Now the Ace High Lodge wanted out of Hanna's lawsuit, which alleged that its clerk should have been in the office, that the motel security should have been better, and so on and so on. Hanna might have had some sort of case on the merits if he had pursued it, but leaving it to languish for so long had exposed him to Betty Jo Puckett's Motion to Dismiss.

Puckett's work looked good. Her law was solid. Statutory limits restricted the ability of plaintiffs to file a lawsuit and then do nothing, as Dave Hanna had done.

Puckett had apparently advised the motel owner well—to lay low for as long as possible and then attack Hanna for failure to prosecute. Nina hadn't met her, but the courtroom grapevine said she had an effective style.

She looked up. Hanna's cheeks flamed, but his eyes were sunken into the sockets. He looked like a big, healthy man who had developed some wasting disease that was ruining him. Nina wondered how long he had been drinking way too much. At least he was sober at eight in the morning. She found it painful to imagine what he'd gone through, how bitter he must feel now.

She cleared her throat. Setting down the Motion to Dismiss, she said, "Your wife seems to have been the classic innocent bystander."

"Did you know she was expecting?"

"Yes."

He shifted in his chair, like the seat hurt him.

"What do you plan to do now?" Nina asked him.

"Slink away, I guess."

"The Lodge wants attorney's fees."

"I might get socked with their lawyer fees?"

"Perhaps."

Dave Hanna put his hand on his heart and said, "Let me get this straight. They want *me* to pay them? How much money are we talking about?"

"I don't know. I could guess, from the amount of work I see here, possibly several thousand dollars."

"If I do nothing, what will happen?"

"You'll probably have to pay their fees."

During a long silence Hanna deliberated about whether to—what? Confide in her? Walk out on her? "Well?" he asked finally.

Nina raised her eyebrows.

"What do you think?"

"It isn't hopeless," Nina said.

"There isn't a damn thing I can do to stop them. Is there?"

"You can fight the motion. The Code of Civil Procedure does require that a suit like yours be dismissed two years after service on the defendant with no action. But it hasn't been quite two years. It's still in the discretion of the court."

Hanna blurted, "Look, lady. I understand you need to drum up business. Maybe you hope we've got a stash of dough hidden away. I hate to say this, but we don't. Bennett demanded a hundred fifty dollars an hour and five thousand up front, and called himself cheap. I don't want to bankrupt Roger and Chelsi. And I'm broke, like I keep telling you."

"We'll take care of the money, Uncle Dave," Chelsi said.

"I will need a retainer," Nina said, thinking of Sandy, who would hold her accountable. She came up with the lowest amount she could manage. "Two thousand, billed against my hours. I also charge a hundred fifty an hour. There may be expenses. If we manage to keep the case going, those expenses could mount up fast."

"Done," Chelsi said, whipping out her checkbook. Hanna bowed his head, looked at the rug. "It's not for revenge," Chelsi said. "It's not for money. It's for my aunt. You know?"

Nina nodded. She pushed the button, as though Sandy hadn't left the door open a crack and been listening the whole time.

After Hanna had signed an agreement and left with Chelsi, Nina adjusted her suit coat and hung her new briefcase over her shoulder.

"You think we can make money on this?" Sandy said. She reposed like a Buddha in her Aeron chair, detached, hands folded calmly on the desk over Nina's notes.

"I do. Fast money. That's if we can get past this motion to dismiss. The motel clerk should have been in the office. The area should have been less of an ambush invitation. There may have been other incidents—this kind of crime occurs in clusters. Maybe the motel should have been on notice."

"The client's unreliable."

"Yes. But his relatives seem to have him in line. I think some money might help him, Sandy. Rehab. Grief counseling. Whatever. I trust Chelsi to steer him right."

"Where do you want to start?"

"Let's get the police reports and check to see if there were similar crimes reported in the area a couple of years ago. File a notice that I'm in as Hanna's attorney and send a copy of the notice to Betty Jo Puckett. She represents the Ace High Motel."

"Betty Jo Puckett?"

"You know her?"

"I met her. She has a problem in the tact department."

Nina smiled, saying, "Report anything else you hear."

"Before you go, what else do you need?"

"Get the file made up. I'll get going on drafting the Response to the Motion to Dismiss after court. There are a long line of precedents regarding innkeeper liability for inadequate security. Sandy, remember Connie Francis?"

"The singer? Nineteen-sixties. 'Lipstick on Your Collar.' That wasn't even her biggest hit. But even now it strikes a chord with me." Sandy's husband Joe and she had broken up for many years and only recently remarried.

"She won an early motel-security case. The damages award was in the seven figures. I don't think it was in California, though. The trial took place in the mid-seventies. See if you can locate the case on Lexis."

"She was robbed?"

"She was raped. During the early seventies, I think, while staying in a hotel room. It was brutal. I think it ended her career."

Neither woman spoke for a moment. Then Sandy said, "So some turkey fired off a wild one during a stickup and killed a third-grade teacher. Do we go looking for him, or just nick the motel?"

"We go looking."

"Good."

"We get started, at least."

"Shall I call Paul?"

"He's tied up."

"You'll need an investigator, and he's the best."

But for many reasons, Nina did not want Paul van

Wagoner involved. She did not wish to see his handsome face, his flirty manner, his sexual vibrations. She was over him, at least for the moment. Someday, Paul could enter her life neutered into professional cronyism. Until then, he needed to stay filed in the Great Memory file.

She said with emphasis, "Do not call Paul."

"Okay, okay. I heard about another good investigator who might be available."

"Good. See what you can do." Nina trotted down the hall and climbed into her old Bronco. Five minutes until court. She bumped off the curb into the street.

There's an advantage to small-town law. She would make it to court right on time.